Book Trader

With her arms about his neck, she laughed breathlessly, and he cradled her as he might have held a child, gazing down into her lovely face.

The laughter died from her eyes, to be replaced by a look of inexpressible tenderness. The bonds of honour that had so unyieldingly restrained him, melted away, and with a small sigh he bent to her lips.

It would have been simple enough for Rachel to swing her head away; holding her as he was, he could not have compelled her. Instead, she lifted her face. Tristram kissed her and, with awed reverence, felt her respond to him.

In that tempestuous instant, Rachel knew how she had yearned for his embrace and knew also dizzying joy, such as she had never before experienced. For an enchanted space she was lost, drifting ecstatically in a dream so perfect, so wonderfully sweet as to obliterate all else.

Another Fawcett Crest Book
by Patricia Veryan

SOME BRIEF FOLLY

PATRICIA VERYAN
FEATHER CASTLES

FAWCETT CREST • NEW YORK

A Fawcett Crest Book
Published by Ballantine Books

Copyright © 1982 by Patricia Veryan

Library of Congress Catalog Card Number: 81-21542

ISBN 0-449-20337-9

This edition published by arrangement with St. Martin's Press

Manufactured in the United States of America

First Ballantine Books Edition: October 1983

For Christine—who started it all.

At dusk, smoke still billowed into the sullen skies near the vil-
lage called Waterloo, and the air seemed to reek of death. The
roar of cannon had ceased at last, and gradually a welter of new
sounds succeeded those mighty voices of battle. They seemed
quiet, by comparison, although in their own way, they were the
more terrible. The road from Brussels was cluttered with the
aftermath of the titanic struggle: dead horses, abandoned carts
and wagons, baggage torn asunder by greedy hands that had
scattered haphazardly anything not worth the looting. Most
ghastly of all were the survivors; some staggering along with
arms across the shoulders of comrades, some crawling painfully through the mud, or lying helplessly, unable to go on,
clutching bloody makeshift bandages and crying piteously for
water. Others, perhaps more fortunate, neither moved nor
pleaded for aid, but sprawled silently, pathetic in their sleep
from which there would be no awakening.

Most who travelled that nightmarish thoroughfare were coming away from the carnage of the battlefield. A steady stream,
however, headed for that very carnage; pale-faced, grim-lipped
men, going to search for injured friends and relatives, or to find
and tenderly bear off their dead.

The heart-rending cries of the wounded hushed all at once,
awe causing stumbling feet to halt and weary eyes to turn to
where a phaeton picked its way through the debris. Incongru-
ous in this brutal confusion, a girl sat in the open vehicle beside
the ample girth of an elderly nun. She wore a simple pelisse of
beige stuff, the hood having fallen back to reveal hair of a light
dusty brown, curling softly about the perfect oval of a delicately featured countenance. Her eyes, wide set under arching

brows, were a deep, clear blue. And although the little chin had an intrepid tilt and there was strength in the firm mouth, to the exhausted men she was as ethereal as beautiful, a stark contrast to the chaos that surrounded her.

A very young soldier, gripping a loosely dangling left arm, reeled towards the phaeton and in a croak of a voice, sobbed, "Water . . . Madonna, in God's name . . . Water . . ." But the phaeton did not check.

Appalled, Rachel Strand cried beseechingly, "Sister, we *must* stop and help them! We *must*!"

Sister Maria Evangeline closed her eyes, and her lips moved in prayer. Glancing back, the groom slowed his team expectantly. But when she looked up, the nun said a sharp, "Drive on, Andrews!"

The groom's eyes slanted from the nun to Miss Strand, and back to the nun. He shook his head with not a little censure at the stern face of this holy woman, but she responded only with a haughty lift of her brows. He sent his whip cracking out over the heads of the nervous horses, and the phaeton bounded forward.

With firm implacability, the nun said, "I warned you, Rachel, when you insisted upon accompanying me, that I seek one man. It is vital that I find him. I will not—*dare* not—be turned aside and should we stop now, I fear— Andrews! Whip them up! Fast! Fast!"

Tightening his lips, the groom obeyed, and the phaeton scattered the desperate little group of the wounded who had converged on it.

Rachel looked back and uttered a cry of pity as a youth, hopping painfully on one foot, his other leg swathed in bloody rags, was sent sprawling. She swung about on the seat, rage in her young face, but tears glistened in the eyes of her companion, and, instead of the furious denunciation she'd been about to deliver, Rachel placed a compassionate hand on the sturdy arm and murmured, "I should have understood how much harder it must be for you, dear soul. Always so gentle and kind. But—oh, is it not *hideous*? So . . . so . . ."

"—So ghastly," the nun finished, unsteadily. "And especially for such eyes as yours, my child! When I allowed you to

2

step into the phaeton I had thought we might chat for just a few minutes, for there is something I am most eager to—'' She broke off, sighing. ''But, I had no right to— I should never have allowed you to come!''

''But I want to help. In Brussels there are many to aid the poor souls who get thus far, but if your history lessons spoke truly, and I'm sure they did, on the battlefield they will be desperate for water.''

Quite apart from her history books, Sister Maria Evangeline was not unacquainted with battlefields. Her frown deepened. ''I should have told Andrews to remove you by force. He is vexed with me that I have not done so.''

The groom gave a grunt of agreement. Rachel, herself dreading what might lie ahead, clasped her hands resolutely and said nothing.

''At all events,'' the nun resumed, ''they say thousands have fallen. Our four water bottles will prove all too few, I do not doubt.''

Rachel was not deceived by the harsh tone and after a moment said thoughtfully, ''If thousands have fallen, how can you hope to find your friend?''

''Because I *must* find him! With God's help, I *will* find him!''

It was getting dark, and Rachel thought there was little hope that the faith of her dear friend and erstwhile teacher would be justified, but she made no comment, sitting quietly while the phaeton pushed on through a continuing nightmare of sights so harrowing that both women were sickened.

Unfaltering, the nun scanned the face of each man they passed. ''Lord! How many there are!'' she muttered. ''Andrews—remember, he will be wearing rifle green. Poor souls . . . oh, the poor souls!'' And moved by a sudden thought, ''Child—how came you to be wandering about the streets of Brussels, alone?''

''We were to have met Dr. Ulrich. Until Thursday night nobody really thought there would be a battle, you know, so we waited. But we heard the cannon from Quatre Bras on Friday afternoon—so dreadful! And this morning, even worse. And

3

when the wounded began to straggle into Brussels—well, you saw how many ladies ran outside to try and help."

"*We?* My heavens! Never say Charity is there?"

"But, of course, for that is why we came, and why I insisted upon waiting. But heaven knows what became of the doctor."

Aghast, the nun exclaimed, "And you left her there, alone? Rachel! She cannot walk! What if we lose this battle?"

"You silly goose," smiled the girl. "As if I would leave my dear sister alone. Guy is with her."

"And he let you go?" Sister Maria Evangeline snorted a contemptuous, "Hah!"

"He was carrying a wounded Ensign into the house. The confusion was indescribable. He had no idea I had wandered off. And no matter what you say, I believe you know that Guy is a fine and honourable gentleman. As for Wellington losing, surely that possibility is remote. But—if it should happen, then Guy will carry my sister to safety."

"Such trust is to be admired." The sarcasm in the good Sister's voice was pronounced and brought a faint pucker to Rachel's brow. "But what of yourself, miss?" she went on. "Does Claude know that his affianced bride rushes to a battlefield with never a thought for her own safety?"

"Claude was unable to come. This morning he sent word that we must proceed to Ostend in the event Dr. Ulrich is unable to reach us, and that he will bring the doctor to Sussex as soon as possible." With a touch of defiance she added, "And I am very sure that Claude would expect me to do whatever I may to aid these brave men."

Sister Maria Evangeline clung to the side and stood to obtain a better view of a gun carriage jolting along with a cargo of seriously wounded officers. Surveying those ravaged young faces in grim silence, she was thinking that Miss Rachel Strand was either hopelessly besotted by the tender passion, or had surprisingly little knowledge of the character of her betrothed.

Captain Sir Simon Buchanan, his broken right hand tucked into the front of his torn and dusty red jacket, bent over a tumbled heap of the dead, his red-rimmed eyes searching among them anxiously. The thick dark hair of the young Colonel he turned had caused his heart to pound with dread, but the quiet face was not that of the man he sought, and sighing, he straightened and led his bay mare on again. It was almost dark, the dimness shedding a welcome veil over the horrors of the battlefield littered with its dead and dying. Few tended the wounded; for the most part their piteous cries went all unheeded. The water they prayed for was not to be had for miles around, and most of the men beginning to drift among them were there not to offer help, but to loot and murder.

Buchanan sought on doggedly, himself barely able to set one foot before the other, and aware he must not linger, lest he also fall prey to the scavengers. He hardened his heart against the pleas that beset him from every side, but the feeble clutch of a hand at his muddied boot sent a pang of anguish through him. Pulling free, he said gruffly, "I cannot help you, poor fellow. If I'm to find my closest friend, I—"

"Well, damn your eyes, Buck! You might at least . . . tell me . . . who won?"

Startled, the Captain bent lower, and gazed into grey eyes dark-shadowed with exhaustion, yet having an indomitable twinkle in their depths that was unmistakable. With a leap of the heart, he exclaimed, "St. Clair! Are you badly wounded?"

"Not . . . wounded at all." Captain Lord Lucian St. Clair lay propped against his dead horse, and said with a quivering grin, "A bit . . . sharpish there for a while . . . wasn't it?"

Buchanan's eyes lit with appreciation of this incredible understatement, but he merely agreed that it had indeed been "a slight tussle." And, recalling St. Clair's initial question, added, "Nosey pulled us out of it, as usual. The Frogs are in full retreat." St. Clair's breathless cheer widened his smile, and he asked, "What's to do, Lucian? Resting, old fellow?"

"Gudgeon! Blasted nag rolled . . . over me."

Much shocked, Buchanan peered at the deceased animal. "Not Caliph?"

"Well, if that ain't just like you! You might at least enquire if my back is broken!"

"Yes, I will. But—was it Caliph?"

St. Clair chuckled. "No, thank heaven. That lunatic's too wild for battle. Now, get on with you, or you shall lose what's

5

left of the light. I'll be up in a trice and . . . I've got my pistol ready, so do not fret. I collect it's poor Tristram Leith you seek, eh?''

Buchanan stiffened. ''Yes. You've seen him?''

''Saw him fall. Sorry, Buck. The shell exploded directly above him. He's finished I'm afraid. Got him in the face, poor devil.'' His rumpled blond locks jerked to the northward. ''Over there, somewhere. Have a care, old fellow. Vultures are among us.''

His heart aching, Buchanan took the time to ascertain that, astonishingly, St. Clair appeared unhurt and his pistol was indeed loaded. Then, he resumed his own sad quest.

They were close to the battlefield now. Scarcely daring to look about her, Rachel was shaking, her teeth chattering as with ague. Everywhere she turned were the dead and dying, and—more terribly—furtive, shadowy shapes that flitted about to dreadful purpose. Young voices upraised in painful pleading were cut off by the flash of steel, or rose into choked screaming that turned her knees to water. Numbed with horror, she heard the groom explode harshly, ''We never should've brought the young lady along, ma'am! Turn back, I say! We'll be lucky do we get away alive, even now! Turn back! 'Fore it do be too late for any of us!''

''No,'' Rachel quavered staunchly. ''We—must help the . . . the poor creatures. Oh, Lord!'' Shuddering, she turned from the pile of half-naked bodies before her. ''How frightful! Such savagery is—''

''Stand back there!'' Andrews flourished his whip, but three tattered shapes leapt to the heads of the team. A fourth ran forward, and all turned their glowing eyes towards the two women.

Sister Maria Evangeline fumbled beneath her habit and brought forth a large horse pistol. ''Get back, you spawns of Satan!'' she cried, fierce and dauntless. ''I've no wish to shoot, but—''

Another scavenger came at her from the side. The pistol was wrested from her hand. Struggling, Andrews was dragged from his seat, and Rachel gave a muffled shriek as she was torn from the phaeton and crushed suffocatingly against a rank and hairy

6

chest. A man—more beast than human, she thought—was chuckling, nuzzling at her throat. And she was too overwrought to even attempt a scream.

A shot rang out, followed immediately by a gurgling cry. She was on her knees, but free! A large man, clad only in a torn and bloody shirt and tattered breeches, crawled weakly towards them, a smoking pistol in one hand. The three remaining looters raced for him, knives flashing, and even in that dim light, Rachel saw that their rescuer was already badly wounded, his face a mask of dried blood so that she wondered he could see.

The looters surrounded him now. He struck out valiantly with the pistol but, laughing, one of his assailants kicked the weapon from his hand, and another sent a knife streaking down at the arm he flung up in a feeble attempt to protect himself.

Rachel came to her feet. Sister Maria Evangeline ran to grab her hand and hiss, "Into the carriage! Quickly!"

"And leave him to die? No, I shall not!" Rachel scooped up the whip the groom had dropped, swung it out, and ran forward. The wounded man had crumpled to lie sprawled on the ground, and the looters, laughing, were bending above him.

"Filth!" Rachel cried shrilly, and brought the whip whistling around.

The first man, sword upraised to stab his helpless victim, gave a yowl of pain and shock as the lash cut across his back. His two friends spun about, crouched and ready for action, but seeing the girl and the whip already curling back for another swing, they grinned and, dodging that whistling thong, started for her.

"Question is," drawled a lazy voice beside her ear, "which one o' ye I blows the gizzard out of, first?"

That lusting charge halted. The looters glared, cursed, and cursing still, melted into the darkness.

Sister Maria Evangeline's "Diccon!" was more a sob than a word.

Rachel threw a glance at the newcomer and had a brief impression of a tall, lean, youngish individual, with an unruly shock of curly hair. Then she was running to the still shape of the man who had so bravely defended them. Sinking to her

7

knees beside him, she wrenched the rolled linen bandages from her pocket and tried to wipe some of the blood from his face.

A faint gleam told her his eyes were open. A breathless voice said in French, "So this . . . then, is not . . . Hades?"

"I wouldn't refine on that overmuch, friend," came that deep drawl once more. The man Sister Maria Evangeline had addressed as "Diccon" slipped a hand under Rachel's elbow. "This is no place for you, miss. Come."

"No!" Stubbornly, she wrenched free. "I'll not leave him! He saved us, and they've cut him badly. See how his arm bleeds! We cannot—"

"We'll leave the poor lad some water. It will keep him sane 'til dawn, which is more than could be said for most of these poor devils. Now—"

But again Rachel dodged that long hand and slipped her arm beneath the shoulders of the injured man, struggling to raise him.

"Go!" he gasped faintly, his dark head rolling against her shoulder. "Your friend . . . perfectly right. No place for—for blessed angel such as you . . . Go!"

Looking up at Diccon, Rachel grated, "Help me lift him into the phaeton."

The looters were coming back. Diccon swore under his breath. Sister Maria Evangeline said, "We'll manage. I will help. Oh, if only he were not such a big fellow! Andrews? Where are you? Come!" She clambered into the phaeton, urging, "Hurry, hurry!"

Between them, Diccon and the groom lifted the soldier and disposed him in the phaeton so that he half sat, half lay across the seat with his head in the nun's lap. Rachel squeezed into the vehicle and knelt on the floor, attempting to quench the blood that welled from the wound in the soldier's arm.

The looters rushed them, two wielding swords, and one thrusting a rifle at Diccon, the bayonet gleaming wickedly. Diccon's pistol blasted Rachel's ears. The man with the bayonet howled and went down. Andrews sprang for the driver's seat. A slap of the reins and the frightened horses plunged forward. With a wild dive, Diccon caught the back of the phaeton. The looters jumped clear, and the phaeton was away.

They had been at sea for a very long time, and the storm was so fierce he was unable to hold himself steady in the bunk but was constantly flung against the side, each collision seeming to hurt his throbbing head more than the last. The portholes were closed because of the high running seas, and the tiny cabin was oppressively hot. Yet sometimes the spray managed to penetrate the closed ports and splash, icily refreshing, against his face. With stunning force he was hurled at the side once more and, crying out, awoke from his dream.

A cool hand touched his cheek. A blurred shape bent above him, and a sweetly musical voice said in lilting French, "Lie still, please, sir! You must not toss so."

Puzzled, he stared at that indistinct form until the mists faded a trifle, and he saw again the girl he had thought to see in his dreaming. Gentle of eye, fair of skin, her face a vision of loveliness, her whole being the very personification of feminine grace and purity. Scarcely daring to breathe lest she disappear, he lay very still, but when she started to move back into the mists, asked faintly. "Am I now . . . dead, mademoiselle?"

A smile curved that pretty mouth. "No," she answered gently. "You seem to be very much better, in fact. The road was hopelessly blocked and we could not get back to Brussels, but our groom found this cottage. It has been abandoned, so we pass the night here. Sir—we are greatly indebted to you. May we know your name?"

His name? He frowned painfully. A simple enough question. Tell her, you simpleton! But to think, hurt. And the harder he tried, the more it hurt, so that he sighed at last. "I will tell you, but—not just now, for . . . I cannot quite seem . . . to recall. . . ."

When he looked up again, the girl had gone. He was relatively comfortable, lying in bed in a room that held the echo of a sweet fragrance. Who was that lovely girl? And who, by heaven, was *he*? He closed his eyes, fighting to remember. That he was French, he knew, for he had a vague recollection of conversing with someone in that language, and of a scornful British voice saying, "He's just another ruddy Frog! Scrag the perisher!" But as to what had happened, why he was hurt, and where he lay, he had not the faintest notion. He certainly must have a name. A family. Yet all he could clearly recall was an Englishman sobbingly pleading not to be murdered. His brows twitched together. Murder? Good God! What dark past lay behind him? He moved agitatedly, and had to choke back a groan as that venture sent blinding waves of pain through his head.

Someone was urging him to drink. He begged not to be lifted, but a hand raised his head gently. A cup touched his lips and he forced himself to drink. A warm glow spread through him, and he slid easily into darkness once more.

He dreamed that light was creeping through the small window. He lay idly watching that square glow against the dimness, and as it brightened imperceptibly, noted that the panes were cracked and very dirty. People were talking quietly, but he could distinguish the words. A man, with a deep, cultured voice that was vaguely familiar, and a woman, probably the nun he remembered, who was saying in English ". . . fear for the child. Had I dreamed we would be compelled to spend the entire night out, I'd not have brought her."

"To have done so at all, was purest folly, ma'am, if you will forgive my bluntness. Did it not occur to you that she might see me?"

"Of course it did! Do you take me for a henwit? That is precisely why I allowed her to accompany me, for I am ashamed to admit I hoped to turn your meeting to good account. Diccon— she could be an invaluable ally."

There was a faint hissing sound, as of breath suddenly indrawn. Then the man said mildly, "How easily I am deceived. It had been my thought you were quite fond of the chit."

"Pox on you! Do not drown me in your vitriol! Of course I am fond of her. More—I love her dearly. But the cause is such as to justify any sacrifice. If you are there, and she knows she has someone to count on in an emergency . . ."

A brief silence, and the man said thoughtfully, "The risk would be horrible. If he so much as suspected, her life would not be worth a sou!" And after another short and obviously troubled pause, "What of this one?"

In his dream, the man on the bed knew they were discussing him. He lay very still, and waited.

"He can also be put to good account," the nun replied. "If Guy comes, we will have evidence that we went to minister to the wounded."

"Guy! Do you expect that young devil?"

"He escorts Rachel."

Diccon laughed shortly. "A fine protector! I must take care not to allow him to 'escort' any lady of my house!"

A chair was scraped back. Soft footsteps approached the dreamer, and he sensed he was being scrutinized. One of his hands was taken up, and he allowed it to lie limply in a cool clasp.

"A gentleman, from the look of these hands," Diccon observed. "Who is he, I wonder? Has he said anything at all of himself?"

"I think he cannot recollect, poor man. With a wound like that he may never be right in his head again. And only see what it has wrought upon his face!"

"It has marked him, certainly. He must have been a handsome fellow. Pity. Is he French?"

"Probably. He looks it, don't you think? So dark."

"Many of us trace our lineage to Normandy, ma'am."

"True. But even in delirium he speaks the French tongue. An officer, certainly, but as to rank—who can say? His jacket and boots were gone. Had not his shirt been covered in blood and his breeches muddied and torn, they would have taken those also; I do not doubt. Diccon—what a *frightful* battle! It must go down in history as the most costly of all time. And so little caring for the wounded! So many lives lost for want of a mouthful of water, or a bandage or two. Oh, shall we never learn—"

Her impassioned utterance was cut off as Diccon intervened dryly, "Dear lady, I agree with you, but we have no time for philosophizing. I found my man and learned what I went to learn, and in the very nick of time, for he was impaled by a Prussian lancer moments later! Only by the grace of your friend, God, did not I end under one of those piles of corpses! Now I must leave you, for if Guy sees me I shall be undone before I start! If things go awry for me, remember that our answers lie on the top floor of that damnable palace in Dinan. Not much, but at least we have a beginning!"

"Very well. Take care, my dear. I've no wish for this beginning to be your ending! I will convey your warning to the Horse Guards."

Diccon gave a cynical snort. "Much they will heed you! If General Smollet had his way I would be in Bedlam at this very moment!"

"He says that, I admit, but has not ordered you back home. Shall I try to reach the Regent's ear? Mrs. Fitzherbert might—"

"Little hope there, love. Prinny fancies my adversary his fervent admirer. Well, I must be off. Speak to your burnt offering if you wish, though I confess that to place a girl in such jeopardy goes against the grain with me."

"Burnt offering, indeed! I have no more fondness for the scheme than have you. At all events, I'll not attempt to persuade her to it yet. She still supposes Claude to be her saintly benefactor. Poor deluded innocent!"

"Hmmmm. Is it possible she has not heard of his unlovely clan?"

"Very possibly. Her youth was passed at the Convent School, and since her Papa died she has led a sheltered life, devoted to her sister's care. However, I mean to try and . . ."

The dream was becoming hazy, the words fading into an unintelligible muddle. The soldier sighed wearily and sank deeper into sleep.

Sister Maria Evangeline's voice, upraised in anger, awoke Rachel. She lay on a hard and uncomfortable sofa in a tiny parlour, and for a moment stared in confusion about the stark, unfamiliar room. Recollection came in a rush, and with it anxiety, and she sat up as the nun bustled into the room, neat as a bandbox, carrying a pitcher of steaming water and exclaiming cheerily, "Ah! So you are awake, my love. Can you credit it? That miserable groom of mine fell asleep, 'Just for a bit' says he, wherefore our horses are gone, and the wonder is the phaeton was not taken as well." She set the pitcher on a table that already held bowl, soap, and a towel and added, "A fine pickle! Did you get any sleep?"

Rachel pushed away the blanket that covered her, and stretched. "Yes, for you did not awaken me!" She yawned. "I was to have taken the last watch."

"As well you did not!"

Alarmed by the grimness in the nun's small, hazel eyes, Rachel exclaimed, "Oh, no! Never say he is . . . is . . ."

"He lives, thank the good Lord. But towards dawn he became delirious, and I had to call Diccon, for I could not hold him." She lifted a pudgy hand to quiet Rachel's attempted scold. "You were exhausted, child, as well you might have been after so frightful an experience. Besides, I needed Diccon's strength. I wonder our soldier did not waken you, though, he raved so."

"Of what? Himself? His family, perhaps?"

The nun hesitated, then said reluctantly, "No. He seems obsessed with one thing only."

"A lady?" Rachel smiled. "I do not doubt that."

Sister Maria Evangeline shook her head. "Our rescuer spoke only of—" She paused again and lowered her voice. "Murder."

"Murder!"

"Aye. And you look sadly pulled, child. Come now and wash. Diccon has left, and I've sent Andrews to find some horses or a conveyance to carry us back to the city."

Her spirits quite sunk, Rachel stammered, "But—but what does it mean? You never think the soldier could have— That *he* is—"

"A murderer? Or out of his head, merely? Who knows? He is quieter now, at least, and spoke a few words to me. I collect he fears to be taken prisoner. Does he live that long." Pursing her lips, the nun mused, "The arm is nothing for so fine a physical specimen. But," she gave a small shrug, "the head . . . !"

Rachel stood and hastened to the door, only to check as Sister Maria Evangeline called, "Do not fight God's will, little one. Perhaps it is better that the Frenchman go peacefully."

A rebellious frown on her face, Rachel retaliated, "He may be French, dear ma'am, but he is nonetheless a gallant gentle-

13

man who expended perhaps his last strength in fighting for us. I could not forgive myself were I to do less than my best for him!"

With a flash of her blue eyes, a flaunt of draperies, and a toss of dishevelled curls, she was gone.

Sister Maria Evangeline took herself by the chin. "She has the spirit well enough, Lord. The question is—have I the right? On the other hand—" A twinkle brightened her shrewd eyes. "She did not think to ask that I send word to her future brother-in-law or her beloved sister. Nor did she even enquire as to which side won that frightful battle!" She chuckled. "Do you know, Blessed Father, this chance meeting may augur very well for Rachel." She added with a sigh, "I only hope it may be well for England. You cannot deny, Lord, that I am offering the child one last chance."

The sick man was tossing restlessly, his left hand plucking at the blankets and his head turning endlessly against the bolster. Rachel bent over him, for the first time scanning his features by daylight. Around the bandages his hair was thick and near black. The heavy brows were painfully downdrawn, the long dark lashes accentuating his pallor. She thought him very handsome despite the deep cuts that raked down one side of his face and would certainly scar him; and as helpless as he now was, she gained an impression of power and masculinity, heightened by the square jaw, the strong nose, and rather thin lips. His cheek was alarmingly hot, but as gentle as her touch had been, he looked up, peering at her vaguely at first, then with an expression in his dark eyes that made her feel oddly flustered.

In French, she asked softly, "Are you feeling any better today?"

"Very much, thank you," he lied. "But—I fear I cause you a great amount of trouble. And—I cannot seem to think where I am—nor what has happened."

Relieved that he was able to speak rationally, she drew up a chair, took the cloth from the bowl by the bed and bathed his face carefully. "There was a great battle near the village of Waterloo. We had journeyed to the field in search of—a friend, and—"

"You drove through the forest? At night?" he gasped, incredulous.

Rachel thought, "So he remembers a little." And answered, "It was not quite dark, then. But when we came to the battlefield the light was almost gone. There were looters." She shivered a little, remembering, and went on hurriedly, "We were set upon. Oh, I was so frightened! You were already hurt, sir, but you came and sought to help us. Are you able to tell me now, what is your name? Your regiment, perhaps?"

His brows knit in a painful concentration, and Rachel prompted, "You are French, I believe?"

"I—er . . . think, yes. And you, mademoiselle?"

"My name is Rachel Strand. I live in the south of England, in a county called Sussex, but of late months my sister and I have been residing in Bath, so that she might take the—"

"Bath?" The soldier's eyes brightened eagerly. He started up, then sank back, flinching.

Startled by the reaction, Rachel asked, "Sir—is it possible that you have visited my country?"

"Would that . . . I knew!" Gripping the coverlet, he mumbled, "*Mon Dieu!* Is my mind quite gone? How can I not know who I am?"

Rachel straightened the blankets and smoothed the damp pillow, saying sympathetically, "It must be dreadful, I know, but do try not to worry so. You took a nasty head wound and perhaps it will be a day or two before your memory returns. Now, my friend Sister Maria Evangeline is preparing some breakfast. If you can eat a little, it will strengthen you. Hush!" She put a hand over his lips, quieting his attempt to speak. "You are quite safe here, and we will make every effort to restore you to your own people."

The smile in her eyes was not reflected in his, for the fever was playing tricks on his mind. Instead of the girl's face, the terrified eyes of a young man gazed at him. Arms reached out in desperation, and a trembling voice pleaded brokenly, "Do not murder me! For the love of God! Do not *murder*—" The words were cut off by a ghastly scream. Sweat starting on his brow, the soldier cried out and tossed wildly. He quieted to the feel of something heavenly cold against his burning skin. The girl was

15

bathing his face gently. What an angel she was, so unbelievably fair, her touch so light. He saw her again and her lovely eyes were concerned, her mouth tender. His blurred gaze drifted to her hands. No rings. She was young, of course, yet not too young to have received many offers. What madness to allow his thoughts to wander in that direction! He might be wed, perhaps the father of a hopeful family. And even should he chance to be a bachelor, how dared he look at this pure and beautiful lady when he might well be fit only for the gallows, or Newgate. Newgate? Why had that name come into his mind? Dear God, how it hurt to try and think! His teeth gripped at his lower lip and his dark brows met.

Rachel's tender heart was wrung. She had completely forgotten that she had not yet washed nor tidied her hair, and now realized she must look a fright, but it seemed very unimportant. All that mattered was that she do all she might to ease this brave man's suffering. ''Whatever is it?'' she asked kindly. ''What troubles you so dreadfully?''

''Newgate,'' he groaned. ''What is—Newgate?''

''It—it is a great and very terrible English prison,'' she imparted, unease seizing her because of all the things that might have returned to his memory he had recalled that horrible place.

Her dismay was minute compared to that of the injured man. He flung his good arm across his eyes, shrinking from any further glimpse of a past that seemed appalling.

''Can I help in any way?'' Rachel asked.

For a moment he did not move. Then he lowered his arm and looked into her troubled face. Racked with fevered imaginings, he muttered, ''You should not be here . . . I—think I may be . . . a murderer!''

Rachel had been standing close beside the bed, and she took an instinctive step backwards. Perhaps Sister Maria Evangeline was right; perhaps the French authorities sought him at this very moment! Yet he seemed so gentle; humble in his gratitude, the last type to have committed a vicious crime. And how honest to confess so terrible a thing when he was utterly helpless, and she his only hope. Besides, whatever he had done, there was no altering the fact that she owed him her life, for had he not delayed the looters she might have been carried off before Diccon arrived. And thus, reason overcoming her natural abhorrence, she demurred, "But how can you know that, monsieur? You are very weak and ill, and your memory a little uncertain. Is it not likely that your mind wanders?"

It had, he thought. Just a moment ago he had been far from this time and place. He sighed. "I pray you are right," and lay still, watching the delicious wrinkling of Miss Strand's white brow, and trying to ignore the relentless pain.

"I am sure that you have merely suffered a bad dream," she said reassuringly. "Rest now, and in a little while I shall fetch you a tray." He continued to gaze up at her, and she smiled and scolded gently, "Now this will never do—pray close your eyes, sir!"

He didn't want to close his eyes. He wanted to continue to watch her until every lovely feature was indelibly imprinted upon his mind. She was speaking again, her voice soft and so kind. . . . He could not seem to distinguish the words but, joying in the sound, fell asleep.

2

"*Take him . . . back . . . to England?*" *Sister Maria Evangeline's* hand checked, the porridge slipping from the spoon she held as she stared across the rickety table at Rachel's flushed but resolute face. "You are all about in your head, poor child! Indeed I do not wonder at it, after what you have endured!"

"But only think, dear ma'am. The poor gentleman saved us. He is much too ill to be left alone. And he is convinced we mean to abandon him; I could see it in his eyes." Her own eyes softened as she thought of the soldier, and, noting that look, the good sister thought a small, triumphant, "Aha!" Wherefore, she said with harsh judiciousness, "He'll be fortunate if that is the worst we do, for by rights he should be handed over to the authorities!"

"Oh, no! You would not! You *could* not, when he was so good!"

"I have subjected you to enough of danger, child. I'll not aid you in slipping a wanted murderer out of France."

"He is *not* a murderer! One has but to look at him to know that!"

"Evidently, he is not given to gazing into mirrors, for he confessed, did he not?"

"Well, not exactly. He—"

"And while doubtless supposing himself to be at death's door," the nun swept on relentlessly. "It would not be the first time, love, that a wanted fugitive has hidden himself in the military."

"No, but he was delirious. He cannot recall what really happened."

18

"Convenient," grunted Sister Maria Evangeline dryly. "Were I—"

She was interrupted by the sudden clatter of horses outside, and a voice upraised in sharp command. The two women exchanged guilty glances.

"Oh, my goodness!" gasped Rachel. "Guy!"

Sister Maria Evangeline dropped her spoon altogether and clasped her hands prayerfully. "The moment of truth is come, child!"

Rachel reached out to grip those clasped hands urgently. "Dear ma'am, do not tell him what the soldier said. I beg of you. Promise me you will not—"

There was no time for such a promise, however. The outer door burst open, and Guy Sanguinet stood on the threshold. He was a lean young man, his features regular and pleasant, if touched by cynicism. Although not above middle height, he was distinguished by an air of poised self-confidence. He was clad in a jaunty, high-crowned beaver hat and a driving coat that enhanced his shoulders yet lacked the superabundance of capes that were the mode. His brown hair was wind-blown, and his hazel eyes, filled with anxiety, flashed to the ladies who rose to greet him.

"Rachel!" Hastening to take her outstretched hands and grip them strongly, he broke into a torrent of French. "Do you apprehend that I have been out of my senses with fears for your safety? What in the name of the good God possessed you to rush off in such a way? You had but to ask it and I would have—"

"Forbidden me to go," she interposed, smiling. "Is my sister well?"

"*Mas oui*—but of course. Do not seek to divert my vexation! What Claude will say of all this, I shudder to contemplate!" He turned to the nun and bowed. "Had I but known Miss Strand was safely in your care, dear lady, my mind must have been set at ease, to an extent at least."

A gleam in her eyes, Rachel murmured, "Oh, at least!"

Sister Maria Evangeline darted a grim glance at her. "May one ask how you found us, monsieur? With so much confusion and the roads choked with wounded and refugees."

"I chanced upon your coachman. And I dare to hope that the days of refugees are past, dear Sister." Elation in his voice, he added, "Bonaparte is thoroughly whipped, his armies in full retreat. He can never hope to reform before the Allies have taken Paris!"

"Thank heaven!" Rachel exclaimed. "But—oh, at what fearful cost! Countless thousands lay out there dying in the mud last night, and—"

He gave a gasp of shock. "Last *night*? How in God's name do you know that? Rachel—you were never on the *field*?"

"Many passed this way," the nun put in hurriedly, "and we aided those we might."

With sudden inspiration, Rachel said, "Yes. In fact there is a wounded officer lying in the bedchamber even now. He is in desperate straits and I had hoped we might carry him over to England aboard *La Hautemant*, do you not object."

Guy swung the door to and, stripping off his gloves, observed, "Whether or not I object has little to say to the matter. My brother would object unless I sadly mistake it! Are we to be spared his wrath, you and I, we must at once proceed to Dover. Come now, ladies. Prepare to leave. Fortunately I have my carriage."

Rachel stepped closer to place one hand on his sleeve and look into his face imploringly. "Guy—*please*. I am obligtaed to—" she extemporized hastily, "—to the Captain. He saved us when some villains would have shamed us. And him already wounded!"

"*Mon Dieu!*" he exclaimed, horrified. "I might well have arrived to find you both with your throats cut!"

"Indeed you might, and I acknowledge it was all due to my impulsiveness. Nonetheless, it is done. And—I really *do* stand in his debt."

He frowned worriedly. "Then I also am indebted to the gentleman. So be it! We shall carry your brave rescuer into Brussels at least, and see to it that he rejoins his regiment."

The nun, who had been observing this conversation with faint amusement, folded her arms across her ample bosom and waited.

"*Merci*, Guy!" Rachel exclaimed, delighted. "That is splendid!"

Sanguinet gave a grin and started for the inner door. "I shall look at this Captain. In here . . . ?"

"Yes. Only you might better perhaps address him as—'*le Capitaine.*'"

"What?" He checked in alarm and spun to face her. "The Devil! He's French?"

She nodded, and said innocently, "Will that matter?"

Sanguinet rubbed his chin and frowned. "He will have to be handed over to the military, of course, but—"

"Oh, dear! And his poor Mama so ill!" From the corner of her eye, Rachel saw Sister Maria Evangeline shake her head at the rafters, but plunged on. "He spoke of her so often. His mind wanders, poor creature, but it would seem that she lies in serious condition in—Worthing. He prays to reach her before —it is too late."

"*Worthing?*" Sanguinet echoed, incredulous.

"*Oui*. She is—er—half-English, I gather."

He shrugged. "How unfortunate. I sympathize with the poor fellow. Still—*c'est la guerre*. Sister, if you will be so good as to summon my coachman, between us we will contrive to bear *le Capitaine* to the carriage." He strode into the bedroom, calling over his shoulder, "We must be well on the road before noon."

Rachel turned to the nun. "I know what you are thinking," she whispered. "I told the most shocking untruths, I own it. Only—do not give me away, dear Sister. I beg of you. I *must* do what I may to help the soldier."

The nun folded her hands and observed sternly that no good could come of falsehoods. "At all events, M. Guy will not allow him to board the yacht, so how do you propose to come about?"

Rachel's head tossed higher, and the infectious little grin that had first attracted Claude Sanguinet brightened her face. "*Guy* will come about. Never fear, dear ma'am. When *La Hautemant* sails from Ostend, my poor murderer will be safely aboard!"

"A kiss, you pretty vixen! *Then* the necklace!" Lord Kingston Leith, his handsome features alight with laughter, dodged around the rose velvet chair in the small salon, reached for his latest inamorata, and sent a lamp tumbling. The lady uttered a squeal and fled behind the striped satin sofa. Whooping, Lord Leith snatched up and replaced the lamp and pursued the lady merrily.

A light rain was mizzling the Berkshire air, and Cloudhills seemed well named on this cool June afternoon. Leith's spirits, seldom depressed, were little affected by the weather, however, or in fact by anything. Although widowed these twelve years, and approaching his fifty-second birthday, he was blessed with both looks and vigour and, enjoying his single state to the full, had little desire to terminate it. He was wont to explain to concerned friends that he would never find a lady with whom he could enjoy the bliss that had glorified his first union. The truth of the matter, confided to a chosen few, was that he admired so many ladies it would be well nigh impossible for him to choose from among the pretty creatures. He was as generous as his heart was warm, so that his *chéres amies* never left his protection with rancour; and if his largesse, both to his lady loves and the friends who constantly hung on his sleeve, tended to deplete the family coffers, his son and heir, Colonel The Honourable Tristram Leith, now with Wellington in Belgium, returned to England with sufficient frequency to ensure that the steward kept a firm rein on his lordship's excesses.

Blessed with a son he both admired and deeply loved, a pretty and conformable daughter, many friends, good health, and a large fortune, Leith's lot was a happy one. Cloudhills, the splendid country seat that his late wife had favoured, saw him seldom, for he preferred the excitement of the London scene. He was fond of the sprawling Tudor mansion, however, if only for the memories it evoked of bygone years (in addition to the income the farms and village brought him), and he made it a point to visit the estate at least once each quarter. The skeleton staff he kept at the house year round was well paid. The servants' hall might hum with comment over the fact that his lordship never arrived twice with the same lady on his arm, but the criticism was indulgent rather than censuring and a few really held him to be the irreclaimable here-and-therein the Countess Lieven had several times publicly named him.

His next wild clutch securing his lady, his lordship swept her to him and she gave him his kiss, following which they stood, clasped in each other's arms, laughing breathlessly. A discreet cough interrupted this pleasant diversion. Lord Leith chuckled, "Jove! I fear I am in the suds, m'dear!" And slanting a twinkling glance over his shoulder, asked, "Yes, Chesley?"

Mr. Chesley had been my lord Leith's butler for thirty years. He was an imposing gentleman, but his plump countenance, usually, cherubic, was now markedly pale, and there was a distracted look about him that drove the laughter from his employer's grey eyes. Putting his lady aside, he turned fully, to ask, "What is it, Ches?"

"You have guests arrived, m'lud."

"The deuce!" Leith ejaculated. "*Guests?* Here? Now, who the devil told 'em I was— Who is it? Blast it all, there's no—"

"Mr. and Mrs. Garret Hawkhurst, m'lud. And—"

"Oh, is that all? Garret's a good boy and won't look down his nose at me; no more will his pretty lady. Show them—" He broke off in no little surprise as Garret Hawkhurst, his wife, and brother-in-law entered the room without waiting to be ushered inside. This breach of etiquette brought a vague disquiet to Leith. He turned to his companion, but that discreet lady had slipped out the side door onto the terrace. Mildly relieved, he advanced on his guests, hand outstretched.

"Hawkhurst! How very good of you to come and see me. And your lovely wife. Radiant as ever, m'dear!"

Euphemia Hawkhurst, who had always possessed more of countenance than pure beauty, looked elegant, but today her fine blue eyes were red-rimmed and distressed. She gave him her hand, made her curtsy, and said a quiet, "How do you do, my lord?"

Such formality between them was rare, and Leith eyed the tall young woman uneasily. Her coppery curls seemed darker than usual, but he realized that this was by reason of the fact she was very white. He wondered if her new babe was ill, perhaps.

Hawkhurst had gripped his hand with rather less than his usual bone-crushing power, and the lined face that had been freed of sorrow since Euphemia had entered his life some two years earlier, betrayed deep concern.

Glancing to the third visitor, Leith divined the reason for their lack of spirits. Young Simon Buchanan was hurt again, one arm carried in a sling and his features drawn and haggard. He always had been Euphemia's favourite brother; small wonder she was upset. "What, Buck?" he said, shaking the extended left hand gently. "That right arm of yours again? Best get rid of it, old fellow, or—" The trite words died in his throat. Buchanan was blinking mistily and looked positively anguished. An arrow of ice pierced Leith. His breath snatched away, he thought numbly, "There's been an action."

There had been an undercurrent of excitement in London when he had left the city five days earlier, but he'd paid little heed to speculation that a final confrontation was shaping between Napoleon and Wellington. The duke had outfought the French before, and would do it again if it became necessary, but such an eventuality was unlikely—or so he had thought. Searching the sombre faces of the two men, he began to tremble. Not *Tristram*? Surely—not his dear, gallant, warmhearted son?

Hawkhurst saw terror in the whitening face and, taking his wife's elbow, led her outside. "Perhaps you'd best seek out Sarah, my love. It would be easier if you told her."

Euphemia glanced to Leith's frozen immobility, nodded, and moved quickly from the room.

"Sir," Buchanan said hoarsely. "I wish—there was not the need. I wish I'd not—not to be the one—"

Leith stared at him blindly, a hand half-raising in an automatic need to ease the boy's distress. "A . . . battle?" he asked, through stiff lips.

"Yes, sir," Hawkhurst confirmed, his deep voice grave. "A major action. We came here just as soon as Buck reached us."

Leith blinked. "That was . . . very good of you, Simon." He patted Buchanan's shoulder, trying to grasp this; trying to accept what these two fine young men were breaking as kindly as they knew. "You have been Tristram's closest friends. I—I am most—grateful." His voice broke. He wrenched away, stumbled to the window and looked out, seeing only his son's handsome face and laughing eyes. Tristram *could not* be slain! thought Leith prayerfully. Wounded, perhaps. But—not . . .

"Is he dead?" he asked, the thin thread of his own voice sounding very far away.

Buchanan flinched and his head bowed. Hawkhurst slipped a hand onto his shoulder, and he recovered himself. "I'm terribly sorry, sir. I've brought his things. Couldn't find his jacket. There were looters, you see, and—" Hawkhurst's grip tightened. He bit his lip, and added, "But—I knew you would want to have his dress sword and regimentals. Old Tris . . . always looked so—so splendid in—" A sob choked him. He threw a hand across his eyes and spun about.

Hawkhurst led him to a chair, commanded softly but firmly that he sit and rest, and, walking to the sideboard, proceeded to pour three glasses of cognac. He carried the first to Buchanan, watched his brother-in-law spill a good portion of the tawny liquid, cuffed him gently, then carried the second glass to Leith. Standing behind that rigidly straight figure, he said, "Here, sir. You need it."

Leith turned, having swiftly brushed tears from his haggard features. Hawkhurst thought, "Poor devil. He's aged ten years!" But the hand that accepted the glass was steady, and the voice surprisingly calm when Leith remarked, "Poor Buck. You should not have let him come. He must be sadly pulled after so much travelling."

"I could not have stayed him, sir. Nor would I have tried. But he is quite ill. You'll forgive him for—er, well, he loved old Tris, you know."

Hawkhurst's cool control broke for just an instant, and the depth of the man's grief was a comfort to Leith. "We all loved him," he said huskily. "May God bless his valiant soul. Do they bring him home, Garret?"

Hawkhurst strode hurriedly to the sideboard, took up his glass and dashed off a swallow that made him gasp.

Sadly, Leith said, "I feel that he would want to lie in the family plot here. Do not you agree? Tristram always loved Cloudhills."

Hawkhurst stiffened and met Buchanan's pained glance, and seeing that wretched interchange, his lordship's eyes sharpened. "What is it? When was this engagement? And where?"

"On Sunday," Buchanan muttered. "Near a small village

25

called Waterloo. It lies a little less than ten miles from Brussels, just south of the Forest of Soignes."

"Only three days," said his lordship. "So they've not yet had time to bring . . . my son home."

Again, that exchange of helpless glances. Hawkhurst said carefully, "There were so many casualties, you see, sir. From what Buck has said—"

"The dead and wounded were thickly strewn over two square miles," Buchanan put in dully. "Two square miles!"

"Good God!" Leith gasped. "Is there any estimate of casualties?"

Buchanan did not answer. Hawkhurst said grimly, "We hear—between thirty and forty thousand. And ten thousand horses."

Leith's jaw dropped and he stared in shocked silence.

Hawkhurst went on, "So you can understand, sir, with so many, why the burials began first thing the following morning, and—"

"No!" Leith's cry was wrung from his heart. "Do you tell me that my dear son was thrown into—into a common grave?"

"I'm afraid . . . as far as we can determine—"

"As—as far as you can—determine?" A gleam of hope crept into the agonized grey eyes. "Did none see him fall?"

Fortified by the brandy, Buchanan hove himself out of his chair. "St. Clair did. He said a shell had burst directly above Tristram. And—and that his head—"

"Oh, merciful Christ! He was—decapitated?"

Buchanan paced forward compassionately, his hand going out to the white-faced Leith. "No, no! Do not so tease yourself, sir. Tristram was slain by shell fragments, apparently. Lucian said he likely never knew what hit him."

The dreadful words seemed to hang on the following heavy silence. Leith sank into a chair, hands clasped between his knees, his dark head, remarkably untouched by grey, downbent. At length, he murmured, "Then no one really *knows* he's dead!" He looked up from under his brows. "Not with any certainty. He might very well be alive somewhere!"

Being well acquainted with the ebullient nature of Tristram's sire, Hawkhurst's mouth relaxed into a faint, sad smile.

Buchanan said kindly, "Sir, when we knew Tristram was down—well, I started to search that night. But—being a Staff Officer, you know, he was galloping all over the field. Next day, the men who had served under him were wild with grief. They searched every inch of that ghastly field. I would give my life not to have to say it, but—Tris must have been already . . . buried."

Eyes sparkling, Leith sprang to his feet. "Gammon! if my son still had his uniform they'd not have buried him! He was a Colonel!"

"He likely didn't have anything but his skin, sir," said Buchanan, fearing to encourage an optimism that sooner or later must be cruelly shattered. "There were looters everywhere. Murdering swine with less Christianity than a snake!"

"Even stripped to the butt, no man could take Tristram for anything less than he is—an aristocrat!" Leith's head was up-flung, pride making him show almost as impressive as the broad-shouldered young Adonis he so loved. "No! He is alive! Were he slain I would *feel* it! Perchance he crawled to a remote cottage and they are caring for him. The same thing happened to young Redmond after the Siege of Ciudad Rodrigo, do you not recall? They mourned the boy as dead for days, but his horse had bolted with him and his sergeant found him, miles away in some wretched farmhouse, badly wounded, but alive." His eyes were shining to new purpose, and the two who watched him were mute, neither quite able to bring himself to shatter this forlorn hope. "I must go to Brussels at once," Leith muttered. "I shall hire men to seek at every cottage and house for miles around. No matter how long it takes, we will find him! First though, I must to Town and tell my poor little Sally before some well-meaning fool breaks her heart. She loves her brother so. You will pardon me, my dear fellows? I've to warn my valet. No—please do not leave! I shall return directly, and we will dine together. Do you mean to go home tonight, Buck? I take it Stephanie knows you are come home safe? If you are downpin you should sleep here and we could ride together in the morning." And full of energy, he chattered his way from the room and closed the door behind him.

In the sudden silence, Buchanan tore his incredulous gaze

from the door and found Hawkhurst regarding him with a twisted smile. "By thunder!" gasped the Captain. "He's—"

The door swung open. His lordship's dark head was thrust around it. "By the bye," he said cheerily. "Who won?"

Hawkhurst's smile widened. "We did, sir. Bonaparte's thoroughly beaten."

"Oh, that's good, then," said Leith, and closed the door.

Staring after him, Buchanan finished his interruped sentence. ". . . All about in his upper works!" he decreed.

Hurrying across the Great Hall, Lord Leith paused under the portrait that hung in the place of honour. Long, well-opened dark eyes smiled down at him; thick, slightly curling dark hair, near black, tumbled over a fine brow. The eyebrows were heavy but well shaped, the cheekbones high in a lean planed face with a firm nose, wide sensitive mouth, and squarely strong jaw. Clad in full regimentals, Tristram Leith had been so impressive that a newly presented debutante had once swooned at the very sight of him. Yet despite his looks and his commanding height, he'd never been one to give himself airs, thought his father wistfully, and like many large men was more inclined to be shy than aggressive. An heir to be proud of. But—if it *was* true—if dear Tris was gone . . . Leith sighed, and his shoulders sagged. If it was truth, then he had no heir.

In the salon, Hawkhurst turned to greet his wife, who had come into the room from the terrace. "What were you about, love?" he asked.

"Looking for Sally, but I learned she was with her Aunt in London. I went into the garden and broke the sad news to a—er—guest who was walking in the shrubbery. She asked that I tell Leith she has returned to London, but," her voice quavered, "I could not bear to see him just then. Oh, Garret, did you tell him? Has he accepted it bravely?"

"Bravely?" her brother snorted. "Blithely might be a better word!"

Much shocked, Euphemia cried, "Simon!"

"The man's intellect has become disordered!" Buchanan persisted.

"My heavens!" Horrified, Euphemia searched her husband's face. "Garret, has it so affected the poor soul?"

"No, no," he said comfortingly. "You know Leith. He simply refuses to believe that Tristram is killed. God grant he has the right of it. His optimism is fairly astounding, and even should it prove unjustified, may give him the time to more easily adjust to—"

Again, the door opened. His lordship rushed in, looking utterly distraught. Euphemia shrank against her husband's strong arm, and Buchanan gave the appearance of thoroughly regretting his earlier indictment.

"Do you know, Hawk," Leith demanded, with great indignation, "who it will be?"

The three young people stared at him speechlessly.

"Glick!" he uttered. "Glick! Glick!"

Buchanan took an uneasy step backward.

"No, by God!" exclaimed Leith. "I'll not have that whelp here!"

Understanding returned the smile to Hawkhurst's fine eyes. "Herbert Glick?" he mused. "See your point, sir. Dreadful slowtop!"

The light dawning, Euphemia said sympathetically, "Is Sir Herbert next in line, then?"

"He is! Revolting little Macaroni! I'll not have it!" Fire in his eye, Leith started for the door again, but returned to take Euphemia's hand and kiss it gracefully. "Your pardon, child. I've not expressed my very deep thanks for your kindness in coming here. But you see it is not so sad a duty as you had feared. My son is missing, not slain. I am sure of it!"

Holding his hand in both hers, Euphemia, her warm heart aching, said, "But—dear sir, forgive me—what if it *is* so?"

For an instant his eyes held an unspeakable desolation. Then he said in an awed tone, "By Jove! Then, I collect I would at once prepare myself. If—if it is indeed truth, I shall have no choice." He looked at them one by one in the manner of a faithful hound fearing to be put out on a stormy night. "I should have to—to settle down; take myself a wife, and get another heir." His voice sank almost to a whisper. "Egad."

They were all regarding him with frank incredulity, and he asked, "Do you not think anyone will have me?"

Finding his voice, Hawkhurst stammered, "Wh-why, dear sir, you've never had the least difficulty in finding—ah—fair companions."

"No," Leith agreed. "But—this will be different, don't y'see? Marriage. A lady young enough to—" His shoulders drew back and the light was in his eyes once more. "Well, if I must—I must! None shall say Kingston Leith failed what was due his name! Glick? No, by God! Tristram *will* come home— never doubt it. But, just in case, I mean to start looking around." He shook his head and his voice dropped. "Marriage. Good God!"

Rachel's progress along the companionway was erratic, and as she reached the door to the soldier's cabin, the vessel gave such a lurch that she was compelled to seize the handle to keep from being swept past. Righting herself, she dragged the door open, and went inside.

The soldier lay on his back, eyes closed and brows knit in a deep frown. The cuts on his cheek had begun to heal, and although he still looked pale and ill, the grey tinge was gone from his skin. Rachel closed the door and moved to stand beside him. As if he sensed her presence, he looked up. The frown was banished by the smile that came into his dark eyes but she had seen a dulled look of pain and, speaking his native French, scolded gently, "You have been trying to remember again!"

"No, no," he protested, brightly if inaccurately. "I have been resting here, just as your physician instructed, mademoiselle. If I was thinking of anything at all, it was of your kindness in allowing me to sail with you."

Undeceived, she observed, "I must be less kind, do such deeds cause you to break out with perspiration, sir."

"To tell the truth," he said with an irrepressible twinkle, "it has been something of a tussle to stay in the bunk."

She laughed softly. "I quite believe you. Our Captain was certain it would be only a little rough, yet here is my poor Agatha laid down upon her bunk, convinced she will never see England again. Thus, assuming her duties, I am come to see how her patient goes on.''

The soldier had become quite fond of the plump little abigail. She has fussed over him very kindly during the interminable carriage ride to Ostend and confided that she dreaded the sea voyage. Despite her fears, she had boarded the yacht without complaint and remained dutifully beside him until they left the dock. No sooner had they started across the open sea, however, than she had begun to look miserably unwell and had finally all but galloped from the cabin. He was grateful to the comely woman, and had no wish for her to endure the evils of *mal de mer*, but he could not totally regret her indisposition since it had resulted in this visit from the enchanting Miss Strand.

''How very fortunate for me that you are not similarly afflicted,'' he said, watching that vivid little face and wondering if any lady in his past could possibly have been half as lovely. Her eyes flashed to him. Fearing he had offended, he hastened to add, ''I hope your little sister is not made ill?''

''Have you met Charity, then?'' she asked, surprised. ''I do not seem to recall.''

''She was so kind as to come and see me for a moment while we were in Brussels. I could not but notice how frail she is.''

Almost it was an apology, thought Rachel. As though he felt he'd overstepped the bounds and been called to account. She had not intended to imply disapproval and said lightly, ''And so you worry about her? But how kind in you. She is the dearest girl with the sweetest nature imaginable.''

''She seemed a very gentle lady. Forgive me if I presume, but—has she always been confined to an invalid chair?''

Rachel sighed regretfully. ''No. You would not guess it to see my sister as she is now, but when she was younger she was a dreadful tomboy. Three years ago, her pony fell with her. She almost died and, when she recovered, was unable to walk.'' She checked, her face bleak, then went on. ''She had such a terrible time, but at last, thanks to a friend, we found a fine surgeon who was able to help her.''

''And does he think she will walk again?''

''He says it is possible.'' She clasped her hands and said intensely, ''How I pray she will! But even if that cannot be, I am beyond words grateful that she is at least freed from suffering. She is so brave, and never complained, but until she had the operation I don't think she knew a day without pain. To see her now, happy and laughing again . . .'' She blinked and smiled rather unsteadily. "She is on the bridge at this very moment, doubtless to the delight of the Captain. One of the advantages, you see, of travelling on a private yacht."

"Yes. Er—do you often sail in her?"

"Only when we bring my sister to see the surgeon. M. Sanguinet has been so good as to allow us to travel in this way. It is very much more comfortable for Charity."

"M. Sanguinet." Clearly, she was at the very least, fond of that gentleman. Understandable, thought the soldier, glumly. On their first evening in Brussels, he had awoken to find himself in a luxurious bedchamber and had been puzzling at that circumstance when the dynamic young Frenchman had come in to grip his hand and say a fervent, "I am greatly in your debt, M. le Capitaine, and if there is—" He had interrupted, involuntarily, "But, I am not a Captain, sir," only to be at once devastated by a siege of pain so intense as to preclude any further conversation. The snatches of memory that were granted him were always costly, but this particular punishment had been exceptionally frustrating because he'd been most anxious to have a few words with Guy Sanguinet, and had not seen him since. It was apparent, however, that whatever the man's relationship to the sisters, it must be a close one. Perhaps Rachel was his betrothed. He was certainly a fine-looking fellow and if he was also rich enough to maintain so large a yacht must be a good catch. Stifling a sigh, he said, "I see. Then M. Sanguinet is the gentleman I've to thank for my passage."

"Yes," nodded Rachel, a dimple peeping by reason of the dejection in his eyes. Standing, she amended, "But not *this* M. Sanguinet. Guy's elder brother, Claude, owns *La Hautemant*. He sent Guy to escort us to Brussels, since he was unable to come himself, but I know he will want to thank you personally, because—"

The yacht rolled into a deep trough. Rachel's hold on the end of the bunk had relaxed. Taken off balance, she was thrown forward, and would have fallen had not the soldier grabbed for her and caught her.

Gradually, the vessel righted herself, though every board in her seemed to creak a protest. The wind howled through the rigging. From the hold came muffled crashes that spoke of cargo broken loose and tossed about by the violent movements of the yacht. Yet the uproar seemed remote, the cabin suddenly very quiet as blue eyes met eyes of brown. The soldier made no move to loosen his grip on Rachel's arms, nor did she seek to pull away. For a timeless space they regarded one another, he, leaning on one elbow, holding her so closely that he could breathe the sweet fragrance of her; she, astonished by the power of the hands that had caught her, and hypnotized by the ardent admiration so plain to read in the long, deep eyes.

He became aware suddenly, that his weight rested on his injured arm. He caught his breath and released Rachel hurriedly.

Recovering her scattered wits, she exclaimed, "Oh, my goodness! Again, you have hurt yourself while coming to my rescue!" She took a small bottle from the drawer of the washstand and peered at it uncertainly. "I wonder how much laudanum Agatha was giving you . . ."

"It is of *peu d'importance*," he smiled. "I shall not swallow the beastly brew."

She frowned on him deliciously. "I'll have you know, monsieur soldier, that I am accustomed to nursing invalids, and do not permit that my orders are questioned."

A large, surprisingly authoritative hand reached to remove the bottle from her fingers. He said in a very gentle voice, "No, but you see—I have no wish to sleep, just at this particular moment. I am almost well, and a surer cure would be for you to stay and talk to me."

During her short existence Rachel had faced the bitter tragedy of her adored father's sudden death and, having been left with utter chaos and her brother half a world away, had managed somehow to pull together the remnants of her life and so order it as to provide a pleasant home for her sister. Neither hard-hearted nor inflexible, she had learned to be self-sufficient and not easily swayed. Now, however, knowing she should leave, she said hesitantly, "At all events, I must go and—"

33

"No," he gripped her wrist. "Please do not leave me. I—There are things—er, just a few moments, I beg you!"

He released her hand but looked so desperate she could not refuse him. "Very well. But *only* for a few moments."

"I thank you. Indeed, I have so much for which to thank you. Your bravery in refusing to abandon me on the battlefield was—simply incredible. You nursed me when I must have been a wretched nuisance, and to have transported me to Brussels and persuaded your—er, M. Sanguinet to allow me to travel to England on his yacht—there are no words to—"

"Well, I do hope not!" she interrupted smilingly. "You were most gallant, sir, and it was the least I could do by way of repayment. I do not doubt but that you will find your fears regarding your—your past history, to be groundless. "Still," her eyes sparkeld mischievously, "you did not exactly aid my attempt to smuggle you out of the country, you know."

"Did I not?" He grinned, but then sobered and exclaimed in horror, "*Mon Dieu!* I'd not had the brains to consider it! You may very well have incriminated yourself by allowing me to travel in your company!"

"I wish you will not fly into the boughs. I assure you that if you are discovered, I shall claim you deceived me, and I had no knowledge of what a great villain you are. There. Is that sufficient to calm your conscience?"

He smiled wryly, some of the anxiety leaving his eyes, and Rachel sat down on the opposite bunk and added, "I merely meant that in addition to being *such* a rogue, you are a confirmed marplot. Do you recall informing Monsieur Sanguinet that you are not a Captain? Infamy!"

"Yes, and I thank you for the attempt to lend me some dignity. Had I known my promotion was of your making I'd have accepted it with better grace."

"How do you know it was a promotion? You might very well be a Major."

He chuckled at this. " So long as we are indulging in fancy, I will be a Colonel, at the very least, if you please."

She was slightly stunned by the effect of mirth on that lean face and groped for something to say that was even moderately sensible. "I wonder now if I served you a bad turn. We are not sure if you *are* French, despite the fact that you speak it as though it were your native tongue.''

''As do you, ma'am.''

''Yes, but I had a fiendish French governess who browbeat me from the nursery days until I went to the Seminary.''

''And perhaps I had a similar experience,'' he nodded. ''Is that what you mean?''

''I suppose it is not impossible,'' she said demurely. ''Though I would have supposed you to have had a tutor and to have gone to Oxford rather.''

He was unable to repress a laugh and Rachel exclaimed, ''Ah! Now you do sound almost well again.''

''If I am, it is purely thanks to you.''

She scanned him thoughtfully. He did look better and seemed much more comfortable than he'd been during those first bad days. His expression was remote again, as if his mind wrestled with some knotty problem. She waited, marvelling at how completely at ease she felt in his company; more as though he were some very dear friend, or even a brother to replace her absent and so-loved Justin.

In his turn, the soldier was pondering her kindnesses. How sweetly protective of her to have invented his captaincy. Was it possible that he was indeed an officer? Perhaps of lesser rank? An officer, surely, would not be likely to have committed murder. He smiled, cynically amused by such a hopeful and ridiculous thought. ''What stuff!''

He'd not realized he spoke aloud until Rachel uttered a startled ''*What* did you say?''

''Oh—er, nothing of import, mademoiselle.''

''Nothing of import!'' She rose, her hands clasped, her eyes alight with excitement. ''But—you spoke English! And with no *trace* of an accent!''

He blinked at her stupidly. ''I . . . did?''

''And still are!'' Continuing in the same language, she cried, ''Oh, sir! Can it be possible that you are English?''

''I remember speaking French.'' He pressed a hand to his temple in bewilderment. ''So—I thought—that is, I was sure . . .''

He looked mystified and distressed, and fearing his struggle for recollection might precipitate another of his exhausting attacks, she said hurriedly, "Do not worry at it now. You must be very tired." She walked to the door, becoming aware that *La Hautemant* was behaving in a less violent fashion, and that the storm must be drifting away. Pausing, she turned back. "I will ask just one more question, if I may. Sir—do you *think* in English? Or in French?

He considered for only a second. His eyes widened and he exclaimed, "In English! I *do*, by George! I think in *English*!"

"Our mystery is quite *definitely* solved!" she laughed. "None but an Englishman could say 'by George!' in just that way!"

3

From the depths of the bolted-down armchair in her stateroom, Sister Maria Evangeline wailed, "Come in, child," and as Rachel closed the door and hurried to her, she went on in that voice of affliction, "Can you understand it? The flowers and beasts and birds; the wonders of sunshine and moonlight; so many lovely things. But—why a storm at sea? I ask and ask, but am granted no answer!"

Smiling fondly, Rachel crossed to dampen a towel at the washbasin and returned to dab it at the good sister's greenishly clammy features. "Why disease?" she contributed. "Why famine and flood; or flies; or such savageries as the Spanish Inquisition, wrought in the name of religion?"

The nun raised a drooping hand. "One thing at a time, my Rachel. I am still arguing with Him over a storm at sea, and must not confuse the issue by inserting all these other matters."

"Your arguments must have been well taken, dear one," Rachel laughed. "We have passed through the storm and are even now standing off the Dover Tidal Basin."

"What?" Hope lit the pale face. "Have I truly lived through this unspeakable ordeal? Father—I thank You! When shall we land, child?"

"The Captain seems to have been told we may have to wait for some while. There are so many ships bearing wounded from the battle. They are calling it the Battle of Waterloo—did you know?"

"I had heard La Belle Alliance." The nun waved away the towel and, tottering to the porthole, expressed her profound sympathy for the tortures the wounded must have endured on so frightful a crossing, interrupting herself to cry ecstatically that

37

she could see the cliffs. "Oh, for solid ground under my feet! Did the Captain—" She turned about, and said in startled accents, "The *Captain*? You never went up to the bridge alone, Rachel?"

"Oh, it was safe enough, I assure you. I am a good sailor, and—"

"I had not thought of it in just that way." The nun returned to her chair. "Sit down, child. I am feeling more the thing now, and we should talk. But, first—who is with our gallant murderer?"

Rachel seated herself obediently, experiencing the nervousness that had gripped her in years past when she had been sent to Sister Maria Evangeline's tiny office at the Seminary and had stood with quaking knees before the old desk, dreading the reprimand about to be dealt her. "He is alone, ma'am. But I looked in on him for a few minutes, and—"

"How few?"

So that was it. Vexed because she knew that she was blushing, she answered, "Perhaps ten. No longer. Do you brand me a scarlet woman for such? He is—"

"What *I* brand you is of little account, my dear. It is what others may think that matters."

"I am not a girl straight from the schoolroom, Sister. I have had to fend for myself—and Charity—ever since Papa died. Much I care what gossips may make of so trite a thing!"

"You are a lady of Quality, and *must* care."

Her eyes very bright, Rachel argued fiercely, "I am very poor *ton*, ma'am. As well you know! When my dear father was driven by desperation to—" she bit her lip, her hands clenching, "—to cheat at cards, we were dropped as though we had never existed. That scorn—that merciless disdain killed Papa!"

The nun, her face studiedly enigmatic, was silent. Rachel shot a glance at her and went on, "Do not imagine I defend his behaviour. I know that what he did was inexcusable. But—I know also how bedevilled was the poor soul! It is equally wrong to judge someone until you also have had to sit at the bedside of a dear one who suffers unendingly; to know that help could be found, but lack the funds to command it."

"I would never presume to judge, my dear. But—"

"Well—*they* judged!" Rachel flared, cheeks bright with anger. "And they condemned not only Papa, but Justin. *Justin!* That gentle boy, wholly innocent of any wrongdoing! I was with him in Piccadilly one day when a 'friend' cut him dead, before heaven knows how many people!" Galled by that memory, she twisted a fold of her skirt into a tight knot. "Justin shrugged and told me it didn't signify. It did! He was *white*! I knew how deeply he was hurt! Odious creatures! I could have scratched every one!"

Inwardly in sympathy with the girl's passion, the nun persisted, "The more reason why you should allow no breath of scandal to touch you again. If you cavort about, unescorted, there are always eyes to see and tongues to wag."

"And shall it spread through countless servants' halls that I ventured alone to the bridge of a private yacht, ma'am?" Rachel asked, with a curl of the lip.

"Perhaps." The nun leaned back in her chair, elbows on the arms, and her several chins resting on the fingers of her folded hands. "And if they would gossip at that, think how much they could make of your being alone in a cabin with—"

"With a very sick man?"

"With a very handsome young man," Sister Maria Evangeline corrected. "Who is almost well." She saw Rachel's cheeks flame once again, and the angry eyes lower in sudden confusion. "You are betrothed, dear child. And must consider the feelings of the man you love."

The blue eyes, very wide, flashed to her.

"Claude," reminded the nun mildly.

"Oh." The fiery blush faded, leaving no colour in the girl's cheeks.

Sister Maria Evangeline lowered her hands and bent forward. "You *do* love him?"

Briefly, Rachel had the look of a fawn at bay before a pack of wolves. "I— He has been—so good. And—and—"

"And paid for Charity's surgeon, and all the examinations and medicines since then."

Rachel took a deep breath, and recovered her poise. "Yes," she said defiantly.

The nun settled back again, watching that proud young face

with its uptilted little chin. "My dear—are you not confusing gratitude with the tender passion?"

"I do not know, ma'am," answered Rachel stiffly. "For I have never known the tender passion. Gratitude, I do know. And," she shrugged, "one must be realistic, after all. Who marries for love these days?"

Mr. Shotten's frieze coat, lurid but grease-spotted waistcoat, and dirty fingernails were decidedly out of place in the best parlour of "The Ship" in old Dover town. Wholly unabashed, however, he stuck a straw between his stained teeth, and, his eyes travelling Rachel's shapely figure, said, "All as I knows is Monseer Sanguinet says you was to wait here 'til he gets back. I'm a simple cove. I don't argify with the likes o' Monseer. If *you* feels like argifying with him, Miss, I 'spect as that's yer right, seein's England be a free country, and—"

A gloved hand, holding a gold-chased riding crop, flashed before Mr. Shotten's beefy features. The straw was slashed from his teeth, and his indignant "Ey!" rose into a yowl as the leather cracked across his upraised knuckles.

"How do you dare so address the lady, foulness?" Guy Sanguinet, hazel eyes narrowed with wrath, guided Rachel gently to one side, and superbly indifferent to the awed faces of the maids that peered around the hall door, growled, "Your apologies make, and yourself remove! *Vite!*"

Shotten's beady eyes glittered with hatred, but he essayed a clumsy bow and said defiantly, "Sorry I am if I upset Monseer's—" The crop inched upward, Sanguinet's white teeth gleaming in a savage grin. Shotten stepped back and added with haste, "I mean—Miss Strand. But, Monseer says—"

"My brother, peasant, knows it is I who have escort Miss Strand and her sister. *Oui?*" Shotten merely glowering in a truculent silence, Sanguinet continued, "Then, *assurement*, he know also that the ladies they are safe in my care. You would not," his voice dropped silkily, "presume, this to deny?"

Shotten whistled through his teeth in a soft hissing that betrayed his early years as an ostler. His hatred was very obvious, but after a minute's cogitation, he said, "I 'spect as you'll tell

40

Monseer that I tried *awful* 'ard to do wot he asked of me to do? I 'spect as you'll tell 'im you put yerself above Monseer.''

"Do you know what *I* expect, Shotten?" purred Sanguinet. "I expect that in just ten of the second you will be unable my brother to tell *one* of your ugly words. Now," he stepped closer, smiling into the sullen features before him. "Miss Strand's gentle eyes, you shall cease to offend with the view of your unfortunate carcass. You would wish me to help you in this, perhaps?"

Her "gentle eyes" dancing with delight, Rachel walked to the window and glanced out at the spacious garden. How glad she was that Guy had been beside her when *La Hautemant* at last was granted permission to enter the Tidal Basin and tie up at the dock. Shotten had been waiting, and angry. The man made her skin creep, and only the knowledge that he feared Claude more than anyone living sustained her when she was occasionally obliged to endure his escort. He was leaving now, slouching towards the open door, and mumbling to himself under his breath. With one hand on the doorknob, he turned back.

"P'raps you can tell Monseer," he leered slyly, "why Miss brung that there soldier on Monseer's boat. And why that there soldier looks at Miss like—"

Sanguinet took a long stride forward, and Shotten fled.

Sanguinet slammed the door to, scowled darkly at it for a moment, then faced the girl who stood nervously fidgeting with the lace at her throat.

"Oh!" she exclaimed. "How I dislike that man! Why on earth does Claude employ such a horrid creature?"

Guy shrugged. "Occasionally, only. He belongs to my brother, Parnell." His riding whip tapped at his gleaming topboot, and with a slow frown he said, "His is the type of mind to hold evil thoughts of everyone. Nor is he alone in this." He slanted an oblique glance at her. "Speaking of which—what has become of our heroic *Capitaine?*"

The implication caused Rachel's heart to jump. "Sister Maria Evangeline took him under her wing, I believe," she replied, with a nonchalance that betrayed no hint of her awareness that the soldier occupied a room in this very inn.

Wandering to the fireplace, Sanguinet stared in silence at the empty grate. Rachel watched him uneasily, wondering if by right of their close friendship he was about to censure her, or if he was worried that his having allowed the soldier to accompany them would anger Claude. She had seldom seen the brothers together, but it was obvious that Claude was very much the head of his house, especially where Guy was concerned. Never, by the faintest inference, had Guy implied that a rift existed between them. Rachel had been quick to notice, however, that if she chanced to mention him, a gleam of amusement would come into Claude's eyes; a sardonic amusement. There was no doubt but that Parnell was his favourite, and she sensed that for Guy he held a barely concealed scorn; an impression she found disquieting.

Her knowledge of her betrothed was relatively slight, although she had been acquainted with him since childhood. She had never been quite sure of the way in which her father was linked to Sanguinet's financial enterprises, but that Strand was in some way of service to the younger man, she knew. They shared political persuasions, she'd gathered, and both found horse racing, gambling and beautiful women irresistible. Papa had often been a guest at the Sanguinet estate in Kent, and occasionally Parnell, the middle brother, had visited Strand Hall. When Rachel had left the schoolroom, Papa had made no secret of the fact that he cherished hopes for a marriage between her and Parnell, but try as she would, she had been unable to develop a liking for the Frenchman, and Charity was downright afraid of him. Handsome in a dark, gaunt fashion, he had strangely light eyes and an odd intensity of manner—like a leashed panther, said Charity. When Guy had put in an appearance, however, both sisters had warmed to him at once. They had soon learned that his heart was totally and hopelessly given to Parnell's ward, but he affected no die-away airs, and Rachel liked him as much for his droll humour and quiet, courtly manners, as for his unfailing gentleness with Charity. He spent much time in England on his brother's affairs, but after Rupert Strand's death, his visits to Strand Hall diminished, whereas Claude's became more frequent. Claude was older than Guy, by about ten years. He had never mentioned his age, but Rachel guessed him to be in the neighbourhood of forty. She knew that he was extremely wealthy, a power in international politics and finance, and possessed of a shocking reputation as a rake. But to the daughters of his old friend, he was the soul of sympathy and understanding. Accustomed to command, and surrounded by a small army of efficient servants, he had solved many of Rachel's hitherto insoluble problems with, as it seemed, the merest snap of his fingers. He was poised, elegant, gentle, knowledgeable, and an unfailing source of kindness and support. Cut by Society, and beset on every side by tradesmen, unpaid servants, staggering expenses, and her sister's deteriorating health, Rachel had come to rely more and more heavily on his advice. It was wrong, she knew, to allow him to do so much, but whenever she protested, he had some logical reason for offering assistance. "Am I not a trusted friend of the family?" he would say, rather wistfully. Or, with a shrug of impeccably clad shoulders and a kindly smile warming his light brown eyes, he would sigh, "I—the funds have; you, the children of my dearest friend, the need have. What would you?" When he had suddenly proclaimed that he'd searched Europe and believed he had discovered a man who might help her sister, Rachel had been overwhelmed. And when the surgeon had operated and Charity had been so wonderfully improved, she had gone down on her knees and thanked God for sending Claude Sanguinet to them.

Now, she sat on a sofa and took up a copy of *Ladies Magazine*. She turned the pages idly, her gaze drifting often to the quiet figure of the Frenchman and at last, setting the periodical aside having seen none of it, she said in a pleading voice, "I beg you will not think ill of me, Guy!"

He swung around at once, to view her with undisguised astonishment. "Why should I do this?"

She gave a sigh of relief. "You were so silent. And—I thought perhaps you too, would think I had been—er, that is to say—I swear to you—the soldier has never once uttered a single word to me that was improper!"

"*Très bien!*" He smiled. "He is another such as my brothers, eh? '*Integer vitae scelerisque purus.*' "

The quotation eluded Rachel, but she assumed it to be complimentary, and agreed, "Yes. Claude has been splendid. The best friend we have ever known."

Guy regarded her steadily. "So good a—friend—that you will his wife become."

An odd and unfamiliar acceleration of the pulse caused Rachel's breathing to become hurried. She tightened her fingers a little upon a fold in her gown and promised, "I will try to be a good wife to him."

He did not comment, but his brooding gaze remained fixed upon her. How solemn he was today. Curious, she asked with her sometimes startling frankness, "Guy—what disturbs you? Do you fancy me beneath his touch?"

He gave a shout of laughter and lapsing into French, said, "Never that! Only—I would think it an advantage was a lady—ah, fond of the man she married."

Sister Maria Evangeline's words echoed in Rachel's mind. ". . . Are you not confusing gratitude with the tender passion?" Defiantly, she asserted, "Well, I am! Very fond!"

Far from appearing pleased by so positive a reply, his eyes became sombre and after a moment he asked, "Have you never heard gossip about us, Rachel? Has no friend spoken with you of your betrothal?"

"I have few friends now. Oh, I've heard a few silly rumours, of course. Your brother is a man of large fortune, and always there are those who envy the rich. But, do not worry—I pay no heed to such gabble mongering."

He hesitated, then started towards her, the whip gripped very tightly in his hand. "Rachel—you are so very—" He halted, his head jerking around in irritation as a sharp knock preceded the opening of the door.

Shotten stepped inside and bowed much too low. "A cove's come from Dinan," he announced in his coarse fashion. "I'm orf! Got a job of work t'do."

"By whose orders?" Sanguinet demanded haughtily.

"The one wot pays me wages. Yer brother."

The insolence in the beady eyes was unmistakable. Ignoring it, Guy said, "The one from Dinan—he tell you this?"

"Yus. And he brung a littel word fer you as well, Sir. He's

44

waiting dahnstairs.'' He leered from one to the other, and was gone.

"Animal!" grated Guy. He turned to Rachel. "I shall see what is this 'littel word.' Meanwhile, what must I do? Escort you both back to Strand Hall? Or shall you wait here as Claude have . . . command.''

She looked keenly at him, but his face was bland. "Charity should be taken home as soon as possible. She is very pulled from the long journey and always does so much better in Sussex. I mean to wait for Claude, if you will be so kind as to escort her.''

"I am yours to command,'' he grinned, sweeping her a graceful bow. "So soon as may be, I shall return to your side until my 'splendid' brother come.''

Was she mistaken, thought Rachel, or had she for the first time glimpsed a bitter irony in his eyes? Before she had a chance to decide, he bowed and left her.

The messenger from Dinan brought word that Guy was to go at once to Sanguinet Towers, Claude's great house in Kent, and attend to some pressing problem there. Guy declined to explain the precise nature of the difficulty, but that he was vexed was very obvious. He grumbled in his uncertain English, "This is *honteux!* That is to say—''

"Disgraceful," Rachel supplied.

"*Oui.* Dis-grass-fool that I must abandon. Here. Alone!''

"Alone?" she laughed. "I have Sister Maria Evangeline and my dear Agatha. Between them, I shall be very well chaperoned, *à coup sur!*''

And so, ever gallant, Guy carried Charity off, promising to bear her safely to Strand Hall before himself proceeding to Kent. Rachel waved farewell from the front steps, then returned to her room having every intention to remain inside and work at her tatting. The sunny morning proved irresistible, however. Agatha, who was still recovering from the effects of their Channel crossing, had fallen into a doze in her chair. Rachel did not disturb her. She donned her prettiest bonnet, the poke a foam of lace dyed to the exact pale blue of her muslin gown, and, having draped a white lace shawl across her shoulders, took up her sunshade and went downstairs.

As she passed the desk, the clerk glanced up, smiled, and nodded politely. She thought, however, to detect a mild surprise in his eyes. He likely thought her fast to walk out with neither footman nor abigail. What would Sister Maria Evangeline think? She hesitated, frowned, but finally capitulated and, sighing, turned her steps instead to the rear of the inn, and the pleasant, sequestered gardens.

The sunshine was warm now, and she put up her parasol and started along the walk. Rounding a bend shielded by tall hollyhocks, she came upon a slender gentleman of middle age, intent upon planting a salute on the cheek of a plump lady who giggled coyly as she made a show of warding off his advances. They both were startled by Rachel's sudden advent and became blushfully intent upon a clump of hydrangeas they vociferously admired as rhododendrons. Her eyes sparkling with amusement, Rachel strolled on and, following this capriciously curving path, next encountered a tall gentleman who sat with hands loosely clasped between his knees, apparently absorbed by the progress of a stream of ants across the path.

Rachel halted, her heart for some odd reason commencing to pound erratically. The soldier was clad in a passably fitting brown jacket, rather snug beige breeches and glossy topboots. He had discarded the bandages, and his dark hair was so arranged as to fall across his brow, hiding the head wound. He glanced up. A brilliant smile banished the glumness from his eyes even as it snatched Rachel's breath away. He sprang to his feet, exclaiming, "Miss Rachel! I heard you had left Dover! Oh, but this is famous! May I walk with you? Or—should you prefer to sit here, perhaps?"

Flattered, but strangely offstride, she gave him her hand. Instead of shaking it, he stared down at it for a second, then raised it to his lips. It was not an unfamiliar gesture, yet she began to tremble.

He lifted his head, looking at her gravely; saying nothing, yet saying so much.

"Where do you want me to put the tray, sir?"

Startled, he glanced to the parlourmaid, then took the heavy tray from her hands.

"Oh, sir!" she exclaimed shyly. "I can do that!"

"And very well, I've no doubt," he smiled. "But you must admit that I'm just a trifle larger than you are."

She giggled, her head uptilted as he towered over her. "A *trifle*! Oh, my, but you're a proper caution, sir! Will ye be wanting another cup and saucer for the lady?"

He turned to Rachel. "May I beg that you spare me a few moments? I've something marvellous to tell you."

Turning a deaf ear to conscience, Rachel said, "We-ell . . ."

And thus, very soon, the little maid having provided another napkin and plate as well as the cup and saucer, Rachel handed the soldier his tea and told him he looked "vastly better. Indeed, I had not thought to see you up and about so soon."

"Were it not for you and Sister Maria Evangeline, I doubt you'd have done so," he said earnestly. "She provided me these clothes, bless her! I mean to repay her, of course, but how she ever found 'em, I cannot fathom." His grin flashed, and he added with a twinkle, "I'm not exactly an easy fit."

Rachel chuckled. "I believe that! Now—what is this 'marvellous' news?"

He set aside his cup and said in a voice that rang with excitement, "My name! Part of it, at least!"

"Oh!" Rachel clapped her hands in delight and came near to upsetting the tray balanced on the stone bench between them. The soldier laughed and righted it, and she cried an impatient, "Tell me—do!"

"My first name only, I'm afraid. It is—" He paused, with a boyish desire to increase her anticipation. "—Tristram."

"Tristram!"

How sweetly she spoke his name, and how genuinely overjoyed she seemed to share his small triumph. Watching her, he thought the blue gown with its tiny puff sleeves, swooping neckline and lace-edged flounce admirably became her, while the bonnet set off her bewitching face to perfection. She was as kind and warm-hearted as she was beautiful, and gently born, beyond doubting. There was so much more he longed to know of her. Why did she wait here alone save for her abigail? For whom did she wait? Where was her home? And what were her circumstances? Was she (terrible thought!) promised? But he knew he had not the right to ask any questions at all, and therefore waited silently.

If he did not speak aloud, his eyes spoke for him and, thinking she had never seen such expressive eyes, Rachel's breath began to flutter in her throat so that she said rather hurriedly, "Oh—do listen! Someone must be holding a musicale!"

He listened obediently and with his gaze still fixed upon her face, asked, "Are you fond of music, ma'am?"

"Very fond. Is it not beautiful? I do not know the piece, but it sounds like Haydn."

"Handel, I believe," he corrected dreamily.

So he knew music! He was as yet obviously unaware of that recollection and did not appear to have paid the usual costly price for it. Striving to sound casual, she probed, "You are right. I'm so forgetful about some things. Just today, for instance, I heard a quotation, and for the life of me, cannot translate it. '*Integer vitae scelerisque purus.*' Do you know what it means?"

Tristram was thinking that the curve of her lips should be captured on canvas. And, envying the artist who would be so fortunate as to attempt it, responded, "Loosely translated, it means—someone who leads an upright life and has no vices. A sterling character, I—" But he checked, flinching to a blinding stab of pain, the cup toppling from his hand.

"Oh, I am so sorry!" Rachel cried remorsefully. "I should not have—"

"No, no!" He kept his head downbent for a moment, then looked up again, a trifle breathless, but managing to smile into her frightened eyes. "It is really much less . . . violent than it was. And—of far shorter duration. *Voilà!*" He gestured theatrically. "All gone! Besides, I cannot allow it to get the best of me, you know. I simply *must* find out who I am, what I am, before I can—er—attend to certain other vital matters."

Rachel hid her quite inexplicable blushes by reaching down to pick up the cup he'd dropped. Fortunately, it had fallen on the grass between the stepping-stones of the walkway and was still intact. "You have somewhere to start, now," she said, restoring the cup to the tray, but avoiding his gaze. "Tristram is not a very common name, and there is no doubt but that you were an officer. You must go to the Horse Guards, where you will likely discover your identity in a winking."

With a crooked grin, he said, "And discover also, perhaps, that a noose awaits me."

"Oh, no! You do not really believe that?"

She looked distressed, and he wanted no grimness to spoil this idyll, so said whimsically, "Why, murder's none so dreadful in some cases, Miss Strand. Suppose I was quite run off my legs, fell into the clutches of a cents-per-center, and became so incensed I put a period to him—that would be a public service, eh?"

"Probably," she chuckled. "But do you really think you strangled a money-lender?"

"If I did they'll likely have a medal for me. And only think how much worse it could be. I might instead have done something really frightful—like cheating at cards, for example. Now *that* is surely—" He was aghast to see her face paper white, her eyes enormous against that pallor. "What is it?" he asked sharply. "I was jesting, merely. I didn't really mean I had done such a thing."

"No-no, of—of course you did not. Would you care for some more tea? I can ask the maid for a clean cup."

"Lord, no. That one is immaculate compared to some of the dishes we ate from in Spain, I assure you!" She smiled, but watching the delicate movements of her little hands as she wielded teapot and strainer, he was irked because he had evidently said something that had triggered a shocking memory. The nun had mentioned a brother, Justin, who'd gone out to India. Perhaps he'd *had* to leave England! Perhaps he'd been a gamester, or—

"It must be dreadful for you to know nothing of your past, however you joke about it," said Rachel quietly, handing him his tea. "I think you are being terribly brave."

"Yes, aren't I?" Pleased by the responsive gleam that crept into her eyes, he went on, "Still, I've been thinking, ma'am, that perhaps it is better I don't discover the truth. I might be wed to a large, proud lady of domineering disposition, who would terrify me!"

He was the type, thought Rachel, who would face physical danger unflinchingly, but yet was so gentle he could be cowed by just such a lady. Amused, she pointed out, "You'd not have wed her, surely, did she not have a heart of gold."

"My father forced me to it," he said promptly. "He is a tyrant, I've no doubt, and— Oh, Gad! Suppose she has presented me with several noisy offspring?"

"Several?" she questioned, her eyes dancing. "Four— perhaps?"

"Four! Never say so! But—if twins run in the family, I collect it might be worse!"

"Oh, a good deal worse. In that case, you might have ten! All boys. And wildly undisciplined!"

He shrank and, clasping his brow, said, "That settles it! I'll not go back!"

"What? Sir—how dastardly! You never mean to abandon them all?"

"Self-preservation," he decreed blithely.

Rachel said a stern, "It will not do, sir! Too wicked by half!"

She had entered into his farce so merrily that her dismals seemed quite gone, thank heaven. Managing to sound crestfallen, he pleaded, "You'll never condemn me to such a fate? Can you not build me a kinder past, Miss Strand?"

"May I?" she said eagerly. "Let me see now— Ah! I have it! You *are* wed, but to a reigning Toast. A glorious lady, delightfully accomplished, poised, and so charming you are the envy of all England!"

"Euphemia," he nodded, absently.

Rachel asked a somewhat sharp, "Who?"

"Er—your pardon?"

"You said—'Euphemia.' "

He stared at her in confusion. "No, did I?" Who in the deuce was Euphemia? And—dammit! Why were just these occasional scraps of memory so tantalizingly tossed at him? His smile a little forced, he went on, "Well, Euphemia sounds right for such a Fair, do you not think? It's the Royal Mail to a wheelbarrow, *that's* who I murdered!"

"Euphemia?" Rachel gasped.

"Her lover."

"Lover? But—she's your wife!"

"Ah, but you see I am away for long periods. Yearning for her. Counting the hours we are apart. At last, I'm given a leave. I rush home, gallop up the steps of our palatial mansion—and am trampled underfoot by the exodus."

"Exodus?" she echoed, intrigued.

"Of Euphemia's lovers. Scads of 'em! No—don't laugh, for after all she is a reigning Toast; all of London kissing her little feet. It stands to reason there'd be more than one."

"They—why," she asked mirthfully, "why did you murder only *one*?"

"Hmmnn—see your point. Well, I could probably catch only one—after being trampled like that. But I caught him by the ankle, flung him down, and put an end to the beastly rogue. And—*that's* why I joined up! To hide myself in the anonymity of the rank and file!"

He looked so triumphant that Rachel broke into a peal of laughter. "*What* a tragedy! It is fairly heart-rending!"

"Then we won't have it! My apologies, Euphemia, but—farewell!" His smile faded. The words echoed strangely in his ears. "Euphemia—farewell . . ." And suddenly, he saw a pair of laughing, deep blue eyes; a charming female countenance, full of mischief; a tall girl, her hair a shining, coppery hue. A girl he had loved dearly. "By Jove!" he muttered. "So I am not wed, after all!"

Rachel had seen his expression change, and now remarked with studied calm, "So there *is* a Euphemia. Do you know her last name? Perhaps you could find her and discover your identity."

He frowned and concentrated desperately, but it was useless. Apart from that glimpse of her face, and the brief recollection of how deep had been his sorrow when she'd chosen some other fellow, there was nothing. "Alas—I cannot recall. But—I'm not wed! That I do know!"

"Oh. Then you are reprieved, *mon Capitaine*! Your—horde of twins does not exist. At least, for the present."

Her eyes twinkled at him, and he knew that they evoked memories of just such another pair of eyes, and that he loved even more deeply now than he had then. "Yes," he answered. And added, half to himself, "My past will trot itself out, sooner or later. The important thing now is my future—my golden dream."

"It sounds delightful," smiled Rachel. "I hope it may be realized."

Tristram gazed rather blankly at a cluster of daisies nodding white and yellow faces to the sun. For a moment he did not reply, then, lifting his eyes to hers, said gravely, "I pray it will, ma'am."

At about the same moment that Tristram dropped his teacup in the garden, Agatha Summers opened the door to Miss Strand's suite and admitted Sister Maria Evangeline. Her advice that her mistress was gone out for a walk in no way discomposed the nun, "for it is you I came to see, at all events."

Apprehensive, Agatha showed her visitor to a chair and stood before it, with hands clasped; a silent question mark.

"Sit down! Sit down!" commanded the nun in her brisk way. "That's better. Now—what I will say is to remain a confidence between the two of us. Have I your promise?"

"Oh, yes, marm." Agatha laid one plump hand on her generous bosom. "I do solemnly swear—"

"Well, do not. Swearing unnerves me. Tell me, rather— what d'ye think of Claude Sanguinet?"

Her eyes very round, Agatha gulped, "M-Monseigneur? Why—he be a fine gentleman, I'm sure. And very rich. And—" Seeking about, she added lamely, "And none so bad to look on—considering."

"Pish and posh! Be honest with me, girl! D'ye *like* him? Do you think he will make your mistress a good husband? Do you think she *loves* him?"

Agatha fiddled with her apron. Her acquaintance with the nun was small; indeed, she'd seen more of her since Waterloo than in all the years Miss Rachel had been a pupil at the Seminary. Longing to speak out, she said hesitantly, "It bean't my place, marm, to—"

"Make it your place!" Sister Maria Evangeline leaned forward. "One confession for another! I'm out to scuttle the Frenchman. But I need your help!"

"If that be your game, Sister," said Agatha joyfully, "I'm emboldened to say I do not trust him! Nor I don't think as Master Justin ever liked him neither! All smiles and syrup fer Miss Rachel, he is, but never a polite 'how de do' or 'thankee' fer the likes of me! Mrs. Hayward, our housekeeper, do says as he's a Unhung Villin!" She tucked in her chins and nodded solemnly. "And I've heered a whisper here and a grouse there—enough to put two and two together and not come up with five! He don't give me the shivers like his brother Parnell with them moley eyes o' his, but—"

Fascinated by this flood, the nun was moved to interject, "*What* eyes?"

"Moley. All whitish, they be. And 'tis said as he cannot see in daylight hardly, for all his grand manners and good looks! What's more, Mr. Fisher, he's the butler at the Hall and was used to be Mr. Rupert's man, he says as the Sanguinets won't hire no local people at The Towers—nor at their chatho in France, neither! All the help's took on in London or Paris, and a mighty close-mouthed, stand-offish lot they be. Mr. Fisher told Mrs. Hayward—I heered him—that the rag-tags Monseigneur's got about him in France is such as makes his back get all over itchy the minute he sets foot on the estate. Not that he's done it since poor Mr. Rupert passed to his reward. Still," she pursed her lips and nodded meaningfully, "it goes to show. Don't it?"

"It does, indeed," agreed Sister Maria Evangeline, unfailingly impressed by the shrewdness of the British rustic. "But —if I thought Miss Rachel truly cared for him—"

"Care fer him!" snorted Agatha, indignantly. "She don't give the snap of her fingers fer him—saving only that his doctor helped Miss Charity!" She sighed, her hostility fading. "I must own he done us a great service there, and no mistake. If it weren't fer that surgeon o' his, poor little Miss Charity might still be laid down on her bed, so bad as ever."

"True. And Rachel dotes on her sister. It would be logical enough, I suppose, for gratitude to deepen into tender emotion."

Agatha folded her arms and, mincing no words, said an emphatic, "No! I might've thought so, marm. But not since I see the way she looks at the soldier! Now *he's* a gentleman born, and no one can't tell me different! Not a whimper out of him in all that long drive from Brussels to Ostend! And him in downright misery every turn o' the wheels. Always put together a smile, he could. And never did I do the smallest thing to try to help the poor soul, but what he had a 'thank you.' Miss Rachel, she's been a troubled young lady since she come across him. Surely!"

"Troubled? But—I thought you said . . . ?"

"Ar, I did, marm. She knows now what she didn't know afore, I think. What she'll be a'missing of, poor lass. Me heart bleeds fer her, so it does."

"Excellent!" beamed the nun. Leaning closer, she reached to grasp the bewildered Agatha's hand, squeeze it, and murmur conspiratorially, "Then this is what I want you to do . . ."

4

*R*achel *returned from her rather disturbing conversation with* Captain Tristram to find Agatha still laid down upon her bed. The abigail refused the services of an apothecary, moaning that although she was "all over aches and pains" and her throat "scratchy as a hedgehog," she was likely only sickening for a putrid cold. "I'll do, can I just rest, Miss Rachel," she asserted nobly. "Sorry I am to serve ye so—just when ye needs me. But the truth is you'll do well to stay away! We cannot have ye coming down sick—not with M. Claude expected any minute! Sister promised to look in on me. Now you get on out of doors! Such a lovely day as it be. You need a good long walk!"

She had reckoned without her mistress's innate kindness. Rachel refused to leave and fussed over her so anxiously that the scheming Agatha began to fear her deception would be pierced. Sister Maria Evangeline, arriving later in the afternoon, was inwardly aghast to find her former pupil seated beside Agatha's bed, reading to her. The abigail's eyes rolled a message of helpless frustration, but the good Sister merely smiled, murmured placidly that she was sure Agatha would be better "by the end of the week," and departed.

The following morning brought winds and building clouds, and by eleven o'clock rain set in to continue steadily for the rest of the day. Rachel busied herself in writing letters, doing all she might for Agatha, and fighting the memory of a deep voice and two dark eyes that seemed always to hold a smile. Enjoying the luxury of being waited on, Agatha was fretted by conscience and the fear that monseigneur would arrive before her 'illness' had served its purpose. By the next day, however, there was still no word from France, and the brilliant morning would, she prayed, prove Miss Rachel's undoing.

A more tangible persuasion arrived in the shape of Sister Maria Evangeline. Having commiserated at the bedside of "poor Agatha," the lady turned on Rachel and asserted that she looked positively hagged. "Change your dress at once, child, and get yourself into the sunshine! I will stay with Agatha and help her eat these bon-bons I have brought. Nor is there need for you to hurry back, for I've nothing to do the rest of the day and would welcome the opportunity to be occupied."

Rachel thanked her but pointed out that since she had no groom in Dover, and Guy was not yet returned, she had better confine her wanderings to the garden. The nun became quite vehement, however, and announced her intention to go and hire up a groom and hack. "I want no arguments, miss! Have on your habit by the time I return—else I shall spank you, just as I was used to do!"

Since Rachel could not recall ever having been subjected to corporal punishment at the Seminary, this threat elicited nothing more than a ripple of laughter. The prospect of a ride on such a lovely morning lifted her rather depressed spirits, and when the nun came back, she was clad in a dark blue riding habit with Brussels lace foaming at the throat and wrists, and upon her curls a jaunty little hat with long ribbons of matching blue velvet.

"How fetching you look, love," said Sister Maria Evangeline fondly. "What a pity I could not hire a groom." She saw disappointment banish the girl's happy glow and went on airily, "Captain Tristram was about to ride out, however, and has agreed to be your escort."

A flush lit Rachel's cheek. "I trust you did not compel him, ma'am?"

Recalling the soldier's transformation from a polite but rather downcast man to an ecstatic young idiot, the nun smothered a smile and allowed that she'd not found it necessary to "compel" him. "Which was as well," she added, "since I doubt I'd prove equal to the task!"

The gleam in those faded hazel eyes did not escape Rachel.

Blushing, she frowned, "But—I thought you said it was improper in me to—"

"Good heavens, what missishness! To be alone with him in his cabin was one thing! But to ride out in broad daylight with the gentleman who saved our lives, quite another! Besides, I've already told the host that Captain Tristram is an old friend and charged by Monsieur Guy to be of assistance to you in his absence. Now—if you mean to repay my wicked lies by standing there like a ninny—by heaven, *I* shall ride out with him!"

The prospect of the large lady mounted side-saddle drew a giggle from Agatha. Rachel delayed only long enough to adjure her abigail to rest, before hurrying down the hall, riding crop and gloves in her hand, and the train of her habit swept over her arm.

Descending the stairs, she saw Tristram waiting in the vestibule. Her steps slowed. He was turned from her, but his height and the attractively tumbled dark hair were unmistakable. He turned as she approached, revealing a cravat her brother would have marvelled over. She thought with something of a shock that he looked every inch the aristocrat and, for the first time, wondered what his family might think did they learn he was associating with the notorious Rachel Strand. He came eagerly to meet her, and she gave him her hand, conscious of the alarming tremor that raced through her as his long fingers closed about it.

In the yard a groom led promising hacks to them. Tristram threw Rachel up onto the bay gelding, adjusted the stirrup with practiced ease, then swung into the saddle of the big black that the groom innocently assured him "could carry a mountain!"

They rode through the heavily trafficked streets side by side, and not until they were ambling along a country lane did Rachel realize how surely she had been guided. When she complimented him upon this accomplishment, he slanted his twisted grin at her and admitted he'd consulted with the stable hands to obtain detailed instructions of a desirable route.

"Whoever advised you was inspired," she said, glancing around glad-eyed. The lane they followed was a tunnel of mingling greens, the branches of the trees meeting overhead to create a delicately waving canopy through which the sunlight painted ever-changing shadows on the lane. The scents of damp earth, wet bark, and hedge roses sweetened the pure air and, breathing deep of it, Rachel exclaimed, "Oh! How wonderful to be out of doors! Come! I'll race you to the cliffs!" She threw him a look of sparkling mischief, drove home her heels, and the bay sprang forward.

Tristram followed, but kept a check on the big horse who strained and fought the iron hand that held him back so exasperatingly when he knew he should be far ahead of the puny gelding.

They came up with Rachel at the edge of the cliffs. She had slipped from the saddle and stood holding the reins and gazing out across the sea. It was truly a glorious day, a few fluffy clouds decorating a deeply blue sky, a slight breeze ruffling Rachel's curls and setting the ribbons of her hat to dancing behind her. The sea, a rich blue green, was touched here and there with soft little whitecaps, and far off towards France the sails of a ship billowed majestically.

The beauties of the sea and sky were lost upon Tristram. He did not dismount, but sat there marvelling at the perfection of this slim girl; the delicate features and determined little chin, the soft, fair hair, the dainty figure. More important, perhaps, her quick, merry humour that responded so readily to any teasing remark he chanced to make, and the sweetly earnest way she had of instructing him in commonplace matters that were taken for granted by her, but unfamiliar to him. Several times on the way through old Dover town she had undertaken such instruction, and often as she spoke a chord of memory had stirred faintly, and he'd known that the awareness of those things was sleeping somewhere in his battered head. Rachel glanced at him. He realized he was staring and dismounted quickly. "Whew! You're a bruising rider!"

"You let me win," she accused. "Not sporting, sir. However gallant."

"Oh, no. You forget I'm an invalid and have to ride cautiously."

She had not missed the lithe, unconscious grace with which he swung from the saddle, and said, "You do not look an invalid, but it was thoughtless of me. And to bounce about on horseback must hurt your head.''

He threw up one hand, laughing. ''Acquit me of that, I beg you! Have you judged me to have a *very* poor seat?''

She had judged him to ride superbly and, flustered, answered, ''No! I did not mean—'' She checked, her infectious chuckle rippling out as she saw his grin. ''Odious man! You know what I meant. But—does your head pain you?''

''Thank you—no. Save that my brain is so stupid. Is that an island?''

Following his gaze, she exclaimed, ''Good gracious! I see I have my work cut out for me! That is Calais, sir! In France.''

''Oh, is it?'' he asked politely and feasted his eyes upon her profile, wondering if he would ever have the right to tell this darling girl how he adored her.

A seagull swooped low over them, voicing its piercing cries, and shading her eyes to look up at it, Rachel said, ''And—that is—''

''A feather castle,'' he murmured.

Surprised, she asked, ''The gull?''

''Oh—my apologies to him. I had thought you meant the cloud.''

''Is that what you call them? Feather castles? How lovely! Is it part of a quotation, perhaps?''

He frowned, then shrugged wryly. ''Alas, I don't know. Things pop in and out of my mind so haphazardly.'' She was gazing up at those vast white billows sailing high above them and, looking up also, he mused, ''But it's a fine castle, don't you think? Turrets and battlements—the whole article.''

''Yes,'' she smiled. ''An enchanted castle. I wonder if there are feather ladies inside . . . and feather knights.''

''But of course. And they ride feather horses, and joust with feather lances. All lances should be made of feathers. If only in dreams.''

She turned reproachful eyes on him. ''Now you've spoiled it!''

''How so, fair maiden?''

''Because you have inserted reality into a delightful make-believe. All dreams are feathers.''

It was said with a trace of sadness, and unease touched him so that he responded very gently, "The feather castles of our lives? Yet some dreams come true, you know."

"Do they? I wonder." She gave a barely perceptible gesture, as of thrusting away a foolish notion, and said brightly, "Never heed my doldrums, Sir Knight. You are perfectly right, for is it not a dream that we should have such heavenly weather for our ride?"

Any weather would be heavenly he thought, so long as he could be near her. But, "Is that remarkable?" he asked, as they started to walk along the cliffs, the horses thumping amiably behind them. "It is summer time, after all."

Rachel gave a little spurt of laughter. "Perhaps you are fortunate in that your memory is erratic. This England is the dearest place on earth, but a gentleman once described our weather as consisting of ten days fog, twenty days cold, and thirty days rain to every one day of sunshine. And I am inclined to believe he was too generous, at that!"

"He sounds to me like a Friday-faced cawker! French, probably. They're always bragging that their climate is superior to ours."

Rachel said nothing.

"Was I right?" Tristram asked easily. "Was he French?"

Staring with rather fixed concentration at the massive loom of Dover Castle, she replied, "Yes. He is French."

Two days later, Guy Sanguinet had still not returned to Dover, nor had further word come from Claude. Agatha's indisposition had proven stubbornly entrenched so that she kept to her bed and was unable to accompany Rachel on her walks, or her afternoon rides. Aside from anxiety over her abigail's lingering ailment, this did not present Rachel with an insurmountable problem. Captain Tristram was the best of companions; unfailingly attentive and good-natured, unselfish to a fault, contriving always to make her feel that her opinions were valued, and his rich sense of humor complementing her own so perfectly that often the witnessing of some droll little incident would cause their eyes to meet in a mutual sharing of merriment. It was pleasant to rely on his attending to small details for her, but despite his devotion, she soon discovered he could also be firm. At first he'd been so tactful in his dealings with her that she'd scarcely noticed if her wishes were gently redirected. With astonishing rapidity, however, the slight remaining shyness melted away; they were now on the most comfortable of terms, addressed one another on a first-name basis, and not only were able to tease, but to argue without the least fear of creating an unbreachable void.

Walking up the stairs of the inn, stripping off her gloves as she went, Rachel was smiling faintly, thinking of how wickedly Tristram had dissuaded her from purchasing a perfectly ravishing bonnet this very morning. Half-sitting against a credenza at the side of the Salon Elegante, he'd surveyed the lavender bonnet with the faintest trace of a pucker between his dark brows, and murmured lazily, "I cannot say I favour it as well as the blue."

"Oh, but the feathers, Tristram! Are they not dashing? So fluffy."

"And so many. Truly, the blue is more becoming."

"Perhaps. But—no, I cannot resist it!"

"Then do not. In fact, you are very likely right, for now I think on it, my maiden aunt had one very similar that was much admired in Bath. Her friends said it made her look youthful. Yes—definitely, you should purchase it."

Aghast, she had scanned her reflection in the mirror noting for the first time that the feathers *were* rather overdone, and the colour a trifle matronly. Leaning forward to peer questioningly at Tristram, she had surprised the tell-tale twitch beside his mouth and, bursting into laughter, had removed the disputed bonnet. "Wretched creature! You know I could not buy it after so horrid a recommendation! Is he not a villain, Madame? You see how I am manoeuvred to prejudice against the lavender!"

"*Such* a villain!" the proprietor had agreed amusedly and leaned closer to murmur in her ear, "Would I had so cunning a villain to guide *me*, mademoiselle!"

With her hand on the parlour doorknob, Rachel paused. How could Tristram know whether or not he had a maiden aunt? Both that lady and her Bath admirers had been a fabrication she'd been too discomposed to detect! "The rogue!" she exclaimed, and, mentally resolving to call Tristram to account for his heinous conduct, walked into the room.

Sister Maria Evangeline stood to welcome her. "How merry you look, child. Had you a nice shopping expedition? I doubt you may ride this afternoon, for it looks as if it might come on to rain."

"I mean to go to the circulating library, at all events," said Rachel, the smile in her eyes fading to dismay as she saw that Agatha was dressed and hurrying to assist her. Relinquishing her hat and gloves to the abigail, she said with an oddly hollow feeling beneath her ribs, "Why, Agatha. How splendid to see you up and about again."

"Is it not?" the nun restored her bulk to the armchair. "By tomorrow she will be able to relieve Captain Tristram of his duties and go about with you."

"How nice," said Rachel, with a singular lack of enthusiasm. "Now, you must not overdo, Agatha."

"Small fear of that, Miss Rachel. Oh, before I forget, here's a letter come from Monseigneur."

Rachel stood utterly motionless. Staring blankly at the folded paper that was held out to her, she did not see the swift and meaningful exchange of glances between the two women; she saw only Tristram's crooked grin . . . Recovering herself, she took the letter and broke the seal.

Claude had written in French:

My Dearest Rachel—

I am devastated to be so delayed in joining you. However, a matter of business compels me to journey first to Scotland. How may I atone for having kept you in Dover these many days? Will you allow me to suggest that you at once return to Strand Hall? I may thus be at ease in concluding my affairs, nor imagine you crushingly bored, cooped up in that dreary inn.

I mean to bring my Aunt Fleur to Sussex to act as chaperon, and then you and I shall proceed to my Chateau. It will be a treat for you to see your new home for the first time, my dear, and one I can scarce wait to observe. Meanwhile, I have instructed Guy to convey you to Lon-

don at the first opportunity, for I entertain a great deal, and you will wish to purchase some new ball gowns. You must allow me to have the reckoning for these; after all, we are formally betrothed, and it is my right, is it not?

I shall be with you as soon as is humanly possible. Until then,

Adieu, sweet creature,
Yr. devoted
Sanguinet.

"Is something wrong, child?"

"What?" Startled, she found that she was frowning, and summoned a smile. "Oh, no. It is only that Claude sends word he cannot come for a little while, and desires that I return to Strand Hall."

"Does this upset you?"

"Not at all. But—we have no coachman until Guy returns."

"No need to fret," said the nun placidly. "I do not doubt that Captain Tristram is capable of hiring a post-chaise and would likely be willing to escort us back to the Hall."

Rachel looked at her steadily. "I rather suspect we have imposed sufficiently upon the Captain, Sister."

Her eyes innocently wide, Agatha asked, "You never mean to stay here, Miss Rachel? Against Monseigneur's wishes? Eh, but he'll cut up stiff, I'll be bound!"

Neither tone nor words found favour with Rachel. She dealt her abigail a sharp scold and, further irked by the twinkle in Sister Maria Evangeline's eyes, stormed into her bedchamber in complete vexation.

She was still repenting that foolish show of anger when she made her way along the busy street towards Wright's Circulating Library. It had been necessary that she hug Agatha before luncheon, so as to restore her to spirits, and why she should have become so very cross when the poor soul was just recovered from such a nasty cold was quite beyond her power to understand. Sister Maria Evangeline had eaten with them and throughout had maintained an air so saintly smug that Rachel had yearned to scratch her. She was too honest, however, to continue to blame her sense of irritation on either Agatha or the nun. The real irritant had been Claude's letter. She had been a trifle put out when she'd been ordered to wait for him in Dover. To be now desired to return to Sussex and await his convenience; to be instructed to buy some new ball gowns—as though the few she had were not perfectly presentable!—and above all, to be informed that he would have the arrogance to bring a lady she'd never laid eyes on to act as chaperon was little short of infuriating. Further, the letter implied that when she accompanied Claude to Dinan, Charity was to be left in Sussex! It was very clear that she and M. Claude Sanguinet had some caps to pull! She could just imagine Captain Tristram ordering her about so summarily. The anger faded from her eyes and was replaced by a rueful smile. Tristram would manoeuvre her just as surely. Only he would accomplish it with such fiendish tact she'd not realize she had been manoeuvred until it was too late. She stepped aside to avoid three ladies with arms entwined and an obvious disinclination to yield the right of way. Rachel's frown, however, was directed at herself. What nonsense was she now indulging in? Claude was the dearest man imaginable. Thanks to him her beloved sister had been restored to a state of health she'd not dared to hope for. He had been the soul of generosity, and was, as Justin would have said, so very well to pass that he could offer her a life of luxury that most ladies only dreamed of. More to the point, his brilliant—and extremely dear—surgeon had expressed the hope that someday he might restore to Charity the ability to walk! Nothing must interfere with such a prospect! Nothing! Not even— She shut off that dangerous line of conjecture, but a moment later was sighing wistfully. Dear, dear Tristram. So courteous, so gallant. Such an unknown quantity. Were his worst fears realized, the summit of his ambition must be freedom from the spectre of the gallows! Even were he proven innocent, he might yet discover that he was wed after all—having a hopeful family, and with no better prospects than those of a half-pay officer. On the other hand, suppose he was highly born? She stifled another sigh. Worse and worse, for his family could only despise Rachel Strand, the daughter of that scandalous fellow who'd cheated at cards. Rachel Strand, promised to a man almost twice her own

age who, however devoted, had for years been known as a notorious rake.

She blotted out such foolish and pointless speculation, and
her small chin lifted resolutely. She must say her farewells to
Tristram and tell him about Claude. Why she'd not done so, she
could not think. Yes, she could, conscience argued. She had
been so happy and had clung to that happiness, not wanting it to
end. Even now, she approached the library with reluctance.

A uniformed page swung the door open for her, revealing a
large room, the sides and rear devoted to rows of tall bookcases. In the centre were counters on which were spread such
delights as prettily boxed marzipan and toffee, ribbons for mi-
lady's hair, mittens, sunshades defying the omnipresent um-
brellas, some ells of fringe and beads, several dozen pattern
cards, and several pretty workboxes. The library was well pa-
tronized, and convivial groups were seated at a number of small
tables, while neat maids moved deftly among them, bearing
trays laden with teapots and crockery and plates of scones and
pastries.

Rachel was so intent upon locating a familiar tall figure that
she did not notice the stiffening of an angular lady standing before a bookcase, nor the way in which she hurriedly rejoined a
companion and at once engaged her in agitated converse.

Wandering along the narrow aisles at the rear, Rachel came
upon Tristram at last, frowning down at the volume in his hand.
She checked and stood watching for a moment, anticipating the
now-familiar light that would come into his eyes, as though just
the sight of her brightened his world. He looked up and saw
her, but his expression was not one of delight. Instead, he
looked pale and distraught. Alarmed, she hastened to his side.

"What is it? Whatever has upset you?"

"B-berkshire . . ." he whispered painfully, one hand going
to his temple.

"It is a county to the west on London. A very beautiful
county. Have you been there, do you think?"

The book tumbled from his hand. Rachel caught it in the nick
of time and slipped it hurriedly into the nearest opening. He
was swaying, his face livid. Really alarmed now, she took his

65

arm and, glancing up, saw a bonnet shoot swiftly from sight at the end of the row.

"Come," she murmured. "Lean on me, and we will go outside."

He reeled, reached out blindly to steady himself, but instead clutched spasmodically at his head, a muffled groan escaping him. His disoriented movements had sent several volumes toppling. Rachel looked desperately for aid, but no one was in sight now and she hesitated to call for help and create a scene.

"Disgusting!" came the hiss of a woman's voice from beyond the bookcase. "He is inebriated, my dear Emma! At this hour! I have sent for Mr. Wright!"

"Very properly. Did you see the lady with him?"

"*Lady!* Hah! It is just such as she who cause the Quality to be spoken ill of! Are we to collect her fine protector has cast her into the gutter?"

Rachel seemed turned to stone. Not daring to look at Tristram, she stood mute and stricken.

The waspish voice responded, "If one is to judge by her Papa, it—" The confidence died to a murmur and was followed by muffled laughter.

A small, elegant, but irate-appearing gentleman hurried into view, quizzing glass upraised the better to survey Tristram, who was leaning against a shelf with shoulders hunched and eyes closed. "God bless my soul!" the newcomer exclaimed fussily. "What is the gentleman about, ma'am? I am Jonas Wright, and I tell you frankly that I tolerate no crude behaviour in my library. Never a breath of scandal in all the years I have been in business. I must insist—"

Recovering herself, Rachel said tartly, "Stop your silliness, do! The—er, Captain is newly come from Waterloo and far from well."

Mr. Wright eyed Tristram uneasily. For such a big fellow to be carried into the street would cause a fine commotion, and if he collapsed, as he appeared likely to do, he might very well carry the whole case down with him! The young lady was a pretty thing, her anxious blue eyes fine enough to melt the heart of any man. Quality, beyond doubting; her walking dress had Paris writ all over it, and that shawl must have cost sixty guineas if it had cost a groat. His mind made up, he said with a thin smile, "I shall take this arm, ma'am. Can you guide him at all on that side? Poor fellow—at Waterloo, you say? Lucky to be alive, from what I hear. I've a small courtyard in the back. Perhaps the fresh air will revive the Captain."

"Thank you," Rachel said gratefully. "I am sure it will. Tristram, can you walk? This way. Slowly . . ."

"You are very determined," observed Tristram, his voice steadier now as he lay back in the garden chair, "to dignify me with the rank of Captain. Have you also selected my Regiment, ma'am?"

Rachel's calm smile masked inner turmoil. That terrifying greyness was fading from his face. He had almost fainted, but could he have heard those spiteful cats? And, if so, how much had he heard? "Oh, the Life Guards, of course," she replied lightly.

"A Gentleman's Son, am I?" he said with a grin, then winced, his teeth catching his lower lip.

She bent forward to wipe his brow gently with the wet cloth the proprietor had brought her. "Your memory is returning with a vengeance. Goodness, but you pay a price for it!"

"Exorbitant," he agreed ruefully, "for all the good it does me. I am truly sorry, Rachel. I must have made a fine spectacle of myself. You could scarcely be blamed did you refuse ever again to venture forth with me."

She thought, with an inward sigh of relief, "So he did not hear!" This was the perfect opportunity to say her farewells—but how could she further upset him while he was so shaken? Deciding there must be a better time, she said, "It was something about Berkshire that had disturbed you, I think?"

"Yes. And clouds, if you can credit it. And a dark young lady who was, I am sure, my sister. Though I can remember nothing about her save that she was flirting with someone and I was taking her to task for it."

"I expect you bully the poor girl endlessly," Rachel teased, trying to chase the worry from his eyes. "I doubt she's allowed a single friend not of your choosing, or—" She interrupted herself abruptly. "*Clouds*, did you say? I wonder why—unless the weather was extreme bad, perhaps."

He frowned and said a helpless, "I cannot remember. Oh, well—the important thing is that I found you here."

She had told him this morning that she meant to come to the library, and, a dimple peeping, she uttered demurely, "How you could ever have done so, sir, is most remarkable."

"Is it not? A rare gift. I've thought, in fact, that if I cannot trace my past, I might set up as an Illusionist, and tread the boards."

"Tristram the Great!" laughed Rachel. "I shall be your first subject. Tell me, oh mighty mystic, of what am I thinking?"

He put one hand over his eyes. "Let me see . . . Ah! I have it! You are thinking of a lady of Quality whose fine protector has cast her forth! Back into the gutter!"

The quiet courtyard seemed to swing, the treetrunks waving like curtains in a draught. Rachel felt sick and said threadily, "So—you heard what they said."

Tristram chuckled, took up the glass of brandy Mr. Wright had kindly supplied, and finished the small amount remaining. "Not very much of it, thank heaven! What dreadful tongues some women have."

Her heart slowing to a gallop, she observed, "Sometimes they wag truth."

"One can but hope not. I thought Caro Lamb was wild, but even she never obtained 'A Fine Protector'—to my knowledge, at least."

Rachel stiffened and, not noticing that he had been granted another small recollection, said, "She certainly has many admirers, whatever one may call them."

"Yes. But I—" He bit the words off and was silent.

"You are not among them? Ah. A moralist."

"And assuredly the last one to dare throw stones," he admitted.

Perhaps because Rachel was so stricken, she said coldly, "Why, we all have our standards, do we not? Whatever our own failings."

The faint colour left his face. He said nothing, but his hand tightened on the arm of his chair.

Rachel saw the movement, and remorse brought sudden tears to sting her eyes. "Forgive me," she said, her voice trembling.

68

"There is nothing to forgive. You are perfectly right, and I—"

"No! I had no right at all, for— Oh, Tristram, you will discover sooner or later that the name Strand is—is not an honourable one. Indeed, we are shunned throughout England!"

"*What?*" He sat straighter, staring at her in horrified disbelief. Her distress was very obvious, and quick to come to her defence he exclaimed, "I cannot credit that any idiot should shun so lovely a lady! You must not tell me more, but I am quite certain you have *never* done anything dishonourable."

"When Charity was injured," she said, looking fixedly at the small shoe that peeped from beneath her gown, "my poor Papa tried frantically to find a surgeon who would help her. She was in much pain and, as you can imagine, he could not bear to see her suffer. From—from one cause and another, our fortune had dwindled until we could barely afford to keep up the estates and pay our servants. Papa blamed himself for this, and struggled to raise funds. Unsuccessfully, I'm afraid. In the end, he began to gamble without restraint until—driven to desperation—" Her hand wrung, and she paused.

Tristram leaned forward and his large hand reached out to cover her nervous small one. "Do not," he admonished gently. "I think I can guess. He outran the constable, eh?"

She was much comforted, but still unable to look at him, said with a wan smile, "No. He cheated at cards."

Despite himself, he gave a shocked gasp. "My poor girl! So that was why you were distressed when I made that nonsensical remark on the cliffs! But it was none of your doing. Besides, your father must have been driven beyond endurance, poor man." Dizzied by the misty smile that was now bestowed on him, he asked, "Was this why your brother went out to India? To try and raise funds? He must be a fine fellow."

"Yes. Justin is very good. But he was never very strong and I worry so. One hears such tales about the fevers and plagues, and the savage things the natives do!"

"No, no," he smiled, leaning back in his chair once more. "I've no doubt your brother will come home so improved in health you will scarce know him. And a regular nabob who will resolve all your cares with one wave of his hand."

"His beringed hand," she corrected, her eyes beginning to regain their sparkle.

"But, of course," he agreed gravely. "Dozens of rings. And he will ride to your door upon an elephant."

Rachel clapped her hands with delight at the picture this conjured up. "Dare he have a train of slave girls behind him?"

"Oh, absolutely. If you like, we will mount them upon pachyderms also. In fact, it would create even more of a stir, you know, was he to lead such a cavalcade down St. James's and under the windows of that club to which all you ladies must receive vouchers else be slain socially. White's isn't it?"

"No," she exclaimed merrily. "Foolish man! That is Almack's—and I doubt Justin would dare lead his ladies past those hallowed halls!" She stood, and he at once came to his feet. "How kind you are," she murmured, gazing up into his face gratefully. "Thank you for giving me that delightful little Feather Castle."

He bowed over her hand and pressed it very briefly to his lips. And longing to tell her how much more he yearned to be able to give her, said nothing.

Lord Kingston Leith's new satin brocade waistcoat brought an appreciative gleam to the eye of his sister's butler who admitted him to the Berkeley Square residence. Left alone in the ornate drawing room, his lordship wandered across to the gilded harpsichord and touched a key, his grey eyes becoming wistful. Tristram had loved to hear little Sally play the instrument. And in the good old days, when Tris and Galen Hillby and Timothy Van Lindsay had come down for the Long Vacation, what jolly parties and musicales there had been. Especially when Carlotta Bryce had been able to come, with her sister Dora. A sharp tongue had Carlotta, but she played the harp magnificently. And, Dora—he smiled nostalgically. Dora had been plump then, true, but always a delight. A most pleasing little lady, Dora Graham. And how long since he'd thought of her . . .

"Kingston!" The low, tragic cry brought him swinging around to meet his sister, the Countess of Mayne-Waring, who bore down upon him like a galleon in a stiff breeze, her train shushing along the floor behind her. "So you are come home," she said, giving him her hands. "And without our dear one, alas, as I knew you must."

"I was not successful this time, I'll own." He bestowed a brotherly buss on the cheek she raised. "But that has little to say to the matter. I've left a fine team of men searching for the boy. Been home these three days. Came here at once, but you was in the country. Starchy on a repairing lease?"

Lady Drusilla fought back her irritation at this irreverent remark. "I felt the need of a change of scene," she advised dolefully. "Oh, my poor bereaved soul! How well you . . . bear . . ." She faltered into silence, having become aware of his attire, and as stunned by it as he had been startled by the unrelieved gloom of her blacks. "What—*ever*—?" she uttered feebly. "You are not in mourning, King?"

Her reverting to that childish nickname spoke volumes for her state of mind, for she was very conscious of the dignity she owed her station in life, and only in moments of great stress was her majestic demeanour overborne.

Leith pulled up a chair for her, and drawing another close, sat down, confirming, "Of course I ain't. The boy's missing, is all. Why should I put on my blacks for that? Or—do you mourn someone else? Good God! Old Starchy has not—"

"Had Mayne-Waring breathed his last, Kingston," she said quellingly, "you, as my only surviving brother, would have been notified at once. As you well know."

Leith grinned mischievously. Despite her grand manner, Lady Drusilla was fond of him, and her vexation mellowed into anxiety. Kingston had always been a bit rackety, as the saying went. Perhaps the loss of his beloved son had overset his already tottering intellect. She raised a dainty handkerchief to dab the tears from her eyes. They were genuine tears, for Tristram Leith had been an object of no little pride with her. She had, in fact, selected several well-born—and eager—ladies as possible mates for her dashing nephew. And now . . . She sniffed damply.

Her brother edged farther back on his chair. "Dru, if you've taken one of your confounded head colds, I'll be off."

She foiled this plan by giving vent to a sob. "How," she quavered, "can you be so heartless? Your only son!"

"Who will be home before the snow flies. I'll lay you odds—er, well what I mean is— Now, dash it all, you're weeping, Dru! I wish you will not!"

"I will try . . . to oblige you, dear brother. But—but I did love him, you know."

For an instant Lord Leith's air of cheerful aplomb slipped. He sprang up and took a turn about the room, keeping his face averted. When he resumed his chair, however, he seemed as hopeful as ever and said bracingly, "Do not use the past tense, Dru. My agents have already found a clue that Tristram survived the battle."

She gave a gasp and leaned forward, hands clasped to her heart. "Tell me!"

"Well, that's what I come for! One of my fellows located a labourer who'd become suspiciously plump in the pockets after Waterloo. My man took him to a tavern and loosened his tongue to the point he spoke of an incident he'd seen following the battle. Something about two ladies about to be victimized, and a tall, well-built soldier who helped them." He frowned and said in a subdued tone, "The soldier was young and very dark, and an excellent shot, though he was badly wounded about the head. From what St. Clair told young Buchanan, it—it might have been—"

"Oh! What utter fustian!" exploded his sister. She plied her handkerchief again, while Leith watched her glumly. "There must have been hundreds of big dark men with head injuries!" she sniffed, when her sobs eased. "And—as if *ladies* would have ventured near that—that ghastly field! From what we've been told, 'twas a—a veritable slaughterhouse. I vow, I've seldom been more vexed with you, King, to raise my hopes to no purpose. Did I not know you are devoted to the boy, I'd swear this is all a ruse—so that you may continue to pursue every pretty woman your lustful eyes discover!"

"Lustful eyes!" echoed her brother, considerably affronted. "Well, if that don't beat the Dutch! Here am I, doing my level best to sacrifice myself on the altar of—of our lineage, and look at you! Full of distempered starts and as Friday-faced as you can stare! And furthermore—"

Bristling, she interposed, "Is it to 'sacrifice' yourself that you've been providing grist for the mill of every gabble monger in town? I could scarce credit my ears this morning when I was told by two visitors that you was trying to fix your interest with the Chandler woman! An antidote if ever I encountered one!"

A twinkle lit his lordship's grey eyes. He took out his snuff box, tapped it gently, and remarked, "Thought Harriet Chandler was a crony of yours? She's a diamond of the first water—for looks, at least."

"She's well enough," allowed the Countess, grudgingly. "If one can endure to listen to her tell of it. I vow her ravings of how many gentlemen are at her feet and how many compliments come her way, and how original and beyond compare are the gowns her woman creates, are not to be borne!''

Leith took a pinch of snuff, inhaled, flicked a few spilled grains from his sleeve, and muttered, ''At least she can say *something*. The Apperton girl can do nothing but giggle and simper! And as for Aurelia Pritchard— Glorious, but—'' He cast his eyes to the ceiling, despairingly.

''I am glad to hear you admit your follies in those directions, at least,'' the Countess acknowledged. ''A man of your years! Diversion is well enough, but—''

''Diversion? Good God! Did I seek diversion, ma'am, I've a lovely little dasher would take the shine out of—''

''Kingston!''

''—Would take the shine out of The Chandler, The Apperton, *and* Miss Pritchard!'' he finished stubbornly. ''Trouble is, I cannot wed the lass. No background, more's the pity.''

His sister's jaw dropped. A faint squawk escaped her, and she groped feebly for the damp piece of cambric and lace that had slipped from her palsied hand.

Restoring it to her, Leith paced up and down and elaborated, ''D'ye think I enjoy these callow debutantes? 'Tis one thing to squire 'em about; to watch their pretty faces and flirt with 'em, to have 'em flirt with you; and go home to a comfortable chair and a good book or a sensible talk with friends, or even with old Ches. But—*marriage?* Gad! To be shackled with a child with nothing in her head but hair! Had I ever thought of wedlock —which I cannot recall having done since my sweet Jenevra died—but, *had* I done so, I'd have chosen someone closer to my own generation. Oh, you may stare, Dru, but what have these chits to say to me? Can they reminisce of Pitt and his fire and brimstone? Do they recall Charles James Fox—the old rascal? Did they ever see Garrick, or the elegance of powdered heads and the hoop skirts you ladies was used to wear so prettily? They are dull, Drusilla. Vapid, and sweet and gentle and foolish and—*dull!*''

''Lud!'' gasped his sister, flapping her handkerchief at her astounded face. ''I vow I'm all about in my head. Or you are! If you do not care for these girls, then why on earth chase after them?''

"Because, Dru—though it's all gammon, you know—if Tristram has indeed, fallen . . ." He sprang up from the chair he'd only just sunk into, and exploded, "I'll not have Herbert Glick at Cloudhills!"

For a space his sister merely blinked at him. Gradually, however, comprehension dawned, and with horror apparent in her plump features, she said, "My heavens! You are perfectly right, of course! I— Oh, dear! I should never have told Maribel MacNaughton you were short of a sheet."

His lordship stiffened. The fair Maribel was high on his "list," and the young widow's eyes had ofttimes held a gleam he'd fancied was encouragement. "If that ain't a dashed fine set-out!" quoth he, indignantly. "It's me that is short of a sheet—but it's *you* allows my only daughter to caper about all over London with Freddy Foster! A fine rake to be trying to fix his interest with the child!"

"Indeed?" she exclaimed, in the tone that struck terror into the hearts of her maids. "I wish I'd a shilling for the times you have told me what a grand fellow he is!"

"Well, so he is. Splendid sportsman, true and loyal friend, up to every rig and row in town. And a rake, ma'am. Young fellow with looks like his—bound to be a rake."

Lady Drusilla's eyes saddened. "Tristram was—is—the handsomest boy I know . . . save for Camille Damon who hasn't been seen for years. And Tristram was—er, is—not a rake."

Leith flinched, and seeing she had pierced his armour, she was sorry for it, and added hurriedly, "At all events, Foster don't *act* the rake. He's mild as milk 'round the gal, and has been good for her. Poor Sarah. She agrees with your optimism, of course. Or pretends to."

Leith stared at the harpsichord and observed quietly that his son and daughter had always been very devoted.

"They have, indeed. And were you not so busy with your flirtations, King, you would have seen that Sarah was falling into melancholy. Foster is always in spirits, and it's a great feather in her cap to have him paying court. Many a lady in this city has dropped the handkerchief, and many a hopeful Mama has held her breath, praying Foster would take it up. This is the first time in years he has been so attentive to one female—and Sarah knows it.''

"Well, why not? My little Sally's one of the dearest girls in this old Village! Any man would be fortunate to secure her affections.''

"No doubt, but—she is not a beauty, Kingston. And will never be a Toast.''

"Her toast will be burned does she dally with the likes of Foster!''

"For shame! What vulgarity! Temper your terms, I pray, for I am not accustomed to such crudities.''

His lordship threw back his head and laughed aloud, being well aware that her spouse was noted for his uncouth remarks. Vexed by this insensitive performance, the Countess stood and, regarding him as from a great height, intoned, "I shall overlook your behaviour under the circumstances, Leith. However, be warned. Do you attempt to put a halt to Foster's attentions, you will earn my niece's resentment—to say the least of it!''

"Stuff!'' he grinned, standing at once. "The day has yet to dawn when I cannot bring Sally around my thumb.''

Drusilla's chin was very high, her eyes glinting, observing which, he went over and slipped an arm about her rigid form. "Or you either, m'dear. Do not imagine I'm ungrateful for your care of Sally, or for the model you set for her.'' Lady Drusilla's back eased a little, and the severity of her expression relaxed into a reluctant smile.

"Any cockleheaded, green girl with little to recommend her save sauce, who could catch herself an Earl,'' Leith finished disastrously, "cannot but be admired!''

The Honourable Sarah Cumming Leith tilted her jade green parasol a little, ostensibly to protect her dewy cheek from the intrusive rays of a rather weak sun. Seated beside her in his luxurious phaeton, Lord Leith was not deceived. He reached up to part the fringe on that charming and expensive parasol, and asked, "Ain't hiding from your Papa, are you, m'dear?''

At once the concealing article was shifted and, blinking her dark eyes rather rapidly, Sarah assured him that such was not the case. "It is just the sun, dear Papa.''

Leith smiled and took up her mittened hand. "No. It is your brother," he contradicted. She swung her head quickly away. After a moment during which his face was unwontedly sombre, he put one finger beneath her chin and turned her head back again. "You are not a beauty, Sally," he observed judicially.

Despite his rather haphazard notions of parenthood's obligations, and the fact that since returning from the Seminary his daughter had dwelt for the most part with her aunt, Sarah had always known that her father loved her deeply. His visits had been frequent, and down through the years she had spent more time with him than did many daughters who occupied the same house as their sire. The generosity Leith showered upon his barques of frailty was not withheld from his child; Sarah had never lacked either for expensive gifts, or the more meaningful unexpected outings, the heart-warming sudden presentation of some small item that he had "no sooner seen that I knew it was meant for you!" Despite his present gallant display of optimism, she suspected that inwardly his grief was far more acute than her own, and she also knew that this drive through the park was intended to cheer her. To be dealt such an unkind remark, therefore, both astounded and bewildered her, and her eyes widened in dismay.

"But you've a speaking pair of eyes," Leith nodded, "and if your skin is a touch sallow, it's clear. You don't throw out a spot with every change of the wind. You've a charming smile, too, love. There, that one in particular!" And as she broke into a giggle, he added lightly, "Little wonder that devil Foster's pursuing you."

Sarah's smile faded into uncertainty. "You—do not approve, Papa? But he has been so kind." She sighed and, looking down at her mittened hands, added, "Truly, after the news of . . . of dear Tris, my spirits were so sunk, I felt I never should come about. But Sir Freddy could not have been more understanding, nor exerted himself with greater kindness to divert me."

A pucker tugged at Leith's brows, but when her eyes lifted shyly to meet his once more, he only asked a gentle, "Do you love him, my dear?"

She looked utterly confused, her blush deepened, and she floundered, "Why, I do not think—I, er—I had not considered— That is to say— He is a very dear friend, and— It would make me very unhappy were I obliged to— But, Sir Freddy *is* your friend, is he not, sir?''

''Damnation!'' thought Leith. But he patted her hand fondly. ''If there is one thing in all this world I've no wish to do, dear child, it is to make you unhappy.''

''The Jolly Countryman'' was a modern inn, constructed entirely of red brick and, being endowed with such luxuries as water-closets and well-fitting windows, had won Sister Maria Evangeline's unqualified approval. ''Indeed,'' she told Rachel as they returned from a walk following luncheon, ''I would raise no objections were we to overnight here, my love.''

''No, do you find the Hall depressing, ma'am?'' asked Rachel mischievously. ''Perhaps Tristram could find rooms for you in the village.''

''Minx! You know I like your home. It is unusual, though, to find so comfortable an inn. Thank goodness Tristram did so. I'm vastly relieved you asked him to escort us, Rachel. I thought you were quite decided against it.''

Rachel scrutinized the good Sister's bland innocence suspiciously. She had changed her mind while returning from Wright's Library and had asked Tristram to escort them to Sussex. Her reason had been one of pure kindness, for after the miserable attack he had endured she could not think him well enough to be abandoned to search alone for his family. For some reason she was reluctant to explain all this to the nun and said merely, ''Why, you had suggested it, ma'am. And I try always to be guided by you.''

''If that were so,'' said Sister Maria Evangeline, ''you would not be betrothed to Claude Sanguinet.''

Rachel stiffened. ''Do you so dislike him, then?''

They had, by this time, reached the grounds of the inn. Slightly out of breath, the nun halted and sank gratefully onto a convenient bench that had been fashioned from a fallen tree-trunk. She patted the space beside her and panted, ''I am unaccustomed to such strenuous exertions. Sit with me, child. I will tell you what I know of Claude, as I should have done long and

78

long ago, save that you were so dazzled by him I could not bring myself to spoil the pure image you had created.''

"Nor will you now," Rachel affirmed, sitting down obediently. "I owe him too much to be swayed, and so I warn you, dear friend.''

"Truly, I have no wish to sway you. It goes against my every impulse in fact, to tell you anything at all. Nor would I do so, save for the fact I am a Christian woman and could not send you in there without you were fully aware.''

Rachel's nerves began to tighten. Then she laughed, "Good gracious! You make it sound as though I was about to enter Bluebeard's Castle!''

Sister Maria Evangeline did not smile, and after a thoughtful moment began, "I will rank the brothers Sanguinet for you, Rachel. Guy is apparently the least reprehensible, although that may be because he is the youngest and does not show his true colours as yet. Parnell is cruel and vicious and would, I think, have been put away years since, save that he is guided and controlled by Claude—who is a very ruthless and dangerous man.''

Searching that grave countenance, Rachel's eyes began to dance. "Let me guess," she pleaded. "Claude, although an aristo, was also a Bonapartist, and now that our Corsican ogre is thoroughly defeated at last, he means to take up where Bonaparte left off, and make himself emperor of all Europe!''

For once, Sister Maria Evangeline was silenced, and, her own eyes very wide, fairly gaped at her erstwhile pupil.

"Oh, you wretch!" Rachel gave a little trill of mirth. "You are quite as bad as Tristram! Do you know that for a moment I thought you were serious?''

"And—for a moment, I really thought you knew some of the truth of it! Child, child! Do not laugh so! This is no joke. Oh, I know you think me a foolish old woman, but—*listen!* For your own sake, if not for England's!''

At this Rachel gave an irrepressible giggle. "*England?* Claude plots against England? Oh, ma'am—you hoax me!''

Strong hands seized her by the shoulders and shook her so violently that her teeth snapped together. Eyes suddenly fierce glared into her own, and a voice like a rasp of steel grated, "Little fool! Why do you think I was so often gone from the

79

convent? Why do you think I sought so desperately for Diccon that I'd not allow even your presence to keep me from my task, whatever the dangers?''

Rachel was really frightened at last, and wrenching free, she cried resentfully, ''What part Diccon plays in your melodrama I cannot guess! But you go too far, ma'am! I am betrothed to Claude, and—''

''And have you told the soldier of it?''

A hot tide of crimson swept up Rachel's throat. She looked away, stammering, ''Well . . . not yet, but—''

''For shame! To lead that poor boy on until he is so crazy in love with you he can see no other!''

''Oh, no, really! Tristram is courteous, merely. And I feel nothing more for him than—a deep gratitude.''

''Nonsense!'' the nun barked ruthlessly. ''He saved you from heaven knows what degradations, and you *were* grateful. But it is not gratitude that has made your step so light of late! It is not gratitude that causes you to smile into your teacup, or to put sugar in your soup, as you did last night at the table.''

Her face an even deeper scarlet, Rachel faltered, ''I—was just day-dreaming.''

''And about whom? Oh, foolish child, you may lie to yourself, and you may wreck that fine young man's life with your silliness. But you cannot deceive me! I know you too well.''

Despite her blushes, Rachel's chin lifted. ''Then you surely know that, having given my word, I will not—*could* not—jilt the man who saved my sister's life!''

For a moment it seemed the nun would make a sharp rejoinder. Instead, she tightened her lips, gave a small shrug, and sighed, ''Very well—believe what you will. But, hear me you must. At all times I work for God, Rachel. But sometimes I also work for England. And I tell you that Claude Sanguinet is one of the most powerful men in all Europe, and I do believe *the* most dangerous! Human life is of no importance to him. He has been responsible for—''

''No!'' Springing to her feet, her eyes flashing, Rachel exclaimed, ''How can you say such terrible things? Claude was my father's dearest friend! Do you suppose Papa would have presented him to me were he an evil man?''

Sister Maria Evangeline knew a great deal more of the late M. Rupert Strand than she cared to divulge to his daughter, and therefore responded with caution, "Perhaps your father did not know the true nature of the man. I *do* know it. And I warn you that Claude is far from the gentle philanthropist you think him. He has a craving for power, and—"

"I will not listen!" Rachel threw her hands over her ears. A frown darkened the nun's usually mild features, and dropping to her knees beside the bench, Rachel implored, "Oh, pray let us not come to cuffs like this! You know how I love you. But I am more beholden to Claude than I can every repay. Because he is so rich, he has many enemies, but he is a good, kind man, I swear it." The nun sighed, and shook her head, and Rachel went on desperately, "Surely, were he as bad as you suspect, the authorities would move against him."

"And will—so soon as we can present them with proof! Unfortunately, we have been unable to convince them."

"Aha!" Rachel pounced, triumphant. "So they do not believe, either! Oh, dearest, will you not see that you have been misled? It is all so nonsensical!" Struck by a sudden thought, she asked, "If you truly believe these things, surely it would behove you to install a spy in the chateau?"

"Most assuredly."

"And—when I wed Claude and go to his home, I could be of great help to you—no?"

"Of inestimable help."

"And yet you warn me against him. Yes, and you encouraged Tristram's attentions—why, if to turn me from Claude would wreck your own schemes?"

The nun smiled sadly. "St. Matthew said, 'No man can serve two masters.' So it is with me. The welfare of England is far more important than the welfare of any individual. But— sometimes conscience reminds me that my other Master has first claim on me. I gave Tristram every chance, hoping you might see what life *could* offer. Diccon would be most provoked with me!"

Rachel stood and looked down into that broad, earnest face for a long moment. "Well, I am not provoked with you," she said at last, "for I know you meant only the best and believe what you say. I wish you did not. I wish I could make you see how wrong you are. But I *cannot* hurt him, nor believe evil of a gentleman who has shown me only kindness!''

Sister Maria Evangeline nodded resignedly, held up her hands, and was aided to her feet. ''Yours is the voice of the ordinary, law-abiding citizen, who prefers to believe all men are basically decent, and closes his or her eyes to the fact that monsters *do* exist! What a great pity it is so very difficult for a good person to comprehend the passions of unbridled ambition, or the ruthlessness that drives some men to deeds beyond their own understanding.'' She smiled wryly. ''And listen to me—making such a speech! Well, I shall return to Godalming and leave you in peace. No, no! Do not be distressed. I am going not because of our difference of opinion, but because I have allowed many things to lapse whilst I played this little game. Alas, the time for games is done. Good-bye, my sweet innocent.'' She pulled Rachel into a large hug, then added, ''Promise me that if you see Diccon at Claude's chateau in Brittany you will not betray him.''

Clinging to her hand, Rachel tensed and said miserably, ''How can I promise to protect a man who spied on my husband?''

''An innocent man has nothing to fear, little one. And if we find Claude to be innocent after all, why—so much the better, eh? Meanwhile, will you at least agree that should you feel obliged to reveal Diccon's true purpose, you will tell him of it first, so that he will have a chance to get away?''

The implications contained in that request were frightening, or would be was there any truth to the matter. Rachel searched her conscience. To refuse must imply a fear that Claude indeed plotted against England—which was ridiculous. Reluctantly, therefore, she gave her promise.

Thanks to the thriving business enjoyed by ''The Jolly Countryman,'' Tristram was able to engage a post-chaise to convey Sister Maria Evangeline back to her convent. Why the nun had made so sudden a change in her plans, he could not guess, but that the decision had distressed Rachel was very obvious. Suspecting that she had quarrelled with the nun, he tactfully rode escort beside the carriage during this final portion of their journey but made no attempt to converse with her.

For some reason he had formed the impression that Strand Hall was a small country house, but when they arrived in late afternoon, coming through what must once have been a fine park, his preconceived notions were banished. Although obviously run down, the sprawling edifice was still a spectacular sight with its pillared front and the soar of the neo-classical architecture. The pillars were chipped now and broken away in places, the paint was faded and peeling, and the once white stucco of the exterior showed sadly weather-stained. Never impressed by pretension, Tristram thought it a perfect setting for one of Mrs. Radcliffe's novels, and wondered whether Rachel was deeply fond of the place. The setting was charming, certainly; the house being centred in large—if weedy—pleasure gardens, and looking out to the west over rolling, wooded hills. An energetic steward, he thought, might have accomplished much even during Strand's absence, but then, perhaps there were not sufficient funds to support the hiring of such an individual.

The butler wheeled Charity's chair onto the terrace to meet them, and Rachel's depressed spirits appeared to revive as she ran to greet her sister. Tristram was commanded to take dinner with them, and the butler, a lean, greying man named Fisher, was sent off to arrange that a room be prepared so that their guest could rest and refresh himself. Tristram had thought this the end of the idyll and was grateful for a possible extension of this dream that must live forever in his heart. Still, he was a bachelor and no suitable chaperon to hand. He declined, his eyes so clearly betraying a longing to accept, that the housekeeper, who had also come out onto the terrace, warmed to him immediately. Turning to her employer, she discerned a look of dismay in the girl's face and, having an axe of her own to grind, suggested that dinner be moved up. Bravely offering to notify the cook that he must provide an excellent meal within the hour, she said reasonably, "If you was to sit down to table at half past five, Miss Rachel, Captain Tristram could reach the village before dark. We could send a boy to arrange accommodations for him. That should satisfy convention, do you not think, ma'am?''

Rachel's eyes flew to Tristram. ''I think it would answer, Mrs. Hayward. Unless the Captain has other plans.''

He bowed—not to his hostess, but to the amused housekeeper. Then, proffering his arm to Rachel, said, ''I am most grateful to accept.'' Rachel smiled radiantly; Charity took his free hand, and in happy captivity he was led into the house.

The entrance hall was a cold chamber of great size, with fading ceiling paintings and a vast fireplace about which were grouped some rather pitiful sofas. The mantel was cracked, and the enormous tapestry that hung upon one wall did nothing to add warmth to the room, its only redeeming feature being that it appeared to have allowed generations of kittens to swing from its gloomy magnificence. Tristram thought, ''The Priory!'' but memory stopped there.

Fisher returned and led him to the chamber allotted him. It was another outsized room with a ceiling that spoke of a smoking chimney. Sunshine poured through the large windows, however, and it was more than adequate for his present needs. Fisher seemed to take a delight in fussing over him, insisting upon unpacking the valise that held the few belongings the nun had so kindly bestowed upon him, and working such magic with his dusty garments that he felt quite presentable by the time he went downstairs.

There was no sign of the Misses Strand, but a maid approached, dropped a curtsy and told him there was wine in the drawing room did he wish to wait there. Her manner was kind, but her eyes were riveted to his face and, very conscious of his scars, Tristram told her he would instead stroll about the grounds, and retreated.

The afternoon had become warm and rather muggy, and he wandered unhurriedly along the path that led around to the side of the house. An elderly spaniel, sprawling in the shade of an apple tree, gathered itself together and padded over to inspect this new arrival. Tristram stroked the dog and invited it to join him. He was promptly presented with a somewhat misshapen ball; the spaniel retrieved only twice, however, then returned to the shade of the tree as though it considered its obligation fulfilled. Tristram followed the ball he had thrown and began to kick it along absently, thinking of the Misses Strand and how different they were: Rachel, so vibrantly lovely with her shining fair curls and the laughter dancing in those deep blue eyes; Charity, frail and tiny, her thin features lit by great eyes somewhere between green and grey, hair of a light sandy shade banded neatly, and rather austerely, about her head. She was no beauty, nor ever would be unless an improvement in her health effected a drastic change in her looks. Despite her long illness, however, her pale face held a look of gentle patience and she had her sister's merry sense of humour, so that one could not help but both admire and like her.

He had by now come round to the rear of the mansion and, guiding the ball through an area of high shrubs, discovered a barn in about as decrepit a condition as the main house. The ball sailed across the cobblestones and bounced against the side of the barn, and from within a voice called anxiously, "Is that you, Riggs?"

Rachel! His pulse accelerating as it always did when he was near her, he replied, "I don't think so. Though you may be right, at that."

"Tristram? Thank goodness! I came looking for you."

He entered the barn and, blinking in the sudden dimness, discerned her halfway up a ladder that was propped against the hayloft. She held a large box in her hands, and peered over her shoulder at him with a rather embarrassed smile.

"You thought I was up there?" he asked incredulously.

"No, of course not. I heard kittens mewing and came up to see if Pieces had become a mama again."

She looked adorable, he thought, her cheeks flushed as she stood there holding the box, from which emanated feline sounds of indignation, compensating in shrillness for what they lacked in volume. "How naughty of you," he grinned, moving closer. "And in your high-heeled slippers, too!"

"Well, I had changed for dinner and came to show you about the grounds, so it is all your fault that I now find myself in this ridiculous predicament." Smiling, she jerked her head downwards. "My flounce has caught itself on that splinter so that I can move neither up nor down, and—" she gave a rueful shrug, "each time I attempt to free it, these foolish creatures try to escape so that I fear they will fall and kill themselves."

Tristram quickly mounted the rungs of the ladder, freed her gown with deft assurance, then reached around her for the box. She relinquished it gratefully, and he descended, set the box down, and turned back to aid her. The rotting ladder looked none too safe, he thought, and his weight had not benefitted it. Even as he reached out for her, the rung onto which she stepped gave way. Uttering a small shriek, she toppled, but he was ready, and caught her. With her arms about his neck, she laughed breathlessly, and he cradled her as he might have held a child, gazing down into her lovely face.

The laughter died from her eyes, to be replaced by a look of inexpressible tenderness. The bonds of honour that had so unyieldingly restrained him, melted away, and with a small sigh he bent to her lips. It would have been simple enough for Rachel to swing her head away; holding her as he was, he could not have compelled her. Instead, she lifted her face, her lashes sweeping down so that her eyes were half closed. And Tristram kissed her and with awed reverence felt her respond to him.

In that tempestuous instant, Rachel knew how she had yearned for his embrace, and knew also a dizzying joy, such as she had never before experienced. For an enchanted space she was lost, drifting ecstatically in a dream so perfect, so wonderfully sweet as to obliterate all else.

Tristram raised his head, but still holding her tightly, kissed her cheeks, her closed eyes, her brow, whispering his adoration.

Pieces put an end to this rapture. Sailing triumphantly into the barn, bearing the sausage she had stolen from the kitchen, the large multicoloured cat was confronted by the sight of her offspring exploring the floor. She dropped her prize and uttered a piercing yowl of consternation.

Rachel gave a gasp and was abruptly returned to the mundane.

Just as suddenly jolted back to reality, Tristram set her down hurriedly. For a brief, aghast moment, they gazed at one another. Then he turned and stepped away and, driving one fist into his palm, groaned wretchedly, "God forgive me! I should be shot for compromising you so! What have I to offer you?"

Rachel stretched a hand toward his hunched shoulders, but withdrew it. "It was not your fault," she said unsteadily, her eyes blurring with painful tears. "I was . . . equally to blame."

He spun around. "I must first clear my name, and shall go to the Horse Guards at once. But, I doubt, my dearest one, that you were kissed by a murderer. That fear has almost left me, thank God! When I return, I—"

"No!" she interpolated, her voice trembling. "You—you must not—"

"Offer for you? No. Nor will I until I have discovered who and what I am." He stepped closer to seize her nerveless hand and hold it between both his own. "My conduct has been utterly shameful, but I shall add to it, by begging that you will wait a month, beloved. Should I discover that I have neither name or expectations, I will not embarrass you further. But—if my prospects prove not contemptible, will you tell me to whom I must speak?"

"No!" She pulled away, staring up at him with dilating eyes, the pretty blush quite drained from her cheeks. "I should have told you long since. Oh, how I wish I had! Tristram—" She gripped her hands in agitation, drew a deep, quivering breath, and blurted, "I am betrothed!"

He stood motionless, so shocked it was as if she had struck him. Rachel saw his face become drawn and white, while a look of such anguished disbelief came into his eyes that her tears spilled over. "I am so sorry," she whispered. "Oh, I am so very sorry!"

"No cause," he said in a croak of a voice. "None at all. May I know—who? . . ."

"You are not acquainted. He is Guy's brother. Claude Sanguinet."

"I see. Then—his is the yacht we sailed on?"

She nodded mutely.

Tristram's hands were clenched so tightly that the nails drove into his palms. He managed a travesty of a smile. "Rather formidable competition, for a man with—with no identity. Has your engagement been made public?"

"Yes. It was in *The Gazette* last month."

He nodded. It was the death knell to his last faint hope. He tried to say goodbye; to take up her hand with poised dignity and kiss it lightly, and leave. But now he dared not touch her again. Nor could he bring himself to leave her. She looked so stricken, so grieving. Against all his instincts, he gasped, "Rachel—only tell me—do you love him?"

Her head went down. In a muffled voice she answered, "I shall marry him."

Tristram flinched. For a few moments he was rigidly silent. "Forgive me," he said at length. "This is very bad, but—if my name should be cleared and my background proves acceptable . . . Might you—? I mean—were I to call on him and—and explain, could you—give me a chance?"

Half blinded by tears, she blinked up into his imploring eyes, and gulped, "It is—not possible. He has been so—so very good. And—" She gave a helpless gesture, words all but failing her. "It is just—too late, you see."

"Of course. And I am behaving—" he drew a hand across his eyes in a distracted confusion, "—behaving disgracefully. I can only wish you happy, and thank you for all you have done."

Not waiting for a response, he walked blindly to the door, but he could not cross the threshold, not without one last glimpse of his love. She was still standing immobile, a slim, lovely shape in the dusty old barn, the sunlight playing on her pink muslin gown and waking bright gleams along the trails that tears had painted on her cheeks.

Tristram had no consciousness of having moved, but suddenly he was reaching out to her. Her arms went about his neck, and he crushed her close and warm and dear against his heart. He did not speak, nor did he attempt to kiss her. Eyes closed, he bowed his head, feeling the silk of her curls brush his lips, feeling her arms tighten about him. For a long, ecstatic moment they remained thus, clasped in that silent, bittersweet farewell. At last, he put her from him and gazed down into her poignant face. He traced the line of her cheek with one gentle fingertip. Then he strode swiftly from the barn, leaving her alone with Pieces and her kittens.

6

The hand-painted hairbrush and comb were neatly disposed upon the dressing table. A mirrored tray held a variety of dainty little pots and bottles, a hare's foot, and a rather meagre assortment of perfumes. But, seated before the mirror, Rachel availed herself of none of these articles. Her hands were folded in her lap, her lack-lustre eyes gazed blankly at her reflection, and her thoughts were with Tristram. Where was he at this moment? Was he, perhaps, thinking of her as achingly as she thought of him? She had managed to slip into the house yesterday afternoon without being observed. Upstairs, Agatha had looked at her with obvious consternation, but upon being told that Captain Tristram had decided to proceed at once to London, and that dinner could be set back to the usual hour, she had made no comment but gone downstairs at once to inform the cook. And Rachel had wept, shaken by so violent a storm of grief she had wondered her heart did not break. When Agatha returned she had managed to conceal her face in the sheet and had pretended to be asleep. The abigail had tiptoed silently away to spread the word that her mistress was tired out from the journey, and thus Rachel had been granted sufficient time to so restore herself that she had been able to go down to dinner looking only a trifle strained.

She took up her hairbrush and stared at it. How brutally she had hurt him, and with what utter thoughtlessness. She had been happy and so she had prolonged that happiness, selfishly refusing to acknowledge that Tristram might be forming a lasting attachment, even as Sister Maria Evangeline had warned. How stricken he had looked, and how very dear their final embrace. Her eyes filled with tears yet again. She thought yearningly, "Oh, Tristram, Tristram. If only we had met earlier!" But it would have been quite useless. Her first duty was to ensure that her frail sister was as well provided for as was possible. Actually, the vow she'd made at Papa's bedside was no more binding than her own sense of responsibility. A responsibility that would, she knew, have bound Charity just as firmly had their situations been reversed. Dear Charity, how she would grieve if she knew the true state of affairs. And, of course, she must *never* know.

Armed with that resolve, Rachel sighed, lifted the hairbrush and was startled by the wan, pale face reflected in the mirror. This would never do! She was completing a careful application of cosmetics when she heard hoofbeats and the rumble of wheels. Claude's groom had brought word this morning that the carriage would reach Strand Hall in time for dinner; they were early. Well, thank heaven she had been able to restore some semblance of normalcy to her features!

Agatha came swiftly into the room. She scanned her mistress narrowly and, responding to a slight lift of Rachel's delicately arched brows, conveyed an expressionless, "I thought you were resting, miss."

"Is Miss Charity dressed?"

"All ready. And so pretty as a picture. Did you hear? Monseigneur's come. Sooner than we thought."

"How lovely," smiled Rachel.

Agatha folded her arms. "And his aunt," she appended.

The half-amused, half-scornful inflection in that pleasant country voice sent a pang of unease through Rachel. Agatha had been in her service since she'd left the schoolroom, and was utterly devoted. But, although only six years older than her mistress, she treated her with the proprietary air of a long-time retainer. Both voice and manner now implied more problems, and, apprehensive, Rachel hurried downstairs.

Fisher stood at the open front door, the late afternoon sunlight waking a sheen on his silver hair. He was as dignified, his stance regal, as ever, but he did not hear her approach and, turning, revealed his lined countenance wreathed in a rare and large grin. He started as he saw her, and regained his gravity in

91

a flash. "Monsieur Claude Sanguinet," he announced, only slightly unevenly.

"So I understand," nodded Rachel, and walked onto the steps.

She checked, barely stifling a gasp. A luxurious beige carriage picked out in gold and drawn by a magnificent team of matched white horses stood before the house. The coachman was still on the box, staring ahead, his face wooden. An equally wooden-faced groom was handing luggage down to two footmen, while three covertly grinning outriders waited behind the carriage. They all were attired in white and gold livery, unlike any Rachel had previously seen Claude's servants wear. Her betrothed stood on the carriage steps, attempting to extricate an extremely large lady from an embarrassment with the narrow door.

"I cannot readily understand," wailed the lady in French, "how this foolish doorway can have shrunk since we entered the carriage!"

"No more can I, Fleur," murmured Claude Sanguinet smoothly. "Since there is but one other explanation, however, we should, I feel sure, attempt to believe it has achieved such a feat."

So this, thought Rachel, was her chaperon; an even larger lady than Sister Maria Evangeline. At that instant the plumed bonnet tilted upward and two small dark eyes flew to her. A tiny mouth drooped pathetically and a little wail escaped it. With a flood of sympathy, Rachel hastened to greet her guests. "Welcome! Welcome! Oh, is it not the outside of enough how narrow they build carriage doors these days? I vow if one dons an extra pelisse it is as much as one can do to escape! May I be of assistance, Madame?"

Sanguinet has spun around at the sound of her voice. He jumped down, sweeping off his high-crowned beaver to reveal a pleasant face distinguished only by large, light brown eyes. His curling hair was near black and just now rather untidy, but in all else he was quietly elegant, despite the long journey. His build was slender, nor was he above average in height, and yet about him there clung an indefinable air; the self-possessed confidence, bordering on the arrogant, that so often marks those blessed—or cursed—by great wealth.

He took both the hands that Rachel extended, and bent to kiss them, looking up from under his brows with laughter in his eyes, to murmur in much better English than that of his younger brother, "If you chance to have the shoe horn about you, my love."

"For shame, sir!" she chided softly. And turning to the carriage, added in French, "Will you not sit down a moment and allow me to join you, Madame? Fisher—please take Monsieur Sanguinet into the red salon and provide him with some cognac. I am assured he must be ready for a glass after such a ride."

"I am *enchanté*," murmured Claude, bowing to her. "As ever." And he followed the imperturbable butler into the house.

Rachel started up the carriage steps. A lean hand took her elbow and assisted her. Surprised, she glanced down. She had never before seen this man. Unlike the servants, he wore a black jacket and pantaloons, and he wore them well, his lean frame such as would gratify a tailor, although his shoulders lacked breadth and the cut of the pantaloons was not so snug as to reveal whether or not he possessed a well-shaped leg. His shirt was as snow, his cravat a model of excellence. Thick brown hair was brushed straight back from a high forehead, and his features were regular. But in the hard black eyes and the smile that curved the thin mouth, Rachel read unmistakable admiration and a chill shivered warningly down her spine.

"Oh, do go away, Gerard!" cried Madame Beauchard irritably. He bowed and took himself off, and she went on in a lowered tone, "That man gives me always the feeling that I am a mouse and he is a snake! He is Claude's steward in Dinan. No one knows his real name. He is just—" she shrugged and threw out her hands in a Gallic gesture that set all her chins to wobbling, "just—Gerard! And I am Claude's aunt! And you—you are *la très belle jeune fille!* How very kind of you, my dear, to help me!" The little mouth spread into a smile, the small eyes almost disappeared in the folds about them, and two large arms enveloped Rachel in a brief and somewhat smothering hug, through which the monologue swept on. "First impressions, says Claude, are all important. And he did so wish that I impress you!" Her hands went up to cradle her cheeks. "He will be angry! Oh, but he will be angry!"

"No, no," smiled Rachel. "How can one be really angry with one's own family?"

"Then—you will tell him you are not offended?" begged Madame.

Rachel eyed her curiously. How odd that the woman should be so anxious to please her own nephew. Perhaps she was dependent upon Claude's largesse. "Whatever is there to offend me?" She patted the plump hand that plucked at her sleeve. "Now, as to the problem at hand—did you by any chance loosen your stays, ma'am?"

Madame Fleur hove a vast sigh of relief. "You have it, little one. Claude dozed off for a space, and I—oh, it is a torture chamber, is it not, to wear tightly laced stays in a rocking carriage for hour upon hour? I knew I should not be so reckless—not without my maid to truss me up again! But—" she giggled conspiratorially, and edged herself sideways on the narrow seat. "You can manage, my niece-to-be?"

Rachel took the precaution of lowering the shades, then essayed the task. It was quite a tussle, and when she was done, two of her fingernails had paid the supreme penalty, but thanks to her efforts, Madame Fleur was enabled to leave the carriage and enter Strand Hall.

The notes of the music box faded into silence. Hovering above it, her face alight with pleasure, her head tilted so as to hear every tone, Charity clapped her hands, closed the beautifully inlaid lid gently and turned glowing eyes on Sanguinet. "Oh—monsieur! It is exquisite! How may I ever thank you?"

He smiled and said with a careless wave of the hand, "By some of the time speaking my name—not 'monsieur.' Soon I will be your brother, you know."

"Yes. I— Of course, Claude." She blushed. "Oh, but it seems so impertinent!"

"Why?" he laughed. "Do you fancy me a decrepit creature of many years?"

Aghast, she protested, "No, oh no! Indeed I do not. I have never—"

"I am glad of this," he interrupted. A faint boredom crept into his eyes as he took up the glass of cognac from the table beside his chair. "You will wish the small tune to hear again, no?"

Quick to take the hint, Charity asked if she might be excused so as to show her gift to Mrs. Hayward and Agatha. Claude rose at once and went to the open door. "I shall carry the box for you," he offered, as she pulled at the wheels of her chair.

"Thank you, but I can balance it on my knees—so."

"Bravo! You go quite nicely, my dear." And looking enquiringly at Rachel, he asked, "Can she manage herself?"

"Very well," said Rachel, with a touch of asperity.

Claude shut the door, returned to her side and pulled his chair closer to hers. He had changed for dinner, and he really did wear clothes well. But she sometimes thought he seemed older than forty. Seized by guilt at so uncharitable a thought, she said hurriedly, "Charity is overjoyed with her gift. That was most kind of you."

He leaned forward and took up her hand. "It is my thought that while we are away she will perhaps the amusement derive from it."

Rachel tensed and drew back. "I should not leave her, Claude."

"But of course you should, my love. She is much improved, but another journey so soon would be a strain for her. You yourself have said it."

"Yes, but—"

"Let me hear no more of these 'buts.' " He caught her hand again and pressed a kiss upon it. "I wish my future wife to be with for a little time."

"I understand," she said, her cheeks growing hot. "But—"

"Again!" He clicked his tongue reprovingly. "Charity will be perfectly safe. I swear this. Do you desire it, we find a suitable nurse for the poor child. Or two, perhaps."

"She does not need a nurse!" Rachel flashed. Her eyes met his stormily. "She is frail, and—"

"So here you are! Oh—do I perhaps intrude?"

Madame Fleur, awesome in a blue and green striped gown amply provided with knots of darker blue ribbon at flounce and sleeves, surged into the room, paused, and looked coyly from one to the other.

Claude put up his glass and scrutinized her with faint incredulity. "Dear lady, you never fail to—er—astound me." Fleur watched him uncertainly. He lowered the glass and, with the slightest twitch of the lips, went on, "By arriving at precisely the right moment, I mean. I fear I was vexing my affianced. Perhaps with my atrocious English. It is better that we speak French together.

Rachel, who was again put to the blush, was relieved by the garrulous lady's arrival. She had the oddest sense that her relationship with Claude had changed. Perhaps, since their engagement had been published, he now felt more at ease with her, and less constrained to be as gently tactful as in the past. Or was she merely inventing excuses for her own change of heart?

Dinner was a lengthy meal, and the Frenchwoman chattered incessantly throughout, despite the fact that she partook of every dish in both removes. Charity had taken a great liking to her and between them they kept a lively conversation going so that Rachel was required to say little. She responded suitably from time to time, and strove to keep a cheerful countenance, though all too often her thoughts wandered achingly to Tristram. Claude was quiet, but Rachel knew he watched her and perhaps by reason of guilty conscience it seemed to her that his eyes were unusually penetrating. She tried to appear engrossed in Madame Fleur's description of the glorious gown her eldest daughter had worn on her wedding day; a gown provided by her ever-generous nephew.

Fisher deftly appropriated Rachel's plate and was about to place it on the tray the maid carried when Claude raised one hand in a detaining gesture. Fisher paused, glancing at him enquiringly. The remark following, however, was directed to Fleur. "Enough, I beg you, dear ma'am," he murmured gently. "Rachel, my love—you have changed, I think."

Fisher continued with his task, managing to look as though he did not comprehend, although he spoke French fluently.

Rachel was shocked as much by the remark as by her own

earlier anxieties. "No, have I?" she answered with commendable *sang-froid*. "Perhaps you carried too kind a memory of me, sir."

He laughed. "Never that. Does my aunt annoy you?"

Charity gave an audible gasp. Fisher's hand jerked a little as he raised the gravy boat. Astounded, Rachel shot a glance at Fleur and saw such fear in the pudgy, pallid face that her own dismay was increased. "Good gracious!" she exclaimed. "I am only too delighted by madame's presence in our home! How can you ask such a thing?"

"Because," he smiled, "if she does, I shall send her home at once."

"But you *must* not be provoked with him," urged Madame Fleur, holding up her wineglass as Rachel refilled it for her. "It is all my fault. I am a dreadful chatterbox and the poor man was cooped up with me all the way from Scotland. You will not, I hope, think less of him for scolding me."

"I think it unpardonable," Rachel said, replacing the decanter on the silver tray. How she had finished that meal she could not imagine, for she had been fairly seething with anger. Poor Madame Fleur had been utterly crushed, Charity horrified, and the servants provided with a very juicy tidbit for Hall gossip—to all of which Claude had appeared totally indifferent. He had launched blithely into an account of how he had designed the new livery for his servants, in honour of the approaching nuptials, and she had managed to respond politely, if coolly. His eyes had twinkled at her when she led the ladies from the dining room, and a rueful grin had conveyed his awareness that he was in disgrace. Now, returning to her chair, she observed that there was absolutely no need for Madame to take the blame on her own shoulders. Claude, she decreed, deserved to be spanked for such a flagrant breech of manners.

Fleur's small mouth fell open, the wineglass tipping in her hand so that the contents dripped onto the vast expanse that might have constituted a lap save for the lack of an indentation. "S-spanked . . . ?" she gasped, feebly. "*Claude?* I doubt—I doubt he was ever spanked in his entire life!"

"Very obviously," agreed Rachel, nodding toward the spilling wine.

Madame glanced down and jumped. "Oh, my! What a silly girl I am!" She set her glass down and dabbed ineffectually at her gown, but abandoned the effort to say anxiously, "Claude knows that you were displeased, I am sure. He will apologize to me, never doubt it. Since my beloved husband passed to his reward—and me left with six little ones, only think!—Claude has been so helpful, I do not know—" Her fat hands tugged nervously at her handkerchief, "indeed, I cannot imagine how we should go on—without his aid. He is only tired, I expect, for it is not his usual way."

"I'll own I have never known him to behave badly," Rachel acknowledged. "Likely you are right—he is tired. Still, I shall feel obliged to scold him."

Her scold was not dealt quite as firmly as she planned. Soon after Claude came into the drawing room, Charity said her goodnights, and Agatha was summoned to wheel the girl to the footmen who would carry her up to bed. Only moments later, Madame Fleur caught her nephew's eye, interrupted her own discourse on the beauties of the chateau at this time of year, and said that she must go upstairs and find the diamond brooch her dear nephew had given her, so as to show Miss Strand. She would be gone only for a moment.

The door had no sooner closed behind her than Claude came to Rachel's chair, dropped to one knee before her and, smiling up into her surprised eyes, said, "Have I been very bad? If I was blunt, it was because I'd not until now realized how insufferable a burden I foist upon you."

Rachel glanced uneasily to the door. "Claude! For heaven's sake! I beg you will get up!"

He sprang lightly to his feet, placed a hand on either arm of her chair and, bending over her, pleaded, "There. Am I forgiven?"

He looked so contrite. Smiling despite herself, she said, "I suppose it was only that I have never seen you be unkind before."

Something very deep in his eyes stirred—she had an odd and very brief impression that she had seen a glow of anger; but he sighed, dropped his head and muttered disconsolately, "Alas. You will quite cast me off. And—" he reached to his inside pocket, "there is no one to whom I may give this."

A long, flat leather case was placed upon her knees, and a mournful glance slanted at her. There was not a trace of the rage she had thought to glimpse, probably because there had been no rage. She *must* cease yearning for Tristram and inwardly resenting the circumstances that bound her to Claude! He looked the picture of mischief now, watching her with a mixture of trepidation and amusement, like a small boy attempting to charm her from her displeasure. She shut out the voice that whispered, "or *buy* your forgiveness!" and picked up the case. "You have already given me much too—" The words trailed into a gasp. She knew little about pearls, but the lustre of this perfectly matched double strand told its own story. Raising her eyes wonderingly, she breathed, "Oh! They are magnificent!"

"For a magnificent lady," he smiled, and taking them from her, unfastened the jewelled clasp. "May I?"

Rachel stood, turned, and bowed her head. The pearls slipped about her neck. She felt Claude's warm touch as he fastened the clasp. His hands slid onto her bare shoulders, and tightened. He turned her gently, his eyes admiring. "They are lovely against your skin," he murmured. "Your so beautiful English skin." He bent and kissed the necklace and her throat. His lips travelled lower. Rachel began to tremble. He was her betrothed, but—no man had ever touched her so. The dark head was raised. "Do not be afraid, little bird," he breathed, and swept her into his arms. She made herself lift her face and he kissed her. It was quite unlike Tristram's tenderness. She thought numbly, "He is French—their ways are different . . ." yet she knew, somehow, that Guy would not have kissed her in that way.

He was crushing her tighter, his words becoming more impassioned between kisses. She could scarcely breathe; she began to feel sick and dizzy. Quite suddenly, he released her. His eyes searched her face, and he turned away abruptly. Again, his head lowered. As though he fought for control, he said a strained, "I am sorry. I forget—you are the unspoiled child—

and I am one fool. Only—I love you so much, you see. I hope you will have the patience with me, *chérie*."

Sudden tears stung her eyes, and a deep pity engulfed her. He had been so kind—so generous, and she could not love him in return. She forced her shaking knees to obey her and stepped closer to touch his sleeve timidly. "Claude, you deserve so much more than—than I can give you. Perhaps we—"

He spun about and cried in horror, "I have offended you! I will not embrace you again—I swear it—until we are wed! Do not reject me—I implore you!"

Touched, she said, "No, no! What manner of woman do you think me? I am grateful—so grateful for your affection, your—many kindnesses. But—" she hung her head, her cheeks burning, and stammered, "I am rather—shy, you see." And knew that some of the heat in her cheeks was because she remembered Tristram's embrace, and how she had gloried in it, with no shyness at all.

"Of course! My sweet, pure angel! How do you endure me! Now—what is this? Tears? Ah—*ma petite!* Come."

He drew her into his arms, gently this time, his kisses soft upon her curls. When she looked up, he dried her tearful eyes and smiled, "I am forgiven? You will have patience with this so clumsy French fellow?"

She blinked, took his handkerchief and blew her nose with a lack of affectation that restored the twinkle to his eyes. "I only hope," she said huskily, "that a very fine French gentleman will have patience—with me."

Gerard closed the door softly and glanced around the darkened drawing room. Night had brought cooler temperatures, wherefore the indignant kitchen boy had been rousted out of his snug bed so as to light a fire for their guest. The logs were dying now, but by their dim glow Gerard discerned a smoke ring floating upwards from a wing chair beside the hearth. He walked nearer and stood in silence.

"You move like a spirit, Gerard," Sanguinet observed lazily.

"A friendly spirit, monseigneur."

Sanguinet laughed. "The devil, more like! Speaking of

which—where is Devil Dice, or Shotten, or whatever it is he calls himself today?''

"To the best of my knowledge, he is at Sanguinet Towers, monseigneur. With M'sieu Guy."

The cigar was lowered. Sanguinet viewed his minion with faint amusement. "You do not care overmuch for my so estimable brother."

His bland expression unchanged, Gerard said nothing.

"Why?" demanded Sanguinet.

"Because," Gerard answered smoothly, "I serve you, monseigneur. And M'sieu Parnell."

Sanguinet considered that for a moment. "You're a clever devil," he acknowledged. "Show me how clever. When shall we leave for Dinan?"

"It would, dare I so remark, be unwise to hurry the English lady. She is—" the hesitation was minute, "of a haughtiness."

"'True. But haughtiness is so often a mask for fear, my Gerard. And we sail on Thursday. Tomorrow you will ride to Dover and tell my Captain to prepare. *La Hautemant.*"

"I bow," said Gerard, grinning, and did so.

"*Merci.* Oh—and when you have spoken with the Captain, send a man to The Towers, or on to Scotland if Shotten has departed already. He is to return to Dinan as soon as he has done as I instructed. I wish him to advise me on—a certain matter."

Gerard nodded, and, sensing from his master's faint frown that there was more, waited.

After a moment, he prompted, "This matter—it is a threat, perhaps, sir?"

Sanguinet blew another smoke ring and, watching it, murmured, "A small one, if it indeed exists. But, do you know, Gerard, I think we will take with us the little invalid. It would so please my affianced bride—do not you think?"

Gerard's saturnine features were lit by a slow smile.

7

A shout of laughter added to the din in the tap of "The Cat and Dragon." Tristram shifted on the settle beside the recessed hearth and tried to shut out those raucous voices. Five days had passed since he'd ridden away from Strand Hall. Five lonely days, through which he'd wandered uncaringly, having lost all incentive to discover more of his past. Haunted by Rachel's lilting laugh, her beauty, her grace, he was more fiendishly tormented by the sure knowledge that she loved him in return. Day and night he had sought for a solution; often he'd been almost convinced that if he discovered his prospects to be fairly presentable, he should rush back to Strand Hall and fight for his love. But in his heart he knew it was useless. Rachel had accepted the offer of a gentleman who had been very kind to her when she badly needed kindness, who had been instrumental in restoring her loved sister to a semblance of health. And even if she were not so indebted, what right had he to woo her? Whatever his prospects, they could not compare to those of Claude Sanguinet, and to ask her to break her given promise was dishonourable, and could only bring shame and disgrace not upon himself, but on that sweet, pure girl.

She filled his mind to the exclusion of all else. Countless memories plagued him: her fierce valour when she had wielded the whip at Waterloo; her patience and gentleness when she had nursed him; the funny little way she had of peeping curiously up at him when she was not quite sure if he was teasing; her head uptilted as she'd stood at the edge of the cliffs and gazed at the "feather castles" with the sunlight full on her lovely face. The most poignant memory—of her yielding body in his arms that last morning in the barn—made him writhe. He jerked upright. There was nothing he could do—save try to forget her. They were doomed to exist separately through the years. He would—

"Go on, Nipper! Land 'im one in the breadbasket!"

"Black 'is ogle fer'un, little'un!"

These bloodthirsty admonitions, accompanied by howls of laughter and the pleadings of the tavernkeeper that "we won't have no violence, gents, if y' please!" penetrated Tristram's introspection. He stood and wandered closer.

The proprietor of "The Cat and Dragon" was not one to waste money on candles, and the interior was dim. There was, however, sufficient light to determine that two men stood facing one another, their obvious hostility encouraged by a crowd eager for entertainment. While not in the least unwilling to be diverted, Tristram frowned when he saw that the opponents were very poorly matched. One—a great brute of a man—fairly towered over the other, who was little more than a boy, small of stature and of such slight build as to have no chance at all against such a foe.

Wringing his hands in apprehension, the tavernkeeper took in Tristram's height and breadth of shoulder, and noting also the disapprobation of the scarred face, appealed for his aid. "They'll proper wreck this establishment, sir, if some fair-minded man don't stop 'em!"

"Oho!" scoffed the large man. "You picked the right one to try it! That there cove, 'e knows all about wot's *fair*, 'e do!"

Tristram looked narrowly at the speaker and recognized him for the vulgar lout who had obviously disgusted Rachel on the dock at Dover and who'd later been so insolent in "The Ship" that, had he himself not been weak as a cat, he'd have felt compelled to pull the fellow's nose for him. He had no intention of involving Rachel in this low brawl, however obliquely, and thus ignored the implications and drawled, "I know enough to mislike a bout between two men of vastly different weights, Shotten."

Both his opinion and his cultured accents had their effect, and the enthusiasm of the crowd lessened. The smaller of the antagonists, however, thanked the newcomer for his concern, but added, "Never confuse quantity with quality, sir. I am perfectly able to pound some civility into this overripe slab of beef!'' Having said which, he soared through the air to land with a crash against a table and disappear behind it.

Lowering the fist which had initiated that sudden flight, Shotten leapt forward, tore the table away and, grabbing the young man by the scruff of a rather worn collar, hauled him to his knees. A shout went up from the onlookers, but hushed as Shotten's muscular fist was restrained by long fingers that, clasping about the wrist below it, seemed with no effort at all to hold back the equally muscular arm.

"You struck while he was turned away," Tristram pointed out in his deep, quiet voice. "Hardly fair play."

Shotten wrenched free and offered a profane wish that the soldier would keep his ugly mouth in his pocket. "Ain't none o' your bread and butter," he snarled.

"I must . . . second the motion," panted the slight young man, struggling to his feet, and swaying back and forth as he peered at Tristram. "My brawl, sir. Must . . . ask . . ." Here, he sagged so far forward that Tristram was obliged to place a hand against his chest to steady him. "Must . . ." he repeated, his voice barely audible, "request—"

Shotten grinned, reached out and knocked Tristram's supporting arm clear.

The young man crumpled to the floor but at once commenced a dogged effort to regain his feet. A laugh went up, but the youth's pluck had not escaped the crowd, and there were admiring cries also. The light was brighter here, several of the customers having brought their table candles with them, and thus he was revealed to be older than Tristram had supposed; somewhere in the neighbourhood of three and twenty. His colouring was fair, his light curling hair sadly in need of trimming. Intensely blue eyes were shadowed by fatigue or illness, and his features, very pale, were astonishingly perfect and so delicately carven as to possess an almost girlish beauty. He had succeeded in getting one foot under him when Shotten's boot shoved him backwards once more. "Devil take you . . . fellow!" he gasped indignantly. "How may I . . . knock you down if—you will not let me up?"

"Knock me dahn?" hooted Shotten. "*You?* That's a corker, that is!"

"Even so," said Tristram, "you must let him get up."

"Oh, I must, must I?" sneered Shotten. "Well, I won't. But I'll tell yer what." He paced closer to thrust his beefy features under Tristram's nose. "You can get yer fancy jawing and yer fancy sporting idees outta my way so I can teach that there pretty little chap not ter prig wot don't belong ter him!"

The object of this discussion was by now on his feet and reeling forward. Shotten saw him from the corner of his eye and swung his large fist to backhand the youth, who went down to lie sprawled and, this time, motionless.

"Now—if yer 'ighness don't mind," grinned Shotten, "I'll wipe me boots on that little lad, and—"

Tristram's hand caught his grayish cravat. "I do mind," he said, his eyes grim. "That was a filthy, cowardly blow, and—"

"Outside!" wailed the tavernkeeper, dancing about them in his anxiety. He ran to swing the door open. "Please, gentlemen—much more room out here!"

Tristram glanced to him. Shotten struck hard, his fist catching Tristram below the ear, staggering him. Leaping in with a shout of triumph, Shotten followed up that first unsportsmanlike attack with a solid uppercut to the jaw. Jarred to the edge of unconsciousness, Tristram was propelled backwards through the open door, and fell heavily in the yard.

Howling a unanimous verdict of "Foul!" the crowd followed happily, until the only occupant of the tap was the delicate youth stretched out on the floor.

Triumphant, Shotten ran at his victim and drew back one large boot. This, the patrons of "The Cat and Dragon" would not countenance, and deterred by angry shouts of "Let be, dang ye!" he hesitated, then stood back, his great knotted fists ready.

Tristram came dizzily to his knees. Shotten grinned and aimed a mighty right. How that whistling fist could miss, he was never afterwards able to understand, but miss it did. The next thing he knew, a steel clamp was fastened about his leg and he was down, the breath knocked from his lungs. Tristram stumbled to his feet, shaking his head in an effort to clear it despite the throbbing that warned he was still in no condition to undertake this battle. Shotten lay and got his wind. He was well aware of the soldier's state of health, else he would never have challenged him, for Shotten made it a practice to bet only on a sure thing. He'd been surprised by the ease with which he'd been brought down, but he was still confident. Groaning, he rolled onto his side and, ever cunning, strove feebly to get to his knees, then launched himself in a tigerish spring at the waiting Tristram.

It was eye to eye then, a jarring exchange of blows between two big men, neither lacking experience. The thud of feet, the solid whack of fists, the laboured breathing were the only sounds to disturb the summer night, for the crowd was rapt and silent, watching a contest that would be described for weeks to come. Shotten's power lay in his brute strength; Tristram, well taught in the years memory clouded, brought scientific foot-work to the contest, so that he seemed never to be there when Shotten aimed. Feinting, blocking, dodging, ever elusive, he delivered telling blows that began to wear down his adversary until Shotten, in the midst of a curse, jack-knifed to the left that rammed into his midriff. Tristram jumped in, but whatever else he might be, Shotten had bottom; he straightened and a punishing right seemed to split Tristram's skull. Sickened by the pain of it, he reeled back, Shotten rushing in eagerly. Gasping for breath and half blind, Tristram launched a right jab. Shotten yowled and crimson streamed from his bulbous nose. He was seldom really hurt in a brawl, and he retaliated typically: Tristram was staggered, not by a fist, but by the hissing vitriol of words.

"Perishin' fool! Shining up to Sanguinet's trollop. Thought yer could make her throw *him* over? That's a laugh! She knows which side her bread is buttered, does *that* one!" And seeing his foe white where he was not bruised, and the dark eyes stunned, Shotten laughed and struck with all his strength. Tristram blocked and deflected that savage blow to an extent, but still it smashed his head back. He scarcely felt it. Blinking, he crouched slightly and moved forward. There were those in London's Corinthian set who would have indulged in some heavy wagering had they seen that advance. As it was, the excitement of the onlookers manifested itself in a roar of acclaim dying swiftly to a breathless stillness. Shotten saw the younger man's eyes narrowed and glittering, and in the set of the jaw, the thin line of the bloodied lips, he read death and for the first time was afraid. Edging back, he dodged the jab that shot at him, retaliated with a right that would have levelled his opponent had it connected, then was driven mercilessly by a rain of blows, each seemingly heavier and more telling than the last, until an explosive uppercut lifted him to his toes. He was quite unconscious before he hit the earth.

Murder blazing in his eyes and in his heart, Tristram bent over that still form, then whirled as hands pounded at his shoulders and voices shouted in wild acclaim. The villagers, elated by the fine struggle they had witnessed, were eager to buy the victor a tankard of home brew. But when that deadly glare was turned upon them, they faltered and drew away. A new diversion offered in the ceremonial carrying of Shotten to the trough, into which he was dumped amid much hilarity. The small crowd then proceeded happily to the tap.

Tristram followed, groped his way to a secluded table and sat there, chin on fist, staring at the opposite settle, oblivious of the many curious glances that came his way. An odd lassitude was stealing over him, but aside from the throbbing in his head, he felt little pain from his bruises. He wondered in detached fashion what he would have done to that foul-mouthed vermin had he been alone . . .

"You took my brawl!" quoth an irked voice.

The handsome youth who had precipitated all this stood over him, a large contusion across one cheekbone and a ferocious frown on his face.

"I—cannot deny it," Tristram admitted.

"He had a right, you know."

Raising one swelling hand to his swelling jaw, Tristram allowed with a wry smile that he was aware of that fact.

"I meant," said the young man severely, "he had a right to be provoked."

"Why? Had you blackened his—er—good name, perhaps?"

A gleam of mischief stole into those blue eyes. "Stole his beef." He nodded reinforcingly as he saw incredulity in the scarred face below him. " 'S right. Slipped a slice off his plate while he wasn't looking. Clean as a whistle. Or—almost." He looked ruefully at one scratched hand. "He stabbed me with his fork. Instead of the beef. By mistake, I'll own." The twinkle in his eyes very pronounced, he added, "He was a trifle surprised."

Tristram chuckled. "I can believe it."

"He said that since I'd put his beef away, which I had, no denying, he would put me away. Fair enough. Only he don't *fight* fair!"

"So I learned."

"Did you, by Jove? Last I remember, you were talking to him. Not the slightest use trying to reason with a lout like that. Strike first and—er whatever it is, later!" He put out a slender hand, smiling.

Tristram shook it, started up, and was obliged to lean on the table as the scene swung before his blurring eyes and his head seemed to explode. From a great distance he heard a concerned voice enquiring if he was all right. "Just . . . my head," he said faintly. "Been a bother since Water— Water—" And he forgot where he was for a while.

"Devenish," said the young man, pouring scalding coffee into two mugs. "Alain Devenish, at your service." He set the coffee pot before the blazing fire in his cozy parlour of "The Cat and Dragon," handed the larger mug to Tristram, then settled himself in a wooden rocking chair on the opposite side of the hearth. "The thing is, I cannot go back. The old uncle said that I would never amount to anything save gallows bait, the way I was going. And that I was not to show him my face again 'til I'd proven myself worthy of my name. Deuced hot at hand, is the old boy!"

Tristram blinked into those indignant eyes, sipped the restoring coffee and stretched sleepily in the overstuffed, sagging, but comfortable chair he had been urged to accept. "Your guardian?" he asked.

"Yes. Frightful Tartar. No pleasing him. None. He's been difficult since I was sent down from King's"

"Cambridge?" asked Tristram, then winced, splashing coffee from the mug.

He had already revealed what he might of his own name and

circumstances, and Devenish rescued the mug and peered anxiously at his guest's lowered head. "Your head still give you a twinge now and then?" he asked. "Shouldn't wonder if it did tonight. That clod hit dashed hard."

"It's not that . . . entirely. Only—when I remember something, I seem to—to pay a blasted . . . forfeit." He looked up, with a wry grin. "Bit of a nuisance."

Despite the grin, sweat beaded his forehead, and Devenish, his heart going out to the man, said, "And it has been like this since Waterloo?"

"Not so often of late. Fortunately. And I am getting snatches of memory. Now—" he retrieved his coffee, "tell me, if you will, why you were sent down."

"Silly nonsense. How was I to know the Proctor would break his ankle?"

A glimmer of amusement lit Tristram's tired eyes. "Lay on, Macduff."

"Yes—well, that's what we did, as a matter of fact. The old boy fancied himself an athlete. He used to roust us all out of bed at the crack of dawn every dashed day and make us run around The Backs with no shirts until we damn near froze. So, one morning we—I—covered the soles of his shoes with glue." He chuckled reminiscently. "Didn't think it had worked at first, but as he trotted along, he started to gather up all sorts of stuff. Before you could wink an eye, his feet were as wide as they were long. Clumsy chap fell over them."

"And—broke his ankle?"

Devenish nodded, trying to look contrite, but his eyes were twinkling. "Yes. Sorry to say."

"And you—owned up?"

"Well . . . yes."

"And got sent down." Tristram laughed. "I wonder you were not bought a pair of colours and packed off to the Peninsula!"

"Was. The colours, at least. But I only got myself another Proctor."

"Captain?"

"Major. Blasted martinet. The Peninsula would have been grand, but instead I did my soldiering in Hyde Park, Richmond

Park, Wimbledon Common. All in full regalia, no matter how beastly hot the weather. How that old devil loved to make us drill for hours, while he snored in the shade. Then he would mount up, whip out his sabre, hold it at arm's length, and prance out in front, natty and neat, while we exhausted slaves followed. The fellow was so puffed up in his own conceit, there was no bearing it." His eyes became grim suddenly. "Used to call me—'My Pretty.' " He fixed Tristram with a challenging stare, but that worthy, having a very good idea of the price Devenish must pay for his unbelievable looks, was commendably unsmiling.

"I trust," he said gravely, "you evened the score?"

The twinkle returned. "Didn't I, though! One of my fellows claimed to have been a locksmith, though I suspect milling kens was more his line. You'd not believe the tools he carried—one of which was—a fine saw." His eyes danced, and a corner of his beautifully shaped mouth twitched.

Staring at him blankly, Tristram began to grin. "Not—the sabre?"

Devenish nodded irrepressibly. "Almost clear through! Then we slipped it back into the scabbard, and in a few hours, off we went to the Parade Ground. Had I known the Duke would be there . . ."

"Oh, gad! *Wellington*?"

"Quite unexpectedly. It was after Toulouse, you see. At all events, what was done, was done. Never had our Major ridden so straight. A regular wooden image! Then, just as we approached the reviewing party, out came the sabre! It began to sag almost at once. And just—just as we passed Old Hooky—" he chortled uncontrollably, "it—it fell right off!"

Tristram gave a shout of laughter. "Would that I'd seen it!"

"Hooky saw it. You should have heard him howl!" Wiping his eyes, Devenish gasped, "I was not cashiered, exactly. But the Major made it so hot for me, I was obliged to sell out. Still—deuce take it—it was worth every second!"

Rather breathless, Tristram remarked, "And—your guardian?"

"As you might expect. Cast me forth, and all that sort of fustian. I wouldn't mind so much—only . . ." Devenish looked rather fixedly at the banked-up fire and said, "I rather miss the old tyrant. And Yolande—and Miss Farthing. Just occasionally."

Yolande . . . Yolande . . . Tristram frowned. He had known someone by that name—somewhere. "Your sisters?"

"Cousin. Yolande, that is. Yolande Drummond. She lives at Park Parapine." He sighed. "Nice chit. Miss Farthing's my mare." Brightening with an effort, he added, "And also the sum total of my fortune at the moment."

Tristram glanced around this parlour that must certainly be the best "The Cat and Dragon" had to offer. "Then—you must allow me to help pay for all this."

"Not in the least necessary, old fellow. You have already paid for it."

Tristram clapped a hand to the purse Sister Maria Evangeline had so generously provided. It was considerably lighter. Peering at his depleted fortune, he said indignantly, "The devil! You had no right, sir!"

"Oh, none at all. If you like," Devenish said hopefully, "you can call me out for it."

The crossing was rough, and with each mile Rachel's heart grew heavier, so that she finally feigned illness, and retired to her cabin. Madame Fleur was genuinely afflicted, and Claude instructed his Captain to put in at Cherbourg rather than attempt the reefs of Normandy in such weather. They passed the night in a comfortable inn, and it came as no surprise to Rachel when, after breakfast, M. Gerard procured a very well-sprung carriage for their journey southward, together with a second coach to convey the servants and the luggage. The drive was long and monotonous however, and the weather gloomy, and when they approached their destination, Rachel thought the countryside very parched and barren, despite the occasional spatters of rain. Claude was pleasant as always, providing them with a running commentary concerning the province through which they passed, and speaking proudly of its colorful history.

Despite herself, Rachel's attention wandered, and she was mildly startled when Charity exclaimed, "Did you hear that, dearest? Monsieur Claude is descended from the ancient kings of Brittany! You are marrying into a royal family!"

"Is that indeed so, Claude?" Rachel asked, surprised. "You never mentioned it."

He shrugged. "One does not go about bragging of one's ancestors. You also are from a fine old house, my love, *n'est-ce pas*?"

Her smile was forced. What he said was true; the name Strand had once been a proud one. But now, she thought sadly, trampled in the dust.

They left the coast and headed inland. There were few habitations to be seen, and the terrain was very broken and rocky. With sinking heart, Rachel thought it lonely and inhospitable, so different from the beautiful French countryside she knew or her lush and gentle Sussex. Up hill and down, rumble and jolt and jingle, until quite suddenly they plunged into thick woods, and soon the way ahead was blocked by giant iron gates hung from white stone pillars, and with a high wall leading off in either direction. Just inside the gates, and to one side of the drive, was a lodge, and three men in black livery sat at a table before it, throwing dice. They all sprang up as the carriage approached, and ran to open the gates. The carriage swept through; Gerard, who rode with the outriders, pausing to call that a second vehicle followed. Rachel caught only a fleeting glimpse of the men, but they seemed to her a grim lot, their shouts of welcome, which were accompanied by neither smiles nor enthusiasm, appearing a concession to protocol rather than an evidence of affection.

Immediately, there was a vast improvement in the scenery. These woods were well-thinned, the undergrowth lush but confined to pleasantly shaped shrubs and fern. Leaving the leafy shade, they came out into an area of downsloping turf, dotted with little arbours and neatly tended flower beds. As if in welcome, the sun came out, drawing a flash from the top of a broad hill that lifted ahead, much of it concealed by trees. Claude, seated beside Rachel, drew her hand through his arm. "See how even the sunshine greets you, my dear," he said kindly. "It knows you come to your future home. I must explain that my Papa built the chateau. He scoured the world for the *objets*

112

d'art you will see. The drivepath we follow loops around the hill through many gardens, each true to its own theme, and separated from the others by trees. The first of these we are now entering. Beyond is the Baghdad Garden.''

The trees fell away. Rachel's gasp was echoed by a delightful exclamation from Charity. They were in an area of indescribable beauty, a place of exotic shrubs, mosaic-tiled walks and statuary that of itself must be worth a fortune. The lawns were like rippling green velvet, and gardeners laboured among flower beds that were riots of colour. The path wound gently upward, revealing its wonders gradually. Rachel gasped again when a mosque came into view. It was scaled down to the size of a cottage, but startlingly authentic, even to the gilded towers and minarets.

''Oh!'' she cried. ''*Never* have I seen so lovely a sight!''

''You have but begun!'' proclaimed Madame Fleur exuberantly. ''Beyond the next wood is—'' She stopped as Claude glanced at her, and then finished lamely, ''A lot more.''

Several men were scattered about, busily at work, and Charity, awed, said, ''You must have an army of gardeners here, Monsieur Claude.''

''An unhappy necessity,'' he smiled.

They were entering another wooded belt. Coming into the open, Claude announced, rather in the manner of a conjurer pulling rabbits from a hat, ''The Cathay Garden!''

Here were quaint winding streams, crossed by stepping-stones, and edged with flowers. The shrubs and trees were of unique delicacy and conformation, and even the turf was different, being of a darker, more dense, and springy texture. Dominating this peaceful garden a great bronze Buddha, oxidized by the dampness to a dusty light green, sat atop a black onyx platform, and nearby, black swans floated regally along the stream. There was scarcely time to fully appreciate these beauties before the next curve brought an even more exquisite sight, an enchanting pagoda beside a large pool, with a red lacquered bridge arching over the lily-strewn surface. The huge tree that shaded the pagoda was gnarled and twisted, and the branches stretching protectively over the enameled roof were bare of leaves save for occasional flat clumps that created a most attractive form, perfectly complementing the oriental architecture.

And so it went, the carriage moving steadily upward through the Grecian garden where marble ruins and statuary were scattered about plantings of classic symmetry, dominated by another pool—a long rectangle this time, providing a mirror-like reflection of the superb temple that loomed beside it; through the Egyptian garden with its sphinx and bullrushes and papyrus; the English garden, complete with moated, miniature castle and charming flowers; each seemingly more lovely than the last.

The sisters were captivated and had exhausted their store of superlatives when the carriage rounded the last curve. The chateau, bursting upon their sight like the final crashing chord of a symphony, was the *pièce de résistance*. A sprawl of white marble, fronted by wide steps, it stood proudly on the crest of the hill. The architecture was Italian rather than French, the main block being set back between the forward-reaching wings on either side, thus creating a wide court which was lined with fountains. The sun was stronger now, and its beams awoke sparkles from the sweeping sprays and brightened the white walls so that the house shone like a thing of faerie.

The coachman blew up a blast on his yard of tin as the carriage circled a wide, level area devoted to an extensive maze where more gardeners trimmed the tall hedge walls. Servants appeared on the broad steps and began to hurry down to them. The carriage stopped. The door was thrown open, and a magnificent being in ivory satin and powder let down the steps. Claude sprang out and handed Rachel down. She paused, looking dazedly at the great, gleaming structure above her.

"Well, *chérie*," he murmured in her ear. "What do you think of it all?"

She thought it a palace, so magnificent as to be terrifying, and experienced a deep yearning for the dear dilapidations of Strand Hall. But she *must* put away such thoughts! She had entered this bargain willingly, and it was both pointless and unfair to her betrothed to do anything less than make the best of it. "I think it superb," she said quietly.

Claude nodded. "Yes. But—just wait until you see the suite that I have had prepared for you!"

As lovely as was the exterior, inside, the chateau was indeed like a palace. The entrance hall was oval, the domed ceiling arranged into six panels radiating from the central star, each panel embellished with paintings of exotic birds fluttering about well-endowed and nude ladies. The floor was of pink marble, having in the centre a large oval Persian carpet woven in tones of red and white. Two enormous chandeliers graced this large chamber, and charming statuary was set about, interspersed with benches and intricately carven chests. Wide corridors led from either side towards the other areas of the ground floor, and at the rear a staircase flowed gracefully around the contour of the wall to spill its widening red-carpeted steps onto the roseate floor. Glancing down the corridors, Rachel gained an impression of red and gold and crystal; of exquisite chandeliers; walls lined with gilded chests whereon were priceless porcelains, jade and marbles; sparkling mirrors within filigreed Chinese Chippendale frames. Everything rich, tasteful, and regal.

A very large footman carried Charity into the house and followed as Claude and Madame Fleur led the way upstairs.

"Had I only thought," Claude sighed, "I could have made arrangements for a downstairs room to be equipped for your sister's needs. Alas, there are steps everywhere, but she need never feel constrained. My servants have so little to occupy them that they will delight to carry the poor child about."

He had spoken in a loud whisper that Rachel was sure Charity had heard. She fought a surge of irritation, reminding herself that he doubtless fancied he had been all consideration, but she could have shaken him for such tactlessness. Like most invalids, Charity was less distressed by her own illness than by her dread of being a burden to others. Rachel, who went to great lengths lest her sister harbour such a suspicion, forced a smile and enquired in a rather brittle voice as to how many rooms the chateau boasted.

"Approximately ninety. Not as many as you may have supposed, but you will have noticed that both wings have only the ground and first floor. Only the main block has another floor, and that, I must confess, I keep all to myself; it is where I conduct my many—concerns and because of the extremely confidential nature of some of my ventures, is necessarily kept locked. However, I shall be very eager to conduct you through the rest of the chateau when you are rested, my love." He bowed over her hand. "I leave you now. If there is anything—*anything* you desire, I pray you will call for it at once."

He smiled upon Charity and hurried away, to be succeeded by a middle-aged housekeeper clad in a gown of dark blue linen fastened to the throat with small mother-of-pearl buttons. She spoke politely, but with brevity, and did not so far unbend as to reveal her name. The sisters were assigned a suite having bedchambers on each side of a central *petit salon.* There was also a spacious dressing room where a cot had been set up for Agatha, so that she could be near to Mademoiselle Charity at night. Listening politely to these arrangements, Rachel was past being surprised when the woman flung open a panelled door. The petit salon was delightful, the walls papered in a design of pale pink flowers interspersed with gold *fleurs-de-lis.* The furnishings were from the era of Louis XIV, upholstered in soft pinks and greens. Charity's room was blue and white and charmingly feminine. Having viewed it, the small procession journeyed across the petit salon to the bedchamber allotted to Rachel. It was large and sumptuous, but not oppressively so. A dainty canopied bed with a small sofa at its foot; thick carpets; a cozy fireplace framed with Italian painted tiles and flanked by two small wing chairs; ample chests and two large clothes-presses, and wide windows looking out over the side of the hill that fell away in a sheer drop below. Rachel crossed to the small table before the windows, enjoying the breeze that ruffled her hair as she removed her bonnet.

"It is all—so exquisite!" said Charity. "Dearest—do you—" She broke off as Agatha uttered an exclamation of surprise.

The abigail stood before one of the presses, staring in bewilderment at the neat row of dresses and ball gowns. "Well! I never did!" she gasped. "One might think as you wasn't never going home again, Miss Rachel!"

8

"*Do* you know, Dev," said Tristram thoughtfully, "we have been three days journeying together, and I've not yet called you out."

Attempting to settle himself more comfortably against the hayrick on this warm July morning, Devenish inspected his left hand and replied, "Had you expected to have done so?"

"I cannot deny it. I marvel, in fact, at my restraint. Never in my life—or as much of it as I can recollect—have I encountered such a firebrand! *Must* you challenge everyone we meet?"

"Firebrand?" snorted Devenish, indignantly. "Was it my fault that clod of a farmer attacked us last evening? *He* was the one named you a 'gert creature,' and—"

"And *you* were the one objected. Had you not retaliated in kind—"

"I did but say he was a yokelly jack-at-warts. Which was purest truth—did you see the one on the end of his nose? The trouble with you is, Tris, that you waste your time in trying to reason with these upstarts." He addressed his companion earnestly. "You must learn to be more firm. More decisive. If a man offends you—knock him down. *Then* you can reason, old fellow. Mark my words, you'll get nowhere in life do you not change your ways." Pleased with this little lecture, he nodded and resumed his inspection of his hand.

"You struck first last night," Tristram remarked mildly. "And instead of the warm bed I'd almost convinced the land-lord we should have, we paid almost as much for the privilege of racking up in a stable." He scratched his ribs and added with a rueful smile, "Some of whose occupants I fear still accompany us."

"Blasted fellow was a rogue! Gouging the public, just as I told the greedy mawworm! When I think—" In the midst of a heated gesture, Devenish winced and swore.

Tristram sat up. "Let me see that."

"It's the thumb, I think," Devenish held out his hand. "Trifle puffy."

"A trifle dislocated. Baconbrain! Why could you not have told me? Hold on."

"Hey! Wait!"

Tristram did not wait and, having pulled hard, was enveloped in a flood of profanity. He lay back, and when Devenish ran out of breath, asked, "Did it do?"

"Blast your eyes! You half killed—"

This exaggeration was cut off by the frenzied barking of a large black and tan dog that came at them, lips curling back from long and efficient-looking fangs, and hair standing on end all across powerful shoulders.

Tristram sprang to his feet. Looking desperately about for a weapon, he found none. "Dev!" he exclaimed. "Get up, you clunch! It's likely the farmer's hound. We're trespassing, and—"

"Come on, you old fool," Devenish said lazily and extended one hand, palm up towards that double row of gnashing teeth.

The dog crouched lower. The growls in its throat were deep and murderous. Tristram took a pace nearer his friend.

"Be still," said Devenish, perfectly calm. "There's no danger to me."

Tristram stood motionless, but watchful.

Narrowed eyes gleaming malevolently, the dog prepared to spring.

"For God's sake!" breathed Tristram, readying for violent action.

"Here, boy!" The slender fingers snapped, scant inches from those powerful jaws.

Growling deep in its throat, the dog's long tail began to wag. The fearsome rumble stopped. The upcurled lip relaxed. The bristling hair lowered.

Slowly, easily, Devenish touched the wolfish head, then

tugged at one rather mangled ear. The dog whined, moved closer, and butted its head under that caressing hand.

"I'll be . . . damned!" gasped Tristram.

Devenish grinned up at him. "I've a bit of a way with animals."

Tristram had detected a new sound. "I trust you've a bit of a way with farm labourers. I fancy your friend here was the advance guard."

Devenish sprang up. "You stay, old fellow," he ordered, and the dog lay down at once.

"Come on!" urged Tristram. "Those rakes don't look any too friendly!"

The farmhands proved a lusty crew, armed with an unnerving array of implements from pitchforks to shovels, and it was some time before their prey dared slow to a walk. Long after he had regained his wind, however, Tristram was silent, his brow furrowed, and the occasional remarks of his companion earning only an abstracted grunt by way of answer.

"Women?" Devenish asked. "They're the devil, are they not?"

Tristram smiled faintly. "Matter of fact, I was thinking of a man. Dev—are you by any chance acquainted with a fellow named Sanguinet?"

"By God—I am not!" Devenish responded, considerably affronted. His ire faded when he saw that Tristram watched him with an almost fearful intensity. The matter must be important, he deduced, and elaborated. "The father was said to be tutor to the Fiend Incarnate. He's dead these five years and more. Unhappily, before he slipped his wind, he sired three sons. Of Guy, the youngest, I know little save that he has fought several duels and is considered deadly. Parnell, the middle brother, is universally despised, and universally catered to. They've wealth beyond imagination, besides which, rumour has it that those who cross them suffer strange and often fatal reverses. My Tyrant claims that Claude, the eldest of 'em, is a monster *veritablement*!"

The ghastly suspicion that had bedevilled him ever since Shotten had voiced his poison, strengthened its grip. Tristram asked, with an attempt at nonchalance, "Dangerous? Oh—to the women, you mean?"

"No. But, he is, I'll admit. How any woman could stomach him is more than I can fathom, for his reputation is perfectly horrible. Money, I suppose. He has an English chit for a playmate at the moment. A beauty, so I hear. Her family's smoky, to say the least of it, but—that she would sink to his level is downright shocking!" He shook his head righteously, happily unaware of the menace of two glinting eyes. "He means to marry her, apparently. Lord knows why—unless he wants to wed into England's society. He's not picked a prime example, but—beggars can't be choosers, and with his past, no matchmaking Mama of the *ton* would allow her daughter within arm's length of the creature. The only other explanation is that the slut's in a delicate condition and blackmailing the dirty bas—" He choked. A hand of iron had gripped his cravat and dragged him to within inches of a face he scarcely recognized, so contorted was it with passion.

"Apologize! You filthy, lying swine!" grated Tristram.

Devenish spluttered, "You're ripe—for Bedlam! Let go!"

"Take back what you said—damn your soul!"

"The . . . the devil I . . . will!"

The murderous grip tightened. Not all Devenish's struggles were of any avail, and a red haze was clouding his vision when he was flung away so violently that he staggered.

"By God!" Tristram snarled. "Did I not outweigh you . . ."

Devenish stood swaying, clutching his throat, and gasping for breath. But in a very few seconds he hurled himself at his tormentor. Tristram placed one hand squarely in the middle of the enraged man's chest, and held it there.

"Fight! You addlewitted hedgebird! You—you man-milliner!" Devenish roared, arms flailing madly. "Damn you—fight!"

"If I did, I'd likely kill you."

"Indeed?" Devenish's struggles ceased. He drew himself up and, as Tristram lowered his restraining hand, requested regally, "Name your seconds!"

"How in the deuce can I name seconds when I don't know with whom I am acquainted?"

The lofty hauteur was at once submerged in rage. "Then—devil take you, we'll fight without seconds. Here and now!" He flung back his hand, but Tristram caught and held his wrist. "I'll not fight a green boy," he said. His own rare fury had waned, and recalling what Rachel had said of her family's disgrace, he watched Devenish thoughtfully through a torrent of outrage during which he was advised that it was too much, quite the outside of enough, and, "I'll have your blood for it! Damme if I don't! You damn near throttled me, blast you! And for no reason! You asked a question. I did my best to give you a civil answer and—"

"And is it your practice to speak ill of a lady of Quality?"

The perfect features flushed scarlet. The blue eyes slid away. "It is not. Nor did I. The Strand girl is not—"

"Have a care!"

Devenish stared at him. Was that the way of it, then? But it was no excuse, regardless! "You have questioned my honour, sir," he said grandly. "You *must* answer to me!"

Those fateful words could not have been spoken with more disdain by a Prince of the blood. Devenish was more than a little superb in his youthful pride and courage. But his old beaver hat was stained and battered, his face bruised and not too clean, and the shoulder of his coat was torn. A twinkle crept into Tristram's dark eyes, and he asked in a gentler tone, "How do you know I am a gentleman? Perhaps I'm not worthy of your steel."

Devenish saw the twinkle and interpreted it as mockery. Seething, he wheeled, suddenly swung around, and backhanded Tristram hard across the mouth.

Tristram gasped and staggered slightly. The boy was stronger than he'd thought! Devenish's flush had faded. He looked grim and white, and very determined. The cold feel of blood on his chin, Tristram bowed and started off.

With a howl of frustration, Devenish sprang after him. "Stop!" he demanded, trotting anxiously along beside his adversary. "Have you *no* sense of proper conduct? Stop! I am five and twenty—*not* a green boy! Dammit, man. I doubt you're above four or five years my senior—eh? *Will* you stop! I've struck you in the face—drawn your cork, too, begad! You *can not* simply walk away from that!''

Tristram could, and did. Baffled, Devenish halted, watching him, then ran in furious pursuit. Sighing, Tristram turned. Devenish raced at him, fists clenched. At the last instant, Tristram stepped lightly to one side. Unable to stop his furious charge, Devenish shot into the deep ditch beside the hedge.

Tristram surveyed him gravely as he sprawled, winded, amid the brambles. ''Good day to you, sir,'' he said, and went his way, faint, breathless curses following him.

What was the name of the village, or even the county through which he now wandered, Tristram had no idea. He knew that several days has passed since he'd parted from Devenish, and he had a vague knowledge that they had been riotous in the extreme. He remembered several inns and himself shouting, ''Ale all round!'' Some kind soul had guided his wavering feet to a room where he had been allowed to sleep. The next night, he had shared accommodations with a gentle-eyed carthorse. He had talked at length with that patient animal, explaining that it could not be truth. Rachel Strand was a pure and virtuous lady. She *could* not be—she *was* not—the mistress of such as Claude Sanguinet. No! Never! The carthorse had flicked an ear, his gaze plainly pitying. And Tristram had remembered many little incidents to erode his trust. Her obvious familiarity with the yacht, the vicious remarks of those two women in the library— aimed at Rachel, he now knew. By her very evasion, she had admitted she did not love her affianced. But, ''I shall marry him,'' she'd said. ''I shall marry him.'' She adored Charity, and it was very possible that she was wedding Sanguinet to provide for her sister. But she had known a father's love; she had a brother—she certainly must be aware of Claude's foul reputation. No lady could sell herself to such a man—whatever her reason. Nor was it necessary. There were other, far more palatable alternatives. Rachel was the loveliest woman he'd ever seen. She could have her pick from among the Cits and Nabobs, that was beyond doubting. Much they would care for her father's disgrace! And better a decent merchant, than a ''nobleman'' of Claude's stamp! Because of his own clouded memory, it did not occur to him that a sheltered girl would have no way of meeting such men, nor that advances from a stranger would have frightened her. He decided wretchedly that, knowing what Claude was, she had cared not. Loving another man, she had clung to her Croesus. "I shall wed him . . ." No matter how vile, how depraved! "He has been so good . . ." He has been so generous, she meant! Sodden days and nights had followed. Bereft of hope, he had now lost the one thing that had sustained him. The pure angel he had worshipped did not exist. He had given his heart to a jade no better than a harlot, and less honest! A woman who sold herself to a man scorned by her own kind despite his riches—a renowned rake and libertine. Heartsick and tormented he had journeyed alone, yet not alone, for he walked ever with despair.

He was coming into this nameless village—a quaint old place, dozing in mellow dignity under a warm afternoon sun. And it was borne in upon him that he was, against all the laws of broken hearts and shattered hopes, hungry. He took out his purse and was not surprised to find that it contained a piece of string and a button. Perhaps he could work for his dinner. Armed with this sterling ambition, he walked on, becoming aware as he went that there was a great deal of excitement nearby, for he could hear angry voices upraised above a murmur indicative of a crowd.

Intrigued, he quickened his stride until he reached the village green and, by means of soft words and the smile that won others to instant and willing cooperation, discovered the cause of the uproar. He shook his head and sighed. He might have known.

A boy held a showy chestnut horse in front of the livery stable, and watched with interest the furious argument being waged between a husky farmer and Mr. Alain Devenish. On either side of the farmer stood younger and, if anything, brawnier versions of himself, while close by, watching with obvious irritation, was a soberly clad gentleman of middle years, spare frame, and sour expression.

The farmer's knotted fist was flourished under Devenish's haughtily elevated nostrils. "We doan't want no puffed-up town boy the likes o' you, a'coming in among us wi' your fancy ways and nasty accersations!'' he bellowed.

Devenish countered coolly, ''No more do I propose to stand idly by and allow a slippery customer like yourself to dupe a poor old duffer, who—''

''*Slippery customer?*'' roared the farmer, giving Devenish a shove that was at once, and with gusto, returned.

''*Poor . . . old . . . duffer?*'' squawked the soberly dressed gentleman in nasal and outraged repugnance. ''By Jupiter, you young mushroom! How dare you!''

''*Mushroom?*'' echoed Devenish, in turn revolted. ''Why, you ungrateful shagbag! Here I've delivered you from purchasing a ten-year-old—''

''Five-year-old!'' snarled the farmer.

''—ten-year-old hack that's all show and no go! And instead of offering a touch of gratitude, you— Be damned if I don't pull your nose for you!''

''Ye dang rude little shrimp of a dandy!'' offered the farmer.

It was the last straw. Devenish sprang at the farmer, who stood head and shoulders taller and was some four stone heavier than himself.

Tristram groaned and put a hand over his eyes.

The farmer uttered a howl and mopped at a suddenly crimson nose. As one man, his two large offspring took up the cudgels. Dancing about, shouting epithets, fists flying, eyes alight, Devenish was here, there, and everywhere, in the process of which, he chanced to alight upon the neatly shod foot of the well-dressed gentleman. Another yowl rent the air. The gentleman entered the lists, cane flailing. Devenish, beset on every side, fought gamely.

''Pluck to the backbone,'' muttered Tristram. ''Blast the little bantam!'' He stepped forward to grip first the collar of one large shirt, and then another. To the accompaniment of gleeful shouts from the crowd, he brought the bullet heads of the farmer's boys together. Hard. Stepping over them, he addressed himself to their sire.

''Sir,'' said he, politely, ''if you would be so kind—let him get up now.''

''Oh, yus I won't!'' responded the farmer, continuing his

pursuit of banging Devenish's curly head upon the cobble-stones.

Tristram sighed. A few seconds later, while the farmer slid down the livery wall, wondering what he was doing there, Tristram turned to the well-dressed gentleman who was gainfully employed in prodding Devenish with his cane each time that young man strove to rise. "I feel sure *you* will listen to reason, sir," said Tristram softly, his tone implying that only the two of them were capable of dealing with the situation.

The gentleman's gaze travelled from the dusty boots to the tousled dark locks of this new arrival. "A large young man," thought he, perceptively. His attention next turned to the flounderings of the farmer's sons, and to their father, who was making quite a show of dusting himself off while awaiting the renewed mobility of his hefty offspring. "Are you, ah—acquainted with this rabble-rousing young troublemaker?" the gentleman enquired, waving his cane toward Devenish.

"Do not just stand there—*talking!*" adjured Devenish breathlessly. "Give him one . . . in the breadbasket!"

With a glance at the bruised countenance of his erstwhile companion, Tristram admitted, "Regrettably, I am, sir."

"Ar! Knows what ye do mean, sir," agreed the farmer, leering at Devenish's frustrated indignation. " 'E be a curst know-it-all from Lunon, as doan't know nothing! I be of a mind to toss 'un in the duckpond."

"I quite understand," Tristram sympathized. "But—to give the devil his due, it's not all his fault. You see—" he thought rapidly, "it was the vow that started all the trouble."

'Intrigued, the crowd pressed in closer.

"Vow, indeed!" snorted Devenish, wrenching his arm free of Tristram's supporting hold and at once tottering erratically. His attempt to fix his companion with a searing glare was equally ineffectual, since his eyes were by now so swollen that he could scarcely see the lane they followed. "If ever I heard such a bag of moonshine! I'll have you know, sir, that it was never necessary for my Guardian to place me under a vow of truth. I am not—nor ever have been given to falsehoods!"

"No, but they were made curious," Tristram pointed out.

"And thus their tempers cooled a trifle until they were able to be amused by my fabrications."

It *had* been funny. Devenish himself had become engrossed in Tristram's whimsical recounting of the "horrors" that had befallen him as a result of the oath he'd taken to tell only the truth for thirty days. By the time the fallacious tale was told, the crowd had been hilarious. "Oh, they were amused all right," he grumbled. "And little wonder, for you made me seem a veritable gudgeon."

"Perhaps, but we are away and with no bones broken."

"I'd no wish to be 'away'! Nor to have to listen to your jawing instead of enjoying a jolly good scrap!"

"Poor odds," Tristram pointed out dryly. "Fifty to one."

"What matter?" But uncomfortably aware that he was behaving like a fool, Devenish flushed and grated, "And *now* what are you smirking at? Blast you!"

"I'm over here, Dev," said Tristram, patiently turning Devenish from the signpost he addressed.

"Oh. Oh—well then, confound you, be somewhere else! I've no least wish to continue in your company!"

"Then, if you will sit down there," Tristram indicated a nearby stile, "I'll try to discover your road. Are you for Town? Or—?"

"That—nor I—is, er—*are*—no concern of yours," Devenish responded grandly, contriving to keep his dignity in spite of the grammatical quagmire.

He did a little better at locating the stile and perched upon it with what was, he hoped, easy grace.

Tristram watched him for a minute, then started off. He probably shouldn't leave the proud young fool; he was ninetenths blind. Lord knows what pickle he would get into!

He had gone a very short distance when a barely audible shout sent him running back. On the far side of the lane from the stile, Devenish was sprawled in the ditch. Tristram hauled him up, exclaiming, "Blast it all! How can I leave you? You're blind as a bat!"

Devenish sat on the edge of the ditch, head down, remarkable for his silence. Then— "Tris," he mumbled with unwonted humility, "you were right—about the way I spoke of—

Miss Strand. Damned ungentlemanly. And—I had no thought to hit you so curst hard. Can you forgive me?''

"Cawker!" Tristram took the outstretched hand and wrung it gladly. And as they started along the lane, side by side, asked, "Have you any lettuce?"

"Spent my last sixpence on a glorious luncheon, old boy. What about your purse?"

"Leased to moths, I fear. I was less sensible, but just as profligate as you. We'll have to see if we can work for the price of some steak for your eyes. It'll be dark soon. Can you walk a little faster, d'you think?"

Devenish assured him he could run a race and, hobbling along, his body one large ache, said, "Tris, it ain't none of my bread and butter, and you certainly don't have to tell me. But— are you, ah—acquainted with Rachel Strand?"

A grimness came into Tristram's dark eyes. "I once was," he said. "Or—so I thought." He sighed. "You've a right to know. I first met her . . . ."

The main ballroom of Mrs. Maribel MacNaughton's great house on John Street was becoming rather oppressively warm, and the floor so crowded that to essay the waltz entailed little more than to stand and move one's feet up and down. It was with regret, nonetheless, that Lord Leith removed his arm from about the waist of his fair partner and hostess and led her from the floor.

Mrs. MacNaughton was a pretty woman with naturally curling brown hair and regular features. Her brown eyes were rather hard, but she was blessed with a petite figure that, being curved in all the proper places, won her almost as many admirers as did the fact that she had inherited a sizable fortune. She had a host of friends and was seen everywhere, since she was considered, by the gentlemen at least, a charming addition to any party. Only one thing did the widow lack, in her own eyes, and that was a title. Unaware that Leith knew of, and was amused by, her ambition, she was reasonably certain that she was in a fair way to achieving it, and, smiling up at the lord whose lady she meant to become, asked, "How do you like my summer ball, sir?"

Leith's eyes had alighted on a certain gentleman who had been very much in his thoughts these past few days, and it was with a fatal vagueness that he murmured, "Delightful, dear lady."

"Thank you. How good it was of my dear brother to play host," she acknowledged. "It is most difficult to be a widow, you know."

If his plan worked, thought Leith, he'd divert Foster's attentions from little Sarah without finding it necessary to downright run him off. No wish to offend Foster. Good fellow. And was he extremely subtle about it all, Sally would be quite— The widow, he apprehended, was eyeing him reproachfully. Unwilling to admit he'd not heard all of her remark, and eager to make amends, he said, "Why, then, we must put a stop to such difficulties, Maribel."

He was mildly surprised to see her pretty mouth fall open slightly. Whatever the difficulty she had spoken of, she must know he'd be only too pleased to assist. "Silly puss," he said in an undertone. "Did you suppose I would say aught else?"

"Wh-Why, I—I knew you were fond of me," she stammered, scarcely able to credit his so easy capture.

"Of course I am. Extreme fond. Now—never look so astonished, dear lady. I daresay you know what has been in my mind of late, eh? I must have a few words with Foster, but I shall seek you out later. Between us, we'll contrive satisfactorily, I've no doubt."

Had she entertained any doubts, these ambiguous words dispelled them, and a small gasp of triumph escaped her.

Sublimely unaware of the hopes he'd raised, Leith lifted her hand to his lips, kissed it with aflair, and sealed his doom. "I've had to play a waiting game, don't you see?" he confided.

"Poor Leith. Did you feel that was so necessary?"

"Why, I did not wish to make a move until I was sure my little girl's affections were fully engaged."

Fluttering her ivory fan, and with her eyes shyly downcast, she breathed, "They are, Leith."

"Yes. I realize that now." His gaze straying to his daughter, who sat talking with her cousin, he sighed. "And so I must proceed at once—or fail us both."

"Oh, Leith! How masterful you are."

"No, am I?" Slightly taken aback, but not displeased, he said, "Well—perhaps. Even so, wedding bells must wait, under the circumstances. Are you of the same mind?"

Because of poor Tristram, she thought, with a sigh for the younger Leith. "Of course." She tapped him playfully with her fan. "Such an iron control. And yet—so devious. Truly, I'd no idea what was in your mind."

Grinning, he said softly, "Let's hope the gabble mongers don't!"

"The thing is, Freddy," said Leith. "She's not just out of the schoolroom, and—devilish pretty." He drove an elbow into the younger man's ribs and chuckled, "Eh?"

Sir Frederick Foster raised his glass to a singularly keen grey eye and surveyed the delightful person of Miss Brenda Smythe-Carrington. Clad in a gown of white crepe, with an overskirt of pale pink net that became her dark prettiness admirably, she stood beside her grandfather, waiting with no sign of impatience for him to conclude his conversation with the Countess of Mayne-Waring, Miss Smythe-Carrington wore her glossy hair in the very latest short style; her skin was extraordinarily pale, thus accenting her big brown eyes and long lashes, and her figure certainly was faultless. Still, thought Foster sceptically, she was at least twenty, if not thirty, years younger than Leith. He slid an oblique glance at his friend. There was a considerable age difference between the two men also, Foster being three and thirty, but during his father's lifetime, Leith had been a frequent and most welcome visitor at their large house on Grosvenor Street, and being an excellent shot, had never missed a season at the hunting lodge in Yorkshire. Foster had been on the town for better than ten years, and although unutterably bored by it all, was nobody's fool. If Leith, after all these years as a happy bachelor, had decided to become riveted, it was for one reason only—to get himself another heir. Well, he was a fine figure of a man, and even so much younger a lady might find his interest most flattering. Some high-pitched giggles drew Foster's eye to Herbert Glick, posturing with his usual set of featherheads. How furious dear Herbert would be if

Leith remarried. Gratified by that awareness, he said with a faint smile, "You are right, by Jove! Never had noticed what a beauty the girl's become. Deirdre Breckenridge had best look to her laurels, or Miss Smythe-Carrington will outshine her!"

"Why don't you ask her for the next quadrille?" Leith prompted.

Foster turned to him, one eyebrow raised in mild surprise.

"Let me know what you think of her," Leith nodded hopefully.

"Oh, I see. Well, I can tell you now that she's a fine-looking girl."

"Looks ain't everything, y'know. She has a good head on her shoulders. Not a bluestocking, I don't mean—Lord no! But she can conduct a conversation. Not all pish and posh like most of these young women. She has—presence, do not you think?"

Stifling a smile, Foster said, "I think, my friend that I shall ask her for the next quadrille."

Leith watched, elated, as Foster sauntered over to General Smythe-Carrington and his granddaughter. He'd done it! Brenda really was a pretty chit. Once Foster danced with her, he'd be fairly smitten.

Sets were beginning to form for a quadrille, and Foster had evidently been successful, for he was leading The Smythe-Carrington onto the floor.

It was not easy to converse through the movements of the dance, but when they came together, Foster found that Leith had spoken truthfully; the girl was a pleasant conversationalist. When the dance was almost over, he again had her ear for a moment, and imparted, "You've an admirer—or I should say—*another* admirer, ma'am."

She glanced up at him with an arch smile. "Do not leave me in suspense, I beg you."

He murmured, "Kingston Leith."

"Leith!" Her smile fled. As they were swept apart, she shot a look to where her "admirer" stood. He was watching her, and positively beaming. Leith! He was handsome, certainly, but old enough to be her father. Still, he was very rich, so they said. And Grandpapa would not leave her a large portion. Besides, it would be nice to be the wife of a baron. "Lady Kingston Leith." It had a nice ring. He was very much the gentleman, and she had heard that Cloudhills was delightful. Thus, when Foster led her from the floor, she said shyly, "Oh, sir, are you perfectly sure of what you—implied? I am just a silly girl, with little experience of the world. Lord Leith is so dashing—so sophisticated. Are you—*sure* he admires me?"

Vastly diverted, Foster said firmly, "*Very* sure!"

9

The afternoon was warm and having a sultry quality that, together with the clouds beginning to appear west of Dinan, warned of the likelihood of a storm. Serenely oblivious to the vagaries of weather, the Chateau Sanguinet glittered like a proud white jewel atop its hill, the splashing of the fountains in the forecourt the only sounds to disturb the quiet. Several gardeners were busied with the flower beds at the foot of the marble steps, but none of monseigneur's guests were about, save where on the level area below the front of the great house a dainty pink bonnet occasionally came into view between the high hedges of the maze.

Charity Strand twisted in her chair to direct a concerned glance at the pensive face framed by that same bonnet. "Are you not tired of pushing me about, dearest?" she asked. "It is very warm in here."

"It is, rather. Is it too much for you? If I have correctly followed Claude's directions, we are almost to the centre and there is a clear space where, hopefully, we will be able to feel the breeze."

"Optimist!" laughed Charity. "The air barely stirs. Ah! You were right! Here is your clear space. How remarkably broad it is; and only look, dear, there are benches so you may rest. How prettily they are fashioned."

Rachel halted the invalid chair beside one of the gracefully carven wooden seats which she then occupied gratefully. Had she thought it would be so warm in the maze she'd not have brought Charity this way. At luncheon, it had seemed an ideal retreat, for even was Madame Fleur ambient, she'd be unlikely to find them here. Claude's aunt had proven to be a lady of decidedly sedentary habits. Her initial effusive display of affection for her "pretty little English niece-to-be" had soon given way to complaints over Rachel's practice of riding each morning and going for a long walk in the afternoons. "Such energy," moaned Madame, "fairly exhausts one!" Her eagerness to please her nephew was, however, compelling. She had interpreted Claude's remark that he wished his fiancé to be properly chaperoned to mean that the girl must not for an instant be left alone. She hovered about Rachel like a reluctant mother hen, and however well meaning, her companionship had proven a decided trial. The worthy Fleur was remarkable for neither wit nor intelligence, and since she did not care for music or the arts, read only the fashion journals and letters from her numerous offspring, and found politics dull, her conversation was as inane as it was unending. A greater annoyance was the presence at the chateau of Claude's cousin, Monsieur Antoine Benét. This slim and dandified young man was also a remarkably fine artist. He was plunged into raptures over Rachel's beauty and when first they were introduced, clung to her hand, his eyes limpid with delight, while waxing so poetical that she was furiously embarrassed. His interest, it developed, was partly professional, since he had been commissioned by Claude to paint a portrait of the bride-to-be. Unfortunately, his admiration deepened with the passage of time, and in a very few days he declared himself Rachel's first *cicisbeo* and became such a pest she took to avoiding him wherever possible.

Despite such minor annoyances, their first days at the chateau had flown by, for everywhere was beauty and elegance, everywhere new wonders to be seen and admired. Guests began to arrive, and for the next week Madame Fleur was able to relax her vigilance, for Rachel was surrounded by the glittering company. These were people Claude described as "very special"; there were several highly placed military men and their wives, a smattering of diplomats, a Count and his Countess from Italy, a French Chevalier, and a gracious English widow, Lady Arnold, squired by her brother, a Mr. Minchly. The pace was accelerated, the days became a whirl of riding and drives, luncheons on the terrace, sittings for the portrait, walks through the exquisite gardens, croquet, musical afternoons, gay dinner parties followed by dancing or cards, and little time for introspection. Claude had been the soul of tactful consideration, devoted, patient, kindly, and never pressing his attentions on his fiancé. When Rachel had taken him to task by reason of the new garments in her press, he'd murmured, ''But, *ma chérie*, I thought it must be tiresome for you to shop, and I have a niece in rather straitened circumstances who was happy to execute the commission for me. If they do not suit—'' he spread his hands expressively, ''discard them!'' She soon found, however, that the gowns were a godsend. The chateau was a country house in location only. Dinners were at eight at the earliest, and the guests attired as though they dined in London or Paris. The few suitable gowns Rachel had brought with her would have proven sadly inadequate, and she was quickly driven to resort to the supply Claude had so thoughtfully provided.

Charity was thoroughly enjoying herself; she was too young to recall the brilliant gatherings that had once graced Strand Hall and was captivated by the elegant company Claude had summoned. Agatha, too, was happy. She had found an admirer in the person of one of the grooms, a charming Frenchman named Raoul, whose lack of stature was offset by an extremely theatrical manner, a pleasing countenance, and a whimsical twinkle that soon won the favour of the English maid. Rachel was struggling hard to crowd all thought of home and her tall soldier from her mind and was managing to convince herself that life here could be pleasant—if not perfect. Yet, try as she would, she could not be at ease and always it seemed that there was something to cast a shadow over her peace of mind. Small matters sometimes: the feeling that there was an undercurrent just below the polite laughter and merry good humour of their guests, that the extravagant embraces and fond words masked other emotions less seen than sensed. Worse, the feeling that Claude knew of this undercurrent and was amused by it. And if she argued that she imagined it all, she was faced by the matter of the guards. She did not imagine those hard-eyed individuals. When she'd first noticed them about the grounds, she had supposed them to be gamekeepers and wondered that they wore black rather than green. Their true purpose soon became obvious, for their only occupation was to engage in such pursuits as archery, target shooting, or wrestling. The thought of spending her life in an armed camp did not enchant her, but Claude pointed out that the surrounding areas were not affluent, and the fact that his home contained many valuable items presented a strong temptation to the poorer inhabitants. His response to her question as to the rather unorthodox weapons used by his guards was that the men found them interesting and that history was a passion of his. "How sad it is," he sighed one afternoon while they watched a crossbow contest, "that we cannot step back in time. We live in so plebeian an age—a very dull time in the affairs of mankind."

A greater cause of concern for Rachel was that the people living on the estates were not friendly towards her. At first, on her morning rides she had stopped if she encountered children or cottagers. But the children invariably fled to the protection of their parents, and the parents were quiet and reserved, their obvious curiosity mingled with an emotion she was for a while unable to pinpoint, but at last identified as scorn. She had glimpsed the same look in the eyes of the servants, though never when Claude or Gerard was about. She at first supposed this to be occasioned by the fact that she was from Perfidious Albion—as Bonaparte had dubbed Britain—but when she noted a quite different demeanour exhibited to Lady Arnold and her brother, could only conclude that the shame of the Strands had spread even as far as Brittany.

Perversely, the thing that most often worried her was the very matter that had at first given her such joy: Claude's decision that Charity might accompany them to Dinan. At first wholly opposed to the idea on the grounds that a second journey would be too tiring for the frail girl, he had abruptly reversed his stand, saying he'd come to believe that since the sisters were so devoted, to tear one from the other might constitute a worse hazard to Charity's precarious health. For some reason, this did not quite ring true, and Rachel wondered uneasily if, since he was very well acquainted with Dr. Ulrich, the surgeon had confided something of Charity's condition that was being kept from her. A worrisome suspicion, nagging always at the edge of her mind.

Towards the end of that week, the guests began to depart,

and soon Rachel was again occupying herself with the effort to escape Fleur and Antoine—hence this retreat to the maze. It was surprising that the guests had left, and she was puzzling at it when a small hand touched her wrist and a soft little voice accused, "Dearest—you are not happy here!"

Startled, she refuted hurriedly, "Of course I am, you silly goose! How could one not be happy in so lovely a spot?"

Charity scanned her face worriedly, then, apparently reassured, turned to the chateau. "It *is* lovely, isn't it?" she mused. "An enchanted castle."

The words stirred memory. Following her gaze, Rachel saw not only the great house above them, but the fluffy white clouds that drifted over it. Tristram's feather castles. A pang of such intensity lanced through her that she had to clench her hands tightly to keep from betraying herself. She would not think of him! She *would* not!

"I had no idea it would be so enormous, nor so beautiful," Charity went on dreamily. "And to think that you will reign here! Is it not unbelievable?"

Recovering herself, Rachel managed a smile. "You make me sound a queen!"

"You will certainly have a more magnificent palace than some real queens. And have you noticed how well trained are the servants? Monsieur Claude has merely to give them a look, and they literally run to do his bidding."

It was quite true. Rachel had very soon noticed that at the chateau there was no trace of the infuriating tendency of old retainers to bully their employer. Claude was served with excellence; but not with love. So different, she thought nostalgically, to the proprietary air Fisher assumed with Justin, or indeed to the scolds to which she was subjected by her own Agatha. Scolds motivated by love. Impatient with herself, she dismissed such nonsensical notions. Neither Fisher nor her abigail would attempt any such behaviour in front of strangers, and besides, Claude had so many retainers he could scarcely be expected to know each of them personally.

Again lost in thought, she had failed to notice her sister's glance return to her. Confined as she was to her invalid chair, Charity was very responsive to the feelings of others, and, hav-

136

ing no outlet for an intensely romantic nature, wove her dreams about those she loved. Rachel's uncharacteristic preoccupation struck dismay into her gentle, sensitive soul. "Something *is* wrong!" she asserted. "Do not try to fob me off with polite whiskers—I am your sister!" And as Rachel's alarmed eyes met hers, she rushed on, "It is Captain Tristram! I thought all along you had a *tendre* for him. And he was so deep in love with you, it must have been obvious to—"

"Then that was most improper in him!" Rachel intervened sharply. "I am betrothed to Claude!"

"Yes, you are!" Charity wrung her thin hands. "But is it because you love him—or because you love *me*?"

Inwardly reeling, Rachel gasped, "Charity! How can you think such a thing after all Claude has done for us?"

"Oh, forgive me! Is it not dreadful, but—but I know you would not wed for money if you had only yourself to consider."

Good God! thought Rachel and, fighting for composure, said with faint amusement, "So you think me a fortune hunter? I do not doubt the world does also." It was time, she decided, for the small speech she had rehearsed in the night silences for just such a moment. "But, do you know, love," she embarked. "I have come to think that since marriage is undertaken for a lifetime, it should not be entered into only because two people fancy themselves 'in love.' From what I have seen of such ill-planned matches, the magic fades all too soon, and two ordinary human beings discover they have nothing in common save the memory of a brief excursion into self-delusion." That had gone off smoothly, and sounded very sophisticated, she hoped, and ignoring Charity's shocked gasp, she continued, "Since Papa died, Claude has shown me what a true friend he is. Indeed, I cannot think how we should have gone on without him—especially with Justin away."

"So you *were* in love with Captain Tristram," sighed Charity; having seized upon the one piece of this disclosure she knew to have merit.

Rachel threw up her hands in exasperation. "Oh, for heaven's sake! Have you heard nothing I said? Charity—Claude has done me the honour to ask me to become his wife—an honour half the ladies in Europe must have prayed would come their way. I am truly grateful for what he has done for you, dearest, but that was only one of many reasons persuading me to accept his offer. Captain Tristram was—was a fine young man, having much to recommend him. But—I'll not lie to you, it has been a struggle to keep us afloat, and I fear, my little innocent, that the adage, 'Love flies out the window when poverty comes in the door,' is all too true. Besides," she tucked a wisp of Charity's hair under a thick braid, "you would not have me break my given word?"

"Yes!" declared Charity vehemently. "Indeed, I would! If there is no real love here for you!"

"Oh! What a romantical little puss!" Standing, Rachel gripped the bar behind the chair and began to steer it towards the same path by which they had come. "I can see that when you escape the confines of this chair, you will be the biggest flirt in town, and quite put me to the blush with your escapades."

"I have found you!" Holding a vibrant red rose, Claude Sanguinet came around the corner. He was elegant as always, the informal brown jacket excellent by its very simplicity, the topboots mirror-bright. Smiling a welcome, Charity nonetheless surveyed him with keen criticism. His height, his looks, his figure, she judged only average. His eyes were large and lustrous, but she did not care for that particular shade of brown, finding it too light to suit her taste, and their expression of lazy amusement was so unvarying that one could not but wonder if Claude owned another. The thought came into her mind that were he to stand beside Tristram, he would disappear.

"For you, my sweet sister-to-be," he said in his mild voice, bending to hand her the rose.

She accepted it, stammering her thanks and blushing guiltily.

Sanguinet moved to drop a kiss upon Rachel's cheek. "You have my poor Aunt in a taking," he smiled. "I warned you she was a bore."

"Oh, but she is so kind," she answered, reverting to the French Claude preferred them to speak. "It is only—well, this heat would fatigue her, and I—"

"And you are not fatigued," he nodded. "But you *are*

bored, I think. Still, we shall have our ball very soon, and you will be presented to my friends and neighbours as my future wife. There will be many invitations then. Meanwhile, are you finding the estate quite to your liking?''

"Indeed, we are. How proud of it you must be. The gardens are—*incroyable*.''

Pleased, he asked, "Have you one you especially favour?''

"The Cathay Garden, I think. There is such an air of peace about it. What is your choice, Charity?''

"I agree with yours, dear. That little red bridge across the pool is exquisite.''

"Yes, I admit I am not displeased with it,'' Claude said modestly, "although it only crosses a small corner of the pool, you know. I must ask, Rachel, that you do not venture onto it. Oh, it is sturdy enough, but one might slip—and the pool was not man-made, you see. It is bottomless. Two poor fellows, to my knowledge, have drowned there, for the water is so cold that only a few minutes are sufficient to render a man helpless and, unless one chances to be a strong swimmer . . .'' He shrugged.

"How terrible!'' Rachel exclaimed. "Were these recent tragedies?''

"Comparatively. One of my workmen fell in while constructing the bridge.''

"But—could none of his companions help?''

"Oh, *assurement*. But the peasants have a morbid fear of the pool. It was most difficult, in fact, for me to persuade them to construct the bridge.'' He smiled. "One of the advantages of being the only landlord for miles around.''

Rachel glanced at him sharply, and he went on in his lazy way, "At all events, by the time someone had come up with the brilliant notion to throw him a rope, his hands were too cold to permit of his holding onto it.''

"How dreadful!'' Charity shuddered.

"Yes. But pray do not refine on it. His widow received a most generous settlement from me and, I am told, considered it the luckiest day of her life.''

Charity looked shocked. Also offended by so unfeeling a remark, Rachel hurriedly changed the subject. "I was rather surprised when the guests left, Claude. I was sure they would stay for the ball—in fact, I had thought that was why you invited them."

"Oh, no. It is that I like to have people about me. Very often the chateau is filled with guests even when I am away. Gerard knows how to go on. He is most efficient and, fortunately for me, his talents are—diversified. Which reminds me, my love, that I must tear myself away for a week or so. It is very bad, and I beg your forgiveness, but—alas—an urgent matter."

"A—week or so?" Rachel echoed in dismay. "But—the ball is to be this coming Friday, is it not?"

"It was, but I have had to postpone it. Did I not tell you? Oh, how absent-minded I am become! We shall instead receive our guests two weeks from Friday."

Charity rather studiedly gazed at the fold of her gown. Aghast, Rachel cried, "But—I had expected to be home by then. There are so many arrangements to be made."

He smiled indulgently. "You must allow me to handle your arrangements from now on, *chérie*. I had thought we would be wed here. And there is not the necessity for you to return, for anything you need can be brought from Sussex and—"

"Here?" She halted, staring at him.

"Do not say you object, dear Rachel. I have so often pictured you in your bridal dress coming down my beautiful staircase. How glorious you will look."

"But, I—well, yes, I *do* object! I have friends—a few. And family, who must at least be visited. A million things to do. And—oh! this is most vexatious! You should have consulted with me, Claude, before—" She stopped with a startled gasp as a stream of water came through the tall hedge to send mud splattering over the flounce of her gown.

Claude uttered a muffled curse and called angrily, "Come here! *Vite!*" He bent to wipe Rachel's gown with his handkerchief, then looked up as a young gardener hurried to them, hat in hands.

Watching Claude's face, Charity caught a glimpse of a different expression at last, and caught her breath. Rachel, seeing only the back of Claude's head, was more interested in the gardener. The boy's freckles were dark against his white face, the grey eyes wide with fear.

"Monseigneur! Mademoiselle!" he gulped. "M-my humble apologies. I did not know you were just there. Not for the world would I—"

"It is quite all right, " Rachel smiled. "Purely an accident."

He did not so much as glance at her, his apprehensive gaze fixed upon Sanguinet.

"You will be so good," said Claude gently, "as to report to M. Gerard."

Anguish came into the boy's eyes. "But—monseigneur—I beg of you! I did not mean—"

"'That will be all. You may go."

A brief, pleading glance was slanted at Rachel. Then the boy's shoulders slumped, and he walked away.

"Claude . . ." Rachel began, frowning a little.

Turning to her, he chuckled. "Have no fears, my sweet. I'll not have the clumsy fool tied to a post and given six hundred lashes—though I heard of just such a case in your own Army last month."

"I am sure he had no thought to—"

"And I will not have you worrying your pretty head with such matters. That is what we men are for, is it not?" Sanguinet patted her hand absently but, peering downward, muttered, "Do you know that beastly peasant splashed some of his dirt on my boots?"

Tristram left the barn, wherein Devenish still snored, and turned his steps toward the main building of the "Castle and Keg Inn." A pleasant place, this old inn, its whitewashed walls and latticed windows gleaming in the early morning sunlight. It was too far off the beaten track to lure any of the London crowd, yet enjoyed a steady business by reason of the fact that it offered clean beds and good food at a moderate charge. Already, smoke was curling from several chimneys, and as Tristram made his way to the washhouse at the side of the stables, he could hear the clatter of crockery, indicating that preparations for breakfast were under way. The ostlers were beginning to stir, but Tristram was sufficiently early to have the pump to himself. He washed to the waist in the icy water and had finished shaving before the head ostler yawned his way across the yard. "Up early, Captain," the man observed sleepily.

Tristram nodded. "I hope to finish this morning."

"And be on yer way to Lunon." The ostler shook his head and bodingly remarked as how that fearsome metropolis was a den o' iniquity what he'd seen once as a little 'un but had no wish to rest his ogles on again!

The description was not appealing, but carrying his tools and supplies to the ladder propped against the rear of the building, Tristram was no less eager to be on his way. Mrs. Rhys, the owner of the inn, was a widowed Welsh lady. When first confronted by two decidedly down-at-heels young gentlemen, she had told them regretfully that she could not afford to hire any more workers for however brief a time. Devenish had at once doffed his battered hat, swept her a low bow, assured her that they would find work somewhere "along the road," and crumpled at her feet in a dead faint. Her motherly heart had melted at the full sight of his youthful and damaged countenance, and they had since enjoyed her excellent cooking, as well as the warm and fragrant hayloft for a bedchamber, in exchange for replacing the roof shingles.

The work had taken longer than Tristram had expected; they'd been here the better part of a week and, however good the food, pleasant the company, and tranquil the life in this lovely part of the south country, he was becoming impatient to get to the Horse Guards and learn what he might of his past.

He worked steadily and had completed a full row of shingles before he began to feel the warmth of the sun. Pausing in his labours, he looked about him appreciatively. Dawn's haze had burned off, but everything was drenched and a thousand tiny lights winked from the dewdrops. This England, he thought, was very beautiful. So different from the parched lands and searing winds of Spain, or the bleak grandeur of the Pyrenees. He grinned, recalling how Timothy Van Lindsay had stumbled on the precipitous slope of the Santa Cruz and hurtled down the mountainside, causing his friends to scramble after him, fearing to find him dead at the bottom. How Tim had cursed when they came upon him! But not a bone broken—good old— He crouched, one hand flying to his temple and his shoulders hunching against the merciless lances of pain that seemed to splinter through flesh and bone to impale his cringing brain. But he fought it this time, for whatever horrors his past may hold *must* be remembered . . .

He saw a field, wreathed in smoke and littered with dead and dying men and horses. A small group of mounted officers, becoming more distinct as he rode up at breakneck speed to offer a despatch. A lean face beneath a plain cockaded hat; a face brilliant of eye, the strong features dominated by a beak of a nose. A smile flashing up at him, and a harsh bray of a voice rising above the cacophonous din of battle to say, "Colonel, each time I see you, you're astride a different trooper. Have you been badly hit?". . .

Memory had been terribly costly. He was panting and soaked with sweat, and as from a great distance, it seemed, another voice reached him. "Be ye all right up there, Captain Tristram?"

Surreptitiously, he drew his sleeve across his face, and answered unevenly, "All—right and tight, ma'am."

Mrs. Rhys scanned his profile with her keen black eyes and asserted it was not "all right and tight" he looked. "Come ye down, lad. 'Tis precious hard ye've worked all week. Too hard, belike, for now Frank tells me as ye be leaving today, and here I'd hoped as ye'd stay to roof the stables also."

His head having eased a little, Tristram laughed rather breathlessly and backed down the ladder to slip an arm about her plump shoulders. "The truth of the matter is that while I've been hard at work, a certain scalliwag has stolen your heart away. Admit it now, you naughty girl!"

Her comely face became quite pink. With a giggle, she admitted Mr. Alain to be a saucy rogue beyond the doubting. "But what charm has he! Never a cross word, always so merry and bright! I wish—"

"See here!" The object of their discussion hurried around the corner of the building, his bruises less lurid, and his spirits as exuberant as ever. He held what appeared to be an untidy bundle of feathers. "Only look how much better she is!" he urged triumphantly.

"She?" Tristram peered dubiously at the bundle and discovered it to be a scrawny, one-eyed duck that peered back at him with marked suspicion.

"Mrs. O'Crumbs," Devenish nodded. "Did I not tell you? A dog got her."

"Yes, and we was all sure as she would expire," Mrs. Rhys said fondly. "But Mr. Alain saved her. He's a wonderful way with animals, has Mr. Alain."

"And with shingles," boasted that gentleman.

Well aware that a formidable glare was fixed upon the perpetrator of this wanton provocation, Mrs. Rhys chuckled and returned to her kitchen, thus allowing Tristram to say a threatening, "You mentioned your—ah, skill?"

"Can you doubt it? I told Mrs. Rhys we would give her a fine roof, and look at it! Jolly fine, if I say so myself."

"I wonder," Tristram said dryly, "you could keep away from so satisfying an endeavour."

"No wonder about it, old pippin. Cannot abide heights." The blue eyes twinkled merrily, but as Tristram strode menacingly towards him, Devenish clutched Mrs. O'Crumbs and cried, "You'd not raise your hand against a sick duck?"

"No. But I may throw her scoundrelly benefactor clear over the blasted roof I was slumguzzled into repairing!"

"Do not, I beg you," Devenish pleaded laughingly. "I own you to be a superlative carpenter. In fact—here! I ask none of the remuneration. It is all for you. We shall toddle forth on your quest at once. I swear it!"

Tristram took the flimsy he offered. "Ten shillings? A fortune! We'll share it, of course. But you are bound to Newhaven, no?"

"No." Devenish restored his duck to the ground, patted her tail feathers and said blithely, "My cousin can wait. Besides—" He paused, eyes narrowing. "Something amiss? You look a trifle pulled."

"Starved, merely." They started towards the kitchen, Mrs. O'Crumbs weaving along after them. "I was sure," Tristram said, "that you told me you were promised to your cousin for something or other."

"Was. George has a yawl he—er—floats around in from time

to time. He cannot always come by a crew, so I help a bit. And he pays well. The thing is, he'll come about. But you will not."

"The deuce I won't! What gives you that impression?"

"Too complaisant by half, old fellow. Do I not take a hand in matters, you'll likely never even get to Whitehall. And your memory don't seem to—" He interrupted himself to ask curiously, "Was that what wrung you out just now? Had you another bout with your past? You've never remembered where your home is located?"

"Unfortunately, my recollections this time were concerned only with Waterloo."

Genuinely disappointed, Devenish sighed, "Pity."

They entered the kitchen and made their way to the large table. A buxom maid hurried over with a dimpling smile and two mugs of ale. Winking at the blushing girl, Devenish drank and then asked, "Anything special about the battle?"

"Not really." Tristram stretched out his legs, then withdrew them hurriedly. Peering under the table, he discovered the little duck nestled at Devenish's feet. "You and your way with animals!" he said indignantly.

Devenish glanced down and grinned. "Whither I goest—she will go."

Thanking the maid for the laden plate that was set before him, Tristram devoted himself to his breakfast until Devenish asked, "What *did* you remember, then?"

"Eh? Oh, well it seems that I was an officer, after all."

"Were you now. Well, I expect your men took shameful advantage of you. Do you recall your rank? Never tell me you really *are* a Captain?"

"No. Not a Captain, exactly."

"Lieutenant? Nothing wrong with that."

"Oh, no. Nothing. Only—I, er—was a Colonel."

In the act of taking another mouthful of ale, Devenish spluttered and choked. Wiping watery eyes with his napkin, he echoed faintly, "*C-Colonel . . . ?* What—what regiment?"

"I wish I knew."

"But you must have *some* indication. Was your jacket red, d'you recall?"

"No. Not red."

"Ah, a rifleman. Green, was it?"

"Not green, either."

Devenish scowled. Then his eyes widened. "Tris! You're never telling me you *are* a blasted Frog, after all?"

"I don't think so, because on the field I was speaking English to someone."

"Another officer, perhaps?" Devenish leaned forward eagerly. "Aha! Now we're getting somewhere! Can you come at his name? Anything in particular about his rank? Did he wear silver lace? A blue plume in his helmet perhaps? White? Well, for lord's sake, don't just sit there shaking your head! What the deuce *did* the fellow wear? His nightshirt?"

"A plain cockaded hat, and—and a dark coat." Tristram frowned reflectively. "Oh, I do recall he had a rather large nose and seemed to be greatly revered by the officers around him."

Devenish dropped his fork and stared, eyes very wide, and jaw hanging.

"And," Tristram continued in his quiet way, "I remember that my jacket was not at all elaborate. If anything, rather dowdy. A plain blue, in fact."

"Oh . . . my . . . God!" gasped Devenish. "One of the great man's Family!"

Before Tristram had time to question the meaning of this inexplicable remark, the quiet was shattered by a sudden uproar from outside. Shouts mingled with the shrill neighing of an angry horse, and thuds and crashes of the sort made by a plunging animal. Tristram was in the yard in a flash. Making his way through a small group of men gathered in the barn doorway, his superior height enabled him to see Frank, the head ostler, attempting to throw a rope over the head of a magnificent but maddened black horse. Mrs. Rhys, hands clasped in terror, cried, "Oh, Captain, a poor groom do be trapped in there!"

There was no sign of the man and, with a look at those flailing hooves, Tristram asked, "Hurt?"

"Fatally, was you to ask my opinion," offered a spectator. Remarkable for stiffly curling whiskers, this gentleman, who looked to be an affluent farmer, went on cheerfully, "Black brute backed him into a corner and stamped all over him. Dead as a mackerel, was you to ask—"

Coming up behind them, Devenish interpolated urgently, "Frank—let me try."

The ostler ignored him, continuing his desperate efforts and succeeding only in further enraging the animal.

"Frank!" said Tristram.

"Yessir!" Reacting instinctively to that crisp, authoritative command, the man swung about and handed the rope to Tristram, who at once passed it to Devenish. "Go on, Dev," he urged. He was, however, considerably taken aback when Devenish began to open the gate to the stall. So were the spectators—they scrambled for safety as the stallion, a screaming, rearing fury, plunged forward.

Devenish doubled the rope and slipped through the gate into the stall. The stallion's ears lay flat against his head. Great, iron-shod hooves sliced the air above the slender man, and a scream of equine fury rent the air. Coolly unflinching, Devenish slapped the rope under first one, then the other of those flying hooves. "Up," he said encouragingly. "Jolly good, old fellow. My, but you're splendid, ain't you?"

If ever a horse was capable of registering bewilderment, this one was doing so. There was a strangeness about this puny man-creature. No fear came from him; instead one sensed kindness so that there was no need to be afraid. The flattened ears of the stallion relaxed, the screams ceased. Staggering on his powerful hind legs, his rolling eyes surveyed the man uncertainly.

"Care to come down?" Devenish enquired.

The suggestion was accepted. There could be no abject obedience, of course, wherefore there was much stamping, snorting and head-tossing, but through this display there was no attempt to rend or maim.

Devenish began to speak, his voice soft and persuasive. The effect was remarkable. In very short order the proudly arched neck was being stroked, the velvety muzzle whuffled at the man's neck, and the stallion's capitulation was complete.

Realizing that he had been holding his breath, Tristram let it out in a long sigh. An awed muttering acquainted him with the fact that the onlookers had returned. "Dev," he said quietly, "lead him out of there, can you? A couple of you men, bring a hurdle or something we can use to carry the groom."

The men moved away again. Devenish left the stall and, meek as a lamb, the horse followed. Tristram slipped quickly inside and bent over the crumpled shape at the back of the stall. "My poor fellow," he said gently. "Are you much hurt?"

A drawn countenance was lifted; blue eyes, narrowed with pain, peered up at him. A deep voice muttered, "So I found you . . . soldier! Is—is Sister Maria . . . Evangeline here?"

Tristram gasped an astonished, "Diccon!"

10

Popping another fondant into her mouth, Madame Fleur said tragically, "But—*why* must you ride this afternoon, my love? It is so warm! How much more comfortable you would be beneath the trees in the garden. Or even laid down upon your bed, having a lovely little nap."

Rachel drew on her gloves and laughed, "You can do those things for me, dear ma'am. I crave a change of scene, and with Claude away, there is no one to scold you."

Madame Fleur brightened, but settling herself more comfortably upon the chaise longue in the small jade salon, pointed out that when she had begged Rachel to go with her to Rennes and shop, as Claude had desired her, she had refused such a "change of scene."

"Because, I—did *not* desire it," Rachel said lightly, knowing in her heart that she was unwilling to accept any more of Claude's bounty just now.

Madame shook a fat finger. "Beware, child. It does not do to provoke my nephew. Claude wishes you to choose your bride clothes, and—"

"And I shall choose my bride clothes in England, ma'am. As I have told him." She smiled at the look of anxiety in the woman's face and assured her she would not be long. But turning towards the terrace, a small pucker of irritation was between her brows.

"Your woman is with Charity. As always." Madame giggled suddenly. "Save when she is with the groom, Raoul, eh?"

Turning back, Rachel sighed, "So you have noticed it, too. I must speak to the wretched girl. I cannot think what Monseigneur would say did he suspect another wedding was in the offing!''

"La, he would be pleased." Madame's hand hovered over the box of fondants. "He likes the servants to be happy—provided they please him, of course."

"Of course." Rachel drew the riding crop idly through her fingers. "Which reminds me: there was a gardener, a boy really, who splashed mud upon my gown last week, before Claude left."

"Yes. Wretched creature. Claude told me of it. Have no fears, love—you'll not see him again. Claude sent him packing that very night."

"Oh, no! It was an accident, merely. And I understood that the boy's grandmother had worked on the estate all her life, and the cottage was given her for her retirement."

"And much fuss she made, foolish old crone. One might have thought she'd not another roof in all France to shelter her."

"Perhaps she has not!" Rachel snapped, hotly. "She was frail, I heard. How very unkind to turn them out for so unimportant a thing!"

"Unimportant?" Madame looked at her in consternation. "But—he splashed mud on Claude's boots, my love!"

Rachel could have shaken her, but it was, she saw, quite useless. She left before she lost her temper. Entering the stables, her eyes were stormy, and the frown in them deepened when she saw Gerard waiting beside her bay gelding, while Raoul led out a black mare.

"Bonjour, mademoiselle." At once noting the vexation in her eyes, Raoul gave a minuscule shrug, his droll grin managing to convey both helplessness and apology.

Gerard said, "If one may be permitted to remark it, Mademoiselle is looking very beautiful this afternoon." His admiring gaze flickered over Rachel's pale green habit in such a way that she at once feared Agatha had left a button unsecured somewhere. From the moment of their first encounter, this slight, watchful man had both frightened and repelled her. Now, she ignored his impertinence and said levelly, "I understood most of the guests had left."

"Yes, and it is my fear," he purred, very obviously waiting to throw her up into the saddle, "that monseigneur would not wish you to ride unescorted."

"Is it?" The words dripped ice. Overcoming her aversion, Rachel placed her foot in his hand and he tossed her up, holding her little boot an instant too long as he set it in the stirrup. Infuriated, she jerked the reins and the fleet bay gelding danced back a few steps, causing Gerard to jump clear. Rachel said, "I do not feel the need of an escort, just the same."

His mouth tightened, but he answered a soft, "Alas. Monsieur Benét must be quite shattered," and watched her mockingly, knowing she had thought he himself meant to accompany her, and that she could scarcely refuse to ride with Claude's cousin.

Rachel bit her lip. The affected Macaroni was only a small improvement over Gerard, and she had so hoped to be alone this afternoon. She badly needed a brisk ride and a chance to try to order her thoughts. Now she would be engulfed by an endless flow of inanities and her brisk ride would degenerate into a sedate amble, for a gallop must disturb the style of Antoine Benét's hair and could not be contemplated.

Her fears proved all too well justified. Monsieur Benét arrived clad in a riding coat of puce, frogged to the throat, and having a short military collar. His breeches were cream, his riding boots with their white tops, gleamed, and he removed his curly-brimmed hat to reveal pale hair immaculately waved and pomaded so that not a single strand was out of place. Having bowed with a flourish, his soulful eyes scanned Rachel admiringly. She was, he opined, superb; a very poem of ecstacy. She would set Paris afire when Claude took her there as his bride. And how happy he was to serve as her escort during his cousin's absence, despite the heat of the afternoon, and the fact that he really should be working at his easel. Nonetheless, this one delightful task must take precedence over all. He would see to it that Miss Rachel was not lonely or bored. But it was, of course, impossible to be bored on this magnificent estate. Miss Rachel could never have seen anything to equal it. Miss Rachel might, in fact, did she wish to please her future husband, take out her sketchbook and attempt some simple scenes.

He paused for breath, and Rachel quickly inserted a suggestion that they leave the stables. Benét seemed rather surprised to discover they had not as yet done so, but having walked to the mounting block, he contrived to climb to the saddle without too seriously disturbing the set of his breeches. Masterfully then he led the way from the yard—at a saunter that caused Rachel to set her teeth. She was unable to protest, however, for his monologue flowed on as though it had never ceased. The Grecian Garden, he kindly pointed out, could provide inspiration by the hour to the artistically inclined. With an expansive gesture, he simpered, "A true artist, naturally, needs no elaborate landscape to inspire him, for beauty is in the most simple of things. Take—my hand, for example." He eyed it admiringly, holding the fingers gracefully arched. "Like a winged bird," he mused. "Is it not?"

Rachel battled a compelling need to laugh. "I had a pet bird once," she said. "But it was full of mites." Benét's complacent smile faded, and sternly suppressing a giggle, she relented and went on, "No, I do not think I would liken such talented hands to a bird."

At once the artist's rather affronted expression mellowed. "Mademoiselle is too kind."

"Mademoiselle is also curious. When may I see my portrait?"

He chuckled and raised one "winged bird" to emphasize an affected scold that she must be patient. "My estimable cousin having commissioned this great work, his shall be the first eyes to gaze upon its perfection."

"Good God!" she thought, and asked aloud, "It is finished, then?"

He brought thumb and forefinger together. "The merest *pinch* have remain! A whisper only. Than—*voilà!* Claude he will see—and marvel."

"How eager you are to win his approval," she smiled. "You must be extremely fond of your cousin."

Antoine's lower lip sagged in a manner that caused his negligible chin to totally disappear. "Fond . . . ?" he echoed. "*Fond—of Claude?*"

"Good gracious," she said mischievously. "Have I opened Pandora's box? You are enemies, perhaps?"

At this, the blue eyes all but started from their sockets. "*Mon Dieu!* Do not, I beg you, think such a thing! A man may make an enemy of kings or princes—of the Pope even. But—of *monseigneur?* Heaven forfend!"

Rachel gave an uneasy trill of laughter. "How merciless you make him sound."

He caught her wrist, the colour draining from his pointed face, and bleated, "You will not *say* this? He would never forgive! Miss Rachel—you jest, you laugh, but you do not perhaps, fully understand. Promise—swear to me that you will not repeat this thing to my cousin!"

His voice was positively shrill, his grip beginning to hurt. Freeing herself and striving for a lighter note, she said, "Shall we strike a bargain? You will take me up to see my portrait, and I will tell Claude you described him as a veritable saint."

Benét gave a sigh of relief. "*Tres bien!* The portrait shall be carried downstairs. There—we have reach a happy compromise, no?"

"I do not wish to put you to all that trouble. I shall just come up, and—"

"No!" The note of hysteria was in his voice again. Meeting her startled glance, he wet his lips and muttered, "It is in Claude's private suite on the second floor."

"I quite understand. You have a studio up there, do you not?"

"Yes. It would not be proper."

"Why ever not? Claude is not in residence. And even were he, we do not go to a bedchamber, but to an artist's work room. Further, you are my fiancé's cousin. Now, what could possibly be—"

"You do not understand. It is not—*you*. It is anybody! *No one* is allowed up there. Not even my aunt—Madame Beauchard!"

The foolish creature was actually perspiring! What nonsense—and carrying the conventions beyond the bounds, she thought. Unable to resist teasing him, she said with a twinkle, "But—I am to be Claude's wife. It is, perhaps, that he has another lady hiding up there?"

"Horrors! No! Claude's mistresses are not kept at—" The amused gleam vanished from Rachel's eyes and her chin lifted, seeing which Benét produced a lace-edged handkerchief and mopped his brow. "Better you do not go up there, mademoiselle. I wish to God I had not, for he may think I would—" He bit the words off, his pallor increasing. "Ah! Pay me no heed. It is—just . . . the heat! It is the heat. You will not relay to him—that is, I did not intend—but my accursed tongue! It will prove my undoing, I know it! And I will end in the quiet pool, like—" He gave a little yelp and, clapping a hand over his mouth, regarded her with utter tragedy.

Rachel was put in mind of a scared rabbit. "You are unwell, monsieur," she said kindly. "Perhaps you should return to the house."

"*Oui*," he gulped, gratefully, a nervous twitch appearing beneath one eye. "You are all understanding. I am, as you perceive, distraught. You will excuse . . . I must seek my valet. I need rest, and a powder to calm me. You forgive that I leave you? A thousand pardons, but it is, you comprehend, my artistic sensitivity." He swept off his hat and essayed a jerky bow. "Adieu, mademoiselle."

Rachel stared after him as he turned his horse back towards the chateau and rode off, his seat a disaster. Shaking her head, she urged the bay to a canter. Why on earth should the poor man have become so petrified simply because she had expressed the intention to go up and see the portrait? And why was he so afraid of Claude? Why was Madame so afraid of Claude?

She rode through the verdant countryside, a place of gentle hills and soft valleys interspersed with rich farmland. A beautiful sight, but one that only deepened the trouble in her eyes. Once, during a ride with Claude, she had remarked on the contrast between his lush acres and the barren countryside surrounding them. He'd said this was the result of a proper use of water. "I am blessed, you see, by the possession of several fine wells, in addition to the stream."

"But does the stream not continue past your lands?"

"No, it goes underground about half a mile inside my lodge gates."

"I see. Still, if the local farmers dug wells, could they not have such irrigation?"

"It is a possibility, but—so far as I'm aware—the only wells rise on my property. And," he grinned conspiratorially, "can you credit it? The stupid peasants refuse to meet my price."

Lost in thought, she was recalled to the present as her mount shied in fright. A guard had stepped from a copse of trees, a large hound cavorting around him. Rachel had heard dogs baying distantly, but this was the first one she had seen and, a typical British faunophile, she kicked her heels home, turning the bay towards them. The hound underwent a frightening metamorphosis. Even as the guard snatched vainly for its leash, it raced at the bay, teeth bared, eyes glaring and savage. Frightened, the bay neighed and plunged. Rachel fought the animal's attempt to bolt. The guard whistled shrilly, and at the last instant the hound dropped to a crouch, still snarling fiercely at Rachel.

The guard ran up and seized the dog's leash, apologizing profusely for the incident. "The dogs are not usually out during the daytime, but this one, he must have a thorn removed from his pad, so I take him home."

Stunned by the ferocity now held in check, Rachel asked, "Are there many guard dogs?"

"*Oui*, mademoiselle. It is necessary." Obviously hoping to please her, he said, "Monseigneur is the great and wealthy man. In his chateau are many lovely things and secrets of State, also. One may not guess of the evil thieves that are kept away by me and my comrades, and our hounds. Monseigneur has, I am sure, warned Mademoiselle not to go into the grounds after dark unless he has ordered the hounds kept in?"

She smiled, nodded, and rode on. But she was thinking that Claude had said nothing about the hounds. He must have feared to alarm her, and doubtless there were servants about to stop her, did she start to go into the grounds at night. The thought lingered, and she could not dismiss it. "Servants . . . to stop me . . . to stop me."

The ride ceased to charm, and her desire for private thought had waned. She returned at a canter to the chateau, the rush of wind past her face dispelling the nebulous fears that lurked at the back of her mind.

As she entered the stableyard, Gerard stepped from the shadows and took the reins. Irritated, she kicked her foot from the stirrup and began to slide from the saddle. He was very quick. He caught her, but did not put her down immediately, holding her above him instead with surprising strength, his hot eyes flickering over her.

"How—*dare* you!" she raged. "Put me down at once! And do you *ever* touch me again, monseigneur will hear of it!"

Gerard became as white as she was flushed. He restored her to her feet and stepped back. "I cast myself on your mercy, mademoiselle," he said, humbly. "I was lost in—in admiration. But I had no thought to offend."

Seething, she swept past and into the clean sunlight. But she took with her an impression of a sidelong glance from black eyes in which ardour had been replaced by malevolence. And she knew she had made an enemy.

Having tended Diccon's broken ribs and sundry lacerations, the apothecary departed, warning that on no account must the victim be moved for at least two weeks. Tristram had been asked to remain in the small room to which the injured man had been carried, in order to assist the apothecary. He had admired the patient's endurance, for only when the verdict was rendered had Diccon betrayed distress. Once they were alone, however, he indulged in a blast of frustrated cursing, and having blasphemously railed against the perversity of Fate, enquired as to the whereabouts of Sister Maria Evangeline.

It was the second time he had asked and, like a half-forgotten dream, something concerning this man and the nun stirred in Tristram's mind. He failed to capture the elusive impression, and replied, "So far as I'm aware, the lady is back at her convent. And if you whip yourself into such a state, friend, you'll be laid down on your back for longer than two weeks."

"She is not!" said Diccon, fretfully. "I went there. She never returned." He groaned. "Damme, what a humble broth this is!" His hand gripped at the coverlet. He was clearly in much pain, his pale face shining with perspiration, yet his agitation of mind appeared to render all else of little significance.

Raising his tall frame from the bench against the wall, Tristram stepped closer to the bed. "The apothecary charged you not to talk. If you keep on—"

"Devil take it, man! D'ye think I hunted you out for no better purpose than to lie here like a—a curst effigy?" Diccon's head tossed against the pillows. His eyes were beginning to acquire the glitter of fever, and he muttered, "Of all the stupid, clod crushing things! To have bent to pick up my purse just as a mouse ran in front of that confounded brute!"

"Is that how he cornered you? I had thought perhaps you didn't know your business. As a groom, that is."

Diccon lay still, and slanted a narrowed glance at him. The soldier's eyes were amused, and the scarred features held a quite different expression to the bewildered look of helplessness he remembered. There was an assured tilt to the head now; a firmer set to the wide mouth. "You see more than I thought," he acknowledged. "Do you know who you are?"

"No. But I have remembered a few things. That I was a Colonel, for instance. My friend, the one who got the horse away from you, seems to think I was one of Wellington's aides-de-camp."

Diccon exclaimed an enthusiastic, "Does he, by God! Then your identity will be simple enough to discover."

"So I think. To which end I mean to go at once to the Horse Guards."

"Very good. After you find the nun for me."

"My regrets," Tristram smiled. "But I would prefer not to delay my own investigations further. I have—"

"I'll remind you, Colonel, that I helped haul you off that bloody field. And even had I not done so, as an officer your first obligation is to your country."

Considerably taken aback, Tristram frowned. "To my country? What the devil? Who are you? No groom, so don't try to gammon me."

A sudden wry grin lit Diccon's drawn face. "As you say, sir. You outrank me. By two steps, in fact."

Tirstram moved closer, leaned both hands on the bedrail and

directed a piercing stare at the invalid. "What's all the dust about, Major?"

Astounded by the suddenly commanding manner, Diccon thought, "Oh, he's a Colonel, all right!" and aloud answered, "I'm after the Sanguinets, sir. Have been in fact, for over a year. It has become a—a sort of personal crusade."

"Personal?"

Diccon gave a bitter snort. "Aye. And thankless. I'm thought ripe for Bedlam at the Horse Guards. My commanding officer less than half believes me, and the only reason I'm allowed to continue my enquiries is that someone in the high echelons of Whitehall had a naval officer for a nephew and suspects Parnell Sanguinet may have had a hand in his sudden demise."

"The nephew was murdered?"

"Shot by a highwayman, ostensibly, but under rather smoky circumstances. Thus, a highwayman's savagery grants me the chance to unmask one of the greatest villains of our century—can I only bring it off!"

His hands suddenly icy cold, and his voice very quiet, Tristram asked, "How is Miss Strand implicated in this?"

"She is—" Diccon's hesitation was very brief, "a key figure."

"I . . . see. Then—she knows what he is."

Something in those halting but unemotional words awoke a sympathy in Diccon's seldom touched heart. He tried to shrug, winced, and gasped painfully, "Don't see how she could—help knowing."

"No. Of course." Tristram took a breath, squared his shoulders and asked coolly, "What do you suspect he's up to?"

"I'll make it brief, sir. Thanks to a highly-placed conniver in London, Claude Sanguinet was presented to the Regent. Claude can be the most polished, charming aristocrat one could wish to meet. Their friendship prospered, and in time the Prince was pleased to accept some small gifts from him. A Rubens; a Rembrandt; a Cellini bowl." He met Tristram's startled eyes and nodded wryly. "Prinny's mad for art, and short of funds. Sanguinet has thus thoroughly ingratiated himself, but

158

Prinny's not so stupid as he looks, and I think our Frenchman grows impatient.''

''You—*think?*''

''I *know!* He hatches something, but—what, I do *not* know. He's power mad. His sire was a murderous despot. Claude differs from him in one respect: The old man wanted riches. Claude wants power. He'll stop at nothing to attain it.''

His face set and grim, Tristram was briefly silent. Then he asked, ''Where do you gather your information?''

''At the chateau in Dinan. It lies some few miles inland from the Brittany coast. The unlamented Sanguinet *père* built himself a palace surrounded by an enormous estate. Claude now rules it, and those so unfortunate to dwell there, with a hand of iron. Through a cunning little trick, I managed to be taken on as a groom. I have been with him almost a year now, and to an extent am trusted. I was able to learn something at last, and when I was sent over with the horse, hoped to pass my knowledge on to Sister Maria Evangeline. I learned she was last seen in company with you, so went to Strand Hall, and thence traced you here. And now I'm smashed and foundered when it is of the utmost urgency that I return to Dinan!''

Tristram straightened. ''You have my sympathy, Major. But—''

Scowling up at him, Diccon rasped, ''I want a sight more than your sympathy, Colonel! That girl fancies me to be in Dinan. I must get word to her that—''

Tristram smiled thinly, and in turn interrupted, ''If your people could track me here, they can certainly get word to Strand Hall.''

''Rachel Strand is not in Sussex. She has been in Dinan these past two weeks and more.''

Tristram said nothing, but his tall frame stiffened, and his hand on the bedrail tightened spasmodically. ''By her own choice,'' he said. ''Good day.''

''I heard she threw you over,'' sneered Diccon. ''You forget that she also saved your life.''

En route to the door, Tristram froze.

''And now you turn your back on both her, and your country. A fine gratitude. Sir.''

Tristram swung around and looked at him levelly. "Miss Strand has chosen her—life and her mate. And it does not appear that my country is very much interested in your theories, Major. However, I will strive to find the nun—shall that satisfy you?"

Diccon grunted and grumbled, but at length said, "It shall have to, I collect. Very well. Tell her—it has to do with the painting on the second floor."

"What has? What painting?"

Shifting painfully, Diccon groaned, "Fiend take it! If I knew, I would tell you! All I have is that somehow the plot is connected with a painting on the second floor. A work Sanguinet has commissioned. Colonel—you'll not fail?"

Tristram said woodenly, "I'll do my best. That is all I can promise."

"Me sensibilities is offended," said the carter huffily, turning his wagon into the yard of a large half-timbered inn called "The Pink Palfrey." "Besides which," he rested an irked glance on Devenish, "I ain't in the business to cart no half-ducks about."

"She is not a half-duck!" Devenish protested indignantly, clasping Mrs. O'Crumbs to his bosom. "And furthermore, I don't think you've the sensibility of an earwig!"

"Oh, you don't, don't yer?" the carter said with a sad want of originality, climbing down from his high perch.

"No, I do not!" Devenish reiterated. He clambered over the tail. "Anyone who finds suet pudding palatable is an utter oaf!"

"And any cove," opined the carter, setting aside his whip and rolling up his shirtsleeves, "any cove wot says good British suet pudding is a 'bomination wot should be fed only to stray warthogs—which is wot you says—any cove wot says that, is a slimy toad wot wouldn't know muck fer rolling in it!"

"Here!" sputtered Devenish, his fair curls all but standing on end as he thrust Mrs. O'Crumbs under the preoccupied Tristram's nose. "Hold her!" And struggling to extricate himself from his tattered coat, he panted encouragement for the carter to sport his canvas, put up his mauleys, stand and fight like a man!

"Hey!" Tristram returned to reality and sprang lightly down from the wagon. "Let be! God, Dev! Are you at it again?"

"Curst rogue took our lettuce!" snarled Devenish, plucking frantically at one recalcitrant sleeve. "Now he will not live up to his bargain!"

The carter, taking in Tristram's height and breadth of shoulder, reached for a cudgel. Tristram seized Devenish by the arm. "It is just as well. I've decided not to go to town, at all events." He retrieved Mrs. O'Crumbs who had been deposited in the wagon again and coolly ignored the carter's recommendation that he pop Devenish in a bottle and cork it. "You could let 'im orf on Guy Fawkes' Day," leered the carter. "Reg'lar shower o' sparks 'e'd make." He tossed an arm in a wide arc. "Whiizzz!"

"I'll c-cork you!" raged Devenish. "Damn you, Tris! Let me go!"

"If'n he does, I'll wrap this 'round yer ear 'oles," the carter promised, flourishing his cudgel.

He was powerfully built, if short of stature, and very near to losing his temper. However, Tristram managed to convince him that to attract the attention of the village constable over so trite a matter would result in unnecessary delays for them all. He dragged Devenish away. The carter tossed a disparaging remark over his shoulder, having to do with moth-eaten ducks, and he and Devenish exchanged pleasantries until they were separated by distance. His mouth open for a final sally, Devenish thought better of it; partly because he was becoming hoarse, and partly because Tristram looked decidedly grim. "What d'you mean—decided not to go to town?" he demanded as they started into the lane. "I thought you was desperate to get to Whitehall?"

"I was. But the more I think of it, the more I realize they would likely forbid me to search for the nun. Diccon said no one will believe his warnings about Sanguinet."

"Then, what shall you do? Send a message to the convent?"

"I fancy Diccon already did so. No. I'll go to Dinan."

Devenish's jaw dropped. "You'll . . . go to—the devil! How d'you propose to get there?"

Tristram began to count out their meagre funds. He looked up and said with a rueful grin, "Not enough to pay for passage, I fear. Unless—did you not say your cousin has a boat? Might he allow us to work our way across the Channel?"

"No doubt of that. And he makes a regular run to Dinard. But—for lord's sake, why, man?"

Restoring the cash to his purse, Tristram shoved his hands into his pockets and walked on. "After Miss Strand brought me off from Waterloo," he said slowly, "I fell asleep and dreamed a strange sort of dream. It has been rather annoying me. You know how it is."

"Gad, do I not! I recall a dream I had wherein I cornered Old Boney, took off my glove and flung it in his face. And just at that moment I heard something and turned around to find a whole regiment of Ney's blasted cavalry galloping straight at me! Sabres drawn! I ran like fury, with them thundering on my heels, but—dash it all! I never did recall what happened! Do go on, old fellow."

"Well, I finally did recall my dream. Just now, while we were riding with our friendly carter. Diccon and Sister Maria Evangeline were talking about Miss Strand. Only—it was no dream." He was silent, his black brows pulling into a dark line across his forehead.

Devenish waited uneasily. From what he'd heard, there was no telling what outrageous conduct Tristram might have learned of.

"They're fanatics, of course," Tristram muttered. "I suppose they're a necessary type—God knows, they're courageous. But they would sacrifice anyone to England's cause. And—I've an idea they've sent that girl in there to spy for them."

"Good God!" breathed Devenish. "Surely you must be wrong. A girl—all alone? Besides—if she's as fond of Sanguinet as you think, she's not likely to betray the fellow."

"True. But I believe she loves England very deeply. If she *should* try to discover something and Sanguinet found out . . ." His lips tightened; he turned to Devenish, his eyes

162

very stern. "She's just a girl, in a strange country and with an invalid sister on her hands. She fancies Diccon is there if she gets into a real scrape. Only he's not, Dev."

Devenish's lively imagination ran riot, so horrifying him that he exclaimed, "Oh, pshaw! There's likely nothing to this tale beyond Diccon's hope for a promotion. Miss Strand knows what she's about. You're not responsible."

"I'm alive. Save for her, I might not be."

"Hmmm. Well, even if you should reach Dinan, what hope would you have of getting into the chateau or finding out anything?"

"I don't know. But something will occur to me."

Devenish persisted, stubbornly, "And—then?"

"Then—if Miss Strand's position is endangered, I'll simply take her and her sister away from the mess."

"You'll . . . simply . . ." Devenish gulped, his eyes as wide as his mouth. Recovering, he burst out, "You're downright looby, that's what it is! They've likely got a special cell in Bedlam reserved for you! For lord's sake, Tris! Nobody *takes* anything from Claude Sanguinet! His estate, so I understand, is a regular fortress! It would be a blasted miracle could you gain entry. And if you did, and he so much as suspected what you were about, he'd have you flogged and thrown to the dogs for sport!"

Tristram threw back his head and shouted with laughter.

The little black mare was full of spirit, and frisked about playfully when she was pulled up at the edge of the woods. Rachel, however, was pale and nervous and held the reins with an unwontedly heavy hand. Watching her, Raoul said, "Mademoiselle is up betimes this morning."

Speaking in her own tongue, as he did, she said, "Yes. I was wishful to speak with you. Alone." She looked at him and found the dark eyes fixed on her gravely. "Agatha," she said, after a brief hesitation, "tells me that—that you are a good man, Raoul."

His sun-bronzed cheeks flushed slightly. "Miss Agatha have tell me much of her mistress. You see, mademoiselle, how very good I have the English! Who is loved by my Agatha, is by me also loved. Mademoiselle now has a friend. One who will strive for her to utmost." He struck himself on the chest. "I. Raoul. Myself." A faint smile appearing on the lovely face beside him, he went on, "But it does not do for to stop. Many eyes the estate have. We can the more safely speak once down the hill we are."

Rachel urged the mare on, and they passed through the cool, quiet woods, and came out onto the open slope beyond, bright, but still slightly misted in the early morning.

"We are far from the hill now." Raoul moved up to ride slightly behind her and asked, "How I may serve my Agatha's so beautiful lady?"

Smiling at this impudence, she answered, "By telling me where a man named Diccon is employed on the estate."

For an instant he did not answer. Then he said a rather flat, "He is the head groom, mademoiselle."

His demeanour had changed. Perhaps she should say no more. But—she *must!* Sister Maria Evangeline had said she could turn to Diccon, and if she did not speak to someone, she would surely worry herself into a decline! "I—chance to be acquainted with his—family," she lied, her lips stiff and uncooperative. "Where may I find him?"

Another pause. Then, he shrugged. "Alas, is impossible, mademoiselle. Diccon is back to England gone."

With a small, shocked cry, she pulled the mare to a halt and turned a pale face to him. "No, no! He cannot have done so! I was told—" She stopped abruptly.

Raoul searched her face keenly. A smile lit his features. "Does mademoiselle not ride on, our converse it yet may be remarked. Ah, this is better. My good friend Diccon would have pleased himself. Always, he hope you come to him."

Her shattered hopes reviving, she asked, "Your good friend? You know Diccon well?"

"Raoul knows everything!" he announced proudly. "Diccon is not what he seem. No more is Raoul. Mademoiselle will please now to laugh and her face turn away again. *Merci.* What have set over mademoiselle?"

She said shakenly, "You mean—overset." And her mind whirled with conjecture. Dare she confide in this man? If her

164

growing fears were justified, dare she? Agatha liked him—loved him, in fact. And trusted him. "I woke up in the night," she revealed. "I do not know what woke me, but I suddenly remembered something Monsieur Benét had said to me yesterday. It was . . . horrible. I cannot think why I did not pay attention to it before, but—it had to do with—with being afraid of a pool."

Raoul nodded solemnly and reined up to ride beside her. "We can be more comfortable," he said. "It is truth about this pool. The Pagoda Pool. *Tiens!* Is an evil pond, that one! I will tell you something of it. This Raoul, he have once a good friend, a fine gentleman by the name—Philippe, who work as footman in the chateau. Philippe, he is ask something to one day carry upstairs. Mistaking what is meant, he go on to the second floor which is for some cause unlocked. He then come upon Monsieur Benét in a room with the door open. You know this foolish one? This so small man, he sit and dab with paints. To me, Philippe say it was a picture most stupid. More than this he never say, for he is called away and then removed outside to work. They build the red little bridge by the Pagoda. This is not work for my Philippe. I see his face. It is not happy. It is afraid. Philippe he go on the second floor and see monseigneur's so foolish kinsman. He have anger monseigneur."

Rachel's heart was thundering. "But—surely," she faltered, "that cannot be? Why would he be punished for so small a mistake?"

"I do not know, mademoiselle. Even my Diccon—he does not know. But—one thing I do know. Philippe is dead."

"Wh-what . . . ?" Rachel whispered, horrified.

"*Oui*, mademoiselle. They say he fall into the pool. He is not the first."

"Oh—my God! How—awful! But perhaps, it was just . . . an accident."

He gave a scornful grunt. "Raoul have not so many friends, and first, he say to himself, 'Raoul, leave this evil place!' Then, he answer himself, 'No! Philippe was too good of friend to die for no reason. Raoul will stay and see what he shall see.' Then, Monsieur Diccon arrive. He and Raoul become fine friends, but this Diccon, he have the eyes that crawl inside a man's head, and soon, what Raoul knows, Diccon also knows. We shake the hands and swear to be comrades and foil this bad monseigneur however we might. Diccon, he is very brave, and Raoul also; who knows what together we may work? Before he take a fine horse to Monsieur Parnell in England, Diccon say, 'Raoul, if the English lady is in distress, you will help her.' So—how may I help?''

Rachel did not answer. Her resolutely suppressed doubts and half-formed impressions were condensing into a terrible suspicion that made her breath flutter in her throat and her bones become weak as jelly. Was Claude one of those individuals whose kindness and love is extended to one person only, and who show quite another face to the rest of the world? Her attempt to convince herself that she must judge by what she herself had seen, and not be swayed by the opinions of others, was doomed. Sister Maria Evangeline had sought to warn her; her own instincts had warned her. Her picture of Claude as a kindly, benevolent protector, someone who would ensure Charity's well-being, was gone, replaced by a picture the more sinister because of his mild and gentle manner. The recollection of how he had kissed her, of his caresses, made her skin crawl. She could not wed him! She *could* not! However disgraceful, better to be ruined for ever than to marry a man who terrified and revolted her! She *must* get them back to England. But her beloved sister's health was so precarious. Only yesterday Dr. Ulrich had paid a brief visit and said Charity seemed to have taken a slight downturn and was on no account to try and walk as she so longed to do. Charity had been downcast and withdrawn since he left, her cheerful gaiety banished by a weary listlessness and a complete lack of appetite that was frightening. Despite her efforts to be brave, sudden tears stung Rachel's eyes. She had tried so hard, subjugating her own hopes so as to provide for Charity, but her well-meant efforts seemed to have resulted in disaster. If only, she thought forlornly, Justin were here. Or dear Tristram. And God forbid they should be, for if Claude was as merciless as she now suspected, any opposition could only be extremely dangerous. She must handle this alone, but she felt so crushed and confused. Whatever *could* she do?

Raoul had seen that proud back wilt and, his kind heart touched, said staunchly, "Mademoiselle will not now despair. Raoul is here! We will contrive, I have said it! What do you wish?"

She pulled up her head and, blinking away her tears, said in a very small voice, "I wish to go home. Before monseigneur returns. Can you help me?"

"With anything, mademoiselle. Within my power. This is not within my power. Raoul cannot the miracle perform. For Diccon we must wait, and in the meantime, should monseigneur come, mademoiselle must be careful—very careful. Never must mademoiselle forget her sister is here also. To get her safely away against the wish of monseigneur, this would be of the impossible."

A shiver slid between Rachel's shoulder blades. "I—will do as you say," she gulped. "Thank you. You are very brave, Raoul."

"*Oui*," he agreed. "I am. Which is well, for this monseigneur is not good for your England, *n'est-ce pas*? Someone his schemes must stop."

Then this was true as well! Sister Maria Evangeline had not exaggerated. Claude really *did* plot against England. Feeling as though she were sinking in quicksand, Rachel said feebly, "B-but—England is not your country."

"This is true. My France have her differences with all Europe, alas, and many, many young men have die. It is done now. It must not again come. This Raoul, he will fight bravely to stop so bad a thing." He paused, then added softly, "Diccon, he hope mademoiselle might be willing to also help."

Rachel shrank. "But . . . how? I—I could not hurt monseigneur."

"If he has done nothing bad, how may you hurt him, mademoiselle? All Diccon hoped was for a key. You know where is monseigneur's bedchamber?"

"Yes. But—heavens! I've not been near it!"

"Of course. Now in the carving of the mantel is a little place concealed that may be opened by twisting of a rosette. And in this tiny place is a key to the door that close off the stairs to the top floor. If mademoiselle—"

167

Shuddering, Rachel cried, "No! I *could* not! I am not brave —what if I should be seen? And the servants are everywhere. Monseigneur—in spite of everything, has done so much for my sister. Oh, do not ask it, Raoul. I *could* not!"

He stifled a sigh. She was, after all, a woman. One could not expect too much.

11

It was a rather sultry mid-morning when Tristram and Deven-
ish arrived at the cove where the yawl lay moored. They were
greeted with reserve by Mr. George Kimble, and watched without enthusiasm by three taciturn men engaged in loading an apparently inexhaustible supply of barrels into the hold. The master of the *Ma Fille* was a stockily built young man with a ruddy
complexion and blond hair already beginning to thin. His countenance was pleasant, although he lacked the spectacular good
looks of his cousin, the only trace of family likeness mani-
festing itself in the deep blue of his eyes.

"I've found a new slave for you, old George," said Devenish blithely.

With his bland gaze steady on Tristram, Mr. Kimble declined the offer. "I am not," said he, "in need of new crewmen
just now."

"The devil you ain't!" Devenish exploded, bending to
snatch up Mrs. O'Crumbs, who had waddled to join them.
"Than you can do without me, either! And—"

"Look! Look!" shouted one of the men on the yawl. "A
one-eyed duck!"

Yells of excitement arose. Kimble's jaw dropped and he
stared, glassy-eyed.

And suddenly, it seemed he was indeed able to take on a new
crewman. Tristram was assigned to help load the barrels, and
Devenish and his cousin undertook a low-voiced and intent discussion. It was all a trifle smoky, thought Tristram, but since
Kimble was again making the run to Dinard, it was much too
providential to be questioned.

Two nights later, standing on the heaving deck and enjoying

the feel of salt spray in his face, Tristram gazed toward distant France and wondered how Rachel would react when they met.

"I'm a man of my word, I'll own, friend," remarked a quiet voice at his elbow. "But did I work you so hard you are too tired to eat?"

Tristram smiled and shook his head. "My lack of appetite has little to do with your demands of us, Mr. Kimble. However, I never dreamed so many barrels could be packed down below. Why in the deuce do you not tie up to a regular dock? I'd think the fees worth every penny, compared to what we went through."

"Would you," said Kimble speculatively, his eyes holding an amused gleam. "My cousin told me about your trouble with memory. You'll find no dock on the other side, either. You'll not forget you're promised to help us offload?"

"I'll not forget. It was pure luck for me that you chanced to be sailing to Dinard, and I'm most grateful you took me on."

Kimble chuckled, his pipe glowing redly in the darkness. "It was purest luck the men decided it was a good sign. They might just as easily have held it to be a warning of imminent disaster,"

"A good sign? Oh—the duck, you mean?"

"Yes. My incorrigible cousin's feathered friend. The truth is that only her arrival won you passage." Tristram's puzzlement brought another chuckle. "Never look so conflummerated. We pick up our cargo at an old tavern called *Le Canard Borgne*."

" 'The One-Eyed Duck'? Gad! And to think I scolded Dev for bringing the creature along!"

"Do you journey far with him, it's probably the least you'll get. The boy attracts livestock—" He broke off as the vessel lurched suddenly.

Tristram grabbed the rail. "We'll not enounter a really bad swell at this season, shall we?"

Kimble shot him a keen glance. "I see you've sailed these waters before. No, the worst of the tides are past, but I must leave you. This is a tricky coast."

It was tricky indeed, for soon the sea was a churning race, with billows of foam roaring around the great rocks that loomed menacingly along the shoreline. Clinging to the rail, Tristram began to wonder if he'd ever reach the chateau at all, and, echoing his thoughts, Devenish struggled to his side, holding his frightened pet under his coat and shouting that at least she would be able to swim for it!

Quite suddenly, however, the violent pitching of the yawl eased, and they approached the darker bulk of the coastline over smoothly rippling waves. The beach was dark, and Kimble grumbled, "Yves is late again!" Tristram scarcely heard the anchor splash into the water, and at once the offloading began. This proved a simpler process than he'd anticipated, the barrels being secured together by ropes threaded through rings on their sides, then lowered into the sea and floated along behind the dinghy. The men worked quickly and quietly, but when one of the barrels slipped from Tristram's cold and inexperienced hands to land with a loud splash, Kimble's head jerked around and he rasped, "Quiet!" his face one big scowl! The recipient of several irked glares, Tristram muttered an apology, and his suspicion that Devenish had plunged him into a decidedly havey-cavey business was confirmed.

Soon, they were on the mist-shrouded beach, hauling in the barrels and stacking them neatly. This proved difficult work for Devenish who was concerned lest Mrs. O'Crumbs wander off in the darkness and become lost. Irked by his cousin's slow progress, Kimble grated, "For lord's sake, Dev! Stick the dratted bird into one of the tubs and get to work!"

Devenish protested, but obeyed, and Mrs. O'Crumbs was safely, if indignantly confined to a small barrel.

Half an hour later, short of breath, Tristram said, "That's the last of 'em. How do we get them to the inn?"

"Why, we will be most happy to assist," offered a triumphant French voice.

Tristram swung around. The biggest musket barrel it had ever been his misfortune to encounter was an inch from his nose.

"Excisemen!" roared a diminishing voice.

A shot rang out and the beach was suddenly swarming with struggling men, a few lanterns dimly illuminating the wild melee. From the corner of his eye, Tristram caught a glimpse of Kimble whizzing into the surf, a large man in hot pursuit. He and Devenish were hopelessly caught, however, unable to move with that musket held so steadily on them, the grimly smiling face beyond it leaving no doubt but that it would be fired if they attempted escape.

"So many times, messieurs," nodded their sturdily built captor, "I am tricked; my trap it is sprung, my prey flits safely away. So many times, you land where I am not. This time, I ask myself where I would be the least likely to land with the tides as they are tonight. *Hein!* I think, I know where I would *not* be. So—here I am, and *voilà!* Here are you, also!"

"How unfortunate," said Tristram. "The barrels, you see, are empty. Is it illegal to bring empty barrels ashore, monsieur?"

"Aha!" Devenish cried gleefully, "He is right! You should have waited until they were full, my poor slowtop!"

The Exciseman glowered at him. "By the saints, but you're saucy rogues! And do not imagine yourselves reprieved. The tubs doubtless reek of brandy, however empty they may be."

A cohort came up, holding a small barrel. "To judge from the weight, this one it is not quite empty, Jean-Pierre."

Devenish stiffened, his mouth opening. Tristram said swiftly, "Dev! Be silent!" And as his friend turned a startled face to him, added, "Admit nothing!" and winked the eye that was beyond the range of the Exciseman's sight.

Devenish's lips twitched. He shrugged, and hung his head as one totally dejected.

"I collect," Tristram signed, "that you fellows mean to sample—" He checked, and went on clumsily, "Er—I mean, take that with you."

The two officials exchanged brief, conspiratorial glances.

"It is our duty," said Jean-Pierre, importantly, "to sample the goods, no, Louis?"

Louis lost no time in seconding the motion. He wrenched the lid off, then raised the barrel eagerly to his lips.

Mrs. O'Crumbs was not in the best of humours. She had endured a horridly lengthy sojourn in a stuffy vessel, and to add insult to injury, had then been plunked into a reeking barrel. While her master had been kind enough to leave the lid off, she'd been able to bear it, but some fiend had come along and replaced the lid, after which she'd been half-suffocated. When the lid was again wrenched off she was at first too startled to give tongue. Propelled forward as the barrel was tilted, she gave more than tongue, and Louis uttered a scream of terror and pain as her strong beak clamped angrily onto the end of his nose. He flung the barrel aside. Fluttering her wings frenziedly, Mrs. O'Crumbs was launched at Jean-Pierre, who yelled and jumped back. Tristram sprang forward, and a clenched fist (which was later to be designated a sledgehammer) caught Jean-Pierre beneath his chin, silencing his outcries. Simultaneously, Devenish seized the barrel and applied it vigorously to Louis's downbent head. The two Excisemen sank quietly to the beach. A shout warned of more trouble. Devenish scooped up Mrs. O'Crumbs.

"Shall we toddle?" he suggested.

They did.

Dominer, situated upon a gentle hill in the Cotswolds, was widely held to be one of the loveliest estates in all England. It had been some time since Kingston Leith had visited the great house, and he had accepted Garret Hawkhurst's invitation with alacrity, partly in the hope that for a while it would help him to forget his growing fears for Tristram's survival, and partly because London was become rather uncomfortable. He was attempting to explain this strange phenomenon to Mrs. Dora Graham as they sat in the luxurious yet welcoming gold lounge, awaiting the arrival of the rest of the family in this pleasant hour before dinner. The day had been warm, and the sun had not yet gone down, the pink rays that slanted through the great windows lighting Mrs. Graham's auburn locks and sending little gleams dancing through the decanter and onto the mahogany of the occasional table. It seemed to Leith that Dora's hair was a trifle less red than in days gone by, but perhaps memory played him false. Besides, like himself, the dear lady was getting just a little past youth.

"The main trouble," he said plaintively, "is Drusilla. Always was inclined to be fusty, y'know."

"So is the Earl." Her pale blue eyes fastened to his face, Mrs. Graham reached blindly for her wineglass, took up a small vase instead, and was startled when the rose it held invaded her eye. "Good gracious! Did you put a rose in my glass, Leith? How very romantic you are! Always was." She removed the rose, then stared at the vase uncertainly.

Leith took the vase from her plump hand and said with a chuckle, "Dora, Dora! Absent-minded as ever!" Restoring her wineglass, and amused by this typical lapse, he went on, "You're right about Starchy, though. Dreadful bore."

"Starchy?" she echoed dubiously.

"Palmer. My brother-in-law. The Earl of Mayne-Waring."

She uttered a trill of laughter. "What a perfect name for him! And how shocked poor Drusilla would be! Leith, you're a rascal. But, oh how very good it is to have you here and chat about old friends, old times."

"Old friends, well enough, Dora," he said rather disconsolately. "It's the new friends tend to have the odd kick in their gallop. Or so m'sister holds."

"How so?"

"Well, I've been—ah—looking about, you see. Not that dear Tristram ain't coming home. You know he will . . ." He searched her face anxiously. "Don't you?" Although inwardly appalled, she smiled and nodded with such assurance that he was heartened, and went on, "Thing is— Just in case— Well, there's young Glick. Cannot have him at Cloudhills. Wouldn't be fitting. Tradition's a funny thing, Dora. Much we may laugh at it, but still—what's due the family is—well, is due. So," he sighed heavily, "there you are,"

She stared at him, her brows knit. "Perhaps you'd best fill my glass, Leith. My wits are no match for yours."

He was only too pleased to oblige, refilling his own glass also. After taking a few sips, Dora seemed more able to comprehend that a new heir must be provided, and was suitably sympathetic regarding Drusilla's henwitted behaviour. "If she don't understand your 'sponsibilities, it's because of her gibble-gabble cronies," she opined, nodding owlishly. "Been filling her head with windfalls."

"Windmills," Leith corrected, but he applauded this excellent verdict and extolled Mrs. Graham's understanding to the point that the blush on her smooth cheeks was not entirely the result of the rosy sunlight.

"She's all on end," he confided. "Says I'm being too partic'ler in me attentions. Am I being too—'ticler, d'you think, Dora?"

" 'Course not, Kingston," she assured him fondly. "Always pleasure to have you. Pleasure, indeed."

He patted her hand. "Too good. You always was, Dora. 'T'all events, there's safety in numbers, do y'not think?"

"Abs'lutely. 'Speak low if you speak love.' " Leith stared in mystification, and she giggled. "That's what Army Buchanan used to say. Before he was wed, 'course."

"Aye. What a wild young devil Armstrong was. Dora," Leith edged his chair a little closer. "D'you remember that time when Army was walking beside your chair—along the banks of the Serpentine, I think. And—and," he chortled gleefully, "some other beau come tripping 'long?"

"Oh, yes. Such a stately fellow he was, too," she nodded reminiscently.

"Got to admiring you too pointedly, as I recall," grinned Leith.

"It turned out eventually, he was a Cit, Kingston. Designed toothpicks!" This sent them both in whoops. "Poor Army," Dora gasped. "But—it was the Seine, not the Serpentine."

"And Army was just . . . just as wet!" he howled, slapping his knee.

Dora laughed until the tears slipped down her cheeks, and it became necessary for Leith to dry them for her.

Watching from the doorway, Euphemia Hawkhurst's eyes were very soft. She held up a hand to detain her tall husband as he moved quietly to join her. Taking that hand, he kissed it and, his eyes holding the smile the sight of his wife invariably awoke in them, murmured, "How does Leith go on, love?"

"He seems content," she murmured, "but only because— Oh, Garret, the poor dear will not accept it! Is it wrong in us to pretend with him?"

Hawkhurst's gaze turned to the two who chattered so gaily together, and, frowning a little, he said, "Perhaps it gives him time to adjust to the pain of his loss. Perhaps—when it becomes obvious that he must face the fact that Tristram is . . ." And he hesitated, himself unable to speak that dread word.

Euphemia's face crumpled. She hid it against Hawkhurst's splendid dinner jacket, and he dropped a kiss upon the bright tresses that contained a titian no artifice could provide. "Do not, sweetheart," he murmured. "We must try only to be glad we knew him. He'd not have wanted these tears, you know."

"I . . . know," she gulped. "But—is there *no* hope? No hope at all?"

Hawkhurst stifled a sigh. "It is almost six weeks since Waterloo, Mia. God knows, I'd give my right arm to think Tristram was alive. But—" He heard her muffled sob and said bracingly, "If anyone can help poor Leith face up to matters, it's our Dora. Come—let them talk alone a little longer. They've been friends for years. Who knows, that friendship may prove a boon to both of 'em."

Euphemia looked up, wonderingly. Drying her tears, she slipped her hand into his, and they crept silently away.

Rachel sat beside the open *petit salon* window, staring blindly into the peaceful afternoon. For the third time she sighed, and took up her embroidery frame.

Watching her, waiting for the first stitch to be set, Agatha saw the pretty hands sink again and, her heart heavy, put down the torn flounce she mended and asked, "Miss Rachel? Be you worrying over what that silly Raoul said? I nigh boxed his ears when he told me! The impertinence, to dare try and involve you in such a scheme as he and Mr. Diccon have—"

"No, no." Rachel crossed to sit beside the indignant abigail. "It is much more than that. And, Agatha—my sister must know nothing of all this."

"My lamb." Agatha squeezed the hand she held and said fondly. "You do not belong here. Can we go home soon?"

Rachel bit her lip. "Truth to tell, I have very little in the way of funds. And—at all events, it cannot be thought of while Charity is far from well."

Agatha said glumly. "She did seem to take a turn, dear soul. And so quick as it was!"

"Yes. And in no case for a long journey, even if that were

possible. I worry about her, and yet—'' she checked, turning sharply as she heard a small sound behind her. Angered, she came to her feet and said with regal hauteur, ''I failed to hear your knock, Gerard!''

''A thousand pardons, mademoiselle. I knocked very softly, for fear of disturbing Mademoiselle Charity.''

''Must've been so soft as thistledown,'' Agatha muttered, but when Gerard's cold gaze rested on her, she quailed into silence.

Rachel's head was very high. ''Indeed? I assume you intrude for some urgent purpose?''

Amused, and unable to refrain from admiring her, Gerard betrayed neither emotion, saying, ''A messenger has arrived, mademoiselle.''

''From monseigneur?''

''From . . .'' he paused, knowing he was vexing her, and finished with his faint smile, ''from Mr. Justin Strand.''

The embroidery fell from Rachel's hand. ''My brother?'' she gasped, hearing Agatha's excited exclamation.

''So I am advised.''

Her heart leaping, she asked, ''Where is this messenger? Bring him here at once!''

''I would have done this, *naturellement*, but he is not, ah—suitably clad to set foot above stairs.''

''Oh, for heaven's sake!'' She swept past him and walked swiftly along the corridor, her steps muffled by the thick carpets. Dear Justin was come home at last! And just when she so needed him! Hurrying down the winding stairs, she all but ran through the hall. Several footmen came rigidly to attention as she passed, her eyes searching anxiously. There was no sign of anyone other than servants in the entry hall, and she spun about angrily. Gerard watched her from beside the open door that led to the kitchens and the rear of the house. He bowed slightly, his face quite without expression.

Rachel fairly flew past him and down the narrow corridor, a startled kitchenmaid leaping back before her impetuous advance. When she came to the door leading into the small office where the housekeeper interviewed local merchants, Gerard was beside her and, reaching for the handle, murmured, "Allow me, mademoiselle. This is a rough-looking customer."

He entered the room first, blocking the doorway as he said a stern, "Make your respects, fellow. Here is Mademoiselle Strand." And he stepped aside, his cunning eyes riveted to the girl's face.

"Are you—" Rachel began, and stopped, her breath snatched away, shock causing her heart to leap into her throat and every vestige of colour to drain from her face. A hand to her throat, she stared at the tall young man who bowed before her; the strong fine face, the wide-set dark eyes she had never thought to see again.

Tristram had heard the gasp that cut off her eager words and was himself stunned. Rachel was white as death, with dark smudges beneath her glorious eyes, and her face thinner than he remembered; yet her beauty seemed enhanced. For a frozen instant he could only know how lovely she was, the pale jonquil gown accentuating the fair curls and dainty figure. Even though he had prepared himself for this moment, it took a mighty effort of will to present an appearance of cool impassivity. It was very clear that Rachel had not been told his identity. How stricken she looked. He slanted an irked glance at the Frenchman and surprised a gloating triumph on the sallow features. As always, danger sharpened his faculties. He pulled himself together and said politely, "My apologies, ma'am. I should have realized my sudden appearance would shock you. I did not die, after all, you see."

Rachel had betrayed herself, she knew, but an escape route had been offered and she snatched at it. "I am—very glad," she stammered breathlessly. "I will own I was . . . most startled. I had thought—that is, the surgeon was of the opinion . . . I am glad to see he was mistaken."

Tristram laughed easily. "Oh, yes, I confounded him. And went to Strand Hall to thank you for your kindnesses."

"It was the least I could do." Her knees were jelly, but she turned to Gerard and said, "Captain Tristram did me a great service after Waterloo, when the carriage I occupied was attacked by looters."

"We are greatly indebted to *Monsieur le Capitaine*," murmured Gerard, his eyes enigmatic.

"No need, I assure you, sir," smiled Tristram. "Any man would have done the same."

"And it appears you have now done me another service," said Rachel. "Monsieur Gerard says you bring word from my brother? He is back in England?"

"Yes, ma'am. And when he learned I was bound for France, begged that I tell you of his arrival and ask that you return to Sussex as soon as is convenient."

"He doubtless sent a letter to that effect," purred Gerard.

Tristram thought, "Blast! Why did I not think of that?" "Regrettably," he said, "Mr. Strand was abed with a heavy cold. Nothing to worry you, ma'am, but he did not feel inclined to write."

"Oh, no," Rachel laughed nervously. "Justin abominates being obliged to set pen to paper. How eager I am to see him, and my sister will be overjoyed. I shall return to England at once, Gerard. Please order a carriage for us."

"But of course, mademoiselle," Gerard turned to the door and Rachel's wild heartbeat began to calm. See how simple it had been? How absurd that she had imagined he would object!

His hand on the doorknob, Gerard paused and glanced back. "Monseigneur is expected momentarily. He will, of a certainty, wish to thank the gentleman who was of such great service, and doubtless would desire personally to escort you."

"But we cannot be sure when he will return, and I can be back in—"

"Mademoiselle has perhaps forgotten the ball?" he reminded smoothly. "I betray a secret, I fear, but monseigneur is even now in Paris selecting the betrothal ring. He will be quite shattered to find mademoiselle gone away, for he has planned the ball with such care—everything mademoiselle might wish. Many of the guests must travel a great distance and are already en route."

"Even so, does Miss Strand desire to return home and would permit, I would be happy to serve as courier," Tristram asserted, a touch of steel in his voice.

Gerard smiled. "You are too kind, but it is not to be thought of, monsieur. Mademoiselle Strand is my employer's affianced bride. If mademoiselle persists in leaving while monseigneur is absent, *I* must ensure her safe conduct."

"No," said Rachel calmly. Gerard was quite right, for she had not only forgotten the ball, but all sense of propriety and manners. There was no escape for her. The ball was, as he had said, almost upon them, and to run off and leave Claude to face his guests alone would be unforgivable. She held out her hand. "Thank you, Captain. Adieu."

His strong clasp sent a near unbearable pang through her heart. He bowed and released her hand at once.

"*Mais non!*" Gerard protested. "I have to insist that monseiur remain, as our honoured guest. Do you refuse, *Monsieur le Capitaine*, my situation will be lost to me. I know it."

Afraid, Rachel inserted, "Captain Tristram undoubtedly has other commitments, Gerard. We will not add inconvenience to the debt that already exists."

"To the contrary, Miss Strand, it would be my very great pleasure to stay," said Tristram. "However, I cannot think my so small service warrants such a reward."

"But—monseigneur will think so," Gerard contradicted, his crafty eyes very bright. "On that head, I have no doubts whatsoever."

Rachel managed to slip into her bedchamber without disturbing Agatha, who was sitting in the *petit salon*, reading to Charity. She closed the connecting door softly, went at once to the washstand, dampened a cloth and held it to her brow. She must not faint, though to succumb to the reaction that was making her head swim would be a welcome relief. Tears began to mingle with the cold water. She had to choke back a flood of sobs, and for the first time in her life, longed for the restorative of strong spirits. She crossed to the windows and opened them wide. For a moment, she stood there, breathing the cool air, then sank her face into her hands. In heaven's name—what must she do for the best? She could not be *sure* why Tristram had come. There had been a frost in his eyes when he looked at her, but he was here, and that his strength and gallantry were at her command, whether or not he now despised her, she did not doubt for an instant.

She began to pace the room, walking quietly for all her desperate agitation. She was no longer so alone with her problems; someone beloved and reliable and strong was come, someone in whom to confide all her woes, to offer a broad shoulder to weep on. But in her ears rang a distant echo of the words that Sister Maria Evangeline had uttered with such grim intensity: " . . . make you see Claude Sanguinet for the monster he really is . . . one of the most powerful men in all Europe . . . *the* most dangerous! Human life is of no importance to him. He has been responsible for—" For what? She halted, a whimper catching in her throat. Murder? Careless cruelty? Oh, *why* had she not listened to the nun's warning? It had seemed so inconceivable at the time; it had been so hard for her to accept. But even were Sister Maria Evangeline and Diccon, and that funny, strutting, warm-hearted little Raoul, wrong, she knew she must still be afraid of a man who surrounded himself with such people as Gerard and those icy-eyed guards. She wrung her hands and paced on.

If Claude were even half as dangerous as the good Sister suspected, what chance would there be for Tristram? If she told him the truth, he would fight to the death to win her away. And that is what it might well come to, for how could one man hope to carry herself, her maid, and her invalid sister from these closely watched grounds? She huddled on the side of the bed, a small, stricken shape, elbows on her knees and forehead resting on her clenched fists, rocking back and forth in a frenzy of despair. Perhaps she could go to Claude, tell him she wished to return to see Justin, and would come back. But there was no time! The ball was three days hence. She was sure that if she attempted to break her engagement, Claude would not allow her to do so—not while she was here in France. And with Charity to transport, how could she possibly— She gave a sudden gasp of terror. Was *that* why Claude had insisted upon Charity accompanying them? Had he suspected she might attempt to sever their engagement? Did he mean to use Charity as a tool, knowing she was too ill to travel? "Oh . . . God!" she moaned and, remembering Gerard's sly intrusion into their parlour earlier, she sobbed again, a hand pressed to her mouth to stifle the sound. How long had he been standing there before she heard him? How much had he heard?

"What must I do?" she whispered distraught. "Oh, what must I *do*?"

There was no answer, save what she herself could devise. On the one hand, marriage to a man she had come to fear and dislike—but luxury and health for Charity. On the other, a desperate, probably doomed attempt at escape, ending perhaps in the ultimate penalty for the man she loved more than her own life . . .

Her hands lowered, and she sat very still, gazing haggard-eyed at the rich carpet. There *was* no choice. No choice at all.

"Welcome to Versailles!" Devenish sauntered through the connecting door between the rooms and, amused by Tristram's astonished expression, laughed, "Did you ever see the like? Mine is just as luxurious. Does Prinny rest his ogles on this, he'll tear down his Pavilion and build himself a chateau."

The bedchamber was, at the very least, sumptuous. Gold silken hangings descending in billowing loops from the centre of the ceiling, were caught back along the tops of the walls so as to create an opulent, tent-like effect. The draperies were of a paler gold velvet, contained by rust-coloured braided silk ropes. The furnishings were all of cherrywood, embellished with an inlaid trim of intricately wrought mahogany. On the floor were spread thick Aubusson carpets, and the bed was sufficiently outsized that even so tall a man as Tristram would be enabled to stretch out in comfort. Fine paintings, keyed to the prevailing colours of rust and gold were spaced at discreet, if rather unimaginative, intervals upon the walls, while a magnificent gilded mirror was hung above the mantel.

Hands on hips, Tristram gazed about him, and with a quirk of the lips observed, "No barracks room, is it?"

"I thought my uncle's house was ornate," Devenish grinned. "But—this? Egad!" He strolled to sprawl on a chaise longue and choose from a bowl of fruit on the low table beside it. "Bestowed by the groom of the chambers," he imparted, waving a bunch of grapes. "We, my poor soldier, have apparently been taken for visiting potentates."

Tristram glanced down at his rumpled and dusty garments. "Visiting paupers, more like,"

"Worry not. Our man assured me he would provide us with suitable raiment within the hour." Dropping a grape into his mouth, Devenish watched Tristram's tour of inspection and remarked, "If this is the treatment accorded to us, I wonder how the important guests are served."

"The gentleman to whom you took so immediate a dislike at the lodge gate is playing some little May game of his own, I think." Tristram wandered back to sit on the table, and went on. "Else he suspects our real motive in coming here."

"Gerard? Slippery customer, that. Which reminds me—why was I spirited away? I should like to have seen your—er, Miss Strand."

For a moment, Tristram stared blankly at the bowl of fruit. Then he said thoughtfully, "I believe you were removed so that Gerard could be quite sure her reaction was to my presence alone. It was very obvious she'd not been told my name."

"Lord! What a shock for the poor girl! How did she react?"

His face enigmatic, Tristram answered, "Violently. She made a splendid recover, but—I'd the feeling a trap had been sprung exactly as Gerard hoped."

"That fellow needs his greasy head punched! Did you hear him ask me 'What is that *thing*?' Haughty as you please!"

"I did. I also heard you tell him it was not a *thing*, but a duck—as any fool could plainly see."

"Yes, and he piped up with, 'I mislike your tone!' Blasted impudence!"

"You did not help matters by telling him you didn't like one dashed thing about *him*!"

"Help matters? Why the devil should I truckle to such as he?"

"Because we are not boxing the Watch, Dev—to bait these men will not do. I must ask that you do not further antagonize Gerard."

"Oh, must you, indeed?" Devenish sprang up and flared

hotly, "One might suppose me a blundering doddipoll! I came with you, sir—"

"*Why*, I cannot understand. You said you were going back to England with your rum touch of a cousin."

"Well, how the deuce could I do that when he went churning into the waves like a confounded merman?" His anger forgotten, Devenish's contagious grin lit his eyes. "Besides, this has all the earmarks of a juicy adventure. Be dammed if I'll miss it!"

Very conscious of the weight of responsibility for the safety of four other lives, Tristram stood. "We were fortunate to gain access to this palace. To get out with our health will be little short of miraculous. You're a hell of a good man, and I would ask nothing better than to have you side me in a scrap, but for a while at least, this is going to be a subtle game of cat and mouse. Can you not control that fiery temper, you must leave before you endanger us all. No!" He flung up one hand in a gesture so commanding that the again fuming Devenish was surprised into swallowing his enraged response. "Hear me out! The more I see of this situation, the more can I appreciate the concerns of Diccon and the nun. For England, I mean to find out all I can. For myself, I swear to God I'll not leave before those girls are safely clear. I'll have your word, Devenish, that you will do as I say, and muzzle your hasty tongue."

Staring up at him, Devenish was shocked into the awareness that although this tall, aristocratic stranger had not once raised his voice, he felt as though he'd been sternly rebuked. And, oddly, he could but like the man the more for it. "By God, Tris," he breathed. "What a curst trial I am! You've my word, old fellow, of course. On one condition."

Tristram's hand, coming up swiftly to meet his own, paused. One eyebrow lifted, and the ready smile faded into the coolly unfamiliar hauteur.

"Which is," Devenish went on with a rather shy grin, "that you don't call me 'Devenish' in just that way again."

Tristram chuckled. "Only if you overstep the mark with Gerard!" They gripped hands firmly. "By the way," added Tristram, resuming his seat on the table and picking up an apple. "Where is your feathered friend?"

"Under the bed in my room. She don't like this place. No more do I. It's plain I shall be obliged to keep her safe. Would you credit it, whilst I was awaiting you, I saw one of the guards—for I do not doubt but that's what they are—kill a dove!"

"Did you? A good shot?"

"Jolly good. Especially," his eyes hardened, "since his weapon was a crossbow!"

"Now was it, by God!" breathed Tristram.

Devenish went on at some length, expounding on the guard's skill with the medieval weapon, and on his concern for his pet, but Tristram's attention wandered.

How incredibly lovely was Rachel, and how bravely she had met the challenge of his arrival. She had even sought to protect him by giving him the chance to leave in spite of Gerard's manoeuvrings. He felt a twinge of guilt: what a blasted fool to have believed Shotten's poison. He should have known better. Rachel's purity and goodness were written in her sweet face. She must not have been aware of Sanguinet's reputation—that was the only answer. And if that were so—

"Devil take you, Tris!" said Devenish, justifiably irked. "You've not heard one blasted word I said, and what you find so beguiling about that apple you must sit there and smile at it is beyond me!"

His face very red, Tristram took a bite of the beguiling apple.

12

The fussy little gentleman at chambers, at first appalled by Tristram's size, was so fortunate as to unearth some garments left at the chateau by a noble and large guest whose plans to return had not as yet materialized. The fit, while not perfect, was swiftly improved by the talented fingers of Madame Fleur's dresser, with results sufficiently pleasing as to cause little M. Auber not only to rejoice at Captain Tristram's splendid physique, but at his own cleverness in solving the difficulty. Devenish presented less of a problem, and suitable apparel was soon offered for his approval.

As a result, the two young men joined Madame Fleur, the Misses Strand, and Monsieur Benét in the crystal lounge before dinner, with no need to blush for their appearance. The sight of Tristram in evening clothes brought a gleam of admiration to Madame, a wistful smile to the younger Miss Strand, and a sharp yearning to the heart of her sister. Many of Rachel's fears proved ill-founded, however, for while never showing her less than courtesy, Tristram's attentions were bestowed elsewhere. Madame Fleur, at first highly disapproving, was not so elderly as to be impervious to the charm of a dashing young man and was soon chattering merrily with him. Both he and his friend were, she thought, dangerously handsome, but Claude could in no way hold her responsible because that fool Gerard had pitchforked these two young men into close proximity with the Strand girls. In point of fact, much of the blame must lie at Claude's own door. Any man who brought his lovely fiancée to visit his home, only to abandon her and trot off, lord knows where, was no less than a noddicock, and so she would tell him. Perhaps. Meanwhile, she was thoroughly enjoying herself.

Although apparently hanging on Madame Beauchard's every word, Tristram's senses were alert to every movement of the other occupants of this luxurious room. Charity, he had at once noted, looked pale and wan; Rachel, exquisite in a low-cut robe of primrose crepe over a white silk slip, her curls softly clustered about her ears, and with Claude's pearls glowing against her smooth throat, was very animated, her flushed cheeks and bright eyes heightening her beauty so that he could scarce endure to look at her. Her devoted admirer, Monsieur Benét, at once classified in Tristram's mind as a weak-chinned fribble, was exclaiming ecstatically over Devenish's good looks. Under different circumstances, Benét's fulsome praises might have been amusing, but Tristram was too aware of his friend's tight lips and the stormy glint in the blue eyes. Dev was restraining his temper, but—volcano that he was—did that clunch Benét not cease his ravings, it might soon become expedient to intervene.

Adroitly manipulating the conversation, he garnered from the garrulous Madame Beauchard much information that might be of use to him. After the fashion of poor relations, the lady was somewhat less grateful for her cousin's largesse than she was resentful of the need to be so obligated. At first, her remarks were cautious and so honeyed as to conjure up the picture of a loved benefactor whose disposition was as saintly as his generosity was unfailing. Madame, however, was quite partial to "a tiny drop of wine," and Tristram only too willing to ensure her glass was never empty. Under this treatment, she mellowed considerably. The more she mellowed, the more her tongue wagged, and the more her tongue wagged the less saintly became her nephew until Claude's halo dimmed to the point of extinction.

Rachel, meanwhile, talked easily with Devenish, responded dutifully to Charity's occasional remarks, and managed to avoid being drawn into a discussion with Monsieur Benét anent the differences between the features of the new arrivals. Despite these distractions, she missed none of the soft laughter, the increasingly confiding exchanges, the unceasing flow of chatter between Tristram and Fleur. Her nerves were taut as stretched wire, her terrified heart leaping erratically for fear

Benét would comprehend what she guessed Tristram was about. She had seldom been more relieved than when Devenish, seeking to escape Benét, murmured that he must make the better acquaintance of Madame, and Tristram politely changed places with him. Charity, who had been relatively quiet until now, at once engaged Antoine in conversation, under cover of which, Tristram murmured, "Dare I remark that you are looking very lovely tonight, Miss Rachel?"

"Thank you." She leaned forward and as he bent to refill her glass, breathed softly, "I must talk to you. I shall ride early in the morning. The groom, Raoul, will tell you—"

But then Antoine turned to them, his brow furrowed and jealousy written in every line of him.

"I quite agree." Tristram replaced the decanter on its silver tray and went on smoothly, "Never have I seen so lovely an estate."

Benét did not think they had been discussing the estate. "But then," he pouted, "Miss Rachel says you have little recall, *Monsieur le Capitaine*. So how could you know what you have seen?"

"You are very right, monsieur," Tristram agreed gravely. "What I admire here may very well be—so much dross compared to other country homes. Is that what you imply?"

"No!" the artist yelped. "I had no such thought! I assure you, mademoiselle, that I intended no criticism of my cousin's—"

"Criticism of Claude?" Madame Fleur intervened, much shocked. "Whatever are you about, Antoine?"

Paling, Benét all but ran to her side. "Nothing! No, no—it is all a misunderstanding, only. Oh—*how* I am misunderstood of late!"

"Dinner," announced the butler, regally, "is served, Madame."

For Rachel, at least, the meal was both a joy and a nightmare. To be so close to Tristram, to see him smile, hear his deep voice and easy laugh, and even to watch the movements of his hands, was delight, but to maintain her share of the conversation and comment on simple, commonplace matters when she was so torn with worry taxed her nerves to the breaking point.

Never had she been more thankful for Madame Fleur's untiring tongue; never had she waited with such pleasure through Antoine Benét's banalities.

Charity, astounded when she had been told of Tristram's arrival, had immediately clasped her hands and exclaimed, ''Oh! How romantic! He has come to claim his love!'' Despite her sister's refutations, nothing would move her. Tristram had, she was sure, come to Dinan to find Rachel. He had come in despite Claude's wealth and power, risking the certainty of being challenged to a duel for his daring. He was the bravest of men, and her admiration for him had soared to such dangerous levels it had been necessary for Rachel to become quite stern with her. Tristram had chanced to be journeying to France, she said dampingly, and had merely done Justin the favour of bearing his message. If Charity were to, by the slightest hint, suggest there was another reason for his presence here, it might indeed stir a witch's brew. Glowingly undampened, Charity vowed she would be flayed alive sooner than utter a syllable that might create a hazard for the Captain. And with that, Rachel had to be content.

During dinner, Charity behaved perfectly, her own bright chatter helping the taut moments slip past. Quite soon after the gentlemen joined the ladies, however, she began to look tired. Rachel summoned the two brawny footmen; one of whom carried Charity, and the other her chair. Bidding the company goodnight, Rachel also went upstairs and within the hour was in her bed—unhappily, neither to sleep nor dream.

Devenish essayed a mad leap and snatched up Mrs. O'Crumbs a split second before the hound's teeth would have caught her. The guard swore, pulling the dog back as the powerful animal ravened and strove to come at the frightened duck. ''Devil take it!'' cried Devenish, springing clear, ''Call the brute off!''

By the light of the three-quarter moon, Tristram saw another man approaching, and Gerard called, ''Something is amiss, gentlemen?'' Coming up with them, he smiled. ''Ah, I comprehend. I should have warned you. One does not walk the grounds after dark. The dogs do not patrol close to the house, but down here—" he shrugged. "A necessary precaution, you understand."

"I did not see them in time, monsieur," the guard said tonelessly, and turned to Devenish. "That was unwise. The dog near had your arm for his dinner."

"Yes, and at first you made no effort to restrain him, damn your—"

"I apolgize if we violate your rules, Monsieur Gerard." Tristram's voice was chill. "Mr. Devenish and I merely wished to see the grounds by night."

"Your wish is no sooner spoken than granted, messieurs. Pray walk wheresoever you will." Gerard produced a silver whistle from his pocket. "I will instruct the men to take the dogs in for a while." He blew several long blasts and one short and warbling. "There—you will be perfectly safe now. Though —forgive that I suggest it—you might consider returning to the house within the half-hour." His teeth flashed whitely in the darkness. "Goodnight, gentlemen."

Watching the two men move off, Devenish muttered, "Blasted place is like a castle under siege! I wonder how many of those damn great hounds they let loose at night? I've not seen a sign of one before this, have you?"

"No. They must be penned far from the house. The guard was right, though. I'd not want that brute's teeth in my arm. Why did you not employ your famous 'way with animals'?"

His anger gone as swiftly as it had come, Devenish chuckled and, stroking the still outraged Mrs. O'Crumbs, replied, "Don't do to show all one's cards at the start of the game."

"True, but I'd rather you do so than be savaged. Come— we'd best turn back. I'd not put it past Gerard to see how fast we can run!"

"One last look, only. Tris—is it not a fine spectacle? A regular Vauxhall Gardens!"

The hill sloped away from them like some enchanted land, soft lights illumining selected trees or flower beds, and the various structures aglow with colour. The English castle was a soft green, the Egyptian sphinx golden, the Grecian temple pale blue, and far down the hill they could see the red loom of the Pagoda. Tristram's thoughtful gaze flickered over it briefly, then his dark eyes again returned to the chateau. "I think the best time to attempt Claude's private floor would be during the ball—do you agree?"

Devenish slanted an alarmed glance at him, and as they started back towards the white sparkle of the great house, protested, "No, really, Tris. That's coming it a bit too brown. You never mean to attempt it?"

"Oh, yes. Diccon said the key to the entire mess is contained in a painting up there."

"You caper-witted booberkin! Even did you succeed in getting inside— Good God, man! There might likely be fifty guards prowling there!"

"At least," Tristram grinned. "If I cannot get in by the door, I mean to climb in from outside."

"Oho! I wish I might see it! *Regardez vous*, the north and south walls boast neither balcony nor trellis. The west face is in full view of the inner windows from both wings, and the back of the chateau rises sheer from the edge of the hill. One slip, old lad, and you've a two hundred foot fall. Only were you to land on your head could you survive it."

"Granted," said Tristram. "But, seriously, d'you see that tall tree beside the south wing? Were I to climb that—"

"I do indeed see it. Not one branch reaches within ten feet of the wall. You propose to ask Mrs. O'Crumbs to fly you across, perchance?"

"Gudgeon! She'd never agree—she don't like me above half! If I took a rope with me and secured it to a branch, then I might swing across to a window."

"And sail on through! That would properly wake the estate! But before you reached that point, my circus acrobat, have you considered that the chateau is pure white? Picture yourself dangling at the end of a rope, in full view of several guards who are having a frightfully jolly time, lobbing crossbow bolts into your carcass."

"Do you know, Dev," Tristram mused, "I rather doubt a crossbow is a very accurate weapon."

The dawn was fair. One or two clouds, still touched with pink, hung lazily against clear skies, and, gazing up at them from her bedchamber window, Rachel sighed wistfully. It seemed very long ago that Tristram's deep voice had said, ". . . the feather castles of our lives? Yet some dreams do come true, you know."

"Some dreams, my love," she murmured sadly. "Some dreams."

Agatha hurried in and closed the door behind her. "I saw Raoul, miss. He has the horses ready."

"Oh, very good." Rachel turned, smiling cheerily. "And no one else was there yet, I trust?"

"No one, ma'am, and sorry I am that I was so long. Here's you all dressed and your hair done, and everything."

"Have I done dreadfully? You look—" She broke off, searching Agatha's solemn countenance with new anxiety. "What is it?"

"Raoul had a talk with the Captain last night, Miss Rachel." Agatha glanced to the connecting door and moved closer to say *sotto voce*, "The Captain said as Diccon hurt himself in England, and will not come for weeks—months perhaps."

"I feared something of the sort." Unconsciously gripping her hands, Rachel asked, "So Captain Tristram has taken his place, is that it?"

Her eyes very round, Agatha nodded. "Raoul says as they mean to help one another, and that you are not to worry."

"Oh! He never told the Captain—I mean . . . did they speak of—of me?"

"Didn't have time, by what he says, miss." The abigail's eyes softened. "But once he learns you want to go home, the Captain will arrange things, never you fear!"

Distraught, Rachel cried, "That is exactly what I *do* fear! Agatha, you must tell Raoul not to breathe one word to Captain Tristram that would lead him to think I—I am—" She paused, searching for a suitable word.

"Unhappy?" prompted Agatha. "But—miss, you *are*, poor soul! And worried out of your sweet wits besides, as if I wasn't to know! If you was to ask me, the Captain's come like the answer to our prayers!"

Rachel bit her lip and, abandoning pretence, said quietly, "I'll not have him risk his life to correct my foolish mistake."

"Oh—miss!" Agatha paled. "You never think—? Oh, my lor'! You're right! I never thought— But monseigneur would kill any man who tried to take you from him!" She gave a wail of fright. "Oh, help! Whatever is to become of us?"

With a confidence she was far from feeling, Rachel reached out to take the abigail's trembling hands. "We will go home, Agatha. I promise you. Somehow. But—not this way. Promise me you will tell Raoul."

Her eyes tearful, Agatha nodded. "I promise!"

Tristram reached the stableyard only a moment before Rachel. He turned when he heard her light steps and strode to meet her, hat in hand. "Good morning, Miss Rachel," and arming himself against her radiant beauty, said, "I hope you will forgive my appearance. The groom of the chambers does his best, but—" he shrugged wryly.

The bottle green jacket might not ideally complement the blue pantaloons, but Rachel saw him through the eyes of love and thought him superb. His whimsical grin made her heart turn over, and it was with a great effort that she merely nodded, walked past him, and called, "Raoul, would you assist me to mount?"

Tristram said nothing, and his face wooden, Raoul hastened to throw her into the saddle. Tristram mounted with a lithe swing that spoke of the cavalryman and deferred the lead to Rachel. She was silent as they rode down the hill, bearing gradually northward, nor did she utter more than simple commonplaces until they had left house, hill and gardens far behind, and were crossing rolling meadowland with not another soul in sight. Then, drawing her horse to a walk, she nerved herself and asked, "Tristram—why are you here?"

"I might ask you the same," he countered gravely.

"Surely you know the answer to that. I am come to visit my future home."

"And that is all?"

"I don't follow you."

"Do you not?" He rode closer, jaw set and eyes flashing. "For God's sake, Rachel! Don't fence with me. You must know what Sanguinet is!"

She lifted her brows, said a cool, "Of course," and could have wept because of the disgust that chased a momentary shock from his eyes.

"And—knowing the man is a rake, a libertine, a murderous and unscrupulous schemer," he said relentlessly, "knowing this, you yet would wed him?"

She felt lashed by his scorn and found it so hard to speak that her voice was a trifle shrill when she answered. "How very melodramatic you make it sound. Claude is not like that—to me. He has been a kind and generous gentleman."

"Indeed, ma'am? How odd that I'd formed the impression he is not a gentleman in any sense of the word. And that when first I arrived, I'd fancied you most eager to return home."

"Only because you said Justin was there! I mean—that has nothing to do with my marriage. I shall be wed very soon."

"In France?"

"What? Well, possibly." His eyes were so chill, so disdainful. As they should be, of course, but she was wouenedd despite herself, and began to panic. "*Very* possibly," she reiterated. "And I really do not see, Captain, by what right you question me."

"Your pardon." He gave a slight, mocking bow. "It merely appeared strange to me, for when I was at Strand Hall, Mrs. Hayward had no notion that your plans had so drastically changed." Watching her from under his lashes, he saw dismay flash across her face, and murmured, "But I imagine that you have by now advised your brother."

"Justin? Oh, is he really there?" Her hand came out with her old sweet impetuosity to grasp his sleeve; she asked eagerly, "Have you actually seen him, then? I thought it all a sham to get you here."

Despite himself, he could not restrain the hand that flashed to cover her own. "If you thought it a sham, and if there is no cause for melodrama, why did you aid my deception? You knew I was well recovered when we parted!"

"So it *was* a pose!" She drew away from the perilous delight of his touch. "Justin is not at Strand Hall. Claude will hear of it, and what he will do, I dare not think. You had best leave as soon as may be, and—"

"And you have not answered me," he said grimly.

"You know perfectly well that with Gerard looking, and thinking—" Flustered, she broke off. "As to aiding you—all I did was to name you Captain—which may very well be true, no?"

"No, ma'am. In point of fact, my rank is Colonel."

He spoke in his usual quiet drawl, but searching his face Rachel read confirmation there. Perhaps because she was desperately afraid and seemed so ringed about by the deep waters of insincerity and deception, the fear came that he too deceived her, and she shrank a little, whispering, "*Colonel?* Oh—who *are* you?"

"That, alas, is still denied me. But—why so fearful? Do you think I mean to thrust a spoke in the wheel of your betrothed?" He smiled thinly. "You would be perfectly correct."

"And you would be mad to attempt it!" Then, spurred by the sardonic glint in his eyes, she asked, "What do you mean to do?"

"Two things. Firstly, get into that top floor of his, and—"

"No! Oh, no! You *cannot!* The door to the upper flight of stairs is kept locked. Only Claude has the key. And besides, the servants are all about. It would be suicide!"

She had spoken too frantically. A curiosity crept into his eyes. "Why? I understood you to say I was being 'melodramatic.' " Her eyes dropped, and regarding her wistfully, he said in a softer tone, "How very kind in you to be so concerned. I knew somehow, after all that has passed between us, you could not—"

She had lost her poise and her pose and, aware of it, reacted too hastily. "You should also know, sir, that more has passed between my betrothed and me!" She realized belatedly how crude that sounded, and her cheeks flamed. An arrested expression came into Tristram's face and, knowing she had gone too far, she blundered on. "You—you go beyond the line, Captain. My personal affairs are—"

He transferred the reins to his left hand, reached out suddenly and seized her wrist in an iron grip, pulling her close to him. "There's a deal more at stake here than your personal affairs, my girl! But—by God—if I thought— Look at me!" Her wrist

195

was jerked relentlessly. "Now—tell me that you mean to become the bride of that treacherous, conniving little worm! Say it! Swear it!"

He was so close, so very dear. Everything faded save for those compelling dark eyes. Mesmerized by his nearness, yearning to submit to his mastery, she gasped faintly, "I . . . mean to—to wed that conniving little—"

"Hello! Hello, there!"

In their preoccupation with each other, neither had heard the hoofbeats, and both glanced, startled, to the approaching horseman.

Knowing she had all but ruined everything, Rachel gave a gasp of thankfulness.

Tristram, his scowl thunderous, released her, muttering, "Curse and confound the dainty creature!"

All unaware of his mixed reception, and fortunately still some distance off, Antoine Benét waved gaily and urged his mount to a trot.

Rachel, her gaze returning to Tristram's face, said, "Do not waste your time here. Go back to England, before Claude discovers you! There is nothing for you in Dinan."

"The devil there is not! I *shall* go back to England. You have only to say the word, and you and your sister will go with me! But—first, I'll have a look at that second floor!"

"But—I *told* you!" she said desperately. "You cannot even get to the stairs!"

"Right," he acknowledged, his voice very low. "So I mean to climb in from the outside." And, in a louder tone, "Good morning, Monsieur Benét."

"What a gallop!" the artist exclaimed jubilantly, rearranging a disturbed lock of his hair as his horse ambled to join them. "How glad I am that I was able to come up with you! Is this not fun?"

His gaze flickering from the artist's curly-brimmed beaver with its jaunty red feather, to the striped yellow waistcoat and the welter of fobs and seals, Tristram smiled. "I cannot imagine anything more amusing," he admitted.

Gerard was waiting in the stableyard when they returned, and he watched them dismount with a sly twinkle in his black eyes, then followed at a respectful distance. Walking to the house, Rachel attended Benét's vapid chatter with only half an ear. Her mind was still numbed by Tristram's perilous scheme. She began to feel like a caged bird, vainly beating her wings against impregnable bars, for no matter how she strove, the situation seemed to steadily worsen.

A lackey swung open the side door. Tristram's hand was upon Rachel's elbow, guiding her up the steps, that small courtesy so typical of him as to bring a blur of foolish tears to her eyes. She knew she was overwrought and walked a little faster in an effort to conceal her emotions. When Gerard called Benét aside, she did not pause, and Tristram escorted her into the house in silence. The wide expanse of the main hall opened before them.

A slender gentleman rose from a velvet soft, both hands extended. "Welcome home, my love," said Claude Sanguinet.

A moment or two later, Rachel's head stopped spinning, and she was able to focus upon Claude's gentle smile as Tristram bowed before him. She had introduced them somehow, her voice distant in her own ears. Her paralyzing sense of shock had apparently gone undetected, however. Tristram's bow held just the right amount of deference; Claude's was positively humble, following which he put out his hand, exclaiming in French, "Our gallant soldier! Gerard told me of your arrival. I cannot thank you enough for your intrepid defense of my betrothed and her friend. And you were already desperately wounded, I am told?"

Tristram had swiftly taken in every detail of this elegant individual. His age was indeterminate, though no effort had been spared to create an impression of youth. His figure was trim; artfully brushed locks fell across his brow; his voice was soft, his smile wide and welcoming. Yet Tristram had never met a man to whom he'd taken so instant an aversion, and he knew beyond doubting that this mild individual was very far from being what he seemed.

"You do me too much honour, monsieur," he murmured. "I merely chanced to be so fortunate as to render some small and very brief assistance."

"But for which assistance, my reckless—if well intentioned —lady must have been borne off before help could come. How grateful I am to be granted a chance to host you. Pray do not say that you mean to rush away. You *must* allow me the opportunity to in some small measure repay you."

"There is no need," said Tristram.

"I expect the Captain has other demands upon his time, Claude," Rachel put in. "We should not detain him."

Sanguinet smiled, and patted her hand. "Ah, but we should, my dear. Come, Captain Tristram—or must I have my men chain you, and keep you here as my captive guest?"

It was said so kindly, but Rachel felt sick, and for an instant the room dimmed before her eyes.

Tristram laughed easily. "Monsieur is all generosity. But I fear my wardrobe must disgrace so palatial an abode. You have already been more than kind, and my friend and I—"

"The friend. Ah, yes. We must not forget the so estimable friend. Mr. Devenish, is it not? And he has, I am told, a most unusual companion."

"A duck, sir. But if that annoys you . . ."

"Annoys me?" Claude slipped his free hand through Tristram's arm and, walking between them to the stairs, said warmly, "How could anything you do annoy me? I am eternally in your debt. As to clothes, your groom at chambers has already called in the tailor. He awaits you now, and by tomorrow your ball dress shall be ready."

"Tomorrow? Is that possible? I am scarce an easy fit, you know."

"True." Sanguinet's quizzing glass was upraised and swept his guest from boots to crown. "My, but you're a big fellow. Even so—I assure you, the problem is small compared to others we have—ah, dealt with. My people, you see, are hand-picked, and are highly—efficient. Now, you will, I beg, accept my apologies, but my steward has assembled a host of matters requiring my attention. I shall look forward to bettering my acquaintance with you at luncheon."

Tristram bowed, and Claude watched him speculatively as he started up the stairs. Turning to Rachel, he said, "My love, my love, you grow more beautiful each time I behold you! Yet—do I detect a certain—disquiet?"

"I am very glad you have returned," she answered in a low tone. "Gerard insisted Captain Tristram stay. I have tried to be polite, but—"

"But? My dear girl! The gentleman saved your life, no?"

"He was brave, I own. But we repaid him. Guy allowed him to be carried over to England on *La Hautemant*; he was funded and given clothes. Surely, that was sufficient?"

He laughed softly and, twining one of her curls about his finger, mused, "My funny little English girl. How quaint you are. Is there a price on one's life? Your so precious life, especially? His face is sadly marred, I admit. Does that give you a disgust of him? He must have been a well-enough looking fellow at one time, and certainly of gentle birth, for both speech and manners are impeccable. What so displeases you?"

Rachel sighed. "I cannot really say. Except—once, when he was delirious, he spoke of—murder!" She raised frightened eyes to his face. "I cannot but be uneasy in his presence. Claude, I wish you will send him away!"

"A murderer?" He glanced after the now vanished Tristram. "Why, how very interesting. I must certainly learn more of the fellow."

Rachel walked along the corridor with eyes blind to the sumptuous decor and a heart heavy with a sense of impending disaster. Tristram *must not* attempt that desperate assault on the second floor! He would surely be seen, and then— She shivered, trying not to believe what her instinct told her would happen, but she had a sudden mental picture of Gerard's acid smile and cold eyes; of the brutish faces of some of the guards. Dear God—it did not bear thinking of! And surely such things did not happen to ordinary people. But Claude was not an ordinary person. There were ghastly stories concerning British officers captured during the war. A spy would warrant even more savage treatment; especially any man daring to spy on a Sanguinet!

A lackey had flung open the door to her bedchamber, and here she stood, motionless in the corridor, like a total henwit! She murmured her thanks and hurried inside.

Her intention to sit by herself and try to think of a way out was abandoned at once, for from the *petit salon* came the sounds of weeping. Tossing hat, riding whip, and gloves onto the bed, she flew to open the connecting door. Agatha was the lady in distress, kneeling huddled beside Charity's chair while the girl bent forward, trying to comfort her.

"Good heavens!" cried Rachel, hurrying to them. "Whatever is wrong? Is it Raoul?"

"N-no, miss," wailed Agatha, apron to streaming eyes. "It's—it's—"

"It is me," said Charity sternly. "Rachel—were I able to stand, I would shake you! Hard!"

"What . . . on earth?"

"She made me tell," Agatha gulped damply. "M-Miss Charity tricked me, and—"

"And extracted the truth as to what has gone on all these weeks! Though it needed very little to confirm what I already suspected. Rachel—" Sudden tears swam into Charity's shadowed eyes. "Oh—Rachel! How *could* you? How could you think I could—could *bear* to know you had s-sacrificed yourself for—for me?"

"Dearest!" Rachel's own eyes filled. She leaned to embrace her sister, and they wept together, all three, until the ridiculous aspects of this scene striking her, Rachel sniffed, "What a . . . set of watering pots . . . we are!"

Drying her eyes, Agatha stood, and they all began to talk at once. Agatha, striving to justify her "betrayal"; Charity, confessing she had bullied the poor girl into it; and Rachel, assuring them she forgave them.

Clasping her sister's hand tightly, Charity said, "Come—sit here beside me. Now—promise me, darling: No more secrets, else you will make me feel my days are numbered!"

"I promise. And, oh, how wonderful to be able to unburden myself! Now," Rachel smiled mistily, "as proof of my reformation, I will tell you all that I know." She recounted a somewhat edited version of events, omitting only the depth of her fear of Claude. Her revelation of Tristram's plans brought a gasp from Charity, and a small scream from Agatha. "You see," she nodded gravely, "how hopeless it would be. It is not possible that the Colonel could gain entrance from the outside without being observed. And—and if the guards saw him—''

''My poor dear!'' Charity squeezed the hand she held. ''You must be utterly distraught.'' She extended her other hand to Agatha and, looking up from one to the other, said softly, ''We are three sensible women. Between us, surely, we can think of a scheme to help Colonel Tristram!''

Rachel said ruefully, ''You were not taken aback, were you, Charity? Have you suspected Claude all along?''

''No! Oh, no! Nor imagine me an ungrateful wretch, I beg you! But—but I'll own I have found it hard to quite like him. And, oh, forgive me, dearest, but—I always knew that whatever he did for me was not really out of affection. He found me, if anything, rather . . . contemptible.''

Rachel winced. ''I wish you had told me.''

''How could I, when he had been so good? And I could never be sure but that you truly nourished a deep fondness for him. He was such a support to you when Papa died. And—oh, is it not dreadful to feel so wretchedly guilty?''

''It is indeed the horns of a dilemma,'' Rachel admitted, with a sigh.

Agatha, whose expression had become increasingly irate, now put in vehemently, ''Horns is right! And on monsewer's head, was you to ask me! I'm sorry, Miss Rachel, but you hasn't seen him like us servants do! Nor the poor folks what work on his farms and estates. His brother's not as bad as he is, and they call *him* Monsewer Diabolique—did you know it? Parnell, I mean. Not Monsewer Guy. I got nothing 'gainst him.''

''Why, Agatha!'' Rachel exclaimed. ''I'd no idea you entertained so strong a dislike of monseigneur!''

''Dislike's a thin word, ma'am, when it comes to that one! By what my Raoul tells me, there's been many a good man killed what was in Monsewer Claude's path. Not straight out, you understand. But accidents-like. Carriages what goes and drives theirselves off of hillsides. Men just chancing to drop into pools and drown. Diplomatists driv to doing away with their poor sorry selves 'cause they was made to do what they knowed better'n to do! And—hands? Lor', Miss Rachel!

There's no serving maid in this chateau but what has blushed for liberties taken! I could carry on for an hour, I could!''

"Pray do not," said Rachel, pale and stricken. "Heaven forgive me! What have I brought you both into?"

"Nothing we cannot get out of," Charity asserted bravely. "Do not forget the ball on Saturday. There must be many guests who would not refuse a plea that we be removed from this house!"

Rachel thought that there would likely be not a one among the guests who did not have cause to fear the powerful Sanguinets, but she said only, "And on that same evening, everyone will be downstairs, in or near the ballroom, do you not think?"

"Never doubt it, ma'am," nodded Agatha. "There'll be good food a'plenty on all tables, and none of the servants far from getting their share."

Scanning her sister's thoughtful features intently, Charity asked, "What is it, love? Have you thought of some plan?"

Rachel drew a deep breath and leant forward conspiratorially. "Yes. A very desperate one, yet not I think, so desperate as the Colonel's scheme. But—I shall need your help . . ."

Claude Sanguinet was silent for a long time after Gerard had finished his report. Watching him as he leaned back in the chair behind the desk of this beautifully appointed study, Gerard wondered how it could be that so much power, so much driving ambition, could be contained in so insignificant a specimen. Were it the soldier, now, the nature of the beast might not seem so implausible. Still, Bonaparte was not a big man—nor, it was said, had been Caesar.

"Do you know," murmured Sanguinet, glancing up from the nail he pared delicately. "I am always touched to discover loyalty in my staff."

Gerard inclined his head with grave gratification.

"On the other hand," Sanguinet went on, "my pleasure is reduced does loyalty stem from a less—shall we say, noble?—impulse." He waved the small knife he held and smiled beneficently. "You follow me?"

With an unpleasant dryness of the mouth, Gerard said, "I am

not sure that I do, monseigneur. I thought I was acting in your best interests, and—"

"And yours, also?" Sanguinet resumed the care of his nails and, after a very quiet moment, observed, "Forgive, if memory serves me ill, but—was there not one Colette? A bewitching creature who brought enchantment to my nights a few years back?" A swift glance was directed at the stiffly immobile man before the desk. "When she ceased to—enchant, I gave her to you. Did I not?"

"You are unfailingly generous, monseigneur."

"Ah, well done! Still, do you know, I have forgot what became of the child. You did not wed her, I think?"

He knew. Damn him, he knew! Rage so consumed Gerard that he quivered with it, but his voice was even and colourless when he spoke. "She ran away, monseigneur."

"'So she did! How clumsy of me to resurrect so unsettling a memory. Indeed, it astounded me at the time that she could be so lacking in judgment as to choose a—what was the fellow?"

"A baker. Sir."

"A baker. To choose such, over yourself!" Sanguinet clicked his tongue. "Inexplicable."

A small pulse beginning to flicker beside his right eye, Gerard said, "His baking days are done, monseigneur."

"Yes. Such a pity. But—it grieves me, Gerard, to say so gauche a thing, but—however soon she ceases to enchant me, I shall not give away—my wife." And he leaned back, regarding his steward with a faint smile, the little knife waving gently back and forth.

"I—I do not take your meaning, monseigneur."

"I suspect that is because there is—nothing to . . . take, my dear Gerard. Still, I must try to be less obscure in my remarks. Now, as to our soldier—is he lover—or spy? I was at first surprised you had allowed him to stay. But you have done well. He is a worthy opponent, I think. I wonder what is his family? Do you know this?"

"No, sir."

"And, would-be Nabob, Justin Strand. Have you set about discovering his whereabouts?"

"I have, sir."

"How delightful." Claude smiled comfortably. "I think we may have a most pleasant week-end, Gerard. Most pleasant."

His face schooled to cool impassivity, Gerard reflected that the week-end would be so much more pleasant did he rid the world of the aristocratic savage behind the desk. On the other hand, Sanguinet paid so well. And when his plans were brought to fruition the rewards would be enormous.

Claude glanced up. Gerard smiled, bowed, and left him.

13

The great chandelier that hung above the dining table blazed with the light of its fifty candles; the crystal prisms sparkled like diamonds, and the mirrors lining both long walls reflected the luxurious room so that it seemed lit by a hundred rather than one chandelier. This being the small, or family, dining room, the table was a mere fifteen feet in length and, seated at its head, Claude smiled from Rachel at his right hand, to Tristram, at his left. "How gratifying this is," he said in his gentle way. "If you but knew, *Monsieur le Capitaine*, how I have yearned to meet the gentleman who rendered my lady so great a service." He bestowed an adoring smile on the quiet Rachel. "If only I might be of some equal service. For instance—to restore your lost memory. How vexing that must be. I heard that at the onset you scarce knew whether you were French or English, and indeed your French is better than that of many of my countrymen." With a whimsical arch of the brows, he asked, "Are you—*quite* sure upon which side you fought, sir?"

"I can be sure of nothing, actually," said Tristram, refusing the escargots the manservant offered. "I suspect I am English, however. I trust that does not distress monseigneur?"

"How can you say this? No, no. I am, *au contraire*, most fond of your—Perfidious Albion."

Claude rested a fond glance on his betrothed, but the glance that was slanted at him from further down the table was far from fond, seeing which Tristram tensed, and Antoine Benét, seated directly across from Devenish, simpered, "You should not use this term, my dear Claude. You have offended Monsieur Alain."

"No—but I am shattered!" cried Claude. "Monsieur will forgive me, I trust. I intended no offence."

Scarlet, as all eyes turned to him, Devenish stammered, "Not at all. I did not—I mean, I—"

"Ah, then it is our naughty Antoine." Claude's pained anxiety relaxed into a smile. "He is put out, do you know, because I have placed *Monsieur le Capitaine* in the place of honour. Now, never look so horrified, my dear Antoine. I am not displeased with you. Perhaps we may persuade Monsieur Devenish to pose for a portrait. That would placate you—no?"

Benét's dismay eased, and with an eager gleam brightening his weak eyes, he agreed, "It would delight me, cousin. But you mistake, do you suppose me in any way distressed by my position at table." He beamed across at Devenish. "Monsieur Alain—so French a name, is it not delicious?—*will* you sit for me? It is the dearest wish of my heart. To transfer such perfection of feature to canvas—ah, an artist's dream!" He cast his eyes ceiling-ward and placed one white hand upon his thin chest to express his rapture.

"Good . . . God!" muttered Devenish, squirming, and with his own eyes miserably fixed upon his plate.

"Regard me this, I implore you, *mes amis*," urged Benét, now fluttering his hand aloft to summon all attention. "Note the line of the nose—your head lift up, I entreat, Monsieur Alain. The chin—so firm and yet so shapely. The tender mouth, the—"

"Enough! Enough!" laughed Claude. "Our poor Devenish will quite murder you, Antoine. Oh! Your pardon, Captain Tristram! Again, I commit the *faux pas*!"

By not so much as the flicker of an eyelash did Tristram betray himself, but Devenish directed a startled look at him, seeing which, Claude's lazy smile widened.

"*Faux pas?*" Tristram repeated blankly. "But—how so, monsieur?"

"You must call me 'Claude.' And you must also please disregard my—bow drawn at random as it were. A clumsy attempt to prod your reluctant memory, my dear sir. And all apparently, to no avail. That such as yourself should be so afflicted is quite insupportable. I cannot and will not allow it to continue! No—do

206

not seek to dissuade me! My physician, Dr. Ulrich, arrives to-morrow, and I mean to insist that he examine you. He may have some—er, technique to jog your power of recall.''

Rachel smothered a gasp. Devenish was openly frowning at his host. Tristram thought, ''Why, you devious little weasel!'' and said aloud, ''There are no words to express my feelings, monseigneur.''

An appreciative gleam lit Claude's eyes, and he raised one hand in a slight gesture reminiscent of a fencer acknowledging a hit.

''Nor to express my impatience,'' struck in Antoine's affected falsetto. ''I am beside myself, fairly beside myself! Claude—I demand your aid! Intercede with this so splendid but atrociously shy Devenish! Upon canvas I must put—''

''But I am crushed,'' Rachel intervened, alarmed by the savage irritation in Devenish's taut features. ''You have not yet finished *my* portrait, Antoine!''

In the act of raising his wineglass, Claude checked for an instant. He set the glass down and, before Antoine could respond, asked, ''And do you like what you have seen of your portrait, my dear?''

''She has not seen it!'' Benét struck in, his eyes frightened. ''I did not let her go up there, Claude! You know I—''

''But—why ever not?'' Claude's tone was bland as ever, but watching him, Tristram saw a brief but quelling glare. ''Really, Antoine, you speak as though— Guy!'' He sprang to his feet, smiling warmly to the man who had wandered into the room only to halt, staring in astonishment at Tristram. ''Welcome, my dear brother!''

''What—in God's name . . . ?'' gasped Guy Sanguinet.

''Ah, yes. You are acquainted with *Monsieur le Capitaine*, so I am informed,'' Claude nodded.

''Yes. But—''

''I came with a message for Miss Strand,'' Tristram offered, coming to his feet.

''From her brother,'' Claude nodded. ''Do, pray be seated, Guy—I cannot have my poor guests inconvenienced. Ah, that is better. You doubtless saw Justin Strand, since you are newly arrived from England, eh?''

Those dread words seemed to Rachel to hang suspended upon the fragrant air. It appeared to her that even the flames of the candles ceased their flickering as she waited, like one frozen, for the inevitable denouement.

"*Oui*," said Guy, frowningly. "But I'd no notion he had seen you, soldier."

Rachel had to sink her nails into her palms to conceal her overwhelming relief. Devenish's jaw dropped ludicrously. Claude smiled his suave smile and was silent.

Inwardly astonished, Tristram said, "Just before I sailed. He is most anxious that his sisters go home at once." Despite his calm assurance, his brain was racing. Justin Strand had apparently been so accommodating as to return to England. Guy's narrow scrutiny, however, might well presage an accusation. It was all too likely that the man knew he'd not so much as laid eyes on Strand, in which case it might become necessary to fight his way out. His gaze flickered about the table. Benét would present no problem, and Claude was not the athletic type, though he probably had a derringer concealed somewhere about his person. Guy, while an innocent by comparison to his brother, presented the greater physical threat, and those two large footmen at the doors had the same hardness of eye that marked the guards. It would be a close-run thing, he acknowledged grimly, even with Dev siding him.

"Strand is naturally eager to see his sisters," Guy agreed. Tristram met his eyes in a level stare, and he went on, "Though you do not appear to be rushing them away, sir."

Wondering what this young Frenchman was about, Tristram shrugged. "Your brother was so kind as to press me to stay, though I have assured him there is no least obligation."

"Oh, he has," Claude confirmed. "Repeatedly. One might almost fancy him eager to leave us. But," he leaned to seize Tristram's shoulder and shake it jovially, "you must allow me, *mon Capitaine*, to be the best judge of how much I—ah, owe you." His smile flashed, then he transferred his attention to his brother. "Speaking of which, Guy, I have but now discovered that you were so thoughtful as to convey Captain Tristram to England aboard my yacht. I could wish you had written me of it, so that I might have sought him out sooner." Guy looked at him steadily, but said nothing, and Claude went on, "Miss Charity, are you well enough to sing for us? Did you know, Monsieur Devenish, that my brother is quite an accomplished musician?"

Devenish, feeling limp, admitted he was unaware of this fact since he had not as yet been privileged to meet Monsieur Guy. This omission having been corrected, the dinner proceeded without apparent incident. Of the eight people gathered about that beautifully set table however, only two were unaware of the deadly undercurrent to the pleasant conversation, and thus able to do justice to the excellent repast monseigneur's chef had created.

Throughout the interval during which the ladies waited in the oval drawing room for the arrival of the gentlemen, Madame Fleur chattered animatedly. Rachel, her nerves strung tight, helped Charity leaf through a collection of music that a wooden-faced footman had provided. When at last the gentlemen joined them, Rachel's searching gaze could discern no sign of tension. Claude rested one hand lightly upon his brother's shoulder, and they all were laughing at some remark Benét had made.

Two lackeys carried in a spinet, and the next hour passed quite charmingly. Guy proved to be a fine musician, even as Claude had claimed, and Charity's clear little voice, easily drowned by a less skilled accompanist, was flatteringly complemented by his music.

Never, in all Rachel's knowledge of him, had Claude been more attentive than he was that evening. His eyes constantly sought her out; his every concern was for her comfort, her enjoyment; he was very obviously the devoted and adoring lover. Yet, striving to respond suitably to this flattering behaviour, managing to appear shyly appreciative of it, Rachel's attention often wandered. Despite her firm resolve to banish all useless dreams, her bedevilled mind seemed of its own volition to constantly draw comparisons between the two men: Claude's full, well-shaped lips and the smile that endlessly hovered there, but never quite succeeded in warming the bland, blank eyes. Tristram, his wide mouth grave, but laughter twinkling in his eyes as he bent to answer a sally from the usually shy Charity. Claude, expounding with obvious and rather tiresome pride upon his chateau and the lands about it; Tristram, quietly ensuring that Madame Fleur was comfortably settled and a screen placed to shield her from a draught on this rather chill evening. And when Madame, who'd not known of Devenish's pet, heard Mrs. O'Crumbs mentioned and with knit brows strove to place "the lady" and was sure she not only knew her, but had made her come-out in the same year, it was to Tristram that Rachel's hilarious glance flashed, and his the laughing eyes that met her own and made her heart turn over.

When the refreshments were brought in at ten o'clock, Claude took Rachel by the hand and, with a conspiratorial wink and a murmur of apology to his guests, led her from the room. She avoided Tristram's cool gaze, her heart thundering with dread. If Claude meant to embrace her again, as he had in Sussex, how would she endure it? But endure she must—to all intents and purposes she was his affianced bride—he had every right to expect a kiss . . . or two.

A glorious lackey swung open the doors of a small salon—a place of crystal and gold and red velvet. They passed inside; the doors were softly closed, and they were alone.

"You cannot know how I missed you, *chérie*," Claude breathed, kissing her hand. "Without you, my world is *ennui*." His lips travelled to her wrist, and she could not repress a shudder. Claude's brown eyes seemed to take on a reddish hue. "So you feel it, too," he asked huskily. "How glad I am to find you not without passion, my little one. I had feared you were a cold Englishwoman, but—" He swung her to him, his arms proving much stronger than she would have dreamed. Fighting a sense of revulsion, she forced herself to compliance. Once again, his mouth was insatiable, and she was reminded of a greedy animal rather than a lover. She closed her mind to anything but the need to lull his suspicion and somehow bore with him until he released her.

She felt sickened and degraded and swayed a little, and from under his brows his eyes darted at her with so strange a look that she was terrified into gasping, "My! But you—quite take my breath away. How very strong you are."

210

She had struck the right note. Visibly pleased, he relaxed and, straightening his hair, even as she was doing, said, "I can see that I have won more of a woman than I'd dared to hope. Ah, but we shall have a happy time of it, you and I. Now—" He reached to an inner pocket. "Close your eyes and put out your hand, my love."

She obeyed. A ring was slipped onto her finger, and Claude murmured, "*Voilà!*—see what I have found for you."

Rachel looked down and saw a huge emerald, much too large for her small hand, glittering in the candlelight. "Oh . . . !" she faltered, "It is—superb! It—it must be worth a great deal."

"It once adorned the hand of an Empress." His eyes became remote and a queer little smile lit his eyes. Then, as though recollecting himself, he went on, "Come now, we must not keep our guests waiting, and besides, I know how you women love to show off such trinkets."

He bowed her from the room. Passing him, Rachel stepped into the hallway of a palace. The warm air was softly perfumed; she wore a gown that was a cloud of pale blue satin and gauze; upon her feet were jewelled slippers, and on her finger the emerald of an Empress. Countless women would have envied her. But all she prayed for was a safe escape for her love—and later, another escape, one that seemed as remote as it would be difficult.

"Of all the cockaleery, swivel-nosed courtcards!" raged Devenish, striding about the bedchamber and flinging out his arms in the excess of his fury. "Did you see the little worm, Tris? He wants to put me on canvas! *I'll* put him on canvas! Flat on his back! And I'll paint *him*! From head to foot! Blue—with red stripes—so that sensible folk will have time to get clear of his path! The beastly little fella's queer in his attic, I tell you!"

"Can you refer to our estimable artist?" asked Tristram, innocently.

"Estimable? He's a fribble is what he is. Hell and devil confound him! I yearn—I positively pant—"

"You do indeed, Dev." Tristram kicked off his pumps and, stretching out on the luxurious feather bed, folded his hands behind his head and mused, "Best slow down, old fellow, before you melt something."

Quiet as it was, that utterance sobered the agitated young man. He frowned at Tristram, crossed to the bed and, hands on hips, said bitterly, "I have suffered greatly at your hands, Colonel. But, by Jupiter! do you mean to subject me to posing for that toad-eating little twiddlepoop, you can—"

"I have no such intention. I doubt we'd have time, even if . . ." Tristram paused thoughtfully.

"Aye. Claude suspects, that's very plain. Oily snake! He is all that men say of him. When he looks at me with that gentle smile, I feel my backbone shiver. I vow I'd sooner be in a pit with a wild boar than rouse his ire!"

"Sorry, Dev. I don't have any wild boars about me. But I'm damned sure we shall rouse friend Claude's ire. One way or t'other."

"You mean to attempt the climb!" Devenish perched on the side of the bed. "When?"

"The night of the ball. I think we have until then. Raoul will find me a rope, and we'll smuggle it up here."

"Why? If you mean to come in from the tree, I would suppose—"

"It occurred to me, Dev, that we might be able to fashion a loop and swing it up so as to catch the gargoyle over the window above mine. I'm on the end of the south wing, and Claude's sanctum sanctorum is just above, had you realized? You've seen the gargoyles, of course—there's one over each window. Most convenient."

Devenish had not noticed such adornments but stared at his friend incredulously. "You'd risk your neck on so chancy a thing? What if the rope don't hold?" He stalked to the window and leaned out to peer anxiously at the gargoyle, jutting high above him. " 'T'would be devilish difficult to snag, and—" He drew back and called softly, "I regret to advise that there are mice feet all over your jolly scheme. Blow out the candles and come and see."

Tristram hastened to comply, then strode to the window. Heeding Devenish's warning that he take care, he pulled the curtain back slightly. Below, two guards sprawled on the lawn.

He could see the occasional red glows of cigars burning, and the moon's fitful light revealed a gleam of metal beside them.

"Blast!" he muttered.

"Happenstance, d'you think?"

"I doubt it."

"So do I. Jove! Look there! Crossbows!"

"Yes. They're relatively silent. Claude is taking no chance of our slipping away." His brow furrowed, Tristram turned back into the room. "I am perfectly sure he has sent men scurrying to Sussex to talk with Strand."

"But—why? I thought Guy backed your tale quite well."

"He did. But it is possible that Strand was not in England when I claim to have seen him."

"The deuce! Then—Guy would have known. And he certainly would have told Claude!"

"Perhaps not." Tristram wandered to the mantel and relit two candelabra. A muted "quack" greeted him, and he bent to stroke Mrs. O'Crumbs, who had settled herself in the grate. "He's a different stamp to his brothers, would you not say?"

"I'd not! Much of a muchness. There's bad blood there. Was you to ask me, Guy has already told Claude we are spies, and *that* is why we've the guards outside. We're virtual prisoners, my tulip."

"Oh, yes." Tristram stood, nodding. "We have been from the moment we arrived. But I disagree with you about Guy. So far, I believe Claude is not sure whether we are here purely because of my—my hopeless passion for Rachel. Or whether we pose some more sinister threat."

Noting the rueful grin, Devenish was silent. He was very sure that Tristram still cherished a hopeless passion for the beautiful Rachel Strand. What a perfectly ghastly coil for him! When Rachel had returned to the drawing room on Claude's arm this evening, with that valise-sized emerald flashing on her hand, he'd scarce dared look at Tristram. Had he himself been the man so tormented, had Yolande flaunted herself before him wearing so priceless a gift from a man she'd sold herself to, by George, but he'd have challenged the swine there and then! But old Tris was taking it like the sportsman he was. Not a whine, not a whimper. In point of fact, he looked downright— He gave a start, Tristram's faintly amused grin returned him to reality. "Oh—yes. Er, sinister threat, you said? Well, God save us all, does he suspect that, he'll snuff us both!"

"I agree. If his suspicions deepen, he'll call an end to it and discover as much as he can from us before we're disposed of."

It was a grim prospect. Devenish resumed his seat on the bed and lapsed into a brown study. Watching him, Tristram wished with all his heart that he had persuaded the man to return to England. He walked over to the bed and said remorsefully, "I've pulled you into a fine bog, have I not? My apologies."

The fair head swung upward. The blue eyes were fairly blazing with excitement. "To the contrary!" Devenish exclaimed. "I cannot thank you enough! I never got to the Peninsula, or even served with the Army of Occupation after Toulouse. But for you, I'd never in all my life have had the chance at such a hey-go-mad adventure! Tris!" He jumped up and began to pump Tristram's hand up and down. "You're a right one! True blue and bang up to the knocker—dashed if you ain't!"

Laughing into that beaming young face, Tristram said, "Cawker! I might have known I'd not get a logical reaction from you!"

"Most illogical," observed Claude Sanguinet. He had shed his evening wear in favour of a black satin dressing gown and, comfortably reposing upon a chaise longue in the *petit salon* next to his bedchamber, held up a glass of liqueur and watched the candlelight gleam through the green wine. "One does not 'forget' to mention such matters as the near abduction of a man's fiancée, and the spiriting away of her benefactor. I shall ask you again, dear my brother, why I was not informed."

Guy, still clad in his evening clothes, rested one shoulder against the mantel and answered coolly, "I considered the fellow had rendered us a service. Rachel suspected he was a criminal and sought in France, so I suggested we take him over to England. I'll own that in the stress of the moment I did not stop to consider that you might disapprove of a felon travelling aboard *La Hautemant*." He took a mouthful of wine and added dryly, "Such a radical departure from your usual—exclusive company of aristocratic cutthroats!"

214

Claude smiled at him over his glass. "Was this why you omitted all mention of the matter from your letter? You grow devious—dear Guy. Tell me now of Justin Strand. He really is in England?"

"Why, yes. Did not the soldier bring a message from—"

"I don't know. He says he did. Did he?"

"If you doubt it, why tolerate him?"

"Why, because he amuses me, of course. And Rachel regards him—ah—fondly, would you say?"

"No. I'd not thought that."

"Dear brother." Claude chuckled. "You are so predictable. How did you find things at The Towers?"

Deep within Guy's hazel eyes a wary light was born, but he said merely, "I was able to placate the local people. You should instruct your guards, Claude, to be less brutal with simple poachers. What you do in Dinan you cannot do in Chatham."

"Nonsense. Has one sufficient money one can do anything—anywhere. What of my Parnell and the lovely Annabelle?" His eyes danced. "Aha! I have but to mention her name and you are inflamed, *n'est-ce pas*?"

Guy flushed. "I might be less inflamed did Parnell treat her as his *ward*!"

"Instead of as a lover? Well, he is bewitched by the chit, and his blood hot, you cannot deny it."

"Oh, can I not!" Standing clear of the mantel Guy faced his brother squarely. "He has the blood of a snake and pursues Annebelle not from genuine affection, but lust. He has certainly not outrun the constable, and—"

"Outrun the—constable? But, what a very British expression. You become ever more Anglicized. I wonder why?" Guy's lips tightened but he said nothing and Claude mused, "Insofar as Annabelle is concerned, I have ofttimes wondered if the problem is not that—Parnell merely does what you yourself lack the initiative to do." He swung his legs from the chaise and stood stretching lazily. "I shall retire." He went toward his bedchamber.

Eyes bright with anger, Guy strode to catch his arm and wrench him to a halt. "Annabelle does not care for me in—in

215

that way. If she did, then—by heaven!—*no* man would stop me."

With a bored smile, Claude straightened his sleeve. "I would stop you, Guy. It is my intent that this irksome girl shall wed one of us. I myself am not so inclined. Parnell is, and can subdue her—unfortunate disposition. Thus, he shall become her bridegroom. Now, before you utter the impassioned speech that fairly chokes you, consider, I pray, how upset your dear *Grandmère* would be were I to drop a few—a very few words in her aged ear."

The high colour faded from Guy's face, leaving him very pale. For a space he stood utterly still and silent. Then he asked a clipped, "Is that all?" and set his glass upon the mantel, preparing to depart.

"I trust it is all. But—I will be explicit. I do not care to see a triangle develop in the matter of Annabelle. The situation is contained. You will therefore refrain from further interference with my little—machinations."

Guy said through his teeth, "Do not refine on that overmuch. Should your 'machinations' become as contemptible as they have in the case of poor Rachel, I may have no—" He stopped as a hand of iron clamped onto his wrist.

"I really must protest." Claude smiled. " 'Contemptible' —I find I cannot receive with equanimity."

"No? Yet you can entrap Rachel with equanimity. You and your pet surgeon." He tore free and with a curl of the lip, finished, "That is too rank for me!"

"But, of course. You were ever too squeamish to fight for what you desire."

"To the exclusion of all honour and decency? Yes, I thank God!"

Claude stiffened, but his voice as mild as ever, said, "Do you? How very curious. I, on the other hand, must be realistic. And now that this hulking Englishman has come upon the scene . . ."

"*Mon Dieu!* You truly are beneath contempt! You cannot win the girl by fair means, so you sink so low as to—"

Claude's hand moved very fast, and the sound of the blow was like a pistol-shot in the quiet room. Guy staggered back a

216

step, then stood with head down, breathing hard, one hand pressed to his face.

Eyes narrow slits, lips tight over near-closed teeth, Claude gritted, "Insolent whelp! How *dare* you! How dare you use such a tone to me? You—" And he stopped. His tightly clenched fists relaxed and the passion that contorted his features faded. He drew a long, deep breath, and murmured, "By heaven! You made me lose my temper, little bastard. I should have removed my ring, I see; my apologies."

Guy took out his handkerchief. An angry welt was bright on his face and blood trickled slowly from a cut across his cheekbone. His head lowered, he said nothing, but regarded his brother from under his brows.

Meeting that glare, Claude laughed softly. "Sometimes, my dear Guy—seldom, I admit—I entertain a little hope for you."

The rumble of wheels upon the drivepath woke Rachel, as it seemed, a very short time after she had at last fallen asleep. She lay drowsily through several moments of subdued turmoil, but the arrival of a second wagon broke through her consciousness sufficiently to remind her that today was the day of the ball. After the dinner party tonight, her own plan would be put into effect! Her eyes opened very wide and stared blindly at the silken canopy above her.

The door was softly opened, then light flooded the room as the window curtains were drawn. In another second the draperies of the great bed were parted, and Agatha's anxious face peered in at her.

"You're awake, Miss Rachel. Did you sleep, my poor soul? I could not close my eyes! Oh, miss—say you never mean to do it. Say you will not!"

"But I must, Agatha. Else the Colonel will certainly manage to get himself killed." She sat up and, as the abigail plumped the pillows behind her, said with forced lightness, "Well, I see the sun is out. The guests will be arriving soon. All will be chaos downstairs, I am sure."

"Like bedlam," Agatha agreed, placing the breakfast tray across her mistress's lap. "What with preparing all the guest rooms, and the two extra chefs already quarrelling, and that crawly Monsewer Gerard's nose into everything!''

''It will be a busy day for everyone,'' nodded Rachel. It was a day she had come to dread because for some reason this ball had loomed in her mind as the point beyond which her marriage to Claude was irrevocable. Now, it would, she prayed, mark Tristram's escape from the chateau. Later, somehow, she and Charity and Agatha would slip away. In a day or two—perhaps. She would not consider the alternative. . . . This morning, at least, she might be able to go for her ride. Agatha dispelled that hope, however, by informing her that Monsewer Claude was up and had requested she come to his study so soon as was convenient.

Resigned, Rachel donned her prettiest morning dress, a pale pink muslin with white velvet ribbons edging the puff sleeves and threaded through the low neckline. She went downstairs, knowing that she looked well, even if her heart was heavy as lead, and fear her constant companion.

In the study, Claude greeted her affably, but with no sign of the passion that so appalled her. Her hand was kissed, her cheek stroked in almost absent fashion, though her eyes seemed oddly intent. After assuring himself that his bride-to-be had enjoyed a refreshing night's rest, he took up a letter from his desk. ''Parnell,'' he murmured, ''asks that I convey his kindest regards to you. Unhappily, he will not be with us tonight. He is in Scotland.''

''How unfortunate,'' she said, while thinking this a happy circumstance. ''Is he hunting?'' And glancing from the letter he held, to his face, was taken aback by the intent stare he levelled at her.

For a moment he did not respond. Then, folding the letter carefully, he said, ''No. He is fishing. Regrettable, for I had hoped he would bring Annabelle.''

Rachel received an odd impression that she was on very thin ice, though why, she could not tell. ''What a pity. She is his ward, I understand. She was ill for a long time, was she not? And then abroad?''

He nodded. ''Her brother died in a coaching accident. Purest folly. But the girl was heart-broken and went into a decline.

218

Parnell sent her abroad, and she only recently returned. She has refused all invitations, however, and is now, in fact, staying at the Seminary where she received much of her education. I believe," he smiled at Rachel blandly, "you were a pupil there, also. Perhaps your friend—ah—the nun . . . ?"

"Sister Maria Evangeline?"

"Yes. Perhaps the lady told you something of Annabelle?"

Rachel knit her brows in genuine mystification. "No—I cannot recall she ever mentioned her. How odd. I wonder why she would not have spoken to me of her."

He shrugged. "It is of no importance. Now—many of the guests are expected by noon, and I must greet them. But not for the world would I deny you your morning outing, so you need not have donned that charming gown instead of your riding habit. I have asked Guy to escort you and your sister and our two British guests on a drive. My brother knows much of the history of the estate and can be quite entertaining, and I hope he may amuse Charity. Poor little child—it quite wrings my heart to see her so pale. The fresh air and sunshine will be good for her, do you not agree?"

"Yes, and it is most kind in you. But—surely I should be here with you?"

"And so you shall be—at luncheon, and this evening. I know how you enjoy your ride so—off with you, my dear. And never worry about Guy—he will be *enchanté*."

When the door closed behind his affianced, Claude leaned back in his chair, one hand propping his chin and a speculative light in his eyes. "You heard?" he asked.

Shotten emerged from behind an exquisite Coromandel screen in a corner of the room. "Yessir. Don't sound like she knows nothing."

"Hmmmn, perhaps my suspicions of the nun are unwarranted."

"Well, you wasn't wrong about that there soldier, sir. He's got an eye fer—"

"The man who did not find Miss Strand a lovely sight, would be an idiot, Shotten. If that is the Captain's only reason for being here, he presents a very small problem indeed. Meanwhile, however, I'll have him out of the way when Monteil and

Garvey arrive—I must warn them, just in case—'' He started as someone knocked on the door, and jerked his head to the screen. Shotten hurriedly retreated behind it, and Claude called, "*Entrez, s'il vous plaît.*"

Guy entered. He endured in silence an inspection of his cheek and expressions of remorse he knew to be as insincere as they were effusive. When he was next informed of his morning's duties, he appeared far from "*enchanté,*" for his dark brows twitched into a frown.

"You are displeased?" Claude observed mildly. "May one ask if you are greatly inconvenienced? I can require Gerard to do the pretty, if this is the case."

The idea of the acid Gerard "doing the pretty" drew a derisive snort from Guy. "I will go. But—one thing puzzles me. Why throw them together if you think him enamoured of her?"

"Because, my dear," smiled Claude, "you will be there to—er—safeguard my interests, and I should be *most* interested to learn of our Captain's behaviour towards my betrothed. Besides, I am a generous man. They may say their farewells in peace."

"What do you mean? Have you learned something?"

"It is merely that I prefer my affianced bride not be distressed—*before* our ball. Afterwards, when the guests are all gone, carrying with them the picture of my happy English lady, why—then—" He shrugged, his eyes taking on the red glow that had so frightened Rachel. "Then we will see the end of it."

"The end of what?" Guy watched his brother uneasily. "I'll not stand still for more murders, and so I warn you!"

"Then—ride, my boy. The curricle awaits, for the little invalid's sake. And our poor lover-like Captain must be chafing at the bit."

Frowning still, Guy moved to the door. "Incidentally," he said over his shoulder, "you are wrong about his rank. I once asked him, and he could not recall what it had been—save only that he was not a Captain."

Creeping out from his hiding place as the door closed, Shotten saw the scowl on the face of his employer and asked in his crude fashion, "Now wot's put the cat in wi' the chicks?"

"One can but marvel," said Claude caustically, "that my dim-witted kinsman did not into my bowl drop that *on dit* before this!"

"Wot, sir? About the soldier? It won't make no difference whether he was a Captain or a Lieutenant or dog's meat, when we've done wi' the perisher!"

"Fool! Have you not seen how the man carries himself ? The arrogance? The pride of bearing? Our soldier no Lieutenant was! If he is not a Captain, his rank is one or two steps above it. And if *this* is so, we play a more complex game than I had hoped. I fear, Shotten, that he a British spy may be—sent here from Whitehall!"

Shotten cursed. "And—if he is?"

"Alas," sighed Claude. "I will not the alternative have, eh? Before our gallant Englishman and his so charming friend—er, leave us, they must tell me all about it."

14

"*But*, *the temple and the pagoda*," said Charity, a becoming colour in her cheeks as she leaned forward on the seat of the curricle, "were they both constructed at the same time, Guy?"

"No. Several years apart, actually. The pagoda was designed by a Chinese scholar—the temple by a Greek. The whole was in the making for the better part of thirty years, and Claude still is improving it."

"And the pool beside the pagoda," Tristram put in, reining his horse closer to the curricle, "is bottomless, I'm told."

"Correct," said Guy, his mouth becoming grim.

Devenish retrieved Mrs. O'Crumbs from between Charity's feet and put her into the basket he'd borrowed for the purpose of taking his pet about. "A poor fellow tumbled in, eh?" he asked innocently.

"Two men, to my knowledge," Guy admitted.

"How horrid!" shuddered Charity. "Must we go there?"

"*Mais non!*" Guy turned on the driver's seat to smile back at her and ask kindly, "Where would you wish to go, little lady?"

"To the meadows where Rachel rode a day or so ago. Oh, how I should love to ride again."

"Then so you shall!" said Tristram. "Stop, if you please, monsieur."

The carriage halted. Tristram swung from the saddle, walked to Charity's side and reached up invitingly. She gave a little squeak of excitement.

Rachel gasped, "No! You must not! The doctor said—"

"Oh, *please*, Rachel!" cried Charity imploringly. "I should like it of all things! Please." Not waiting for a response, she leaned to Tristram, was swept up effortlessly, lifted to the saddle and settled there. Inwardly dismayed because she weighed so little, Tristram mounted behind her and, having put one strong arm firmly about her, asked, "Comfortable, Miss Charity?"

"Yes! Oh, yes! Oh—how splendid this is!"

She was not afraid, he realized admiringly. In spite of the accident that had crippled her, she was able to mount a horse without fear and trembling!

He touched his spurs lightly to his horse's sides. Nothing loath, the roan broke into an easy canter. Up the hill they went and down the far side, and were far across the rolling meadow before Tristram reined to a walk. "Forgive me," he smiled in response to the girl's cry of disappointment. "But—I deceived you, you know. I had reasons of my own for spiriting you away. Could we talk for a moment?" A wary light came into Charity's eyes. Seeing it, he took up her hand and pleaded, "Will you not trust me? I care only for your sister's happiness—and safety. If I could be assured she truly cares for Sanguinet, I would—" He stopped speaking, his lips tightening.

"You would give her up—whatever your own feelings?" prompted Charity.

He nodded glumly. "I'd have no other choice. Nor would I mind so much, if I knew she was happy. But—"

Her frail hand clasped his more firmly. She searched his eyes and saw such a depth of sorrow there that her mind was made up. "She is breaking her heart for you," she said recklessly.

Tristram gave a gasp, and the incredulous joy that lit his face brought a lump to her throat.

"Ma'am! Do you mean it? Are you quite—You must know my affections are—" He ceased this exuberant if disjointed utterance and burst out eagerly, "Oh, the devil! I love her, Miss Charity!"

"Yes. I know. And I believe your feelings are fully returned, sir."

"My lord!" Beaming, he said, "I'd begun to suspect she played a part, but— Ah!" a shadow touching his happiness, he asked, "She is here for England, then?"

"No. Not originally, at least. She is here for my sake. When Papa died, she swore to care for me, you see. And I have been an endless worry and a fearful expense. Dear Rachel struggled bravely to meet the bills, but it was a losing battle, When Claude offered, I suspect she thought her acceptance would ensure my future. But, now—Colonel, she strives to hide it, but she is so very unhappy, and longs to go home."

The weight of the world had lifted from Tristram's shoulders. Repressing the urge to cheer, he instead murmured, "Little idiot. Why did she not tell me?"

"Because she thinks there is no hope for you to get us away, and she knows you would try. She fears Monsieur Claude now, and dreads lest you should be hurt or—worse, in the attempt."

"Now, by God!" he breathed, his eyes shining. He raised Charity's hand and kissed it. "I am eternally in your debt, ma'am. You are not to fret, now. We'll come about and win safely free, never fear."

The curricle came up with them, and there was no chance for further confidences. Tristram, his world aglow, could scarcely keep his eyes from Rachel's lovely face, but he did not address her, remaining blissfully silent while Charity and Devenish chattered.

They reached a hilltop commanding a fine view of the surrounding countryside and the distant azure gleam that was the sea. The sky was cloudless; a cool breeze tossed the tall grasses and ruffled the leaves of the trees, and everywhere was a pastoral tranquility somewhat at odds with the inner thoughts of the riders. Guy drew the team to a halt. Devenish jumped from the curricle and set Mrs. O'Crumbs down where she might peck and forage about in the damp earth. Guy assisted Rachael to alight, and Tristram called Devenish over and guided Charity down to him. Then, dismounting with a lithe spring, he said, "Dev, engage Guy's attention for a minute."

"How the deuce am I to do that? And why?"

"Dolt! Just do it!"

Charity giggled. Abruptly comprehending, Devenish said, "Oh! Right you are, *mon* Colonel!" And carrying his fair burden to a sunny spot, called "Monsieur—could you give me a helping hand?"

Rachel, pulling a fur rug from the back of the curricle, was suddenly seized by two strong arms. "Your turn, m'dear,"

224

said a deep, beloved voice, and before she knew what was happening, she was perched on the roan's saddle and Tristram swinging up behind her. "My God!" she gasped. "Tristram! No!"

But already the roan was galloping away, Guy's startled shout ringing out behind them.

Her heart convulsing, she cried, "Oh! You are mad! Guy will tell Claude, and—"

"Be still!" growled Tristram, his lips brushing her ear.

"I shall not!" she cried tearfully. "Put me down this instant!"

For answer, he reined up on the far side of a copse of beeches, sprang from the saddle, and dragged her to him. "My valiant, idiotic, darling girl!" he murmured, his eyes adoring her.

"I am not!" sobbed Rachel, distraught. "I am—I mean—you must not—"

Tristram bent his head, Rachel's attempt to reason with him was foiled as one large hand reached up to seize her hair and pull her head back. He found her lips. There was nothing else, then. Nothing but his strength and nearness, the tenderness so different from Claude's greedy mouth, the wild thundering of her heart, the soaring joy that made her soul fly dizzily heavenward and blotted out all thought of caution or fear, leaving only the rapture—the prayer that this moment might never end.

But end it did. Limp, short of breath, her eyes still closed, she rested her cheek against his cravat, hearing the message of his rapidly beating heart, knowing that forever she was his, and revelling in that knowledge.

"My precious, beautiful, foolish sweetheart," Tristram sighed, kissing her hair. "How I worship you!" Rachel pulled away, her lips parting, and he put his hand across them, admonishing gravely, "No more fustian, love. It is much too late for that."

She knew it for truth and with a little moan of despair took refuge in his cravat once more. "I tried so hard!"

"Yes. And properly had me gammoned, you would-be martyr."

"Charity told you! Oh, how *could* she serve me so?"

"I think I knew before she told me. I looked into your eyes last night when you came into the room with that revolting man, and that enormous emerald blinding us all." He smiled fondly. "You glanced at me only once. But—poor girl, you looked as if you were drowning."

Her arms tightened about him. "I was," she sobbed. "I was! But—it didn't matter quite as dreadfully, because I thought—I thought you would—"

"Run away like a craven and leave you in this exquisite bedlam? Never!" He put one finger beneath her chin, tilting her head up. Her eyes were swimming with tears, but the smile she gave him was so full of love he was dizzied by it. For another moment he claimed her lips, then, briefly, clasped her tight and safe against him. "Now," he said, leading her to an upthrusting root and sitting beside her. "We have little time, love. *Will* Guy tell his brother I have abducted you?"

"I doubt it. He is a very good sort of man."

"I thought as much. What happened to his face? A disagreement with Claude?"

"Heavens! I never thought— He said he stumbled against the edge of the mantel!"

"Unlikely. And if that is how the land lies, we have one less worry. Now, tell me quickly, does Claude suspect that Dev and I are here for some other reason than because I love you?" His eyes smiled down into hers as he said the last three words, and he took up her hand and kissed it.

"Yes. Oh, my darling, I fear he does! I've seen him watching you with such a speculative expression. And Gerard would poison Claude against you even were there nothing between us—purely to revenge himself upon me."

"I see. Rachel—you understand that I must make a push to discover what Claude is about?"

"Of course, you are an officer."

"Even if I were not, I—" His eyes lowered and he said awkwardly, "Well, England is—England, d'you see? And—"

"And you," she murmured, "are—you."

Her reward for that lover-like observation left her with a strong suspicion that at least two of her ribs had been fused to her spine.

226

Recovering some degree of sense, Tristram said huskily, "It will be tonight or never."

"Yes. So I thought. With the house full of guests."

"Exactly. Everyone will be occupied, and no doubt the servants will claim their share of the celebration. I shall slip outside, and—"

"No—wait!" She clutched his lapel, looking up into his face tensely. "I have a better plan, my dear. I believe I can steal a key to the top floor."

He stiffened, fear for her seizing his heart with fingers of ice. "How?"

"Diccon told Raoul that Claude carries the key with him always, but he has another hidden in his bedchamber. Gerard uses it when Claude is away."

"And you know where to find it? Tell me! I'll not have you setting foot in that room!"

"Better I do so a thousand times than have you take so terrible a chance as to try and climb in from the tree!" She saw the stormy look in his eyes and went on desperately, "Dearest love—do not deny me this chance to help you to be of use to my dear country. Only think—were I discovered—"

"The devil! That's just what I *am* thinking! No, Rachel! I'll not have it! It's too risky!"

"But, Tristram—listen to me! If *I* were to be caught, I could always say I had come to ask him something. We—" Her eyes fell away from his daunting frown, and she blushed, and faltered, "We are, after all, engaged to be married. And—and however odd it might seem, it is not so beyond accepting as it would be were *you* to be discovered there! Once I have the key, I will find some way to get it to you. And then—" She trembled suddenly. "And then—die, every second that I wait!"

He held her close, appalled by her scheme, arguing against it, but knowing in his heart it was their best hope, and eventually agreeing to it only with the understanding that she not attempt it without letting him know. "We will have a signal," he argued stubbornly. "You can wear a shawl or feathers in your hair, or some such, and when you discard them, it will be our signal you mean to go upstairs. Dev or I will be alert then, and at the first sign of trouble, will come to you. And another

227

thing—" He took her by the shoulders, his face very stern. "I'll have your word you'll not attempt anything if that slippery rogue, Gerard, is near you! If I—" He broke off, looking sharply towards the sounds of approaching wheels. "Here they come! Your word, love! Or I'll not allow you to attempt it at all!"

He stood and pulled her to her feet, and she said quickly, "But—what shall we do if I do not have a chance to get up there?"

"Follow my original plan. By God, I think I'd sooner than have you—"

"No!" And glorying in his concern for her, in the love that shone so clearly in his steadfast eyes, in the wonder of having his strength to support and cherish her, she breathed, "I swear, my Tristram. I swear."

Luncheon was served alfresco, a long table having been set up on the terrace. It was a pleasant meal, for several of the guests had already arrived and they constituted a distinguished gathering. There were three highly placed diplomats from Belgium, France, and Holland; a German General; an Italian Count and his Countess; a renowned and eccentric inventor who was related to Claude in some way, and who escorted an extremely well-endowed lady of middle age whom he persisted in introducing as his "aunt"; a French Chevalier with a bitter mouth and brooding eyes, also related to Claude; and a Swiss gentleman named Monteil, quiet of manner, with dark, watchful eyes, who exuded wealth, and who was, Guy imparted to Devenish, "in munitions."

Tristram made not the slightest attempt to communicate with Rachel and, when he was able to decently excuse himself, returned to his bedchamber with Devenish to discuss plans for the night ahead. Devenish was afire with enthusiasm. Once they had the key, he felt it would be less than no time before they were on their way home to England, for they'd soon discover all Claude's secrets, and be off.

"With the girls," said Tristram.

"Of course!"

"How?"

228

Devenish stared at him. "What?"

"I wish you will tell me, for I've wracked my brains and—short of stealing the carriage of one of the other guests, and hiding the girls under the seats—I cannot come at an answer!"

"Oh. Well—that's it! That's just what we shall do!"

"Right under the noses of all the grooms and guards—to say nothing of the coachmen and grooms of the guests!"

Devenish looked stunned, but fortunately was not obliged to provide an alternative suggestion, since the groom of the chambers arrived with their ball clothes. True to his promise, the tailor had completed Tristram's attire and done a most creditable job. Devenish grumbled that his own pantaloons were so loose he "could conceal a crossbow in the dratted things!" But although Tristram assured him that were they any tighter he would be unable to sit down, he was not reassured. When the groom left them, he confessed he was worried about Mrs. O'Crumbs. "I wish I could take her down with me," he said, locating the duck asleep in a half-opened drawer. "If we've got to run for it, I'll not abandon her, Tris. They'd have her for dinner tomorrow!"

"With all our lives at stake, and England's security in jeopardy," Tristram said in mild exasperation, "all you can think of is that bird!"

"She is my pet!" Devenish bristled. "And I'll take leave to remind you, Colonel, that were it not for the dear little soul, my cousin would not have allowed you on board *Ma Fille*—and *then* where would you be?"

Tristram laughed, bowed, and acknowledged, "True. You have my humble apology." He stroked the duck's motley feathers while the "dear little soul" eyed him with hostility. "Very well. Take her down to Raoul—or better, ask Agatha to take her down there for you. You'd likely have a better chance to collect her from the stables."

"Good thought, old fellow. Agatha can slip her down the servants' stairs at the back." He scratched Mrs. O'Crumbs' neck, and she swung her head to gaze up at him with what must only be complete devotion. "Silly old lady," he murmured fondly, "did you think Alain meant to abandon you in this nest of vipers?"

Tristram shook his head wonderingly. "Look at her doting expression! By Jove! One would swear she understood every word you said!"

"Perhaps she does. I'll tell you one thing, Tris. Most folks don't talk to their animals. And the more you do talk to them, the more you'll find they respond. Which reminds me—I wonder what you'll find up on Claude's sacrosanct top floor. How I should love to go with you. Are you quite sure—"

"Quite sure," said Tristram firmly. "I need a rearguard, Dev. I'd not dare venture up there, did I not know you were guarding my back. The one thing I ask, above all others, is that should I be caught, you'll do all you can to get the girls away—even if it means slipping away yourself so as to return with help. I'm quite sure I do not need to ask that, however."

Devenish's indignant expression eased to a grin. "Good. For you don't. And it appears to me, friend, you jump the wrong hedge—our first concern is to get you up those stairs without four or five of Claude's trained herd following you. You ain't exactly the type can slip past unnoticed, y'know."

"True. My best chance will be to get to the back stairs. To do that I'll need a diversion. And you, my friend, have been placed in charge of Diversions!"

By eight o'clock, when they were to gather for a light supper, the great house hummed with chatter, the rustle of silks and satins and taffetas, and the click of high heels that occasionally wandered from the carpets. The air was sweet with fragrance, for flowers were everywhere. On the stairs, Tristram and Devenish encountered a charming group composed of a French nobleman, his wife and their two marriageable daughters. The girls were shy and their parents gracious, but there was a trace of strain about Monsieur le Comte, and his Comtesse looked nervous and unhappy. Unwilling guests, thought Tristram, and wondered what hold Claude had on the gentleman, and how many of the guests would be here tonight were it a matter of choice.

A touch on his elbow alerted him to the presence of Guy Sanguinet, and he dropped back to walk with him. Despite cosmetics, the cut on Guy's face was still visible, and he seemed subdued, his sombre gaze flickering over Tristram's snowy cravat, the plain jacket that set off the broad shoulders to admiration, and the knee breeches that fit like a second skin over the well-shaped legs. "For your own sake, monsieur," he said softly, "I could wish you did not look so well."

"Your brother's tailor is most skilled. And I believe I owe you my thanks, sir. I gather you have not informed Claude of my—er—escapade with Miss Strand this morning."

Guy looked at him steadily. "I would not advise you to repeat it, Captain. Further, I would suggest you leave here—at your very *earliest* opportunity! Ah, Madame Aunt—how pretty you are. May we escort you?"

The white and gold drawing room, itself a thing of beauty, was the more lovely now by reason of the colourful gowns of the ladies; the pastel shades worn by the unmarried girls enriched here and there by the brighter hues of the matrons' gowns, and the purples and blacks of the dowagers. The arrival of the three young bachelors created quite a stir, many coy glances coming their way, while fans fluttered and whispered comments were exchanged. Tristram saw nothing of this, however, his eyes flashing to Claude, elegant as usual, escorting a vision in a very simple, Grecian style ball dress of cream silk, the bodice crossed with bands of blue French beads beneath which the skirt fell in a long flowing line of voluminous yet clinging fabric. The great emerald glittered against Rachel's ungloved hand, but no brighter than her eyes tonight. Entranced, he thought that no other lady could possibly be more beautiful.

"Jupiter!" muttered Devenish. "What the deuce is *he* doing here?"

Wrenching his eyes from his love, Tristram was in time to see a slender man across the room, in the act of turning away. "Who is he?"

"Garvey. See there? The curly-haired dark Dandy, wearing the red jacket."

"So that's the famous James Garvey. Friend of Prinny's, isn't he?"

"Yes. And a deuced rum customer, so I've heard. He was

staring at you damn near goggle-eyed, Tris. I'll warrant he knows you!''

"Jove! Then I shall have to have a word with him."

This ambition was destined to be thwarted, temporarily at least, when the dinner gong was sounded and Claude, with Rachel on his arm, led his guests to the dining room.

The dinner was both light and delightful. The conversation was bright and witty, the room a picture of elegance. Concentrating politely upon the remarks of the ladies to his left and right, Tristram was conscious always of Rachel's beauty, and of the benign affability that cloaked Claude Sanguinet. Farther down the table, Devenish was doing his best to ignore Antoine Benét, seated directly opposite, and so ill mannered as to try to engage him in conversation across the table. Charity was not present and, since he knew she was in the habit of coming down for dinner, Tristram wondered rather anxiously if her ride had overtired her.

Seated beside Claude, Rachel had to fight her eyes away from Tristram, but all through her dutiful attention to her betrothed, her thoughts were with her love. The knowledge of what might lie ahead brought a cold dampness to her palms and a trembling she was able to control only by reminding herself that he loved her, that whatever was to be faced, they would face together.

When the time came to leave the gentlemen to their brandy and cigars, her heart began to beat erratically. Soon now—very soon, she must play her part in their scheme. If only she had been able to warn Tristram of her change in plans, but this way was better—she was sure. In the drawing room her acceptance by the other ladies was the same as she had been accorded at luncheon. To her face they were polite, gushing, and slightly condescending. Were she to catch them unawares, however, they were whispering behind their fans, or giggling together, their sidelong glances obviously directed at her. Such behaviour, which once would have hurt her, she found laughable. Their barbs could not so much as touch her, for she was quite secure now. She belonged to a true gentleman and none of these posturing, frightened people who came to pay homage to the man who owned them could arouse any other than a feeling of pity.

A formidable, purple-clad dowager was favouring her with a description of "Dear Claude's" hotel in Paris when Agatha edged into the room and beckoned shyly. Excusing herself, Rachel went to the obviously agitated abigail.

"Have I come at the right time, ma'am?" Agatha whispered, clasping her hands tragically. "Oh, do I seem proper cast down with despair?"

"You do," murmured Rachel. "But not *too* cast down, dear Agatha. My sister is ill—not expiring!" She nodded, patted Agatha's hand, and sent her off. Returning to Madame Fleur, she explained softly that Charity was become unwell. She must go upstairs for a little while, but would doubtless be down again before the gentlemen joined them.

"No, my love." Madame started up determinedly from her chair. "I will go. You are the guest of honour, and Claude would expect that I help."

"You are so kind," Rachel smiled gratefully. "And I doubt it is contagious after all."

Madame paled and sat back again. "Con . . . tagious . . . ?"

"Just a rash, I don't doubt. Now, ma'am, have no fears, I shall say nothing. You know how people tend to panic if they hear of anyone throwing out a spot or two—as though scarlet fever was inevitable. Charity has been a little sick, poor darling, but—"

"Oh, my!" gasped Madame. "If I could but get out of this ridiculous chair! But I suppose she would be more comfortable with you beside her, poor child. Dr. Ulrich should have been here long since, wretched man! I shall send him upstairs directly he arrives."

A moment later, hurrying up the grand sweep of the staircase, Rachel was watched by only two lackeys hovering beside the front doors and knew she had timed this well; the servants were enjoying their own feast below stairs.

She ran into the bedchamber and embraced Charity, who lay in bed propped with pillows, reading Cowper. Her sister's hands were very cold and, peering into that thin, pale face, Rachel said, "Do not worry so, love. Everyone is safely occupied. Madame means to send Dr. Ulrich to you when he reaches here. You must tell him—"

"Yes, yes. Never fear, I know how to be the invalid. Go now—I shall not breathe easy until you are come back safely!"

Rachel left at once. The hall was empty. From downstairs drifted a few faint strains of music as the orchestra rehearsed a tune for the ball that would commence in a little over an hour. She hurried along and around the corner into the south wing. There were rooms on each side for a way, and far at the end, the large door across the hall that led to the master suite. Her mouth was dry suddenly, and her breathing fast and shallow. The door seemed to fly towards her. Suppose it was locked? And good heavens! Why had she not thought of that possibility? She sped on and at last stood before that fateful door, her knees trembling with the fear that someone behind her was watching. She threw a terrified glance over her shoulder, but the hall stretched away, luxurious, serene, and unoccupied. Her scratches and then a bold knock brought no response and with a fluttering gasp of relief she turned the handle of the door. It opened soundlessly. She went inside, and seeing no one, closed the door and leaned back against it, breath seeming to elude her.

She stood in a sumptuous parlour. The walls were hung with a glossy black paper upon which red lions, rampant, alternated with red *fleurs de lis*, and here and there a golden crown. The furniture was just as impressive: a huge desk with red leather chair, teakwood bookcases and chests, several red armchairs, and thick black carpets. Two lamps were lighted, their wicks turned low, the red glass shades creating rich pools of brightness in the dramatic room. Rachel ran to the fireplace. Raoul had said the hidden compartment was opened by turning a rosette in the mantel carving, but *this* mantel was not carven, being instead a sweep of white marble ingrained here and there with red. The fireplace to which Raoul had referred must be in the bedchamber. Gathering her courage, Rachel moved towards a door at the left and leaned her ear against it. What if she opened it to find herself face to face with Claude's valet? She scratched softly and waited, scarcely daring to breathe, her ears straining, but she could detect no sound and she opened the door cautiously. Another majestic room still in the prevailing

234

black and red, stretched before her. The main piece of furniture was a great bed with rich curtains of crimson velvet tied back to reveal a crimson velvet eiderdown with long black tassels at the corners. Her awed glance travelled from a large brass lion, rampant, hanging on the wall at the head of the bed, to the winged chairs on each side of the fireplace wherein the fire was laid, but not yet lit. The mantel was old and elaborately carven, and again, above it was a splendid wood carving of a rampant lion, a crowned lion, the gems in the crown looking very real, as they probably were. That carving alone, thought Rachel, must be worth a king's ransom! The fireplace was enormous, and the mantel therefore very wide, the entire length of it rich with flowers and leaves and twining branches. There were at least a dozen rosettes, but she decided to start with those at each end. She twisted, pulled, and pushed the one on the left, to no avail, and hurried to the right end. At her second twist her foot slipped off the extended hearth and as she instinctively clung to the rosette it swung back and to her unspeakable relief revealed a small aperture in which were two little boxes and a key. She snatched up the key, but curiosity overcame her and she picked up one of the boxes. It was a miniature chest, leather bound and edged with gilt. She opened it and discovered another key. This one was very large and looked extremely old, the stem being wrought into the shape of a thistle. Certainly, it was not the key she sought, and to stand here poking about like a mutton-head, as Justin would say, was reckless in the extreme. She replaced the box, closed the secret door, and turned around.

She gave a small scream. The key fell from her suddenly nerveless fingers, as she shrank back against the fireplace, half fainting from shock.

One of the wing chairs was not empty! A man sat there, half hidden by the dimness, silent and unmoving. Panting and sick, Rachel swayed before him, waiting for him to get up and strike her, or curse her.

"Please," she implored weakly. "I—have no—no excuse to—"

And she stopped, hope beginning to reawaken. He was so still . . . She crept forward a pace, peering. It was Dr. Ulrich!

235

A half-empty glass sagged in one limp hand, and his breathing was soft and rhythmical. He was fast asleep!

She felt limp with relief, and threw up one hand to stifle the joyous sob that rose to her lips. Then, retrieving the key, she started for the door.

Her fingers had grasped the handle when the line of light beneath the door brightened and she heard the outer door close. With a choke of horror, she spun round. Where could she hide? If she crouched on this side of the bed, the newcomer would see her directly he opened the door. If she hid on the far side, the doctor would see her when he awoke! Frantic, she raced to the bed, knelt, and rolled underneath. She had no sooner ceased to move than she saw a man's legs go past.

Claude's voice sneered, "So here you are! Drinking yourself into a stupor, as usual? It will not help your conscience—if you have one."

Blinking away tears of fright, Rachel thought frantically, Suppose he had come for the key? Suppose he found her? She could not say she had come to talk with him—and waited under the bed!

Ulrich yawned and, stretching, answered, "Save your vitriol for your poor brother, *mein* Claude."

"What the devil d'you mean by that? I am very generous to Guy."

"Generous mit your fist, eh? I see him ven in I come."

"And so you naturally assume I struck him!" Claude sounded wounded.

"*Ach!* My apologies! It vas Miss Charity—no doubt?"

"If you must have it, Herr High-Principled Physician—my so admirable brother had the temerity to object to your—ah, treatment of that very lady. It became necessary that I remind him he is in no position to object to anything I do."

Ulrich clicked his tongue. "For shame! Iss not enough you must all of his life blackmail the boy? You now strike him? You should haf take off your ring, *mein* Claude—at the least."

"Yes, I'll own that. Still, it is of no great moment. Ulrich, I have an unexpected guest I am in hopes you may identify. He calls himself Captain Tristram, but is I suspect a British officer of a higher rank than Captain. You may have seen him about Whitehall. He is a tall fellow, and—"

"Und that alone is enough to make you hate him, *ja*, Claude?" Ulrich chuckled. "Vell, I haf seen him. I look into your dining room and see that pious hypocrite Monteil at work! *Mein Gott!* He haf look his long nose down at *me* and ven I think of the lives vot *he* has— Ach, enough! I up here came, und your chef, he send me food. Your Captain I know not, but—he is a fine big fellow, I think."

"If one is an admirer of such great clods," Claude acknowledged scornfully. "He will look less fine when I've done with him! I must learn why he is here. It is not for the girl, of that I am certain."

"Vot is this?" Ulrich shifted in obvious alarm. "You think he vos from Vitehall sent? If vord of your plan reaches that dummkopf of a Regent . . . !"

"Any words our 'fine big fellow' speaks, dear friend, will be for my ears alone. After which his last words will be silenced by the Pagoda Pool!"

Rachel closed her eyes, wondering how she could ever have been so blind as to imagine this murderous individual a kindly gentleman.

"Now, why," purred Claude, "do you look so squeamish? Of what account are the deaths of two adventurers when set against my cause?"

"Bonaparte had a cause," the doctor said sombrely, "and dead were t'ousand upon t'ousand."

"Console yourself. Your only task is to attend our dainty Charity. You thoroughly bungled last time, Ulrich. You must do better. I do not tolerate bunglers."

"Vas is das 'bungle'?" the doctor demanded huffily. "The girl suffer a setback, haf she not?"

Rachel caught her breath, her horrified eyes opening very wide.

"Too brief of a setback," Claude criticized. "Gerard tells me that our intrepid Englishman took her up onto his saddle today. At that rate she will be walking within the week. And *that*—I cannot have!"

"Vy not? You are good as ved!"

"Perhaps. I could have compelled Rachel to marry me long before this. But always, my dear Ulrich, there is the crude way and the shrewd way. If at all possible I prefer to do the thing in style and without the irritation of a reluctant bride. Unfortunately, I am meanwhile at the mercy of any whim the chit may take into her lovely head. She is grateful to me—but not, I fear, deep in love. Were her sister to effect a miraculous recovery, I am not at all sure . . ."

"You haf seriously think she vould give up this—palace? Your vealth und power, und position? *Ach*!—not likely!"

"Not for some. But she is the kind of simpleton would prefer love and a cottage. Bourgeois nonsense."

The doctor grunted. "If she is der simpleton, vy choose her?"

It was a question Rachel had pondered many times, though not in just that way, and she waited for Claude's reply.

"She is English," he answered slowly, "and well born. She has no self-righteous Mama to warn me off, her brother is come home too late to interfere, and her father, fool that he was, not only blackened the family name, but conveniently ruined them, with very little help from me. When the debts are paid she will be socially acceptable once more. And I shall be the more palatable to the populace with a British wife. Besides—she is very beautiful and has a touch more spirit than I had suspected. She may amuse me for a while."

"*Ja*. This I understand. Better to keep her in need of my expensive services, eh?"

"Much better. Go and minister to your patient, noble healer. And see that this time she remains ill for long enough that she will be unable to journey to England. It will provide me a fine excuse to have the wedding conducted here. I've no wish to cross swords with Justin Strand at this moment."

"Nor can he do this. Der boy iss laid down upon his bed mit malaria, I hear, and in no condition to argue mit no vun!"

"Excellent! I must return to my guests." There was the sound of chairs scraping back, then Claude said, "Oh—one other small matter. Have you, in your bag there, something to relieve my so valiant brother's mind of its worries for a while?"

"*Himmel!* You vish Guy to be ill also?"

"Say rather, I wish him at rest. Oh, never look so horrified, my good fool! Temporarily, only."

"This I understand not! I vould think your brother you keep at your side just in the case of troubles."

"Were I dealing with Parnell, you would be very right. Guy, Herr Doctor, is another matter. I am not at all sure just where his sympathies lie. Someday," Claude's voice became an introspective murmur, "someday, I may find it necessary to—ah—remove him. Permanently." He added briskly, "But for now, a potion, perhaps? Something sufficient to cause him to retreat to his bed until morning?"

Appalled, Rachel heard the fasteners on the doctor's bag snap, followed by a rattling of tins and bottles.

"Here," Ulrich grunted. "Vun of these drops in his vine. *Vun only*, mind! *Mein* Claude, you would the Borgias put to shame!"

Sanguinet chuckled. "*Merci*. Now, off with you. And stay with the girl."

They walked past the bed, the door opened and closed, and a moment later Rachel heard the click of the outer door. And she did not move—she *could* not move, she was so numbed by the savagery she had overheard. How could *any* man be so base as to condemn a lovely young girl to the life of a helpless invalid, purely to entrap her sister into marriage? Dr. Ulrich had been employed to win her gratitude by performing the operation but then had seen to it that Charity made no further progress. "Oh! How vile!" she whispered, her eyes smarting with tears of rage. The memory of the long months of anxiety; of these past few weeks of heartbreak; the thought of Justin, ill and worrying; the knowledge that there was nothing she could do to warn Guy, of whom she had become so fond, conspired to infuriate her further. But even as she lay here, seething, Dr. Ulrich was with her Charity! She scrambled out from beneath the bed. Stepping quickly to the door, she was heartened by one realization: she had no need to indulge one further qualm of guilt for the sake of Claude Sanguinet!

Dr. Ulrich straightened from examining his patient and glanced up when Rachel hurried into the bedchamber. His broad face was flushed, and the watery blue eyes had a slightly glazed look. He was a tall man who had allowed middle age to impair his waistline severely, but he was not impervious to beauty, and the sight of Rachel in her ball gown brought a beaming grin and a hurried attempt to tidy his thinning grey hair. "Vy, how pretty it is you haf look, *mein fraulein*," he said.

His speech was slurred, and Rachel apprehended that he was more drunk than she had thought. Strengthened by her blazing anger, she gave him a bright smile and advanced, putting out her hand. "How do you do, doctor? And how fortunate you are come, since my sister has been rather out of sorts."

She withdrew her hand from his moist clasp and, stepping closer to the bed, winked in response to Charity's searching look. "How do you go on, dearest? I hope you are not still being silly about taking whatever medicine Dr. Ulrich thinks best for you." She gazed intently into her sister's puzzled eyes and tightened her grip warningly on Charity's wrist.

"Eh? eh?" the doctor said with a jovial grin. "You haf not fear your old friend, haf you, *mein* Charity? *Ach*—just a spoonful of my potion und you vill be better in less than . . . less . . ." He concentrated owlishly on the spoon he held waveringly over a tumbler of water. "Do not," he said drawing back and blinking at his unsteady hand, "haf fears, little vun, that it vill leave the bad taste in your pretty mouth. It haf no . . . taste at all."

Rachel, meanwhile, was striving to convey by means of grimaces that Charity must rebel. At first utterly bewildered, her sister now said rather feebly, "Oh, no—must I?" And seeing Rachel's delighted look, emitted a screeching, "Well, I won't! I won't!"

Astonished by such uncharacteristic behaviour, the doctor looked up, and Rachel chose that moment to stagger back as though Charity had struggled with her. She collided with Ulrich. The spoon fell, but he retained his hold on the bottle. Her profuse apologies were met with a knowing chuckle, the remark that the doctor had dealt with far more difficult patients, and that she was to have no fears, he knew exactly how to proceed.

Rachel had prayed to dislodge the bottle from his hand, and as Ulrich took up his wineglass she waited her chance to sabotage the medicine bottle. She was again thwarted, however, for he kept tight hold of it. Desperate, she signalled behind her back, and as Charity, dutiful, if mystified, let out another shriek and appeared about to have a spasm, Rachel said, "Doctor, how can I express my mortification? You have been so good. Why she should behave in such a way is beyond my understanding. Poor man, you look tired. Will you not sit and rest for a moment?" She lowered her voice to a half-whisper. "Allow me to try my hand with the medicine. I can soothe her, I feel sure. Agatha—would you please bring over that large chair for Dr. Ulrich?"

"No, no!" Ulrich set down the bottle and proceeded rather erratically to the chair Agatha was attempting to lift. "I am stronger than you, my dear. I vill do it."

Rachel seized her chance and snatched up the medicine bottle. Her original intention to drop it had been succeeded by a more diabolical plan, and she instead poured a goodly amount into the doctor's wine. Taking up the spoon, she whirled to Charity, calling over her shoulder, "One teaspoonful, doctor? Come now—no nonsense, Charity."

"No. Better it should be . . . two," he puffed, struggling with the chair. "I do not care for my little vun so pale the face to have!"

"You wicked old villain!" thought Rachel, and cajoled, "Open wide, dearest." Effectively blocking Ulrich's view, she said, "That's a good girl!" She turned, proclaiming, "All finished, doctor. Now I really must go downstairs. Perhaps you could stay here for just a little while? I shall have some more wine sent up."

Predictably enough, he offered no objection to this plan. Rachel kissed Charity and then hastened into her own bedchamber, motioning to Agatha to follow. The instant the door closed, she threw her arms about the abigail. "I have it! I *have* it!" she exulted, holding up the key.

"Oh, praise God!" cried Agatha, clasping her hands joyously. "But—whatever have you done to that poor old man in there?"

"He is a wicked schemer! Charity is not near so ill as we have been led to believe. Ulrich has been *poisoning* her!" Agatha uttered a strangled scream at this. "Hush!" Rachel whispered. "I cannot stay to tell you the whole now, but should Doctor Ulrich become ill, even very ill, do *not* send for help! The wretch deserves to suffer! Now—have you spoken to Raoul? Does he know that Colonel Tristram means to make the attempt tonight?"

"Yes, miss. He says he can have horses saddled and ready, in case we need them, though how he can do it is more than I can guess. Oh, Miss Rachel—I do be that afeared! Suppose the Colonel is caught? Whatever will become of us?"

That grim thought turned Rachel's knees to jelly. "Pray he is not," she urged. "Now, here is the key, but the Colonel does not know I went after it. When the receiving line is finished, and during a dance, you must take it downstairs and ask to speak to Mr. Devenish. If anyone argues, tell them you've a message from Miss Charity, or something. You should be able to slip the key to him, do you think, Agatha?"

Agatha paled, but said staunchly, "I'll manage, Miss Rachel!"

Tristram succeeded in claiming Garvey's attention when Claude left the dining room for a few moments. Garvey replied negatively to an enquiry as to whether they had met before and turned rather deliberately to the gentleman at his right hand, terminating the conversation. Tristram was not surprised. It had early become apparent that most of the guests were in Claude's pocket, and if Claude had warned Garvey of his suspicions, the man was unlikely to be helpful. The chances of anyone being willing to help the girls get off the estate were slight indeed. But get away they would! He and Dev and Raoul would manage, somehow. The aspect of it all that most worried him was Rachel's going to that blasted bedchamber. The thought that Claude or Gerard might discover her made him sweat, and more than ever he inclined to the determination to forbid the attempt and proceed with his initial plan.

Antoine Benét put an end to such introspection by regaling him with a plaintive account of the frustrations of an artist.

242

"Always, *mon Capitaine*, I am at the beck and call of one or other of my cousins, or my ridiculous aunt, and my talent it must shrivel for the lack of use! Now—I look at your friend Monsieur Devenish, and—I yearn! I clamour! I—"

Whatever else he did was not to be divulged, for at that moment Claude returned to suggest they rejoin the ladies.

As they made their way along the hall, Devenish fell into place beside Tristram. "Any inspirations, old pippin?" he murmured hopefully.

"None. Have you?"

"No." Devenish sighed. "What we need is a wooden horse!"

15

It seemed to Rachel that the line of guests was never-ending. Where they had managed to find accommodations, she could not imagine, for despite the size of the chateau, a relatively small proportion of those invited were staying there. For what seemed an eternity she stood beside Claude, acknowledging the congratulations of those elegant ladies and gentlemen who shook hands with Claude, herself, and a wilting Madame Beauchard. A waltz was in full swing when they at last were able to enter the ballroom. The great chandeliers blazed with light, throwing the exquisitely plastered blue and white ceiling into sharp relief. The room was enormous, but beautifully proportioned, the walls of a pale blue-green were embellished with giant gold relief figures of Grecian deities, alternating with large floral arrangements, great sparkling gilt-framed mirrors, and tall windows. In the midst of this luxurious setting were the dancers, the bright gowns of the ladies swirling, the gentlemen poised and immaculate as they guided their fair partners unerringly to the strains of the lilting music.

Under any other circumstances, Rachel would have found the sight enchanting, but now her eyes sought only one dark head and soon located Tristram dancing with a very pretty girl who looked Scandinavian with her flaxen hair and light complexion. Rachel experienced a pang, not of jealousy but of fear because danger was becoming ever more imminent for him, and because he was so tall. That feature, which undoubtedly won him the envy of most of the gentlemen and the added admiration of the ladies also made him so disastrously easy to detect.

Although she was the centre of attention tonight, the minutes seemed to drag past on leaden feet. At a little past the hour of

244

midnight she was waltzing with Monsieur Monteil. For all his wealth and polish, the Swiss was cold and what Justin would have termed a dead bore. At least, he did not engage her attention, a circumstance for which Rachel was grateful when she saw Agatha appear at the doors and summon a footman. Devenish was not dancing; he stood chatting with the French couple who had earlier seemed so stiff and ill-at-ease. The footman made his way to them, and soon Devenish followed him to the abigail. The dance ended, Monteil restored Rachel to Claude, and in a moment or two, Devenish came over. He told her politely that her abigail had been unable to speak with her, so had charged him to convey the message that her sister was sleeping comfortably and Dr. Ulrich would stay with her until the ball was over.

Claude thanked him profusely. Devenish protested that he was only too glad to be of service. He bowed, dazzled them with his smile, and moved off, not by the flicker of an eyelid revealing that a small key of great consequence resided in his waistcoat pocket.

The evening wore on, and Rachel's nervousness increased with every tick of the clock. Torn between the fear that Tristram might not be able to slip away, and the even more chilling fear that he would, she had to struggle to appear at ease. She stood up with Claude for a *boulanger*, went into supper with the German General, and had just been claimed by an elderly and distinguished Frenchman and led into a set for the quadrille, when an unexpected diversion offered, in the form of a small commotion at one side of the room. Two gentlemen were arguing, one heatedly, one—the munitions maker, Monsieur Monteil—with acid cynicism. Claude exchanged a meaningful glance with Gerard, and they moved toward the disturbance. Necks craned, and a hum of speculation arose. The heated gentleman was becoming quite loud, and it appeared that considerable tact would be required to placate him.

The music struck up in rather hurried fashion, and the dance began. Progressing through the movements, Rachel saw Monteil looking very grave as he conversed with a Spanish officer whose splendid uniform seemed literally covered with medals. Antoine Benét was partnering a very pretty dark girl in an adjoining set. Madame Fleur sat against the wall, gossiping happily with the rotund Comtesse D'Azarpé, and Claude and Gerard appeared to be winning their battle to calm the angry gentleman.

Of Tristram, there was no sign.

Tristram thrust the bar of soap into Devenish's hand and, peering around the tall grandfather clock at the two stalwarts near the front doors, murmured, "Why you want it is more than I can fathom."

Devenish lifted his brows and said airily, "Wanted me to create a diversion so you could hop up the back stairs, did you not?"

"I'd not specified a freshly laundered diversion."

"I, sir," imparted Devenish, "am a gentleman of taste." Saying which, he bit off a chunk of the soap.

"Good God!" gasped Tristram. "Dev—poor fellow. Perhaps you had best lie down."

"Oh, I mean to," Devenish nodded, a sparkle coming into his rather watery eyes as he masticated the soap. He slipped the cake into his pocket. "Do not dawdle," he hiccuped, and walked with uncertain gait down the corridor and across the main hall.

Two powdered heads turned warily to regard Devenish's wavering approach. He picked up speed, headed straight for the doors. One of the footmen stepped before him, jaw set, lips tight, eyes cold. Devenish stopped. His body jerked, and he emitted a bubbling croak. The footman, prepared for cold steel, bare knuckles, or bullets, was not prepared for this. He recoiled, his brutal face paling.

Tristram, his eyes dancing with merriment, waited for no more, but started swiftly toward the rear stairs. A remark uttered in shrill horror, wafted after him. "*Sacre bleu!* He foams at the mouth! He have the very bad seizure!"

Chuckling, Tristram took the stairs two at a time. The flight terminated at the northeastern corner of the first floor, from which vantage point he could see the entire length of the halls along the north wing and the main block. Both were bare of either servants or guests. He strode along briskly, staying close against the wall when he reached the main stairs. They also were empty, and just beyond was the forbidden panelled door. He slipped the key into the lock, opened the door to a silent dimness, and stepped inside, pulling the door to behind him. He was in a small landing, from which stairs rose in a sharp spiral, quite unlike the broad curve of the lower flight. To his right, a small table held a broad candle burning steadily in a hurricane glass. He moved to the stairs. These were not carpeted, the wood gleaming richly in the dim light, and he climbed as swiftly and silently as possible. Above was the brighter glow of the upper hall. Ears straining, he paused when his eyes were above floor level and peered around. And then stood motionless, staring incredulously at the scene that stretched away to either side of him. He had stepped into another time, for all here was medieval, from the torches that flickered in several wall sconces to the gleaming suits of armour, and mighty swords and shields that were hung along the half-timbered walls. The floors were of random-width planks, uncarpeted. At intervals great banners were suspended from the ceiling, each bearing the heraldry of a noble house, not all French, he noted with a frown, for some were of ancient British houses. He climbed the last few stairs and hesitated. To each side stretched a line of heavy gothic doors, behind one of which was the painting he sought. Beginning in the middle, he walked lightly to the first door past the stairs and put his ear against it. The stillness was deathlike, and he realized that he was holding his breath. He lifted the iron latch carefully and eased the door open. He beheld the chamber of a feudal monarch: faded but magnificent arras hung on the walls; the floors shone and were spread here and there with animal skins. A massive bed was set on a wide dais in the centre of the room, great war axes and lances were hung here and there between the tapestries, and all the furnishings were intricately carven relics of the past. Despite its splendour, however, the room had a brooding air that made him eager to leave it. He backed out and closed the door.

There were six more rooms at this end of the hall, and he counted another six beyond the stairs. Any one, or all of them, might be occupied, but that chance must be taken. With his hand on the next latch, he paused. Faint but unmistakable, he

247

caught a whiff of oil paint. Triumphant, he very literally followed his nose to the last door, which stood slightly open. He pushed it wider and whispered an elated, "Excelsior!" The room was equipped as an artist's studio, the only furnishings being a long bench, a high stool, some easels, and two work tables under windows now hidden behind closed curtains. A branch of candles and a tinder box had been left on a small but ponderous carven table by the door. Tristram lit the candles, swung the door shut, and scanned the room, holding the candles high.

There were three canvases. One, a portrait of Rachel was in the very early stages, certainly not—as Antoine had told her—nearing completion. The other two were unlike any art he had ever seen and, curious, he drew nearer. They were very large, loosely attached to plain board backings, and each required the support of two sturdy easels. One faced the door, the other was placed where the daylight from the window would fall upon it. Tristram peered at the nearest painting. It was apparently almost finished, because the top was already framed, a strange sort of frame consisting of a round wooden bar. He saw then that the sides were also enclosed, but by flat black strips, and the most curious aspect of all was the shape of the painting, for the lower edge was cut in sharply at each side, about two feet from the bottom, so that only a narrow central panel remained, this also being edged by the black stripping of the sides. The subject matter was as outlandish as the shape, resembling nothing so much as the windows of a large room viewed at night from between two dimly seen benches.

Baffled, he decided it simply could not be completed. Perhaps the wood edging was merely some kind of shaping or stretcher. He made his way to the second painting. The shape, size, subject, and framing were identical to that of the first. He shook his head, frankly astonished, then returned to the first easel. He had seen many dark works by the early masters, and whereas in seconds the details of those fine paintings seemed to leap out at the viewer, in this instance even after holding his gaze steady for several minutes, he could discern nothing more than those two dim benches and the far window. He could only conclude that both works had been brought to an identical stage, with more detail to be added at some future date. It was clear from the odd conformation of the canvases that they had been fashioned to fit into some recess or between certain items of furniture, but why anyone would want two paintings having identical subject matter, or how such unattractive art works could possibly constitute a threat to England, was an enigma. Unless Antoine Benét had used these dull scenes to cover something that had been on the canvas previously! He paced closer, his eyes narrowing, and was so engrossed by this new thought that he failed to notice the flame of the candles flicker.

"I was right, Shotten," purred a smooth voice behind him. "He does not know what to make of—"

Tristram gasped with shock, but his reaction was quicksilver. He flung the candle branch aside, seized the painting and easel and hurled them at the group of men in the doorway.

"No!" screeched Sanguinet. Attempting to dodge, two men came into violent collision and sprawled on the floor. An odd, high-pitched metallic twang sounded, and Tristram felt a sharp tug at his sleeve, but he was already gripping a small but heavy table and sent it whizzing after the art work. He had a blurred impression of shouts and a crash, of more men floundering on the floor, and of Claude Sanguinet wresting a crossbow from one of them. Even as he launched himself at that crowded doorway, Tristram realized his candles provided the illumination for this revelation; they had landed on one of the benches and a merry blaze was licking up from the oily rags scattered there. He cleared the cursing tangle of men with a running leap; his hair brushed the top of the door jamb, and he was in the hall and racing for the stairs.

Furious cries rang out behind him. He'd have little chance if Claude succeeded in loosing another crossbow bolt at him. He snatched a lance from the wall as he ran, and sent a suit of armour crashing to the tiles. They were hot on his heels now, and he heard Claude scream, "Put out that fire! Imbeciles! Do not kill him!"

Two of the "footmen" bounded up the stairs and ran for him, daggers gleaming in their hands. He swung his lance. Grinning, they separated to each side of the wide corridor, so that he could threaten only one at a time. Grinning also, Tristram reversed his grip, holding the lance horizontally before him and charging full tilt. A dagger whistled at him, but he ducked even as he ran, and it missed. The lance did not; it caught them at a goodly speed and they were slammed backwards. The impact smashed the lance against Tristram's ribs, staggering him, but he recovered and sprinted to the stairs. The spiral would be deadly in a fight, but luckily no one else appeared to challenge him, and he plunged down with desperate haste. The door was unlocked and he was through it in a flash, staying a quivering second while they thundered after him, to turn the key and leave it in the lock. He caught his breath thankfully; that would buy him a few seconds—enough perhaps, to—

He slowed almost before he had started off again, and halted.

Three people stood a short way along the corridor. One of the guards, and Gerard, his grin exultant, his left arm about the shoulders of a paper-white Rachel, and in his right hand a long, wickedly shining knife.

"It is only fair to warn you, *Monsieur le Capitaine*," he warned, "that I have a score to settle."

The maddened confusion from behind the locked door exploded into a burst of shouts as the door opened, then quieted abruptly.

"The chit is of no use to me now," called Sanguinet.

Gerard's grin broadened and he started to lift the knife toward Rachel's face.

"Do be so good as to drop the lance," requested Sanguinet, politely.

Rachel's white lips formed the word "No!" but looking into her agonized eyes, Tristram dropped the lance.

"Look at me!" demanded Sanguinet.

Tristram tore his gaze from Rachel, and turned. He caught a glimpse of Shotten's triumphant face, the butt of a musket whipping down at him, and Claude, smiling. A violent impact brought a distant sense of pain, and shattered the hall into a thousand brightly glittering fragments . . .

The cannonade was deafening and showed no sign of abating, even after these long, terrible hours. A shell burst very close by. The trooper screamed, stumbled, and went down,

Tristram flinging himself clear in the nick of time. He landed across the body of a Prussian, a pistol still lying beneath one lifeless hand. Tristram took up the weapon, staggered over to put the horse out of its misery, then was shocked to see Ensign Charles Quincy sitting propped against a shattered gun carriage, watching him with a faint smile on his muddied face.

"Hello, Quincy." He knelt beside the wounded boy. "Is it very bad, old fellow? We must have you off the field."

"No need for . . . for that, Colonel," said Quincy, faint but indomitable. "It—it *is* you, Leith?"

Tristram flinched inwardly, and noting the dimming eyes, knew that yet another fine young life had been claimed by this incredibly savage battle. "Yes," he said gently. "It's me."

"I've . . . message," gasped Quincy. "Carrying it to—to Colborne. Could you . . . ?"

"Of course." Leith took the paper from the feeble hand. "Chin up," he smiled bracingly. "Do not worry about—" And he broke off, his assurances no longer of use to this valiant son of one of his father's oldest friends.

Shoulders slumping, he thought dully that it did not hurt as much now. The grief of seeing one after another of his comrades slain must have numbed his mind. Ignoring the cacophonous uproar raging about him, he closed the sightless eyes gently, wondering with a vague detachment why he himself still lived. His head and shoulder were slightly cut, but otherwise he was only bruised here and there. Remarkable, considering that three horses had been killed under him today. He'd been thrown over the head of one, and briefly stunned by the exploding shell that had killed another. He'd lost count of how many of his friends had fallen. He had held his favourite subaltern's hand as the young man died, and dismounted several times to assist with terribly wounded men. Never before—not even at St. Pierre—had he seen such losses. They'd been cut to pieces by Ney's cannon, and mauled by his cavalry charges. The field was littered with dead and dying—yet the slaughter went on and on, as though there would be no end to it until the last man was slain.

Leith shook his dizzied head. He must get to Woodford with his orders, or—

251

A hand tugged at his shoulder. "Colonel?" said an insistent voice. "Are you—? Oh, my God! Not—not poor little Quincy? Then— they're all gone! Winters, and Bailey, and—Sir! You're hurt!"

"Nothing vital."

"But—you're all blood!"

"No—am I?" Tristram peered downward and found his blue jacket hideously blotched and stained. "By Jove, so I am. Well, it's not mine. At least, not much of it. Here," he thrust Quincy's papers at Lieutenant Jonathan Rayburne, and managed to stand, only to reel uncertainly. He drew a hand across his eyes. "I'm a trifle winded, I'm afraid. Get this to Colborne, like a good chap, will you? But—first, help me find another trooper. I've orders for Woodford, or I'd—"

The Lieutenant recoiled, his youthful face strained and terrified. "I'm for Brussels, whilst I can! We all shall die here, Leith. There's no hope now, and I'll not—"

"Don't be a fool! You're tired, is all. Old Nosey will not let us down! Now—off with you, man."

Rayburne edged back, his dilating eyes riveted to the tattered figure of the tall staff officer.

"Not that way, you fool!" Tristram staggered forward and caught his arm. "You'll *not* desert, damn you! How do you think your father would feel, to know you'd turned yellow? Buck up, Jon! Now, go—"

Rayburne began to fight him frenziedly, raining blows at his head, and shrieking, "You mean to murder me is what it is! Leith! Let me go! For Lord's sake—do not murder me! Please —do not murder me!" He ran off, wildly.

A shell screamed through that carnage, and Tristram knew it would be very close. His last awareness was of the sudden and complete absence of all sound . . .

He opened his eyes. His head felt as though the shell had split his skull open, the pain so intense he was half blinded by it. Gradually, he realized that he was not as cold as he'd expected to be; nor could he smell the smoke and powder, or hear the cries and groans of the wounded. Was he deafened, perhaps? But that could not be, for he could hear talk close by. A soft, persuasive male voice, and a girl, her words angry but holding a note of fear. He tried vainly to distinguish her, then drew a sleeve across his eyes and comprehended that his own blood had blinded him. Now, he could see more clearly, and was puzzled to find that he lay on a sofa in a room, vaguely familiar, and decorated with ancient weapons and tapestries.

". . . have held true to my part of our bargain," the man was asserting in an injured tone. "No one can say I've not. You have had all that money could buy, Rachel."

The name snatched Tristram's breath away. He struggled onto one elbow and saw Claude Sanguinet gripping the arms of a girl with a pale, beautiful face and terrified blue eyes, but her chin proudly uptilted, withal.

Memory returned in a rush. He was Tristram Leith! He had a fond and noble father, a lovely sister, many friends and relations, and was heir to a great fortune and several estates, most beloved of which was Cloudhills in Berkshire. And he was not guilty of murdering anyone—thank God! But outweighing all these things in importance was the girl who said scornfully, "I have been hoodwinked from the start! Your rascally surgeon helped Charity once, I grant you. But has since ensured that she remain an invalid—has deliberately drugged her into illness so that I was made to think her only hope was for constant medical care. So I would be coerced into wedding you!" Her eyes flashed and she uttered a contemptuous, "Despicable!"

"Naughty puss!" Sanguinet released her so roughly that she staggered against Gerard, who immediately seized and held her. "How did you learn this? From that drunken sot, Ulrich? Oh, you had much better tell me now, my love. Also, I shall require to know why this British officer is here, how he came by the key to the second floor, and where he learned of my screens." He moved a step closer to the slender girl. "I do dislike the thought of hurting you, my betrothed, but—"

Tristram swung his feet down from the sofa and sat up. "Sanguinet!"

From behind, someone grabbed him by the hair and his head was jerked back agonizingly. Dimly, he knew that Sanguinet had crossed to stand before him.

"Well, well. Our soldier has awoken. Gently, Shotten! Your hand is too heavy. Only look at how you've delayed me." The

253

kindly face smiled gently on the man whose dark eyes met his own with fierce defiance despite the blood that streaked the scarred features. Sanguinet went on expansively, "Now that you are awake, *mon Capitaine* . . ."

"Fully. My name is Leith. Tristram Leith. And if you want my advice, Sanguinet—"

"Do I? I think not. However, I will own you have surprised me. So you're Kingston Leith's heir, are you? But how very obliging. Everyone imagines you dead, which simplifies matters. Now, what I *do* want from you, my dear fellow, is information." Claude's gaze slanted to Shotten, who again tugged Leith's thick hair savagely, causing Rachel to gasp, and the captive's eyes to close for an anguished instant. "Gently, Shotten!" Claude repeated. "You lack finesse. There is absolutely no need to hurt our intrepid Englishman. He will tell us, readily enough." He smiled. "Do not look so derisive, Leith. This is perfectly true. You see—we have a trump card." He nodded towards Rachel.

Tristram's heart constricted. Surely even so ruthless a despot as Claude Sanguinet would not harm a lady?

There came a sudden muffled thumping. Gerard's head tilted, and he glanced about uncertainly. Tristram's keen ear, however, had already detected the direction from which the sounds had come. His fist swung around with all his power behind it, and Shotten staggered back, clutching his middle and gasping for breath. Tristram sprang to his feet. A guard, about to leap for him, checked aghast, as a scrambling thump preceded a great black cloud that billowed from the fireplace.

Claude staggered back, choking. Rachel clawed at Gerard's hand upon her arm, her nails digging deep. His yowl was cut off abruptly as Tristram rammed home a right to the jaw that collapsed him. A blackened apparition coughed its way from the hearth and tossed a generous handful of soot into Sanguinet's eyes. The guard yelled and ran for the door. Tristram leapt after him. Claude dragged his sleeve across his streaming eyes and made a dive for the knife Gerard had dropped. With a scratchy whoop, Devenish jumped to stamp hard on those outstretched fingers, then kick out savagely, silencing Claude's yowl and sending him to join Gerard on the sullied rugs. Tristram had already reduced the guard to a crumpled heap, and, her face smudged with soot, Rachel flew to his ready arm. "My darling! My darling! Are you much hurt?" she asked frantically, caressing his bloodied cheek.

"No, I assure you. Matter of fact, our Claude did me the favour of restoring my memory. Now—tell me quickly, how many are outside?"

"Two, I think. Claude told Gerard the fewer who know of this night's work, the better. But—love, we must go to Charity. She and Agatha are locked in our room, threatened that I will be hurt if they dare make a sound!"

"By Gad! Fella's downright indecent!" snorted Devenish, using Claude's pristine sheet to wipe some of the black from his face.

Shotten was mumbling incoherently and sitting up. Tristram jerked him to his feet. Devenish uttered a triumphant exclamation and snatched a mace from the wall, only to stagger at the weight of it.

"Behind the door, Dev!" said Tristram. "Now, Mr. Shotten—you will call in your comrades." He pressed the razor-sharp dagger against the flabby jowls. "The slightest misstep . . ." he said softly.

Tremblingly eager to be of service, Shotten yelled in execrable French, "Paul! André! Come quick!"

"Dreadful!" said Tristram critically, and the hilt of the knife thudded against Shotten's bullet head, restoring him to slumber.

Paul and André plunged into the room to be faced by a tall, grim, bloody man with lethal fists. Paul met the challenge unhesitatingly. André whirled to the door and was confronted by a black apparition wielding a mace and screeching a demented "*Aaieee!*" Stupefied, André's hesitation was just sufficient for the mace to swing, and André was granted a respite from worry.

"Rachel," said Tristram breathlessly, passing one of the daggers to her. "Cut the sheet into strips, love. We must tie these carrion, Dev."

They set to work at once, Claude being the first to be trussed up and gagged.

"You were splendid," said Tristram, blinking a little because of the pounding in his head as he bent to secure a knot. "Whatever made you think of coming down the chimney?"

"Didn't. They put me outside after I suffered my delicious seizure, so I shinned up the tree and tried to swing in through the window as you'd originally planned, you'll mind. Good thing you didn't attempt it, Tris. The blasted rope broke! Dashed shoddy workmanship. Hold this knot a minute, will you? Luckily, I fell right on top of one of the guards who was toddling about in search of someone to impale. He was, as you might say, thunderstruck!"

Rachel gave a gurgle of laughter. "But"—she handed Tristram another strip of sheeting—"how ever did you get into the chimney?"

"Wasn't easy, ma'am. Shall I start on Gerard, Tris? I went up the tree again—all the way to the top, but it began to sway about like the deuce. Then I thought of encouraging it, and when I was close to the roof, I jumped. The only way in that I could find was through the chimneys. I'd never have managed had I been built on the gargantuan lines of some people I'll not name." He flashed a murky grin at Tristram. "It's a regular maze in there! I crawled about for hours, it seemed, but luckily, I'd a tinder box with me. Almost set fire to some of the soot, once. Gave me a nasty turn, I don't mind telling you! Then, I chanced to hear our garrulous host gloating, so I decided to—ah, drop in."

"Remind me to thank you properly, when we're out of this." Tristram turned his attention to Shotten. "Oh, by the bye, my name's Leith."

"Good God! Not Lord Leith's son and heir?"

Rachel darted a swift and startled glance at Tristram, stared at him for a moment as he nodded, then asked tremblingly, "Do you need any more strips, dearest?"

"This little lot will do nicely, thank you. Dev—did you have a look at Benét's paintings?"

"I should jolly well hope not! Haven't the slightest desire to, what's more!"

"Well, you must, for I can make neither head nor tail of 'em!"

256

They worked swiftly, then Tristram stood. "Rachel—come love. Just a quick look and we'll go to Charity."

They left their securely tied victims and hurried along the silent corridor to Benét's workroom. Inside, Tristram found that the painting he'd used as a projectile had been carefully restored to its easel and was seemingly little the worse for wear.

Devenish sniffed and remarked that something was burning.

"There was a small fire," Tristram explained. "Well now, Dev," he held up a branch of candles. "What the devil are they?"

"Blasted rum, is what," Devenish decreed, peering curiously. "Who'd want to hang rubbishing stuff like that?"

"Hang it!" Rachel said scornfully. "I'd not hang it in a stable!"

Tristram stared at her. "In a stable . . . !" he breathed. "That's it! And now I recollect that Claude *said* they were screens! They are, by God!" His elation faded into puzzlement. "But—why? Well, London must answer that question."

Devenish asked, "What in the name of the Bishop's goat are you babbling about?"

"Not now, Dev. No time. See if you can get Rachel back to—" He checked, surveying his friend judicially. "Jove! You look like some demented dervish. I'd best go. You stay here and fashion a rope of the curtains, or something, so as to lower these two delightful works of art out of the window. Take them off the boards and roll them in a sheet and—"

Devenish and Rachel exchanged alarmed glances. "It's his head, poor fella," quoth Devenish.

"Dearest," said Rachel, "you never mean to take them with us? We shall be lucky to escape, ourselves, especially with my loved sister to get clear. I do not see why—"

"Trust me, love," he smiled, bending to drop a kiss upon her brow.

"It'll take more than a buss to make *me* trust you," Devenish grunted.

Tristram laughed, then stepped to swing open the door and peer into the hall. All was quiet. He turned back into the room. "Sweetheart, on second thought, I'd best give a hand here.

Dare you creep to the top of the stairs and warn us if anyone comes? We'll not be a moment.''

Glad to be of help, Rachel nodded and ran quickly into the corridor. Tristram assisted Devenish to remove a painting from the easel. ''I did not want Rachel to hear this, in case I'm mistaken about these screens. If I'm right, we may get the girls safely away, but you and I will have to find our own route. Everything will depend upon your doing *exactly* as I say, Dev.''

Charity uttered a sob of relief when the *petit salon* door opened to admit her sister and Tristram. Rachel ran to her outstretched arms and tried to comfort her. Agatha, bending above a faintly wailing Dr. Ulrich, exclaimed, ''Thank the good Lord! We've been proper beside of ourselves! Oh, Sir! Your head!''

''Never mind that. Agatha, you must go at once to Raoul. Tell him to bring the new black carriage as close to the side door as possible. If he's questioned, he can say that Miss Charity became very ill and Ulrich wants her taken to his hospital —or some such. Hurry now, there's a good girl.''

Smiling at him admiringly, she nodded and fled.

Tristram crossed to the mirror above the mantel and scanned his reflection. His face was bloodstained, but the large lump he cautiously investigated was hidden by his tumbled locks, and the cut had not bled so profusely as to result in splashes on his shirt or jacket.

Rachel hurried to him with a bowl of water and a cloth and said urgently, ''Come and sit here, dearest,'' and when he had obeyed, began to bathe his face.

''What's the matter with Ulrich?'' he asked.

''I gave him the 'medicine' he intended for Charity. You see how it has restored him!'' And slanting a contemptuous glance at the doctor, she said grimly, ''Wretched man! You deserve a deal more than you now suffer!''

''Yes. The plague, at least.'' Tristram added thoughtfully, ''Does Claude know you drugged him?''

''No. He obviously thought him in his cups.''

He chuckled and looked up at her, his eyes dancing despite

the fierce throbbing in his head. "It will serve, Rachel! By God, but it will serve us well!" He stayed her gentle hand for an instant, to kiss it. "With your help, love, by dawn we shall be en route home to our grey and rainy little island!"

16

"*Oh*, there *you are, Captain!*" *cried Madame Fleur, in ex*-aggerated relief. "It is quite unlike Claude to leave his guests, and I've not seen him this half-hour and more! Oh, my goodness! I'd not stopped to think! Is it the poor little Strand girl? I declare I have been quite overset with anxiety for the dear child! Is she—er—very ill?"

"Hush, ma'am," Tristram said in a dramatically low tone, leading her to one side of the ballroom. "Claude wishes it to go no further than the few of us who know." He glanced around again as though every ear in that hot and crowded room was stretched to them, then gestured to the hall. When they stood in the middle of that large chamber, he went on, "Your nephew asks that you be so good as to help us get the poor girl to the doctor."

"Wh-what . . . ?" she stammered, her eyes widening with fright. "Oh—lud! Rachel *said* something about its being c-contagious, but—"

"Sshh!" Tristram glanced to the two interested footmen beside the doors. "There is no cause for panic."

"P-panic? Oh—no, no. B-but I thought Doctor Ulrich *had* arrived."

"So he has. Unhappily, it appears he also had thrown out a rash and is now in near as bad case as the girl."

"R-r-rash . . . ? S-scarlet fever . . . ?" she gulped. "Oh, God! Not—*the pox?*"

"Monsieur Gerard has ridden for another physician, but you can appreciate it will take time, ma'am. And now that Rachel is feeling in queer stirrups, Claude wants both ladies sent at once into Dinan. The abigail cannot manage by herself, and Claude does not wish word to spread to the servants. You understand.''

"Oh, I do. I do. But—but, do you know, Captain, I am— feeling rather unwell, myself. I think I had best go and lie down upon my bed.''

"But, you cannot, ma'am! Monseigneur had hoped you could ride in the carriage with—''

"Quite impossible! Claude shall have to do that! I must to my chamber!''

"Claude has been put into isolation by Dr. Ulrich. He fears he may also have contracted the disease. It is so curst swift, you see. Madame—'' He caught her arm as she backed away. "You must not abandon me! I've no authority here!''

She wrung her hands distractedly. "If only Guy were here, but— *Tiens!* He was taken ill shortly after dinner and has not stirred from his room since! Is—is he . . . too . . . ?''

Surprised by this intelligence, Tristram dropped his eyes, shrugged, and said nothing. His very silence fanned the flames.

"Oh, what a wretched business this is!'' wailed Madame. "I knew no good would come of it. One cannot trust the English! Your pardon, sir, but fact is fact! How any girl of breeding could invite hundreds of guests to her engagement ball, and then expose them to the plague!'' She threw up her hands. "It is beyond my understanding. Antoine! Antoine! Over here, fool-ish creature!''

Tristram's feeble and insincere plea for caution was ignored. No sooner had the exquisite Antoine joined them than his aunt proceeded to regale him with details that grew ever more lurid. When she ceased speaking, he was as pale as she and recalled an engagement in Paris that would necessitate his leaving this very hour.

Tristram scolded severely, "This is ridiculous! You are monseigneur's kindred. One, or both of you, *must* help. Miss Rachel is able to walk, but her sister must be carried down, and monseigneur wishes us to use the back stairs so as not to alarm the guests.''

Antoine fussed and Madame whined, but the end result was that the two sturdy footmen were summoned and, with faint, knowing grins, followed Madam, Tristram, and Benét up the stairs.

Agatha answered Benét's cautious knock at the door of the *petit salon*. Her face was very white, and the shadows Rachel had carefully painted under her eyes made her look as if she'd not slept for a week. "Thank heaven you are come!" she exclaimed tremulously. "Miss Charity's very bad, Mr. Benét, and Miss Rachel so ill, sweet lamb! Are these men to carry them to the carriage?"

"That," one of the footmen spoke up, his sneering grin fixed on Tristram, "must wait for what Doctor Ulrich says—eh, Léon?"

His broad-shouldered colleague nodded grimly.

"Excellent," said Tristram. "I'm glad to see you're not afraid."

Some of the mockery faded from the man's hard eyes, replaced by an uneasy look, but his friend smirked, "You intend to accompany the ladies, I have no doubt?"

"I?" Tristram fell back a step. "Er—well, I would be overjoyed. But monseignéur required only that their abigail accompany them."

It was a telling stroke. Obviously unnerved, Claude's minions yet clung to their intention to receive Dr. Ulrich's orders. Agatha waved them impatiently into the room and closed the door. "The doctor is laid down upon Miss Rachel's bed, poor man," she offered. "This way, you two!"

She opened the door into the bedchamber. The one called Leon took one look at the doctor's limp form and fairly lept back. "*Mon Dieu!* Do but look at his face! It is the pox!"

His comrade viewed that livid, spotted countenance, crossed himself and retreated precipitately. "D-do you wish us to carry the English mademoiselle downstairs, doctor?" he croaked.

Ulrich opened one bleary eye and mumbled incoherently.

"Enough!" said Tristram. "The ladies are ill, and you stand here shivering. Agatha—do the Misses Strand have their cloaks? Miss Charity must be wrapped in a blanket as well and carried to the carriage. Do you not agree, Monsieur Benét?" But when he turned around, by some strange chance both the artist and his aunt seemed to have been summoned elsewhere.

262

Emulating their example, Léon volunteered nobly to hurry downstairs and open the rear door.

Tristram nodded, stifling a grin as Léon made a dive for the corridor.

In Charity's room, Rachel sat on the bed supporting her sister, whose countenance was so alarming that Tristram could scarcely contain his mirth. The remaining footman gulped something about "summoning aid" and shot from sight.

"By heaven, I believe we've cleared a path to the back door, at least," Tristram said jubilantly. "Will Raoul have the carriage for us, Agatha?"

"Yes, sir. He says as he will. It created such a bobbery when I told him, for word had got out that Miss Charity has 'something catching,' and all the other grooms and stableboys wanted to know what ails her. I said I'd been told not to say nothing."

"Excellent." Tristram swung the "expiring" Charity into his arms and smiled down at her. "Courage, ma'am. We shall do nicely so long as you look sufficiently stricken. Agatha, do you support 'poor' Miss Rachel. Come now."

The wide corridor was deserted. Music could be heard from the ballroom, but it sounded as though many people were gathered in the lower hall, their voices considerably agitated. Tristram led the way, walking swiftly to the rear stairs. If they could just get the girls into the coach, he thought prayerfully, the worst part of the battle would be won. A maid, carrying a jewel box upstairs, took one look at Charity's face, uttered a screech of terror, and ran for her life. At the foot of the stairs a small knot of servants peered at them in horrified awe, several of the women whipping their aprons over their noses and mouths. A grim-faced footman began to push his way through. The housekeeper, wearing bombazine and a lace cap, suddenly screamed, "The pox! It *is*! The pox!" and before that dread cry the scramble to get clear became a riot. The footman, however, was made of sterner stuff. He stayed a distance behind them, but one hand was inside his jacket, and his eyes were alert.

At the end of the hall, Tristram called over his shoulder, "Well, for Lord's sake, man! Come and open the door!"

The man hesitated, then sprang forward to swing the door wide.

Raoul had not failed them. The large black coach, with four matched black horses between the traces, waited. Of Devenish there was no sign.

Seized by a sudden sickening doubt, Rachel murmured, "Tristram—you *will*—"

"Get in, quickly!" he urged, *sotto voce.*

She glanced frantically at the powerful form of the footman, bit her lip and climbed into the coach, Agatha following. Well aware that the footman was only inches behind him, Tristram said, "Here we go, ma'am—mind your head now," and ducking his own head, carried Charity up the steps to deposit her on the seat beside Rachel.

Very white, Rachel put a hand on his sleeve. "You do not mean to come! I *knew* it!" She started up. "I'll not leave without—"

Through the far window, Tristram saw more guards watching, faces suspicious, weapons held ready. He pushed Rachel back down, hard. "You will do as I say!" he commanded sternly. "Do not spoil this, love. I cannot accomplish it any other way. We will join you—never fear."

"No—but—"

He sprang down the steps, and slammed the door, shouting. "Off with you! To the doctor's house—as fast as you can go!"

He had a brief impression of Rachel's horrified and blotchy face at the window, then the horses had leaned into their collars, and the carriage was gaining speed and rolling swiftly down the drivepath.

The footman was very close now, and the little knot of watchers across the yard started forward.

The door suddenly burst open again, and Monsieur Benét rushed out, his man following with valise and dressing case. "Poor girl!" Benét said, twitching with nervousness. "I sympathize. I really do. Do not stand there gibbering, Ransom! My chaise! At once!"

His arrival was but the start of the avalanche. A valet shot past calling for the carriage of the Comte Dolbé; a maid, pale and frightened, summoned the barouche of Monsieur and Madame de Young, and in a flash the yard was crowded with shouting servants, bewildered grooms, and frustrated guards.

Devenish appeared, wearing a fine jacket of maroon velvet, and with his face much cleaner if somewhat grimed here and there. "Claude's," he twinkled in response to Tristram's curious glance. "Didn't think he'd mind. We'd best—"

Above them, a window was suddenly flung up. Claude leaned out, scanning the chaotic scene. The lamplight was not brilliant, but Tristram's height betrayed him, and Claude howled, "Do not let them escape! Imbeciles—*stop them*! At all costs—stop them!"

His guards and more intimate servants knew exactly to whom he referred: his guests did not. As the burly guards surged toward Tristram and Devenish, the guests, sure they were to be forcibly detained, variously shrieked, shouted, or fought back. The power of Sanguinet's wealth and whatever other holds he exercised upon them were wiped away, for not even Claude's rage was to be feared more than the dread spectre of smallpox! The visiting servants resisted even more furiously than did their masters, for Sanguinet had no direct power over them.

Looking up, eyes glinting with amusement at this providential development, Tristram saw Gerard, aiming a musket. The man would not dare shoot, he knew, and laughing openly, he continued toward the stables, undaunted by the three fuming men who stood between him and his objective. Devenish also had looked up, however. He entertained less faith in Gerard's humane impulses than did his friend, and in his eyes, Tristram's head, above any other, presented an all too easy target. "This way!" he shouted and dove around to the back of the house.

"No! Dev!" shouted Tristram, but he was delayed by the new surge of the mob now adding to the hysteria in the yard. "Blast the gudgeon!" he groaned but plunged after the rapidly disappearing Devenish. He caught up with him in the rear shrubbery. "Stupid chawbacon!" he raged. "We could have won through!"

"The devil we could! You tower like a blasted lighthouse! Gerard would have picked you off, easy as winking. If we head north, we may—"

"We *cannot* head north! That's just what Claude would expect. Raoul will come back for us as soon as he gets the girls to safety.''

''You're addlebrained! We'd have no chance to get past the main gates!''

''Why not? Couldn't you install the screens?''

The slope was steep here, and for the moment they were concealed by the tall shrubs, and Devenish stopped walking, to say indignantly, ''Of course. Though it was no mean task, I can tell you! Raoul was talking with the other servants, and I worked like a blasted Trojan, fearing you would arrive with the ladies to find me only half-finished. Instead of which, you took an age!''

''It was necessary. The screens attach to the roof inside the coach, no?''

''Just as you thought. And can be let down so as to enclose a small segment of the interior. Thanks to those 'paintings' that so baffled us, anyone glancing in from outside the carriage sees apparently empty seats and the other window. But the area so enclosed is very small. I doubt it was intended for more than one or two people at most. There'd have been no room for us, in addition to the ladies.''

''Did you tell Raoul to be sure the screens are down before he reaches the gates?''

''D'you take me for a clunch? He will inform the gatekeepers that he was sent by Claude to collect a distinguished latecomer. They'll not stop an empty carriage.''

''Good. Come on!''

Below, was a fairyland of lights. In addition to the usual decorative illuminations, the winding drivepath was brightened by colourful Japanese paper lanterns hung from iron stakes driven into the lawn. The two young men paused briefly, eyeing the daunting course they must travel. A faint squawk sounded, and Tristram said, ''So that's where you were.''

Devenish stroked the duck's feathers fondly. ''Didn't think I would abandon the poor old lady, did you?''

Tristram grinned. ''No. Never that.'' He clapped Devenish on the shoulder, and at once a slim hand came up to cover his own and grip it hard. It was the only acknowledgment they made of the fact they both knew they might well be going to

266

their deaths. Then, they started down, wherever possible keeping to the shrubs and trees, their objective the far-distant main lodge gate.

What a wild, darting, dodgingly erratic flight that was! The wind was rising, and the three-quarter moon was often hidden by cloudrack, but the illuminations rendered the progress of the fugitives exceedingly hazardous. Three times they saw guards, but were able to elude them, partly because of the fascinating distractions of the constant procession of carriages which by every law of society should not be departing for at least three more hours. Flabbergasted, Claude's men gawked at the swiftly travelling vehicles, thus granting Tristram and Devenish the chance to make their perilous darts from trees to shrubs, unobserved. They passed the loom of the miniature English castle, the waters of the moat reflecting the green light that bathed it. Starting on, they crouched again as three guards materialized just ahead—guards so intrigued to observe the abrupt flight of yet another carriage that they were oblivious to the two men who plunged for the shelter of a formal rose bed only yards away. The balance of this garden provided good cover, with its lush flower beds, tall clusters of hollyhocks, and rose arbours, but the Egyptian area was less accommodating, and their progress here was painfully slow and nerve-wracking.

"Where . . ." gasped Devenish, a hand pressed to his side, "is our—Claude?"

"Must be—searching the other way. Now!"

They darted on, and were almost to the trees dividing this and the Grecian gardens when they had to fling themselves down again to avoid detection by two horsemen, galloping madly for the gates.

"Gerard!" panted Tristram. "Who was—other?"

"Didn't . . . see. Are we—properly cut off . . . d'you think?"

Tristram suspected that they were, but did not answer. A few minutes later, they sought the sanctuary of a clump of tall grasses when the horsemen returned as rapidly as before. The next stretch of lawn was long and open, the places of concealment few and far between. Still, the steady stream of fleeing guests was their best ally. Whenever possible, Tristram set a desperate pace, and coming at last to the trees, he was spent and reeling, his head pounding unmercifully. Beside him, Devenish sprawled flat on his back, his voice a sobbing rasp as he admitted he could run no farther. Tristram dropped to his knees. "We've done . . . jolly well . . ." he gasped. "Never thought we would . . . reach this point so—easily."

"Easily!"

"Could be worse. Save for Claude's guests—they might have . . . let the hounds loose."

"True. And I doubt I could've . . . handled that lot! Speaking of guests—" Devenish uttered a soft, wheezing laugh. "There goes another! D'you ever see such a—a panicked exodus? Like a blasted . . . Roman chariot race! Old Claude must have—"

Tristram's hand closed over his mouth shutting off the words, as an approaching French voice said, ". . . have I seen anything to equal it! I tell you this, *mon ami*, something it is very much amiss at the chateau."

"Aye. And the Englishers at the root of it, I'll warrant!"

"Then our eyes we will keep wide, my Jacques, and perchance win ourselves the big reward—no?"

They loomed into sight; tall dark shapes against the lighter darkness of the night sky. The one called Jacques asked, "You will recall monseigneur's instructions? If we ever again see the Englishmen in the gardens at night, it is the case of 'shoot first' and then apologize, eh?"

"I always respect a man," chortled his friend, "who can follow orders."

They moved off, and were almost out of earshot when Mrs. O'Crumbs, objecting to being restrained, uttered an indignant and penetrating squawk.

"Confound it!" breathed Tristram furiously. "You'd best let her go!"

The retreating footsteps halted. A voice exclaimed suspiciously, "What was that?"

Unaware of her peril, the duck lurched out of the trees, pecking hopefully at the grass.

"Well, it was not a whale!" proclaimed Jacques scornfully. "A bit of sport, at all events."

Face grim, Devenish started up. Hauling him down, cursing him softly, Tristram heard the other guard admonish his friend to save his ammunition. "We may stand in need of it before this night is out. *Voilà!* Another carriage and going hellbent! What in the name of *le Bon Dieu* . . . ?"

They wandered off and, scarcely waiting for their departure, Devenish darted out to recapture his pet. "Silly old woman!" he scolded, stroking her neck gently. "Almost you were in a French stewing pot!"

"And almost we were discovered!" growled Tristram.

At once, Devenish flared, "Because of me—is that your meaning? Well, I shall not leave her, sir. So perhaps I'd best free you of my disturbing presence!" He eluded Tristram's restraining hand and charged across the open space toward the trees of the Cathay garden.

Tristram groaned his exasperation and peered after the two guards in an effort to discover whether Devenish's wild flight had been detected. They were walking uphill, however, and did not turn back. He sprinted after Devenish and saw him plunge full tilt into the far belt of trees. When Tristram entered those same trees, he was met by the sounds of desperate combat. Curses in French and English interspersed, together with much trampling about and the thud of blows. Moving swiftly, Tristram saw Devenish, beset by two hefty guards, fighting gamely, but sadly outclassed by his larger and professional assailants. Tristram ran up and tapped one of the guards on the shoulder. The man spun about and was lifted to his toes by the uppercut that connected hard and true to the point of his jaw.

Heartened, Devenish drove a right into the midsection of his opponent and, as the man doubled up, finished him with a flashing left. He then turned to confront his unexpected ally and beamed, "Well met, Sir Knight!"

"You," said Tristram, breathing hard, "are, without a doubt, the most aggravating, strutting damned gamecock, I ever—"

Devenish chortled irrepressibly; Tristram was forced to a reluctant grin, and cautiously, they left the sanctuary of the trees, side by side. "Your head is bleeding again," Devenish advised.

"I cannot wonder," Tristram raised a hand to investigate. "When one has to cope with a bedlamite like—"

"Hey!" Devenish interpolated. "Where's Mrs. O'Crumbs?"

He glanced back. The little duck wove her patient sideways route to them. Devenish froze. Beyond her, two riders broke from the trees, and eastward were several men on foot, running silently to come up with them. His cry of warning was cut off by a metallic twang and, groaning, he sank down, gripping at the steel shaft that protruded from his thigh.

Pistol in hand, Claude rode up, calling, "Well done!" to Gerard, who was replacing a crossbow in the sling about his shoulder.

Tristram stood rigid for an instant, then, accepting the futility of resistance, dropped to one knee beside Devenish who lay propped on one elbow. "Let me see," he said, moving the clutching hand from the wound.

"How glad I am that you are not yet dead," Claude grinned. He fingered his jaw, the bruise apparent even in the darkness. "You, I believe, were the one who kicked me?"

"The honour . . . was mine," Devenish gasped unevenly.

"Honour must always be rewarded," purred Claude. "Perhaps you would now be so kind, *mon Colonel*, as to tell me where you have concealed the Misses Strand and my paintings."

Startled, Tristram looked up from his inspection of Devenish's injury. Surely the man must know that Raoul had driven the girls to safety? On the other hand, between the widespread panic over the outbreak of the "pox," the melee that had raged before the stables and a perhaps justified reluctance of Claude's servants to impart such news, it was possible he did *not* know! The exquisite humour of the situation dawning on Tristram, he burst into a laugh and, glancing down, saw Devenish grin responsively.

Such insouciance astounded Claude. "Perhaps," he said, "it is that I did not make myself clear. I should have added that when you tell me what I ask, I shall remove the bolt from your friend. There are several ways in which that can be accomplished, you know. Regrettably, none pleasant. But some less, shall we say—taxing?—than others.'' He waved a protesting hand. ''Ah—you mistake! Unlike my brother Parnell, I derive no enjoyment from inflicting suffering. It does, in fact, repel me. But,'' he shrugged, ''you see my predicament?''

Tristram frowned down at Devenish. The bolt was cruelly designed so as to inflict the most possible damage when removed, unless it were to be sawn through, which would of itself constitute a gruelling ordeal. Devenish winked indomitably, but he was sweating, his eyes full of pain, and his face white even in the red glow of the Pagoda. ''He needs a doctor,'' Tristram said slowly.

''And I need my fiancée and my paintings.'' Claude smiled. ''Never let it be said that I am unkind. We will carry your friend to the Pagoda and do what we may for him. Meanwhile, Gerard can ride for Dr. Ulrich, though I suspect he is by this time considerably—as you English would say—bosky.''

A grim smile curved Tristram's mouth. So Claude didn't know about Ulrich, either. He must really have ridden out in a hurry!

Claude gestured to Gerard. The steward hesitated briefly, but the runners had now come up with them, and he reined around and rode off. Hope stirred in Tristram's heart. Three guards—and Claude. As if reading his mind, Claude said, ''Michel, you will be so kind as to keep your pistol trained on our gallant Colonel at all times. Meanwhile, call in the men.''

Michel's pistol was aimed obediently. With his free hand he drew a whistle from his tunic and blew three loud blasts, then repeated the signal.

Watching Tristram in amusement, Claude said, ''Do you know, Colonel, you look quite downcast. Have no fear. I honour my obligations. You two men—help Monsieur Devenish.''

Tristram lifted Devenish to his feet, and the guards supported him on either side, his arms across their shoulders. As they started towards the Pagoda, yet another carriage rumbled down the drive. Claude glared after it, then said chattily, ''At first, Leith, I feared you had been sent by your government. But it was Miss Strand all the time, was it not? And the paintings you took purely because you became curious?''

Tristram was thinking that whatever he was going to do, it

271

must be soon, before the rest of the guards converged on them. But—with that pistol at his back, the chances were poor. Sanguinet wanted to boast, obviously. Which might prove useful in case they ever got clear. Therefore, he answered, "I could not understand why such dull paintings were important."

Claude gave a little crow of pleasure. "But of course you could not. They are not paintings, in the true sense of the word. They are screens, my dear fellow, but not for draughts. They fit inside a carriage I have specially built. Can you guess why?"

Looking into those jubilant eyes, Tristram managed to keep his own countenance grave. "Screens? If the glare offends you, why not use curtains?"

Claude laughed delightedly. "Oh, but they are not for the glare. You scowl—you are baffled! Yet, I assure you, my screens are *most* important. To France! Aha! *That* surprises you, I see!" He glanced at the guards and lapsing into English, went on, "The secret I unfold, dear *mon Colonel*. You think you have us beaten, eh? But many among us are loyal to Bonaparte. I have the fortune to win the favour of your Prince—a silly fellow. Still, he someday will be King, and by the populace is thus revered, no?"

"No," answered Tristram, baldly. "He is probably the most unpopular prince England has ever inherited from the House of Hanover."

"Even so, he have represent you so—so irritant small island. Your government, your peasants even, must be much *embarrassé* were he—shall we say—stole?"

Devenish, whose head was sagging, raised it at this, and gasped incredulously, "Crazy . . . as a moonling!"

Equally stunned, Tristram was silent. This deadly information was, he knew, being vouchsafed only because Claude believed there was no chance of his schemes being betrayed. Surely, Devenish must be as aware of their sentence of death—and how he was to bring the poor fellow out of this, he could not guess. "If you are serious," he said scornfully, "pray accept my sympathy. Prinny is guarded at all times. You'd not come near him!"

"You really so think?" Claude asked archly. "Were you aware, my dear friend, that your Prince have built himself a palace at the village named Bright'emstone? Oh, the splendid extravagance, but funds he have into it pour so that he is much criticised. He down there dares not go so often as he wish—a situation that pique him. So I—his friend and admirer—will him show the secret mode of travel. A means to slip to his Pavilion or his new inamorata, with none the wiser being. He is at heart child—wilful, eager, trusting child. Do you doubt his delight? Do you doubt he play my small game?'' Tristram's face was unreadable, but Devenish could not hide his consternation, and Sanguinet chuckled. ''Your fat Prince into my magical carriage he climb, and Pouf!'' he gestured dramatically. ''He disappear! Until I choose to allow he reappear. When my terms are met.'' In French again, he asked ''Now, my dear Devenish, do you not think I shall—as you might say—do the thing?''

Bloody but unbowed, Devenish said, ''I think you're . . . dicked in the nob! They should clap you up, Sanguinet. And likely will!''

They had come to the Pagoda pool now and, even as he spoke, Devenish eyed the smooth black water uneasily. Claude chuckled. ''You admire my pool, no? Is it not restful?'' He turned in the saddle as a rider galloped to him, and demanded, ''Well?''

''There has been an outbreak of pox at the chateau, monseigneur!'' the man announced awfully. ''The little English lady, and—'' He stared at Devenish, his eyes dilating. ''*Mon Dieu!* Only yesterday, he carry her!''

The two men supporting Devenish let go as though he had become a red hot coal, and backed away, wiping frantically at their sullied garments. Devenish crumpled, a muffled cry escaped him, and Tristram at once knelt, trying to ease his position.

''Idiots!'' Claude's benevolent expression became malevolent. ''There is no such outbreak! You are no better than my fine guests, who run like rabbits and shall bitterly repent their stupidity, I assure you! Is there any word of the women, or my paintings?''

''*Oui*, monseigneur, Monsieur le doctor sent the English ladies away in monseigneur's new black coach.''

Sanguinet's eyes widened. Shock and disbelief were replaced by a dawning comprehension, and with it a boiling fury. "Ulrich—*himself*—told my grooms to do this?"

"Why—no, monseigneur." The guard's eyes shifted to Tristram, uneasily. "Miss Strand's woman—she tell Raoul, and he—" Seeing Claude's expression, he added hurriedly, "B-but—they did not go far, monseigneur! I rode to the gates, and the men there said the coach went through quite empty!"

"Peasant!" Claude screamed, beating at him with his riding whip. "Useless . . . brainless . . . animal!"

The guard threw up one arm and cringed. Claude's whip landed hard across the withers of the horse, and the animal reared, with a neigh of pain, then bolted. The rider made no attempt to restrain it, and they shot away, passing Gerard, who rode up, took in the scene, and imparted expressionlessly, "Ulrich has been drugged. He's half dead. I do not know what the result will be."

"And I do not care!" raged Claude, "Is it truth? *Did* they use my carriage as that stupid bastard claimed?"

"Leith sent the women off in it. The guards are coming as fast as possible, but the stables are like a madhouse, and—"

Sanguinet swore blisteringly, and swung to Tristram, his face maniacal. "You knew—damn your soul! You _knew_—and made mock of me!"

Tristram came to his feet, then bowed in a deep and stately obeisance.

Clutching his hurt, Devenish laughed feebly, "Hoist by . . . your own petard, eh, Claude?"

"You find it amusing, do you?" hissed the maddened Sanguinet. "I have another funny little thing for you! Only watch!"

He spurred his horse away. Devenish began to struggle frantically, shouting an imploring, "No! Do not! Please—I *beg* you!" He managed to get to his knees, but crumpled helplessly.

Watching Sanguinet, Tristram stiffened, and swore.

Ever faithful, Mrs. O'Crumbs wove her erratic way in search of her beloved master. And laughing uproariously, Sanguinet rode straight at her. The little duck squawked and flapped her scrawny wings as she darted about in a frantic attempt to escape those flying hooves, but Claude dug home his spurs and his high-strung mount plunged and reared, neighing in fright. Quite suddenly, the uneven contest was won: the tattered wings ceased their frenzied beating; the squawks were silenced.

Devenish groaned and turned his face from that pathetic heap of smashed feathers.

Tristram rested one hand consolingly on his shoulder, then straightened. Head slightly lowered, shoulders a little forward, eyes narrowed, he waited, poised on the balls of his feet, as Sanguinet rode back, jeering, "Was that not the funny joke?"

"Most amusing," said Gerard, unsmilingly.

"Why do you not laugh, English fool?" demanded Sanguinet. His glistening eyes swung to Leith—and widened in alarm. His recognition of peril was belated. With an inarticulate growl of rage, Tristram sprang.

Gerard jerked up his pistol, but, quick as he was, Tristram had already seized Sanguinet's arm, and Claude, his riding whip flailing, was in the line of fire. Ignoring the blows of the whip; scarcely feeling them, Tristram heaved mightily. Sanguinet clung to the pommel with one hand, but his efforts were useless against the Englishman's flaming fury, and he was torn from the saddle. The guards did not stay to assist their lord and master; their fear of the pox outstripped greed or loyalty, and they melted into the night. Strengthened by passion, Tristram swung Claude as though he had been a child. Gerard, who had leapt from the saddle, pistol ready, received his employer's heel just behind the ear, dove gracefully into a peony bed, and did not rise. At the culmination of his swing, Tristram released his hold. With a terrified screech, Claude soared high over the pool and landed with a mighty splash in the centre.

Probably as yet unaware of the threat of smallpox, two more guards burst from the trees, and others were sprinting down the hill. Sanguinet was floundering about, his spluttering shrieks spurring the oncoming men to more frantic haste.

"Up, Dev!" Tristram panted. He slipped a hand under the injured man's arm, and lifted.

Devenish struggled gamely, but his face contorted with pain and he swayed and sank again, his eyes closing.

Tristram swung that sagging form across his shoulder and began to run. A shot rang out, the ball whistling past his ear.

"Never mind *them*!" howled Sanguinet. "*A moi! A moi!* I am drowning!"

Hysteria was strong in that watery command, and the guards raced to the pool, but those following turned aside to pursue the fugitives.

Devenish was a dead weight, and the rage that had bolstered Tristram was diminishing. His head, which had been pounding ever since he was struck down in the chateau, seemed to become more painful with every stride; his vision began to blur with the ceaseless effort; and each breath seared his lungs. He could hear the steady pound of feet behind him. They were not shooting—Claude could not risk his death until those screens were safely recovered. His stride faltered. He must keep on! He *must*! Soon, he was weaving drunkenly; there was a roaring in his ears; to breathe was agony. He couldn't last much longer . . .

"*Colonel! Mon Colonel!* This way! Me—I am come!"

Tristram blinked stupidly at a familiar face, hanging disembodied in the air. Raoul. *Raoul!*

Clambering down from the box of the carriage, the little groom swung the door open. With a sob of thankfulness, Tristram stumbled to him. "I knew . . . you would come . . . for us!" he wheezed.

"*Oui!* But of course. Raoul have come. And in the notch of time!" After which dramatic, if slightly inaccurate announcement, he urged, "Inside! *Vite!* Poor Monsieur Devenish—Raoul will help."

They hauled Devenish inside while the howling guards drew ever closer. It was all Tristram could do to clamber in. Sobbingly exhausted, he sprawled on the squabs. A musket roared, and the ball smashed into the door.

"The screens!" shouted Raoul, scrambling back onto the box.

Tristram dragged himself to his feet, then almost fell as Raoul swung the team and the carriage rocked to the sudden surge of power. Incredible as it seemed, little more than an hour had passed since Devenish had so nobly sunk his teeth into Claude Sanguinet's perfumed soap; however, that hectic space had allowed little chance for conversation and he had neglected to ascertain just how the screens were attached. It had been his thought that the wooden strips along the tops fitted into some kind of track across the carriage roof, but his seeking fingers could discover no such track, and now that they had left the illuminated area of the grounds, only the occasional beam of the lanterns lighting the drivepath lit the interior. Raoul was whipping the team to a thundering gallop; soon they would reach the lodge gates, and still Tristram could not locate the screens. His heart was hammering tensely when at length his fingernails detected grooves. He pushed to no avail, but the thin panel yielded when he slid it to the side, and at once the screen unrolled, the shorter sides flopping down onto the seat cushions, and the long centre section stretching neatly to the floor. There was a small separation between the cushions on each seat, and the screen tucked down inside, while a hook under the rug slipped into a matching hole in the wood trim of the screen, holding it taut. "Halfway home!" he thought, but now the coach was slowing. Gritting his teeth, he sprang to the other side and repeated the process, his fingers seeming clumsy and fumbling. They came to a halt as the screen dropped across Devenish's slumped form. Tristram dragged him inside the dark and tiny concealment, propped him against the squabs, and worked feverishly. He was slipping the hook into place when a gruff voice jeered, "You fairly flew. Monseigneur took your nose off for not collecting his guest, eh?"

"*Mais oui!* Did he not!" Raoul mourned. "This poor fool did just as Monsieur Gerard ordered, only it was quite incorrect. Let me pass with all speed, I beg. Already, I may never be forgiven."

"They came here, asking if you had gone through. What is going on up at—"

Devenish moaned, and stirred weakly. Tristram gasped, clamped a hand over his mouth and held him still, scarcely daring to breathe.

"Who have you got in there?" Another voice, sharp with suspicion.

Nerves tight, Tristram waited.

"Who else but Bonaparte and Ney, and four brigades of cavalry?" scoffed Raoul bravely. "Can you not see, maggotwit, that I carry no one? Do you delay me, I shall inform monseigneur why Raoul he is late!''

"Listen to the bantam!'' The voice was very close now. ''I shall look under the seats nonetheless, for something it is not well tonight. Otherwise why should all the guests run off?''

Readying himself for action, Tristram stood. The screens would assuredly be detected under a close examination.

"Why, the news have leaked out. About the younger Miss Strand. What? You did not know of this?'' Raoul imparted in a solemn tone, ''She and Doctor Ulrich and perhaps her sister also, have been stricken with the pox!'' And, inspired, he added, ''Raoul is much afraid, for he was speaking with the lady but yesterday!''

"*Sacre bleu!*'' The guard retreated rapidly while admonishing Raoul to take the carriage through and not loiter about.

The carriage began to roll once more, Raoul whipping the team to a gallop.

Tristram sank down, drawing a deep breath of relief.

They were away!

17

Three crowded days later, Tristram guided Charity's uncertain steps to a bench in Strand Hall's once luxuriant pleasure garden. "There," he smiled, as she sat down, her wide eyes fixed in triumph on his face. "Did I not tell you that you would be riding before the month is out?"

"Oh—can I believe it?" she said breathlessly. "*Dare* I believe this is really me? And that I walked—I really *walked*!"

"You must assuredly did! And practically unaided! Your brother will—"

Aghast, he stopped speaking, for she had seized his hand and nursed it to her cheek. He felt dampness and when she looked up in response to his stammered protests, saw her eyes abrim with tears. "I just do not know how to thank you," she said chokingly. "You have been so—so splendid. And we, alas, have brought you only sorrow."

Tristram sat beside her, the trouble that lurked at the back of his own eyes becoming more pronounced. "You think she will refuse me?" he asked, offering his handkerchief.

Charity dried her tears and blew her small nose. "In her shoes, I would."

He glanced at her sharply but read only sympathy in her gentle face, and there was no chance to pursue the subject further, for Agatha came to them with word that Justin Strand was now able to receive the Colonel.

Tristram had hoped to catch a glimpse of Rachel, but when he entered the dim coolness of the house there was no sign of her. The butler ushered him to the master bedchamber at the front of the first floor, and closed the door softly behind him.

Walking across the large room, Tristram was engulfed in a

tide of thanks for his efforts in behalf of Rachel and Charity. He shook the thin brown hand Strand offered, obeyed a request that he pull a chair closer to the chaise longue on which the sick man rested, and sat down, scanning the features speculatively. Thick light hair framed a sun-bronzed face that was strong despite its present almost skeletal thinness. Eyes as blue as Rachel's met his gaze unwaveringly; the nose was inclined to be Roman; the jaw firm, and the mouth well chiselled. Not a handsome face, but reflecting a character to which Tristram warmed at once. He threw up one hand to stem the tide and grinned easily. "You had best be done with your thanks, else you may put yourself in a vulnerable position. I am come to ask your permission to pay my addresses to your sister."

Strand smiled, but some of the warmth faded from those intensely blue eyes. "I'm dashed sorry I must lie here like some languishing girl on such an occasion. How does Devenish go on? My sisters tell me he'd a rough time of it."

The evasion, Tristram did not doubt, was deliberate. Accepting it, he said, "I believe he will make a good recovery now he is safely in his cousin's care. You know, I expect, that we were so fortunate as to reach Dinard ahead of Sanguinet's hounds, and that the people at *Le Canard Borgne* hid us in the cellars?"

"Yes. Rachel tells me you persuaded an apothecary to go there and remove the bolt. Poor fellow—was it very bad?"

"Quite bad. He's pluck to the backbone, but luckily fainted before the worst of it. Rachel nursed him devotedly, with the result they now quarrel like brother and sister."

Strand grinned. "She didn't say that. She mentioned that he was shy."

"True. But one cannot for long remain shy with the lady who applies hot fomentations to one's thigh—or holds the bowl when the motion of the seas is ah—unpropitious."

"Oh, gad! A poor sailor, is he? Likely that was worse than all the rest."

"So he told us," Tristram agreed with a twinkle. "I regret to report that he behaved on that occasion with a total lack of valour, and even went so far as to say he wished the bolt had found his heart rather than his leg!"

They both laughed, and Tristram asked quietly, "Are you putting me off because I subjected your sisters to the rigours of a smuggler's ketch on the way home?"

"No, sir." For an instant, Strand was thrown off his stride, and a faint flush appeared beneath his tan. Recovering, he said, "Though, I'll own I cannot quite understand how you were—er—acquainted with smugglers. That is to say, I do not mean to appear censorious, but . . . ."

"I was more than acquainted with them. Devenish and I worked our way to Dinard aboard the yawl of a friendly free trader. We had no choice, actually. Pockets to let, for both of us. And so, you see, on the return journey we were treated as," he smiled, "brethren."

Strand sighed and shook his head regretfully. "I collect there is a great deal yet to be told, and I should dearly love to hear it, but I know you are anxious to get to Whitehall."

"I am. I should have ridden there at once, but I first had to get Devenish safely bestowed, and then return the girls to you."

"For which I am ever in your debt." Transfixed by an unblinking gaze, and realizing this man would not be put off, Strand added a reluctant, "As to your request—my regrets, Leith. But I cannot give my consent."

Tristram's heart sank. "I suppose I expected that. I'll warn you that I am become heartily bored by the Strand pride. I am deep in love with Rachel. I've every reason to believe she feels the same. I mean to wed her—with or without your approval."

"I doubt that, sir." A wry smile curved Strand's mouth. "No—do not eat me! But I cannot feature a man such as yourself essaying a dash to the Border whilst I lie here knocked out of time. More importantly—I know my sister. She will never wed you." His eyes became bleak suddenly. "Not now."

For a long moment, Tristram said nothing. Then he stood and, walking over to the window, observed, "I realize you know nothing of me, Strand, but—"

"Not *know* of you? Everyone knows of you! Tristram Leith—heir to a barony and a fortune; Leith, who acquitted himself so well on the Peninsula he was made one of Wellington's matchless aides-de-camp! Leith—admired by London's gentlemen and the *beau idéal* of her ladies!'' Strand gave a cynical snort. "Much do I know of you, Colonel!"

Genuinely taken aback, Tristram turned to face him. "I thank you for the compliments, but—someone's been hoaxing you. I never heard such farradiddles!"

"Stuff! It's purest truth, whether or not you acknowledge it. I chance to be well acquainted with Jeremy Bolster and Timothy Van Lindsay—I heard them sing your praises long before I knew you were—er—involved with my sister."

"Yes, and a greater pair of booberkins you'd not wish to meet!" His face hot, Leith demanded, "Now listen to me, Strand—if it is this business with Sanguinet that disturbs you— why, people forget. In time—"

"They'll not forget the Strands. My father's reputation alone was sufficient to bring us to ruin. And as to his debts—"

"They can be paid. My father will—"

"The devil he will!" Strand sat up straight, eyes blazing, and two spots of colour lighting his hollow cheeks. "Why in the deuce d'you think I spent these past three years in India? I'll have you know, sir, I'm not an utter failure! Our debts will be paid in full! And if you think that will turn the trick, you're a maggotwit!"

"My apologies if I offended." Tristram strode back to the chaise, his eyes holding a flare that would have warned his subalterns. "I wish to God I could stay and talk some sense into your addled brain. But I must get to the Horse Guards, and then to my father. When those matters are attended to, I'll come back, Strand! I mean to have Rachel for my wife and I don't intend to let the Strand pride stop me!" He thrust out a hand and, it being duly taken, said sternly, "Good day, sir. And I am glad to have met you!"

Strand watched that erect figure march to the door and, with a rueful smile in his eyes called, "Leith—you cannot know how I wish I could give you my blessing."

Tristram turned, flashed a grim stare at him, and left, closing the door quietly behind him.

Rachel sat in a shady corner of the rose arbour, trying to concentrate on the weeds that invaded the once pristine beds, and the amount of work that must be done to restore the estate. Her fingers were nervously braiding the fringe that edged the pink sash of her sprigged muslin gown, and her thoughts strayed constantly to Tristram. He would seek her out at any moment, she knew. She also knew he had spoken with Justin, and what her brother would have said, wherefore her palms were wet, and her heartbeat wildly irregular. Whatever happened, she told herself sternly, she must be firm. She must not weaken, no matter if—

"Good morning, my dear."

The deep voice was quiet, but Rachel's heart bade fair to jump through her ribs and, despite her preparations for this moment, her breath was snatched away. She stood, her knees trembling as she faced him.

"I did not hear you come," she said tritely, fighting to control her nerves and to crush the familiar ache of longing that scourged her whenever she saw him.

Tristram pushed his broad shoulders away from the tree he leaned against and moved towards her. "I was watching you," he admitted, adding with a rather crooked smile, "I am forbidden to pay my addresses, you know."

She looked at him levelly, drinking in every beloved feature, and hearing as from a great distance her own voice say, "I know."

"What utter, rubbishing nonsense it is!" he exploded, anger and frustration uniting to unleash his rare temper. "You love me. I love you. And because of a pride that is foolish beyond permission—"

"Do you refer to the Strand pride, Tristram?" she intervened calmly. "Or to that of your own family?"

"My family would not shun us! My father is kind and understanding, and—"

"And would welcome Rachel Strand as the future Lady Leith? Forgive me if I doubt that."

He all but sprang to seize her by the shoulders and sweep her to him. "Much I care what you doubt!" he rasped, frowning down at her. "Or what my father thinks—or what the whole world thinks! Rachel—in the name of God! Don't allow this worship of pride and position to come between us. Do you think I could ever be happy again without you at my side? Do you think I give a button for the *ton* and their stupid unwritten laws?''

''Yes, I do.'' She smiled suddenly. ''Oh, my very dear—do *you* think I could bear to see you hurt those you love, and who love you? And it *would* hurt them. And humiliate them. Tristram, I have been bred up to the same Code as you. Do you think I do not know what it would do to you to marry to disoblige your family? Do you think I do not know what you owe to your name—to all the Leiths who have gone before you?''

''The devil with them!'' he said desperately and, shaking her a little, ground out, ''*You* are all I want. You are all I need. After all we have endured together, would you condemn us both to a life of misery—for something as pointless as Pride?''

She blinked, and if her lips trembled a little and her voice was shaken, she still said resolutely, ''You seek to condemn me to a worse fate, Tristram. You speak now in anger and—and fear. Oh, yes—I know you love me. But you are too fine a man to love selfishly. Sooner or later, you would repent your father's shame and disappointment. Sooner or later, you would begin to yearn for the world you grew up in—the social order you love. And—and if I had to watch you grieve, or turn from me—begin to . . . hate me . . .''

''*Hate* you?'' he cried, his face twisting with emotion. ''My God, girl! I worship you! Rachel! Do *not* do this!''

Her heart wrung by the pain in his eyes, her tears overflowed. She made no attempt to wipe them away, but gasped threadily, ''I cannot—fight you very well when—I long with all my heart to . . . to accept your offer. But—I beg of you, as a gentleman, do not cause me to—to despise myself! My brother forbade you to speak. You should—''

''Be damned to your brother! I told him I meant to have you for my wife, and—'' He checked. Rachel was wincing, cringing away from his iron hands, and the sight shocked him back to sanity. He gave a muffled groan, released her, and swung away, to stand with head down and shoulders hunched, while passion died and the cold implacability of Reason and Responsibility marched hand in hand to defeat him.

Watching him, still shaken by his ferocity, Rachel's hand went out to him in a yearning gesture, but was withdrawn.

After a moment, he said, very low, "Forgive me, I beg you. That was disgraceful. I—I must be more tired than I knew."

"Of course," she gulped, dashing tears away. "I quite understand. We all have been through a great deal."

"Yes." He faced her again, struggling for a smile. "I must get to the Horse Guards, then see my family. But—" He bit his lip. "I may come again?" He waited through seconds that seemed an eternity. She looked so grieved, so troubled, but to his unspeakable relief, at last, she nodded.

"After you see your father and your family, if you still feel that what you propose would not hurt them—or me—then, you may come, Tristram."

"Against my better judgment," said General Smollet, glaring from under beetling grey brows at the young officer standing so tall and straight before his desk, "against my every instinct, I have heard you out." He leaned forward, brawny hands clasped before him on the desk, and hard grey eyes glinting his disgust. "And I tell you, sir, that—*never* in my entire life, have I heard so reprehensible a pack of nonsense!"

From the instant he had set foot in this venerable old building, Tristram had known he was in trouble. From the sidelong glances of the sergeants, to the amused stares of the officers, had come the message that not only was his survival common knowledge, but that he was not going to be welcomed with open arms. Outright disbelief he had not expected, however, and tensing said curtly, "Sir, with all due respect, everything I have told you is truth. You certainly know I was downed at Waterloo, and—"

"And that having chosen to disappear for six weeks, you finally popped up in France, professing not to know your identity? No, sir! We did not know that! But we know it now. And I confess myself astounded, Colonel. *Astounded*! That you should have the barefaced gall to stand there and mouth me your—your farradiddles!"

Angered, Trisram declared dangerously, "I also am astounded, General. I bring you word of an attempt on the life of the Regent, and—''

Smollet sprang to his feet. ''You bring me fustian, sir! A damnable, slanderous, mingle-mangle, with not a vestige of proof!''

''You ask me for *proof*?'' His chin jutting, Tristram grated, ''May I remind the General that I hold the rank of Colonel? That I was on the Duke's staff? Further, that I was not alone in this? Mr. Devenish, Miss Strand and her sister, the groom, and your own man, Diccon, can vouch for what I have said.''

''How unfortunate!'' snapped the General. Not removing his fixed glare from Tristram, he held up one hand and began to count off on his fingers. ''Mr. Alain Devenish—a young rapscallion who left an unenviable reputation at Eaton, was sent down from University, and damn near cashiered from the military!'' He gave a snort of disgust. ''A fine witness for the defence! Of Miss Rachel Strand and her sister, being a gentleman I shall say nothing. Your groom, Raoul, is known to us—by many names—and has led a colourful life ranging from ivory turner to smuggler! And as for this Diccon whom you rashly categorize as 'my man'—let me assure you that he is nothing of the sort! For years I've warned my colleagues that he is short of a sheet, and since he has now completely disappeared, one can but hope that some public-spirited citizen has had him clapped up!''

Seething, Tristram stifled an impassioned rebuttal and said deliberately, ''Sir, I came here as swiftly as was possible under the circumstances. I expected to be received as an officer, and—''

''And a *gentleman*, sir?'' Resting both hands on the desk, Smollet leaned forward and all but spat out, ''Is *that* what you were about at the Chateau Sanguinet? Behaving like an officer and a *gentleman*? Damme, but one would never have guessed it.''

His narrowed eyes a dark glitter in his pale face, and the dead whiteness about his mouth betraying his fury, Tristram said nothing, not trusting himself to speak.

Smollet gave a gesture of impatience. ''Perhaps I should have warned you. We have already been visited by Marshal

Pierre D'Harnoncourt. He came representing Monsieur Claude Sanguinet, who presently laid down upon his bed with pneumonia. Pneumonia! He may well die—and God help you if he does!''

"God help the world if he does not!" Tristram grated defiantly.

The General's fist crashed onto the desktop. "Oh, have *done*, man! Do you fancy us all fools? There was no *need* for these hair-raising tales of yours! You have served for many years and built a splendid record. You are from a fine old family. Blast it, I have hunted with your father! And a nice bumble broth you've created for *him*! Had you come here and admitted your folly; had you owned up to your, ah—escapade, you would have been disciplined, merely. But to desert in time of war—as we *were* at the time!—to follow the woman back to France; to create a disgusting scandal, and to have the brass to come here with the Cheltenham tragedy you have fabricated in a shameful effort to—''

"That . . . is . . . *not so!*" Very straight, his eyes flashing, Tristram interpolated, "Every word was fact! I give you my word of honour!''

With a snort, the General marched around the desk and thrust his flushed features under Tristram's nose. He was not a tall man, and his grey hair was thinning to reveal a bald head, but his shoulders were broad, his mien fierce, and his rageful disgust genuine, so that he looked very formidable. "Shall you," he ground out, "shall you also give me your word of honour that you journeyed to Dinan purely to investigate Claude Sanguinet and this ridiculous threat you allegedly uncovered? Will you swear that this was your *only* reason for crossing the Channel—on the yawl of a known free trader?''

"It was one of my reasons, but—''

"Will you *swear* you did not go to Dinan simply because Miss Strand was there?''

Tristram's lips tightened. Sanguinet had moved fast and spread his poison well. He said deliberately, "Diccon feared she was in grave danger, and I went because—''

His whiskers fairly bristling, the General snarled, "You went, Leith, in pursuit of a woman of whom you had become hopelessly enamoured! You went—well aware of the fact that you had no business doing so, and that she was betrothed to another man! With guile and deceit you insinuated yourself into the home of a powerful French diplomat.'' He threw up one hand as Tristram attempted to speak, and thundered, ''*You will be silent, sir!*'' Breathing hard, he paused, his baleful gaze fixed on the white, set face of the young giant who towered over him. Then he went on in a more controlled tone, ''Violating every concept of honour and decency, you abandoned your sworn duty, abused Monsieur Sanguinet's gratitude and hospitality, turned his betrothal ball into a madhouse, frightened half the nobility of France into a panicked flight, and—to climax this depraved and despicable conduct, to climax it, I say, you ran off with the woman and tossed her betrothed into a bottomless pool, leaving him there to drown! For shame, sir! For *shame*, I say!''

His fists clenched, a pulse throbbing at his temple, Tristram said in a voice of ice, ''Were you a younger man, Smollet, by God! I would call you out for what you have just said. No! You've had your say. Now—the devil with rank and protocol. Be man enough to hear mine!''

Smollet's face purpled. For a moment he chewed at his lip, spluttered and snorted and twitched with rage. But the cold hauteur of this young Colonel had its way, and he stood glowering as Tristram went on, ''I did *not* abandon my sworn duty, for the simple reason that when I recovered after the battle, I had no knowledge of which side I had fought on. My mother, as you may know, was half-French. I speak that language as well as my own. For reasons I will not enter into, I believed myself to *be* French.''

The dark eyes struck the General like twin rapiers. Smollet stared, grunted, and said with considerably less heat, ''If that is so, I apologize. But it does not excuse the rest.''

''You think I invented it—purely to camouflage my passionate lust for Miss strand. Is that it?''

''It is! And—by thunder, what fine conduct for a British officer!'' He stamped back to his chair and lowered himself into it.

Watching him, longing to shake some sense into his stubborn head, Tristram said, ''I presume you are aware, sir, that

288

Devenish was badly wounded in our escape? Does that tell you nothing?"

"It tells me," barked the General, "that Sanguinet's men are damned poor marksmen! Had you perpetrated such an outrage at *my* home, Leith, I would expect my servants to have shot to kill, and *you* would have been the ones dumped into that pool!"

"Sanguinet's intentions, exactly, General!" His chin high, Tristram asked proudly, "Am I under arrest, sir?"

"If I had my way, you would be! And that young rogue Devenish, with you! However—" Smollet drummed his fingers angrily on the desk. "Sanguinet—poor devil, has requested the matter be kept as quiet as possible, and since you had the sense not to use your name, few knew your identity. Because of those facts, coupled with my respect for your father, and your own hitherto faultless reputation—I will accept your resignation, Colonel Leith!"

The afternoon was warm, the sun shining benignly upon the pleasure gardens at Dominer, and adding warmth to a charming picture. Today, Mr. and Mrs. Garret Thorndyke Hawkhurst held a garden party in honour of the christening of their infant son, and from miles around, the *ton* had come to celebrate the occasion. The famous fountains sent up their lacy sprays; the flower beds were a blaze of carefully nurtured blooms; a gentle breeze fluttered silks and muslins, tossed feathers and the fringes of parasols, and offered gallants the opportunity to drape dainty shawls about the daintier shoulders of their ladies.

In the midst of this riot of colour, oblivious of the happy hubbub or the lilting strains created by the wandering musicians, one gentleman stood alone, staring rather blindly upon a dark red rose. Tristram, thought Lord Leith wearily, had ever loved red roses. Dear Tristram. His heart twisting, he knew the time had come: that he must face the truth—his son was dead, and not even a sight of the grave had been granted him. He must go into mourning, but before he did so, an offer must be made, a marriage arranged as quickly as was possible, for life had become a stale and empty thing, and he dared not risk a year's wait. The only question remaining was—which one? Which one . . . ?

"Brenda Smythe-Carrington?" In another part of the gardens, Sarah Leith, wearing a dark grey gown that brought her many sympathetic glances, said an astonished, "And—my *papa*? Oh, but—dear ma'am, are you sure? He has not spoken to me of it!"

"Nor is he likely to do so," said Lady Anne Hersh, her sharp features arranged into a tight smile. "The gal's not much older than you—eh, Sarah? Your father is after another heir, as all London knows. I'll own I was considerably surprised Carrington countenances it, but then—Leith's a well enough looking man, and plump in the pockets, besides."

Ignoring this vulgarity, Sarah murmured a perplexed, "I cannot credit it! Papa will not admit— That is to say, we all still believe my dear brother to be alive—somewhere." And contradicting this hopeful claim, "Surely, did Papa mean to remarry, he would wait until we are out of mourning."

"Leith ain't about to go into blacks until he's safely leg-shackled," decreed the Earl of Mayne-Waring, knowledgeably. "And I have it on excellent authority he's already offered for Maribel MacNaughton. Proposed to her at her Ball in July, but said he could not announce the betrothal until poor Tristram—" He shrugged. "You understand, Suffield?"

Sir Aubrey Suffield put up his glass and turned to survey Lord Leith's distant figure curiously. He was not a highly perceptive young man, his taste running to horses rather than *affaires de coeur*, but he observed judicially, "Something haveycavey, Palmer. Ain't the thing, y'know."

"No, I don't know, " the Earl demurred, puffing out his cheeks. "She ain't of the first stare, I grant you. But she's pretty enough, and pretty well accepted. And her husband had the good taste to turn up his toes and leave her very flush, so I hear."

"Yes. Quite. But—*I* heard it would be . . ."

"Harriet *Chandler*?" The Dowager Duchess of Banbury gave a trill of amusement and rapped Sir Horace Drake on the chest with her painted ivory fan. She was a large lady, and the fan was applied with vigour, wherefore Sir Horace eyed her without enthusiasm as she asserted, "Never! Why would you even suspect such a nonsensical thing?"

"Because," said Sir Horace, gently massaging his abused chest, "Harriet happens to be my wife's godchild, and she came rushing to the house *aux anges* at ten o'clock last Friday morning, to—"

"*Ten o'clock?* Lud! I might have expected such conduct, though. Her Mama was a feather-wit as well."

"To tell us," Sir Horace went on, rather irritably, "that Leith had all but proposed to her during the Hilby boat party on Thursday afternoon."

The Duchess frowned. She was fond of Leith, and although she was forced to admit that Harriet Chandler was a diamond of the first water, she also considered her to be selfish, and of limited mental power. Harriet was not, however, so lost to propriety as to regale her godmama with farradiddles of this sort. And, the Duchess recalled gloomily, she was a bosom bow of that odious Drusilla Mayne-Waring. Drusilla was just the type to inveigle her cronies into Leith's fortune! Small wonder Harriet had been *aux anges*! " 'All but'?" she probed. "What may that mean?"

"Lord, I don't know. She said he kept asking her what she thought about a man offering for a much younger lady. It was very obvious he was referring to Harriet, and she assured him she could only think any woman would be delighted to receive such an offer—did he mean who she thought he meant."

"And what did the poor fool say to that witch's brew?"

Sir Horace scowled. "You've a sharp tongue, ma'am! I don't scruple to say it!"

"And a nimble brain, besides, Drake. Now—what did Leith say?"

"He said he was quite sure she knew who he meant, and that did the lady in question respond as Harriet promised, his dearest hopes would be fulfilled!"

"Then he is mad!" the Duchess exclaimed, convinced at last. "Stark, raving mad! I tell you, Drake, it must be the shock of his son's death! Oh, never look at me so fustily, man! What I say is not slander, but purest truth. It had *best* be!" She glanced around, then leaned closer and seizing her legal advisor by one elegantly turned lapel, hissed, "I know, for absolute fact, he has offered for . . ."

"Me!" Mrs. Dora Graham was seated upon the balustrade that edged the terrace, a rose-bedecked parasol fluttering above her auburn locks, and clashing hideously with her purple gown.

She put up one hand to hold back her flyaway hair and, moving closer to her good friend the Countess of Carden, whispered, "Leith has told me I have his heart, Lucinda. Is it not foolish, at our age? But—he is so very dear, you know. And—and I . . ." She blushed becomingly.

"Have loved him for years," Lucinda nodded, rather grimly.

"Yes. But we cannot be wed for a time. Not until Tristram, bless his dear soul, has either been found, or—or buried."

Lucinda had heard several of the rumours that had swept the *ton* of late. She pursed her lips, the frown in her eyes deepening, but being truly fond of Dora, nodded and said merely, "Very proper. And you will have my felicitations, dearest, for he's a fine figure of a man. A most excellent leg."

The romantic Dora sighed dreamily, and quoted, " 'See what grace was seated on this brow.' "

More practically minded, Lucinda thought, "Hawkhurst will blow his head off!" And glancing up, saw the object of her ominous thoughts approaching. "Good afternoon, Hawk," she said with the familiarity of old friends. "What a lovely party you have given us."

His grey eyes alight, Hawkhurst took her outstretched hand, thanked her rather hurriedly, and asked, "Have you seen Leith? I've the most splendid news!"

My lord Leith accompanied his host into the quiet house, striving to appear cheerful. In the wide circle of the Great Hall, Euphemia waited, her eyelashes suspiciously wet, and her hands gripping nervously.

"There is someone come to see you, Leith," said Hawkhurst gently, exchanging a meaningful glance with his wife. "He is waiting in the drawing room."

Lord Leith paled. Mia had been weeping; and the "someone" in the drawing room was military, for he'd seen a cockaded hat on the teakwood chest by the front doors. He knew suddenly. Word had come—at last!

Watching that set face anxiously, Euphemia turned worriedly to her husband. No less concerned, Hawkhurst put a hand on Leith's arm. "Sir—perhaps I should tell you that—"

"No." Leith clasped his hand briefly, then drew back his shoulders. "I would sooner hear it—alone, if you please." He walked briskly to the drawing room, paused for one brief second, then opened the doors and went inside, his head well up.

A tall young man stood before the fireplace, staring down broodingly at the fine screen in the hearth. And seeing that tumbled dark hair, the blue of the Staff Officer's uniform, the erect, athletic figure, Leith's heart all but stopped.

Tristram glanced up. The sight of the scarred countenance was too much for Leith. He staggered, and Tristram sprang to support him. A muffled sob broke from the older man. Holding him tightly, Tristram was caught in a crushing hug, and his own eyes grew dim. Neither man said a word through that strong, emotional embrace. Then, scanning Tristram at arm's length, heedless of the tears that streaked his own face, Leith said chokingly, "You . . . curst young scamp! Where the . . . *devil* have you been all this time? And—and what d'you mean by allowing those damned Frogs to rearrange your face?"

"My apologies, sir." Touching his offending cheek, Tristram blinked and admitted, "Must have been a dreadful shock for you. I wonder you acknowledge me."

"So do I," beamed Leith.

They were both still slightly overcome, wherefore they broke into laughter and were again embracing when the doors burst open and a joyfully sobbing Sarah flew to her brother to be seized, swept off her feet, hugged, kissed, and hugged again.

The word had spread, and perhaps because the war had been so long and the casualties so appalling, perhaps because the young Colonel was so well liked, there was no containing the crowd. They poured into the house and flooded the drawing room. Tristram's hand was shaken until it ached, his shoulder pounded, his cheek kissed by every lady who even remotely knew him, and many who knew him not at all.

When at last the uproar had eased a trifle, Lord Kingston worked his way to his son's side and, gripping his arm as though he still could not believe this was really happening, said huskily, "Jove—Tristram—but I'm glad you are come home!"

"D'ye mean to tell me they wouldn't believe you?" Leith

sprang up from his chair to survey his son with outraged indignation. The evenings were commencing to be cool, and at ten o'clock the Hawkhursts' redoubtable butler, Ponsonby, had himself come in to light the fire in this private parlour to which the two men had retired. Watching the red glow illumine his father's irate countenance, Tristram drawled, "It seems my—ah, exploits were known in Whitehall, sir. Sanguinet moved fast."

"Survived your swimming lesson, did he? Unfortunate. Never have liked the tales I heard, though I'd not dreamed him so sinister a creature as you describe."

Tristram had offered his sire a considerably edited version of his adventures, and now said carefully, "Sanguinet is powerful, the French are offended, Whitehall is embarrassed, and I am 'inventing' scurrilous tales only in an attempt to disguise my own shameful conduct."

"Good God!" gasped Leith. "Such stupidity defies belief! What of this fellow—Diccon? Can he not substantiate your story?"

"He might, could I find him." Tristram stretched his long legs and shrugged. "He has vanished."

"But his superiors know of his warnings, damn 'em! By thunder, I've a mind to go and seek out Wellington! He'd listen, I can tell you! Do they mean to do nothing, then?"

"I don't know, sir. I was told to consider myself fortunate I was not placed under arrest." He gave a wry grin. "I've resigned my commission. By request—" He paused at Leith's howl of rage, then added, "I only wore this regalia today because I thought you would expect it."

"Hell and damnation!" Leith exclaimed, driving a fist into his palm. "What typical military lunacy! Those fools at Whitehall should be put away!"

Tristram sank lower in his chair and, with elbows on the arms, leaned his chin on clasped hands and watched his father pace furiously up and down before the hearth, arms waving, and a blistering denunciation of the authorities pouring from his lips. When some of that fury began to ease, Tristram said quietly, "To give 'em their due, sir, I had no proof. The coach was sent off, *sans* coachman, to draw Sanguinet's bullies after it. And our arrival at the inn was a rather desperate business.

295

What with poor Devenish looking near death, and my own head ringing like a church bell, I did not think to keep one of the screens with us. Tell you the truth, I'd not thought I would need proof.''

"No more should you have! Damned if ever I heard of such a set of rum touches! I'll go down to Sussex. Young Devenish ain't too reliable from what I've heard. Downright rackety, in fact, but he might be of some use; or his guardian. Know Tyndale—good man!'' He thought for a moment, then exploded. ''And why in the deuce would you be accused of stealing such Haymarket-ware as the Strand woman? It's regrettable she ain't of good repute so she could have testified for—'' He broke off, staring in surprise as his sleepy son sat up and interpolated a frigid, ''Your pardon, sir, but Miss Strand is the loveliest, most kind and good lady it has ever been my pleasure to know!''

"Oh—er, quite.'' Dismayed, Leith eyed his son uneasily. ''My apologies. I forgot she nursed you when you was hurt. Still, you must face facts, my boy. Might have been wiser, y'know, had you left her there. Sanguinet couldn't—''

"I'd not leave a salamander in the hands of that vicious swine! Much less a lady I love and honour!''

Leith gasped. There was a moment of tense silence. Then, ''I trust,'' said his lordship softly, ''that you were not so ill-advised as to utter such a remark at the Horse Guards?''

"I think you will allow, sir, that I am not of violent temperament. However, I will suffer *no* man to speak ill of the lady.''

"Good God!'' Leith sprang up. ''In whose teeth did you throw it? The War Minister's? Tristram, if you must have your bits o'muslin, for heaven's sake—''

Tristram had come to his feet also and, fronting his father squarely, now interposed, ''Miss Rachel Strand is not a 'bit of muslin,' sir. She is in fact, the lady I wish above all things to make my wife.''

Once more the room became deathly still, only the crackles of the flames resounding through that silence. Unmoving, the two men faced one another, and then, seeing the shock and consternation in the eyes of this man he had so short a time ago been tearfully embracing, Tristram drew a hand across his brow

296

and apologized, "I'm sorry, sir. I had not meant to break it to you in just that way, or at this time. You have had enough to bear, and—"

"It will . . . *not* . . . *do*, Tristram!" Leith's measured words were very quiet, yet cut through his son's utterance like a knife. "If you have given her your heart, she must be a fine lady, indeed, for I know you could not love her else. But—you have an obligation to your house. Marriage with one of—" He saw the flash in the dark eyes, and amended, "Marriage of a Leith to a Strand? No! Never!"

It was Euphemia Hawkhurst's custom to preside over the coffeepot at the breakfast table. This October morning was no exception, and having poured her husband a second cup, she sat stirring it absently and, under his amused eye, added sugar, which he detested, and went on stirring. Hawkhurst smiled, and returned to his preoccupation with the newspaper.

"Something," murmured Euphemia, "has to be done."

He knew the tone, the motivation, and the possible and ghastly imbroglio that might well result. Shrinking a little in his chair, he muttered, "Oh, my God!"

"You should have seen him," advised Euphemia.

Hawkhurst sighed and, laying aside *The Gazette*, said brightly, "My apologies, sweetheart. Would you have wished I come with you to town?"

"At the start of the Season? No!"

Being that most fortunate of men, a husband who was quite sure the wife he idolized adored him, this bald statement merely brought about the lift of one mobile brow.

"Oh, I *well* know how you delight in shopping expeditions!" Euphemia teased. "But Stephanie and I had a lovely time, and when she went back to Buchanan Court, Leith took me up to Cloudhills to see Tristram."

"I see." He asked whimsically, "Regretting your choice, love?"

She laughed. "Idiotic man! But I have always loved him, you know."

"Yes, I know." Chin in hand, he watched her. "You mean to do it again! You will restructure his life, and he shall become

297

one of 'Mia's Mandates'—along with half the Top Ten Thousand!''

Her eyes had become nostalgic and, as though she'd not heard, she asked, ''Do you recall, my dear, two years ago, when you were trying valiantly to drive me away, however shamefully I threw myself at you?''

He sobered. ''And wanting you with every breath? Yes. I'm not like to forget that miserable period of my existence!''

''In that case,'' she nodded gravely, ''You know how Tristram feels.''

Hawkhurst frowned and began to toy with a knife.

''He looks perfectly dreadful,'' Euphemia went on, a note of urgency in her musical voice. ''He is so thin and quiet, and didn't once tease me the entire time I was there. Oh, he pretends to be happy, of course, and insists he is doing splendidly and very busy with his estates, but Chesley is terribly worried about him. He says Tristram refuses almost all invitations and seldom goes to Town. He sits alone at night for hours—reading, but when Chesley looks at the book after Tris retires, he finds it open to the same page as it was the previous day.''

It sounded quite unlike the good-natured, gregarious young man he knew so well. Concerned, Hawkhurst looked up at his wife from under his brows and said slowly, ''If he weds her, he will be quite ruined, Mia.''

''Now—wherever have I heard that before?''

''Yes, love. But happily I was exonerated—*before* we were married.''

''And there are those who still doubt your innocence, Garret.''

The formal use of his name spoke volumes, and relinquishing the knife, he clasped his hands on the table and faced her levelly. ''Madam Wife—how many people's lives have you rearranged? A score? A hundred?'' Hew brow wrinkled deliciously and, resisting the impulse to go and kiss her, he said, ''Has it ever occurred to you to wonder what might have happened had you not—er—''

''Interfered? Why, they would probably have found each other anyway. But after oh, so much more grief and anxiety! I cannot bear to see my friends suffer. And most people are so hopeless when it comes to arranging their own affairs. Take Leith, for instance—Kingston, I mean. He has managed to embroil himself in the most shocking scandal imaginable, but has not the remotest idea of how he did it, and is half out of his wits between worrying about Tristram and—'' She paused, a faraway expression coming into her eyes.

''Eu—phemia . . . !'' said her lord and master, sternly.

She looked up at him, the dimple he could never resist peeping beside her mouth. ''What a feather-wit I am,'' she admitted. ''Do you know, Gary, I believe I shall be able to bring us all off very creditably, after all.''

Hawkhurst sank his head into his hands and groaned. Then, he went and kissed the dimple.

Alain Devenish limped along the garden path towards the drive where Raoul, now happily wed to his Agatha, walked the horses. Pausing for a moment, Devenish glanced back. Strand Hall was not near as shabby now as Tristram had described, the exterior sparkling with fresh paint, the flower beds spaded, the lawn weeded. Even on this blustery October afternoon, it presented a charming picture. Strand had done very well in so short a time. A good fellow was Justin Strand, thought Devenish. They had met today for the first time, but had struck up what he sensed would be a lasting friendship. Strand was deuced proud and unbending, though. Almost as proud as Rachel. Must run in the family. He continued on his way, heartily wishing that he cared not, and glumly aware he cared very much; that Rachel was like the sister he'd never had, and Tristram— He sighed heavily. Poor old Tris.

So lost in thought was he that he failed to notice the luxurious carriage standing on the drivepath behind his curricle, or the tall lady descending from it, and he was startled when a musical voice called, ''Your pardon, sir. But—are you by any chance Mr. Justin Strand?''

''No, ma'am.'' He snatched off his hat and bowed. ''My name is Devenish. Strand's out riding with his sister.''

''Oh, dear.'' The lady made no attempt to restrain her hood, as the wind whipped it from glowing, coppery curls. ''Then Miss Rachel Strand is from home?''

"No, no. It's Charity's gone riding, you see. Rachel is in the potting shed." He thought, "Gad, but she's a handsome female!" and said gallantly, "There's no one else about at the moment, I'm afraid; butler's taken the housekeeper to look at some new furnishings Strand has his eye on, and lord knows where the rest are." He grinned winningly, "But I'll be most pleased to conduct you."

In the potting shed, Rachel stood holding a bulb in one hand and a trowel in the other, staring blindly at her faithful spaniel who sniffed hopefully at a small hole in the wainscoting. The uniform greyness of life had been brightened by Devenish's visit, that exuberant young man banishing such things as sorrow and loneliness, if only for a little while. He was, he'd informed her, happily reconciled with his guardian, and his much-admired cousin Yolande appeared to be encouraging his courtship. The picture he had painted of Tristram, however, had been disturbing. She had imagined her beloved happily reestablished in his military career. The intelligence that he had sold out and dwelt alone at Cloudhills, wrung her heart. Her own suffering had been intense and was unalleviated by the passing of time, but womanlike she had supposed that a man so popular and admired would soon be enmeshed in the coils of some lovely and eligible young lady. To learn that his devotion was instead as deep and steadfast as her own, brought joyous tears to her eyes; but to envision her love grieving and alone was anguish. Had she dealt him so cruel a wound that—

Slippers broke into a wild farrago of barking that caused Rachel to jump almost out of her skin. Both bulb and trowel tumbled and, spinning around, she saw a tall, attractive young woman coming briskly toward her despite the dog's frenzy.

"Slippers!" Rachel ordered breathlessly. "That's enough now!"

Already bored with barking, Slippers desisted and ambled to greet the newcomer.

"Hello, Slippers." The visitor stopped to stroke the dog, even as Rachel reached out to snatch the trowel from her path. They bumped heads and straightened, both laughing. Rachel saw clear blue eyes set in a vivid face framed by windblown

300

curls of light, reddish gold. "Oh, I do hope you are one of my brother's friends," she said impulsively, putting out her hand. "We've not met, have we? I am—"

"I know. You are Rachel Strand. How do you do? My name is Euphemia Hawkhurst. I believe your brother would know me as Euphemia Buchanan, for we met before I married; but I could not claim him for a friend."

"Could you not? Well, *he* does so, I do assure you, and often sings your praises. I'm afraid he is from home, but—"

"Yes," interrupted Euphemia, for the second time. "Mr. Devenish told me. But I did not come to see Justin, my dear. You see," she searched the beautiful face intently, gratified by the dark smudges below the blue eyes, and the smile that could not quite conceal the sorrow that lurked there. "I have a very dear friend," she went on, "named—Tristram."

Rachel gave a little gasp. *That* Euphemia! Her attempt to draw away was foiled, for the impulsive Euphemia drew her into a hug and, looking into the poignant little face, smiled. "Oh, I am so glad we shall be friends! You will not be angry if I tell you that Tristram occupies a very special place in my heart?"

Making no attempt to feign unawareness, Rachel said simply, "No. How could I?" And watching this warm and wonderful girl, thought how much better it would have been for Tristram had he persuaded her to wed him. "He once told me he had offered for you."

Euphemia's heart was wrung by the faintly wistful smile. "Yes, he did. And you are so kind, I think, as to suppose we might have dealt well together. Indeed, I was sorely tempted to accept, for he is such a splendid fellow. But—he did not love me, you see." Her brow furrowed, and she qualified, "Oh, he does love me, and I love him. But—not in that very *special* way. Ah, I see you understand. At all events, we are close friends, and it is because of our friendship that I simply cannot endure to see him as he is now."

Gripping her hands very tightly, Rachel asked, "He—he is not ill?"

Euphemia shook her head. "He is very changed." She sighed worriedly. "He smiles, but his eyes do not. He is like a man—existing only. Without joy, or hope . . . or any reason for living.''

In a strangled voice, Rachel exclaimed, ''How—dreadful. But—but he will come about. And I'll not destroy him, Mrs. Hawkhurst.''

''Please call me Mia. And—my dear, between you, you *have* destroyed him.''

''Oh, n-no!'' Her eyes blurred with tears, Rachel gulped, ''N-never say so! I only sent him away because—because I dreaded to bring disgrace upon him!''

''I know, but you see he was by then so deep in love with you, there could be no other. And he is too kind and honourable to seize his happiness if to do so must break his father's heart. If—if there was a way we could ah—arrange things, would you accept him?''

''*Accept* him! Oh, if you knew—I worship him! Without him, life is—is an emptiness. With him . . . it would be . . .'' Rachel's voice broke on a sob. She wailed, ''Would be—joy unspeakable!''

Euphemia smiled, took out her handkerchief, dried the tear-wet eyes, and turning, called to the tall man who stood so quietly in the doorway. ''You may come in now, Kingston.''

Rachel was not alone in receiving well-intentioned visitors. At the gracious old house in Berkshire, Tristram was host to a steady flow of friends who would drop in casually, stay interminably, and do all in their individual power to cheer a man they obviously had decided was about to go into a final decline. Suspecting a conspiracy, he was both touched and irritated. Some of his friends brought more than themselves. Viscount Lucian St. Clair arrived with a puppy of somewhat dubious bloodlines who was, he imparted proudly, a son of his famous hound, Homer. That the puppy had inherited the traits of his sire became obvious when he set to work to undermine several of the new plum trees the head gardener had installed and, as an afterthought, dug up a few rose bushes. Alain Devenish's contribution was a large cage containing a magnificently coloured and very regal parrot, irreverently named Byron. For three days this distinguished bird did not utter one of the friendly and companionable phrases Devenish had insisted formed part of its vocabulary, although Byron's former owner had gone so far as to offer his word of honour that the parrot was a most garrulous creature. The arrival of the Countess of Mayne-Waring apparently inspired him, for she had no sooner begun to coo and gush "Pretty birdie" at him, than he hopped onto one foot and regaled her with a stream of such foul profanities that the outraged Dowager went into a fit of the vapours and Tristram spent the better part of the evening apologizing for his pet's obscene behaviour.

It was, therefore, not without trepidation that the following morning, while busied in his study, he heard the clatter of hooves and rattle of wheels on the drivepath. His encounter with Claude Sanguinet had stirred a dormant interest in antique weaponry, and he resumed his inspection of a halberd only to look up uneasily when the door swung open.

"General Sir Nevin Smollet," the butler announced impressively.

Tristram stiffened, and came around the desk wondering if Smollet had brought an order for his arrest. Smollet, however, marched in alone. He was resplendent in dress uniform, and his brows and whiskers bristled as ferociously as they had done on the occasion of Tristram's last interview with him. Instinctively bracing himself, Tristram bowed perfunctorily, and said a polite if reluctant, "Good morning, Sir."

"Don't hear a welcome!" Smollet glowered, making no attempt to shake hands. "Cannot blame you. Didn't want to come. Do not like the necessity. Wish I wasn't here!"

Tristram thought, "I wish you weren't either, you obnoxious old bastard!" but he merely lifted his chin a trifle and waited.

"Ain't making it any easier for me," the General pointed out resentfully. He gripped his hands behind him and took a turn about the room. Tristram watched him, curiosity deepening. Smollet had evidently not brought an arresting party, and whatever he had come to say was vexing him, whereas an opportunity to disgrace the man he despised would likely have rendered him jubilant.

"It has come to my ears," Smollet began formally. "Oh, hell and damnation! I've learned that you spoke only truth, Col-

onel! I hate like the very devil to do it, but—admit it I must!''
He stamped to the younger man and stood glaring up at him.
Thrusting out one square, muscular hand, he snarled, "You
were perfectly right. You behaved like an officer and a gentleman. I was wrong. Utterly. A curst idiot, in fact. You will, I
trust, accept my most humble apology.''

The apology was as far from being humble as Tristram could
imagine, Smollet's manner implying that Leith would be at
once taken out and shot if he failed to accept it, but he restrained his mirth, took that strong hand, and shook it firmly.
"I most certainly do accept. Thank you, Sir. I know my father
must be overjoyed when I tell him I am vindicated. May I—''

"No, you may not!'' Smollet interpolated belligerently.
"Cannot tell him. Not yet at all events.'' He cast a pointed
glance to the sideboard and the decanters on the silver tray and,
recalling his manners, Tristram begged that the General be
seated and went over to pour him a glass of Madeira.

Smollet raised his glass in a grim salute, sipped, and sighed
blissfully. Leaning back in his chair he said a tentative, "Sev-
enty-eight?''

"Seventy-six, Sir.'' Tristram half sat on the desk, one long
leg swinging. "From my father's cellars. May I ask why he
should be kept uninformed?''

"You've a head on your shoulders. Why d'you think?''

"I certainly cannot think Sanguinet will try again, if you are
aware of his dealings.''

"You might be right in that event—though I doubt it. He
ain't the kind to halt in mid-campaign. Thing is, he don't know
I'm aware. I've made damned sure of that! He'll try again—
never doubt it. And next time—'' He clenched his left fist and
brought it down hard on the arm of his chair. "I'll have the lunatic!''

Tristram made no comment, but Smollet saw his frown, and
bristled. "You think I will make a mull of it? By God, Sir! I
shall not!''

"Sanguinet is as devious as he is powerful, General. I shudder to think what might happen were he to contrive success-
fully.''

"Personally,'' said Smollet acidly, "I ain't never been one

for shuddering.'' His fierce glare was met by one so cool and unwavering that his eyes fell at last. He grunted, and said with something almost approaching a grin, ''I see you earned your reputation, Colonel.''

''Am I to be reinstated, Sir?''

''Egad—no! I'd not dare. Sanguinet would hear of it, and the wolf would be in with the sheep! The best I can do, Colonel, is to tell you that we'll strive to keep an eye on you. That maniac is not above arranging an accident to you or your lovely lady.'' He saw the younger man's eyes flicker and went on hurriedly, ''I am in touch with your old friend, Diccon, who is now in Normandy. I will require that you contact me at once do you hear so much as a whisper of the Sanguinets. We're alerted now, at the least. Pray God, with all of us working together, the Frenchman may be outwitted. But I fear him—I'll own. I fear him . . .'' He stared broodingly at his glass, then put it down and stood. ''I must go. Took a chance in coming here, but we've reason to believe you are not presently watched.''

Walking with him to the door, Tristram said rather wistfully, ''My father is a most honourable gentleman, as you know, General, If I could just set his mind at rest, he would never—''

''*Dammit—no!* That is an order, Colonel! We deal with the safety of England—not merely the family or reputation of one Staff Officer!'' He turned at the door, accepted his cloak from the butler, and stalked onto the front steps. ''Oh, by the bye, Wellington knows all that I know. Asked me to convey his congratulations. Thinks highly of you.'' He put out his hand again. ''I've your word, Colonel!''

With a wry smile Tristram answered, ''You have my word, General.''

Smollet nodded, stamped down the steps, then stamped back. He reached out and slapped the surprised Tristram on the arm. ''Did damned well in that confounded chateau. Proud of you, my boy!''

Speechless, Tristram blinked, and, watching that fierce gentleman climb into an unmarked carriage and be driven away, felt as though a medal had been conferred upon him.

*O*n a grey afternoon several days after General Smollet's un-expected visit, Tristram rode homeward from the estate of his nearest neighbour to whom he had paid a rather belated courtesy call. His host, though not endowed with great wealth, was blessed with a plump and cheerful wife who had presented her lord with five healthy children. The house had fairly radiated domestic contentment and although he had enjoyed his stay, once he left Tristram's quiet existence was rendered the more bleak by comparison. Heavy-hearted, he dismounted some distance from Cloudhills, looped the reins over the pommel and walked on, the mare treading daintily after him. The wind was growing colder, pushing great thunderclouds before it, and whipping the trees about. His valet, he now recollected, had urged that he wear a greatcoat, but he had not done so, and the breath of the wind was commencing to cut chillingly through his cambric shirt and light frock coat.

A branch fell across the lane ahead, and the mare kicked up her heels and was off, galloping towards food and the warm stables. Her desertion deepened Tristram's loneliness. Much as he loved his ancestral estate, he felt no pressing need to hurry back to it and, having swung easily over a stile, he wandered along slowly, head downbent, until he came to a clump of ancient oaks. He had been travelling steadily uphill, and from this eminence a fine view of the valley could be obtained. He sat on the gnarled old root that had served him since childhood and leaned back against the treetrunk, one hand resting across a drawn-up knee, and brooding eyes fixed unseeingly upon the stormy autumnal scene.

How strange a thing, he mused, was life. Who would have

dreamed that their struggles against Claude Sanguinet would end in neither victory nor defeat, but a sort of limbo; as though the final act was yet to be played. They had, of course, won a victory of sorts in escaping that beautiful but savage chateau. Yet Sanguinet had won a victory also: He was fully recovered of his illness—if he had in fact been ill—freed from all blame, and had—in the public eye, at least—become an object of sympathy, so that he was viewed less censoriously than before. If nothing else, however, they had delayed him and forced him to restructure his carefully laid plans. Smollet had said Diccon was back in Normandy, and that zealous watchdog would be ever vigilant. The risks the man must be taking were horrible to contemplate, but his warnings would not fall on deaf ears now; Smollet would act swiftly the next time Sanguinet struck. And that he *would* strike again at England, Tristram had no doubt whatsoever.

As yet, his own name had not been mentioned in connection with the scandalous doings at Chateau Sanguinet, and he supposed that Whitehall had been able to impose silence upon the few people who had been aware of his identity. He derived little pleasure from being thus spared, for Rachel had become a prime target for gossip, her jilting of Sanguinet earning her widespread condemnation. That beautiful, gentle, so beloved girl was quite ruined. He sighed wretchedly. He had found his true love at last—a love so perfect as to lift him high to heaven, and so brief as to doom him to wander aimlessly through a world without hope, the future stretching out like a grey abyss of purposelessness. Where was Rachel at this very moment? Was she grieving, as he grieved? Was she victim to the same unbearable loneliness that so tormented him?

The wind gusted, and he glanced up at the racing clouds. They were enormous today, billowing before the force of the wind, ever changing, dark with the rain they carried. "My darling girl," he thought yearningly. "If only we were there together, you and I. Safe in a feather castle, where none could part us."

"I wonder if there are feather ladies inside . . . and feather knights."

He smiled sadly. Almost he could hear her again, as she had

spoken on the cliffs that day when he first had glimpsed what life might offer. A happiness too deep, perhaps, for this old world. And— He stiffened. He *had* heard her! Those words had been spoken—not imagined! Scarcely daring to move, he turned his head.

She knelt beside him, her face pale and marked by sorrow, yet lovelier even than he remembered; her gleaming curls framed by a hood edged with chinchilla, her glorious eyes adoring him, and a questioning half-smile hovering on her lips.

He wrenched his head away and put a shaking hand across his eyes. Perhaps the strain of these past weeks had been too much; perhaps she was in his thoughts so often that his mind was giving way—playing tricks on him, again.

Warm fingers touched his hand, drawing it down. A soft fragrance stole to him. A sweet voice murmured, "Oh, my dear love—how very thin you are become!"

And even now, he dared not believe, and whispered uncertainly, "Rachel . . . ? Is it—is it really . . . ?"

"I am here, my darling. Come to beg you to lift this notorious lady to the haven of your love—if you will."

Speechless, he stretched out his arms, and Rachel melted into them, her face eagerly lifting for his kiss.

An eternity later, she looked up and, seeing the dark eyes above her glistening with tears, said tremulously, "How much I love you, but—oh, my Tristram, I *told* them this was wrong!"

"Who—my own, my dearest, most precious girl!" he asked huskily. "Whom did you tell?"

"Your friends. Garret Hawkhurst and his Euphemia. Your sister. Devenish and his uncle. And—your Papa."

"My father?" he gasped, incredulous. "You have met him?"

She nodded, her hands fast locked upon the lapels of his jacket, and his arm tight about her. "He begged me to come here. They were all so worried about you dearest. Though," a trace of her mischievous smile flickered, "I believe Mrs. Hawkhurst has manipulated things very skillfully."

"What? Has my lovely Mia been up to her tricks again? But—how?"

"Well, she told your Papa—oh, and I do so like him, Tristram! He is the kindest of men!'' Being promptly rewarded with a kiss on the temple, she went on, ''Mia told him that because of his disgrace it would not be amiss for—''

''Wait! Wait a bit, love! That is not possible. My father never did anything dishonourable in his entire life.''

''I do not know what you would term 'dishonourable,' '' she said with a demure twinkle, ''but Mia seemed to think that to offer for four ladies at once was rather—*outré.*''

His eyes slightly glassy, Tristram gasped, ''Offer—for . . . *what?*''

She nodded solemnly. ''Four, dearest.''

Astounded, he gazed down at her, then threw back his head and uttered a shout of laughter. The first time he had laughed for years, or so it seemed. ''That devious rascal! And not a word to me! But how on earth does Mia hope to bring him off?''

''She told him that she could save only one of you from notoriety. Of course, he immediately said that must be you. But Mia somehow talked him around her thumb, so that he came to realize you might not—terribly object to—to being disgraced if—that would also ensure—'' She blushed. ''Ensure that—well, that is to say—since you seem to wish to . . . marry me.''

''I—'seem to wish to'—do I?'' he breathed, raising her hand to his lips. ''What fustian you do talk, joy of my life. But—how does that massive understatement help to bring my father out of this bumble broth?''

''Why,'' said Rachel, failing to keep her fingers from caressing the crisp hair at his temple. ''Mia said he must tell his ladies they were not to be disturbed when the *ton* cast us out, as they would when you married me. He and his bride could dwell year round at Cloudhills.'' Her eyes sparkling, she finished, ''Outcast—with us.''

Greatly amused, he exclaimed, ''By Jove! That would turn the trick, all right!''

''Yes. It did. With all but one lady, and I think he will very happily wed her.''

''He—*will?*'' The deuce! How have I missed all this? Who is she?''

''An old friend of yours. Mrs. Dora Graham.''

He gave a whoop of delight. "Oh, but that's famous! Much Dora would care if we are ostracized! And she has cherished a *tendre* for him for years. It will be, of all things— Oh, lord! Sweetheart, we have *all* been rearranged! We are two more sets of 'Mia's Mandates'!"

"Are we, Tristram?" she asked, tenderly smiling at him.

"We are indeed, or will be, when you do me the very great honour of becoming my wife."

She blushed, and said sighfully, "I told you once that I never would wed you. I do dread lest you think me a very biddable girl, my resolution easily overborne."

Despite this dread, she proceeded to illustrate her lack of resolution by raising not the slightest objection when she was rather roughly interrupted. After a long, heavenly moment, she snuggled her face under his chin and closed her eyes rapturously.

They sat there for a long time; loving and loved, in a bliss so deep it seemed holy. And savouring it to the fullest, both were silent.

The dark clouds above them grew darker, and a few drops began to patter down. Tristram stood. "Come, love." He reached down to help Rachel to her feet. "I cannot allow you to be caught in the rain."

She smiled up at him. "It is only a cloud, my dearest."

"Yes," he nodded, gently pulling the hood over her curls. "A very special cloud." And with a new and wonderful possessiveness, drew her hand through his arm.

The wind tossed the treetops, and the rain fell softly, and Tristram and Rachel would not have had it otherwise.

Very close together, they walked up the hill, through their own Feather Castle.

About the Author

Patricia Veryan was born in London, England, and moved to the United States after the Second World War. she now lives and writes in Riverside, California.